"MR. ST. CLAIR,
I DID NOT INVITE YOU IN!"

Ignoring her protest, Damon looked at Lily's indignant reflection in the looking glass on the wall. Her green eyes were fiery, and her full, tempting mouth slightly open.

"It is getting late." She looked pointedly at the door. Except she didn't want him to leave. The realization shocked Lily to her toes.

He turned to her and touched her cheek, as soft as pink silk, with his fingertips. She stared at him, the longing he felt unconsciously mirrored in her eyes. Then, Hawkhurst could not resist doing what he had been yearning to do almost from the first moment he had seen her.

He bent his head and kissed her.

The Lily And The Hawk

MARLENE SUSON

AVON BOOKS ◆ NEW YORK

THE LILY AND THE HAWK is an original publication of Avon Books.
This work has never before appeared in book form. This work is a
novel. Any similarity to actual persons or events is purely coincidental.

AVON BOOKS
A division of
The Hearst Corporation
1350 Avenue of the Americas
New York, New York 10019

Copyright © 1993 by Marlene Suson
Inside cover author photograph by Debbi De Mont
Published by arrangement with the author
Library of Congress Catalog Card Number: 92-97430
ISBN: 0-380-76960-3

First Avon Books Printing: June 1993

AVON TRADEMARK REG. U.S. PAT. OFF. AND IN OTHER COUNTRIES, MARCA
REGISTRADA, HECHO EN U.S.A.

Printed in the U.S.A.

RA   10 9 8 7 6 5 4 3 2 1

In memory of Howard J. Sweeney
The very best of fathers
With love and gratitude

Part One

Bath, England

Chapter 1

~~~~~~~~~~

As the ebony traveling carriage of Damon St. Clair, the Earl of Hawkhurst, hurtled into Bath on an evening in late April, he read again the cryptic note, its ink badly splotched by tears, that had spurred his hasty journey.

Dear Hawkhurst:
  Come at once. Disaster has struck!

  Phoebe

How like the pea-goose, the earl thought irritably, not to give him the smallest clue to the nature of the disaster, leaving him to conjure up unsettling possibilities.

He thrust the note back into his pocket as his coach stopped at York House, the hotel he patronized on his rare visits to Bath.

Passersby turned to stare as Hawkhurst emerged from his equipage with a fluid, loose-limbed grace that belied his exceptional height. It was frequently said that he was well titled. With his sharply etched face, beak of a nose, and dark, glittering eyes that missed nothing, he rather resembled a hawk, and that had become his nickname.

He looked up at the sky where the clouds had turned dark and threatening. An occasional raindrop, a harbinger of what was to come, splattered on the paving stones as he made his way toward the York's door.

Behind him, an excited voice cried, "Hawk, it is you! What a rare piece of luck. I have been desperate to talk to you."

Damon turned to see the round, eager face of his young cousin, Pelham St. Clair, looking for all the world like a Bond Street dandy in his high shirt-points and stylish blue-velvet evening coat that had been padded to simulate a physique its wearer did not possess.

Hawkhurst had never before known his cousin to exhibit any interest in male fashion, and he did not know which surprised him more, Pel's attire or the warmth of his greeting.

Once Hawkhurst had been the boy's idol. But that had been before he had vainly opposed Pel's marriage last year, arguing that a youth still thirteen months short of his majority was too young to take a leg shackle. Since then, his cousin had treated him with cold formality, even addressing him as Lord Hawkhurst.

But now, Pel was all smiles and calling him Hawk again.

"The most amazing thing has happened to me, Hawk."

Pel's wife was expecting their first child, and Damon assumed his cousin was referring to that. "Yes, so I have heard."

"You have?" Pel wailed. "But I have tried so hard to keep it a secret."

"Why would you want to keep your impending fatherhood a secret?" the puzzled earl asked.

Pel sighed in relief. "Then you have not heard."

"No, but now I insist upon knowing," Hawkhurst replied, unhappily certain of what he was about to hear. The remarkable change in his cousin's wardrobe should have been a warning.

"I have fallen madly in love."

It was what Damon had expected. "Have you now?" he said, careful not to betray his true reaction, which would have brought an abrupt end to Pel's confidences. "Tell me about her."

That request was too much for his inarticulate cousin's vocabulary. "She's . . . she's . . . Mere words cannot describe her. She's the . . . the . . ." He floundered about for another moment before concluding with a burst of inspiration, ". . . the most gorgeous creature alive—a goddess among us mere mortals."

"I see," Hawkhurst said dryly. "Does this Venus have a name?"

"Lily Culhane."

Clearly Pel expected his cousin to recognize the name, but Damon was at a loss. "Do I know her?"

"I hope not!" Pel blurted in consternation. "She is an actress."

That explained his cousin's alarm. Hawkhurst had cut a scandalous swath through the greenrooms of English theatres from which he frequently selected his mistresses, and Pel feared he might know Lily Culhane *too* well.

Damon assured his cousin that he had never heard of her, but that did not seem to please Pel either. "Surely, you must have heard of her, Hawk. She is a great actress!"

Hawkhurst, seeing in his cousin's round, serious face all the signs of violent, blind infatuation, suspected sourly that a tree stump could out-act Lily Culhane. Actresses were a greedy lot—no one knew that better than Hawkhurst—and he was certain that this one regarded poor Pel as a plump pigeon ready for a lucrative plucking.

Well, damn her, she had reckoned without Hawk-hurst!

Now he had two problems to deal with before he could leave Bath.

The rain had begun to fall in earnest now, and all along the street, umbrellas were popping open like wildflowers in the spring.

"Come inside," Hawkhurst said to his cousin. "No sense in getting soaked."

"I only have a few minutes," Pel said.

So did Hawkhurst if he was to catch Phoebe before she went out for the evening.

He guided his cousin into one of the hotel's empty lounges, comfortably furnished with japanned chairs and a writing desk. Pel's neckcloth and shirt-points were so high and heavily starched that he could not bend his neck. Consequently, he was forced to lower himself slowly while he groped with his hands to locate the seat of the lacquered chair opposite the earl's.

Hawkhurst suspected a hangman's noose would be more comfortable than his cousin's ridiculous neckwear.

But he kept this thought to himself, inquiring instead, "Where are you going that dictates such sartorial splendor?"

"To the Theatre Royal. Lily is playing Lady Macbeth tonight."

Hawkhurst had assumed the Culhane female was Pel's age or perhaps younger, but if that were the case, she would not be playing Lady Macbeth, a role that would go to more mature and experienced actresses.

Apparently his cousin had fallen into the clutches of a cunning, cynical older woman who, recognizing him for the Johnny Raw he was, would bleed him with endless demands upon his purse.

Even if Hawkhurst had not been Pel's trustee since

his father's death, he liked the youth too much to
let that happen.

"How old is Miss Culhane?" Hawkhurst asked.

"I don't know Mrs. Cul—Lily's age," Pel admitted.

Mrs. Culhane! Good God, the situation was more
dangerous than Damon had suspected. Would he
also have to save his cousin from the wrath of a
vengeful husband? His voice took on a hard edge.
"But she is some years older than you?"

Pel's gaze dropped away from his cousin, and a
bright flush spread across his cheeks. "Yes," he
conceded.

Hawkhurst silently cursed the cunning female
who was heartlessly capitalizing on a young man's
naiveté.

"But," Pel said earnestly, leaning forward in his
chair, "not age or anything else matters when two
people are in love."

"I suspect *Mr.* Culhane would not agree with
you," Damon said dryly.

"I am persuaded that Lily is as unhappily married
as I am!"

"But married you are," Hawkhurst reminded him
quietly. "What of Cecilia? She is your wife, and she
is carrying your child."

Pel flushed guiltily. The pain in his eyes told the
earl that his infatuation with the actress had not entirely blinded him. His conscience was plaguing him,
as well it ought.

"Do not think I will shirk my duty to Cecilia. Oh,
God, Hawk, how I wish I had listened to you when
you counseled me against marrying."

Damon refrained from reminding Pel how he had
stubbornly insisted then, with the misplaced certainty of impetuous youth, that he would never love
any woman but his Cecilia.

"You will say that I was too young to know my
own mind," Pel continued, "but the truth is, Hawk,

that it was Cecilia I did not know! She has changed so much since she has been increasing that I feel as though I am married to a stranger."

"I hear she is having a difficult pregnancy. She will no doubt be her old self again when she is feeling better."

"It is too late!" Pel cried, sounding like a petulant child. "Lily is the great love of my life! I cannot give her up."

Cold rage gripped Hawkhurst as he divined how deeply the female must have sunk her claws into his cousin.

Pel stood up. "I must go. I cannot be late for Lily's performance."

"And I must call on my dear stepmother," Hawkhurst said, accompanying Pel to the door of the lounge.

"But Phoebe isn't in town just now," his cousin exclaimed. "She and the girls are visiting at Hedrick Park. They will not be back until late tonight."

So whatever ill had befallen the young widow had not been sufficiently dreadful to keep her and her stepdaughters from going into the country. That relieved Damon's mind a little.

"Phoebe sent for me, saying that disaster has struck. Do you know what she was talking about, Pel?"

"I have no notion, although . . ." His cousin broke off, looking a little uncomfortable.

"Although what?"

"Well, dash it, sometimes Phoebe gets more upset than circumstances warrant."

How true, the earl thought bitterly, wondering whether that would prove to be the case this time.

Hawkhurst parted from Pel by the reception desk and went up to his suite where he bathed, dined, and donned evening clothes.

When Damon judged that the night's performance at the Theatre Royal was over, he set out for it, intent on launching his campaign to rescue his naive cousin.

His strategy for doing so was as simple as it was disagreeable to him. He would expose Mrs. Culhane to Pel as the faithless, avaricious creature she was by fixing her interest himself. Hawkhurst had no doubt that his title and wealth would win her with little effort on his part.

A grim smile tugged at Hawkhurst's lips. When he was done with Lily Culhane, the unprincipled jade would count the day that she had met Pelham St. Clair as the unluckiest of her life.

At the conclusion of Lady Macbeth's sleepwalking scene, the audience rewarded Lily Culhane's performance with wild applause.

She thought wryly that the easy part of her night's work—giving a vivid and memorable portrayal on-stage—was over. Now came the hard part—her appearance in the theatre's greenroom.

Entertainers were expected to mingle there with aristocratic males who had visiting privileges. For Lily, it took all her considerable acting talent to be polite to these rich rakes seeking a new plaything.

Unlike many actresses of the day who looked upon the stage as a stepping stone to capturing rich and titled lovers, she wished only to perform. Lily wanted to be remembered for her triumphs onstage, not for her conquests off.

Yet she could not avoid the greenroom. To do so was to court unpopularity that she could ill afford. Her income depended on her ability to draw audiences and to sell tickets to her benefit performances.

Unfair though it was, the most socially skillful players, not the most talented, often enjoyed the greatest success and financial reward. And monetary success was important to Lily, who had been seventeen when her parents had been killed, leaving her the sole support of a younger brother and sister.

It had not been easy at first for a girl of her young years to earn enough to keep the three of them together, and she was proud that she had managed with no help from anyone.

When Lily had stalled as long as she dared, lingering in the dressing room well after the other actresses had left, she walked toward the greenroom with all the enthusiasm of a prisoner being led into Newgate.

Her friend and fellow actress, Nell Wayne, came out of the greenroom, attired in a gown of lace over blue silk and a sparkling necklace of faux sapphires that she had borrowed from the theatre's wardrobe.

"There you are, Lily," Nell said. "Your impatient admirers find me a poor substitute and have sent me to find you."

It astonished Lily that any man in the greenroom could prefer herself to a diminutive beauty like Nell who was eight inches shorter than she. Lily felt rather like a clumsy elephant next to her petite friend. Nell had the added advantage of a profusion of golden curls framing her heart-shaped face. Lily's hair, although no longer the hideous carrot color of her childhood, was an unfashionable auburn.

"Your admirers are arguing over whether Lady Macbeth or Isabella in *The Fatal Marriage* is your most difficult role," Nell said.

"My most difficult role is the greenroom," Lily replied tartly.

"No one would suspect you hated it to watch you there," Nell said admiringly. "I wish I possessed half your skill at discouraging roués without offending them."

Although it was true that few actresses could parry offensive innuendos and dishonorable propositions with more deftness than Lily, she despised both the

men who made them and the time she had to spend
in their company.

"You are so good at it," Nell continued, "that I
wager you would be a match for Lord Hawkhurst
himself."

"That detestable rake," Lily snapped. He had
been dubbed "the king of the greenroom" for his
habit of choosing his mistress of the moment from
the ranks of London actresses. And in recent years,
a moment was about as long as his affairs lasted before he moved on to another. Such a man, bent only
on his own pleasure and arrogantly certain no actress could resist him, disgusted Lily.

"I did not think you had ever met him," Nell said.

"I haven't, thank God." Lily did not need to meet
him. She knew precisely what Hawkhurst would be
like—excessively handsome and arrogant with a
golden tongue constantly spinning compliments as
fulsome as they were false. "Should he ever approach me, I would give him a set-down he would
never forget."

"From all reports, you would be the first actress
ever to do so." Nell sighed. "I think I would prefer
him to the present company in the greenroom."

"Don't tell me Yarpole and Broome are there!"
Lily exclaimed anxiously. This boorish pair had been
barred from the greenroom two nights earlier for ungentlemanly conduct toward the actresses.

"No, they have not tried to defy their ban—yet."

Lily did not know which of the pair she found
more despicable. Young Hugo Broome, one of Lord
Olen's offspring, loved to intimidate those weaker
than himself with his own considerable size and his
father's power. Irwin Yarpole, the smaller and clev-
erer of the two, easily manipulated Broome into doing his offensive bidding.

Nell said, "I heard that Hawkhurst once thrashed
Yarpole for his behavior toward an unwilling young

actress and warned that if he saw him again he would give him even worse. 'Tis rumored that Yarpole's terror of the earl is why he quit London for Bath.''

''If the story is true, it is the only laudable thing I have ever heard of Hawkhurst doing,'' Lily said. ''I have no use for him.''

Nell grinned at her. ''Oh, but you do have a use for him, *Mrs.* Culhane.''

Although Lily called herself ''Mrs.,'' there was no Mr. Culhane. She did so to discourage amorous pursuers and unwanted offers of carte blanche. To add weight to her claim of a husband, she wore her mother's thin gold wedding band on her left hand.

If, despite that, an admirer persisted in his attentions, Lily displayed considerable alarm about Mr. Culhane's jealous nature and described in vivid detail his exploits with pistols and fists, which she had confessed to Nell were drawn from the wild tales that circulated about Hawkhurst.

Nell giggled. ''Poor Mr. Culhane would not know what to do without Lord Hawkhurst for inspiration.''

At the greenroom door, Lily wearily looked over the visiting males: eight or so libertines and young Pelham St. Clair. In truth, the rakes were easier for Lily to handle than a calfling like St. Clair. With the lechers, it was all a game, and she was adept at discouraging them, but poor Pel believed himself truly in love with her.

Lily was uncertain of his age, but judged him to be about eighteen or nineteen. She longed to tell the foolish boy bluntly that his pursuit of her was hopeless and he should stop making a cake of himself, but she could not bring herself to be that cruel.

Furthermore, the mulish set of his jaw warned her of his obstinate nature. She feared telling him the truth would only make him all the more stubbornly determined to win her heart. Subtler stratagems were required to depress his interest in her. She had to find a way to make him fall out of love with her.

With a sigh, Lily stepped forward to wage her nightly battle of wits with the greenroom gallants and Pelham St. Clair.

Chapter 2

Hawkhurst paused on the threshold of the greenroom, looking for Mrs. Culhane. He envisioned her as a fading beauty: a petite, delicate blonde with languishing mien, pouting mouth, and soulful blue eyes that would gaze with mendacious adoration at Pel.

He caught sight of just such a creature in a gown of lace and blue silk. A flashy necklace of paste sapphires nestled in her daring décolletage.

But she held his attention for only a moment before it was riveted by another woman who was more striking than beautiful. Her features lacked the classic perfection of the blonde's, but her emerald eyes gleamed with mischief, and her generous mouth curved in a provocative smile. Her luxurious hair, piled high on her head, reminded Damon of fine claret. He judged her to be about twenty-five. Taller than most of the admirers gathered round her, she had the majestic carriage of an Amazonian queen.

Even her dress was a refreshing departure. Her simple gown of green muslin was without adornment. On her, it needed none, Damon thought approvingly. She wore no jewels, real or otherwise.

She looked to have the breeding and bearing of an aristocrat. He wondered whether some particularly daring lady of quality had decided to amuse herself by invading the greenroom.

She was infinitely superior to Mrs. Culhane in her silk and lace and fake sapphires. What a fool Pel was not to see that.

Then Damon saw to his surprise that his cousin was one of the men gathered round the tall woman.

Hell's fire, could it be that she was Mrs. Culhane?

He read his answer in the expression on Pel's face, so transparently adoring that Hawkhurst longed to shake the noddy.

Before the earl had seen Lily Culhane, he had sarcastically referred to her as Venus. Now as he studied the perfect form beneath the clinging green muslin—full breasts, tiny waist, and provocative hips—he thought with self-mocking humor that he had been far more accurate than he had suspected.

But he had been wrong about something else: there was nothing soulful or loving in Mrs. Culhane's eyes when she looked at his cousin. Could it be that Pel had seriously overestimated her interest in him?

The other admirers surrounding her included a young man whose handsome face already showed the effects of his dissipation; two aging reprobates who looked as though they had long been greenroom habitués; and Sir Oswald Ridley, a dandy who had the advantage of being the best-looking—and most likely the richest—of Mrs. Culhane's ill-assorted admirers.

Hawkhurst listened as Sir Oswald tried to persuade Mrs. Culhane to let him take her home in his new carriage, which he assured her was the most magnificent ever seen in Bath.

She said tactfully, "You honor me, but a married woman can permit no one but her husband to take her home at such a late hour."

Sir Oswald went off to flirt pointedly with the

blonde in the fake sapphires. Hawkhurst observed that Ridley's effort to make Mrs. Culhane jealous failed dismally. She did not once bother to glance in his direction.

Eavesdropping shamelessly on her, Damon grew increasingly perplexed. He could not determine which, if any, of her disparate beaux she actually favored. There was nothing coquettish in her manner toward any of them. Mrs. Culhane treated their fulsome tributes with the indifference they deserved. She deflected suggestive remarks and advances with remarkable skill, neither committing herself nor giving offense. He could not help but grudgingly admire how cleverly she handled them.

The woman was more astute than he had suspected, although he liked her no better for this discovery.

Nevertheless, he gave her singular performance an amused, almost imperceptible nod of reluctant approval. He would enjoy matching wits with her. She was not in the common way, and Hawkhurst hastily revised the tactics he intended to use with her. Extravagant compliments would only garner him her scorn.

The task of extricating his cousin from Mrs. Culhane's coils promised to be more challenging than he had anticipated.

And considerably more pleasurable, too.

Lily had stolen one quick, covert glance at the tall stranger when he had first appeared in the doorway to the greenroom.

No London dandy was this one. His sober, unobtrusive dress was not that of a man who frequented greenrooms—or could afford to do so. His coat, as black as his hair, boasted neither ornament nor padding. But then, she thought admiringly, a man with shoulders and chest as powerful as his needed none to enhance his consequence. His white

waistcoat was as plain as his jacket. His neckcloth
was simply tied and his shirt-points lightly starched.

He stood out in stark and—to Lily's eyes—welcome
contrast from the other men in the room, all well-
breeched swells in richly embellished waistcoats,
elaborately tied neckcloths, and evening coats of
robin's-egg blue, bottle-green, and other rainbow
shades.

From the quick glimpse she caught of his frowning face, he appeared to be a man embarked upon a
distasteful mission. In light of his somber dress, she
wondered whether he was a straitlaced country cleric
searching for a young charge he feared had come
here.

Lily longed to examine him more closely, but she
felt his gaze settle on her—and remain fixed there.

After several minutes, no longer able to control
her curiosity, she looked at him again. This time,
she saw his face clearly, and her breath caught.

He might dress like a parson, but he looked like a
high-flying raptor with his hawklike nose and
hooded eyes that seemed to see everything, yet reveal nothing. He was not handsome. His features
were too harsh for that, yet the strong planes and
hollows of his face fascinated her.

Her gaze met his dark eyes beneath intimidating
brows, black and thick. She shivered, whether from
excitement or unease she was uncertain.

He swung away from the door frame where he
had been leaning and came toward her with the
careless, confident grace of a man accustomed to
deference and respect.

No country cleric was this man!

As he approached her, Lily saw that she had been
wrong, too, about his clothes. Although they lacked
the ostentation of the other men's garb, she recognized in their superb fit and fabric the work of an
excellent tailor.

She hastily revised her assessment of him. He must be a country gentleman of comfortable inheritance who eschewed London fashions and frivolities.

So why was he in the greenroom?

His hard eyes, so dark they appeared black, still pinned hers, and her heart fluttered like the wings of a trapped butterfly.

As he reached Lily, she saw that he was even taller than she had thought. Although her own height equaled or exceeded that of most of the men in the room, he towered nearly a half foot above her.

Pel, standing beside Lily, belatedly saw the man. Indignation and jealousy gripped his round young face. And well he might be envious of such a formidable figure.

The stranger seemed to make the two aging profligates beside her uneasy, too.

"Why are *you* here?" Pel demanded, glowering at the man. He showed no inclination to make him known to Lily.

"You are quite rag-mannered tonight, cousin," the stranger said softly. His voice, in contrast to his harsh features, was rich and pleasing to Lily's ear. A faint scent of sandalwood emanated from him. "Pray introduce me to the lady."

Unlike so many male visitors who sought her acquaintance, the stranger did not insult her with a bold, suggestive leer. Even if his dress had not set him apart from the other men, his quiet, polite manner did. She did not meet many true gentlemen in the greenroom.

"This is my cousin, Damon St. Clair," Pel said sullenly. "Damon, Mrs. Culhane."

Lily wondered why Pel's cousin seemed so amused by his introduction. She murmured politely, "Mr. St. Clair."

He gave her an odd, enigmatic half-smile. "My pleasure, Mrs. Culhane."

He did not, however, sound as though it was. She wondered whether he was a high stickler who was appalled that his young cousin would visit a greenroom and had come to rescue him from its depraved and debauching premises.

Pel looked as though he suspected the same, and he repeated petulantly, "Why are you here?"

"I confess that after your description of *Mrs.* Culhane I was overcome by an irresistible curiosity to meet her."

So Pel had told him about her. Knowing the intensity of Pel's infatuation with her and the hyperbolic accolades he heaped upon her, Lily cringed to think what he might have said to his cousin.

She began to understand the reasons for Mr. St. Clair's hostility toward her. His emphasis on "Mrs." told her that he disliked Pel's dangling after a woman he believed to be married, and well he ought to disapprove. She suspected from the coldness in those hooded eyes that he believed all the dreadful tales he had undoubtedly heard about greedy, scheming actresses.

How unjust of him to convict her before he knew her. She said with ironic tartness, "I hope that after what Pel has told you about me, I have not been too great a disappointment."

He shrugged his powerful shoulders. "Not too great."

She was taken aback by his answer. "How complimentary you are!"

"I do not make flattering speeches in order to ingratiate myself. When I pay you compliments, they will be honest ones." His eyes narrowed assessingly. "Or would you prefer that I fill your ears with pretty prevarications?"

Miffed that he would even ask, she retorted, "No, of course not."

Across the room, Sir Oswald Ridley, beckoned urgently to Pel to join him, but the youth ignored him until his cousin said dryly, "Sir Oswald appears anxious to converse with you."

Lily was surprised that Mr. St. Clair recognized that fribble Ridley, for it seemed unlikely a country gentleman, so indifferent to the latest in male fashion, would travel in the first circles of society.

When Sir Oswald started toward them, Pel hastily hurried over to him as though he were eager to keep the dandy from joining Lily and his cousin.

She belatedly thought to introduce Mr. St. Clair to her other two companions, only to discover upon turning to them that they, too, had deserted her. That astonished her, for this aging pair normally stuck to her with the tenacity of leeches.

A sardonic half-smile tugged at Mr. St. Clair's lips. "I suspect that I have driven your other admirers away."

Lily's unruly tongue momentarily overcame her discretion, and she said acidly, "If that is the case, I hope you may come often."

It was his turn to look startled. Then he said coolly, "Having watched you deal with your admirers, Mrs. Culhane, I am certain you need no help from me. You handle them most expertly."

The smile he gave her did not reach those cold, dark eyes that saw too much.

Lily was a little unnerved by his quick comprehension of her strategy. She would be wise not to trust Mr. St. Clair.

Yet she could not remember when she had been so intrigued by a man. She was used to being plied with extravagant praise by male visitors to the greenroom. Their humbug earned them only her scorn, but Mr. St. Clair's plain speaking and his refusal to pay her false compliments piqued her interest.

"You do not look like a man who frequents greenrooms," she remarked.

To her surprise, profound amusement danced in his guarded eyes. "On what do you base that assumption, Mrs. Culhane?"

"You do not dress the part."

"Should I ask Sir Oswald for the name of his tailor?" he inquired dryly.

Lily glanced toward Ridley. He embraced the latest and most exaggerated male attire. His stiffly starched shirt-points rose so high on his face that they were a danger to his eyes; his cravat, large enough to double as a tablecloth, was tied in an intricate style; and his double-breasted coat was heavily padded across his chest and corseted at the waist.

The amusement in Mr. St. Clair's dark eyes as he regarded Sir Oswald told her that he found the costume as silly as she did.

He asked, "Do I disappoint you because I refuse to pad my chest like a pouting pigeon, imprison my waist in a corset that creaks whenever I move, and lock my neck in a pillory-collar with shirt-points that threaten to put out my eyes?"

"Not at all!" Lily, delighted to discover that he shared her sense of the ridiculous, felt herself relaxing. He was such a refreshing change from the crowing peacocks she generally met. She would not have to play the greenroom game with him. It had been so long since she had met a man that she had the smallest desire to know better, but here at last was one. She said approvingly, "I find you eminently sensible."

"Because I do not subscribe to the foolish theory that clothes make the man?"

"Yes, such nonsense!"

The scornful fervor of her reply seemed to surprise him.

She could not resist quizzing him a bit. "I confess, though, that I initially mistook you for a parson."

He actually laughed aloud at that—a deep, robust laugh that erased some of the hardness from his dark eyes and sent a wave of pleasure rippling through Lily.

When his mirth subsided, he said, "I am quite certain that I have never before been mistaken for a man of the cloth."

"But you dress so soberly," she observed archly. "Tell me, Mr. St. Clair, do you not care what the *haute ton* thinks of you?"

"Not if it bases its opinion upon so paltry a measure as my clothes," he answered quite seriously. "If I am to be judged, let it be on my integrity."

His tone told Lily that his integrity was very important to him. Her estimation of him was growing. "What a rarity you are in the greenroom," she commented.

He looked at her as though she confused him.

"What is it?" Lily asked.

"I was pondering how different you seem to be from what I expected."

She could not resist asking, "Pray, sir, have I just been paid an honest compliment?"

"Yes, you have."

This time his smile did not reach his eyes, and Lily felt deliciously warmed by it.

"Actually, I paid you another compliment, you know, when we were introduced. I believed you too intelligent to be swayed by false flattery."

That pleased Lily far more than if he had extolled her as the most beautiful of women. She stared into his smiling eyes. At five and twenty, she was too old to have her heart thumping like a silly schoolgirl's, yet that was what was happening.

Lily saw Sir Oswald Ridley taking his leave of the greenroom, and she wished that Pel would go with him. Instead, the calfling started back toward her. She caught Nell Wayne's eye, transmitting to her a silent message.

Nell hurried to intercept Pel. She caught his arm and led him off to a far corner.

Lily turned back to her companion. He was grinning at her in the most unsettling way, his eyes alight with amusement. How could she not have thought him handsome when she first saw him?

He said softly, "Thank you for sparing us Pel's company for a few more minutes."

Those dark eyes missed nothing. Lily felt herself blushing like a green girl and hastily changed the subject. "Do you live in Bath?"

She hoped that he did, for she wanted to see more of him.

Much more.

"No, thank God, I don't. I find Bath a dead bore."

She swallowed her disappointment. "Why are you here then?"

The laughter suddenly vanished from his eyes, and his mouth hardened. "Family duty."

"Not a pleasant one, I gather."

"No," he admitted, "but I do not shirk my duties."

No, *he* would not. Of that Lily was certain. Caring gentlemen who put duty ahead of pleasure were as rare as unicorns in the greenroom. She spoke from her heart when she told him, "Your family is very fortunate to have you."

A sardonic smile played at the corners of his mouth. "They would not agree with you."

"They are fools then," she blurted.

His eyes narrowed. "I paid you the compliment of not flattering you. Please do the same for me."

"I meant it honestly," she protested.

He did not look as though he believed her, and she cast about for another, less volatile subject. He had said nothing about her performance that night, and she wondered whether it was because he had not liked it. Whatever his opinion, she was certain he would be honest with her.

"What did you think of *Macbeth* tonight?"

"I did not see it."

Any other greenroom caller, even though he had not watched the play either, still would have lavished praise upon her for a magnificent performance.

No, Mr. St. Clair definitely was different. Had he tried to fix her interest with flowery, fraudulent clichés, she would have been on her guard against him, but instead he breached her defenses with his blunt honesty.

"I came to see you tonight, not the play."

That caught her by surprise. "Why?"

"I should think the reason is obvious. Pel is much enamored of you."

Lily wanted to confide in him her fervent desire to be rid of the boy's unwanted attentions, but she feared that such a plainspoken man as Mr. St. Clair would then tell Pel the truth with brutal bluntness. That was not the way to handle the stubborn calfling. So she parried by observing, "Not many men would take the interest you do in a young cousin."

"I told you that I take my family responsibilities very seriously."

His eyes were suddenly as hard and keen and cold as black diamonds. He reminded Lily of a raptor about to swoop down on its prey. She was bewildered and a little unnerved by the sudden change in him.

He said, "I am Pel's closest male relative. Since his father's death, I have been the trustee of his inheritance."

An unpleasant suspicion crept up on Lily. Could it be that Pel's silly infatuation with her was the distasteful reason that Mr. St. Clair had been summoned to Bath?

Dismayed by this possibility, she asked uneasily, "Were you by chance summoned here to save your cousin from the clutches of a harpy?"

"Is my cousin in that peril?" he demanded.

His question stung Lily, even though she knew that some actresses would have taken cruel advantage of Pel's youth and naiveté, and Mr. St. Clair was justified in wanting to save his cousin from such an unhappy—and expensive—experience.

His piercing eyes bored into her. "Answer my question, Mrs. Culhane. Are you a harpy?"

How could he think that of her! "If I were, would I tell you?"

"No, but if you were not, wouldn't you send Pel packing?" he shot back with a look so fierce she shivered a little.

Lily was wounded to the core. How very glad she was now that she had not confided her true feelings about Pel to this maddening man. She said frostily, "I assure you I do not seek to trap innocent youths."

His mouth curved cynically. "You may not have sought to trap him, but he is captivated by you. I do not want to see him hurt."

"Nor do I," Lily said stiffly. Mr. St. Clair did not look as though he believed her. "So Pel *is* the reason you came to Bath."

"No, I was unaware of his interest in you until I ran into him after I arrived." His tone turned sarcastic. "His description of you would have made Venus blush."

"As you can see," she said acidly, "he grossly exaggerated. Now if you will excuse me . . ."

He caught her arm. "Oh, no, I won't let you get away from me so easily." His harsh face suddenly softened into a devastating smile that ambushed Lily's indignation. The eyes that had been hard and midnight-black lightened to the color of rich, dark chocolate, and he asked soothingly, "Can you blame me for being concerned?"

"No," she admitted. No more than she could resist that smile or his suddenly congenial manner.

"Is your husband here tonight, Mrs. Culhane?"

She was instantly on her guard. "No."

"Does he await you at home?"

Lily said in a quelling tone, "I do not discuss Mr. Culhane with other men."

"Yes, I can understand why you would find that awkward. Since your husband is not here to do so, may I escort you home?"

Lily had always flatly rejected such offers, using her purported spouse as the excuse, but Damon St. Clair intrigued her more than any man she had ever met. She could not bring herself to be so unequivocal as she always had been before.

"It is kind of you to offer, but I cannot allow a man I scarcely know to escort me home."

She expected him to try to cajole her into changing her mind. Instead he said gravely, "Yes, a lady cannot be too careful."

Lily suspected that he was mocking her, but his hooded eyes were unreadable. He bowed politely, accepting her edict without objection, and took his leave of the greenroom.

What a provoking man, she thought in mingled exasperation and disappointment as she watched him disappear through the doorway. He might at least have protested her refusal to accompany him.

Pel escaped from Nell and came up to Lily. His scowling demeanor betrayed his deep jealousy of his cousin.

"Don't tell me that you are smitten with him?" he demanded angrily.

Pel's tone told Lily that admitting an interest in his cousin would sink her in his estimation. Since that was exactly what she wanted, she sighed soulfully and said, "I declare, Pel, your cousin is the most exciting man I have ever met."

"But he is so old, and not the least bit handsome or amiable!" For the first time since Lily had met Pel, he looked at her as though she might not be perfect.

She was determined to widen this crack in his idolization of her.

"I cannot understand what women see in my cousin," he complained.

So Lily was not the only female who found Mr. St. Clair intriguing. "That is because you are not a woman."

"I am terribly disappointed in you, Lily," he wailed.

Yes, she thought, pretending to be fascinated by Mr. St. Clair would help discourage Pel's interest in her.

And, actually, it would require no pretense on her part.

Giving Pel a dreamy look, she observed, "I prefer older men."

"I warn you that he is notoriously clutch-fisted—only look at the way he dresses."

"I prefer the way he dresses," she replied truthfully.

Pel, looking thoroughly frustrated and angry, exclaimed, "I warn you, Lily, he has the devil's own reputation with women."

Mr. St. Clair's harsh, rather forbidding countenance and plainspoken manner was so different from that of the handsome, golden-tongued rakes Lily had known that she was convinced poor Pel, consumed by rabid jealousy, was exaggerating. Just as he had exaggerated her attributes to his cousin.

"I beg of you," he cried dramatically, "do not become another one of his conquests."

Irritated that he would recklessly malign his cousin like that, she said sharply, "Really, Pel, you make your poor cousin sound as bad as Lord Hawkhurst!"

Pel looked positively stricken at that. He opened his mouth, then closed it again, turned on his heel, and rushed from the greenroom.

Chapter 3

When Hawkhurst called at Phoebe's home the next morning, he was told that his stepmother was in the breakfast parlor.

"I'll announce myself to her," Damon told the butler.

As he entered the breakfast parlor, its sole occupant, a girl who looked to be still in the schoolroom, sat at the table lingering over a cup of tea. She had the lovely, innocent face of an angel.

Phoebe looked sixteen, Damon thought, and acted six. In fact, she was twenty-three. She had been barely seventeen when his father had made her his third wife. He had left her a widow four months later.

The color and severe lines of the black bombazine gown that Phoebe wore in mourning for her recently deceased mama only accentuated her pale-blonde beauty and her youthfulness.

"Black becomes you, Phoebe," Hawkhurst said to her.

Her cornflower-blue eyes widened when she saw her visitor, and she gasped in unmistakable alarm.

Damon was reminded of a frightened little rabbit about to take flight. He silently railed at his late father for having saddled him with such a childish widgeon of a stepmother.

"What brings you here, Hawkhurst?" Phoebe's voice quavered with nervousness.

"You do," he reminded her. "Kindly enlighten me about the mysterious tragedy that required me to rush here immediately."

She looked at him blankly for a moment before remembrance dawned. "Oh, that."

Recalling his hell-bent trip from London, Hawkhurst said savagely, "Yes, that!"

He was far angrier at himself than at her. How could he have been such a fool? No one knew better than he timid little Phoebe's unfortunate tendency to view commonplace occurrences as great tragedies.

Tears rose in her big, blue eyes as they always did when his tone was harsh with her. "I assure you it was dreadful. Poor Cassandra is quite unstrung by it."

Hawkhurst's gaze hardened at the mention of his half-sister. She was the second most manipulative female he had ever met. Only Cassandra's late mother—his father's second wife—had surpassed her. He had no doubt that she was using Phoebe as her pawn to further some devious purpose of her own.

Phoebe said, "And I assure you that I am very nearly reduced to nervous spasms over it myself."

"When you can remember what it is."

This sardonic comment sent tears trickling down her cheeks.

He admonished her unsympathetically, "You are too old for tears, Phoebe, and too young for spasms."

"Cassandra is right—you are the most unfeeling man!"

"Yes, I am when it comes to females who weep for no good reason," he agreed. "Now, for God's sake, tell me what happened."

"The wheel came off our barouche."

So it had been serious after all. "Were you and my sisters hurt?" he asked with genuine concern.

"We weren't in it, but Cassandra says we would have been killed had we been." Phoebe shuddered. "She says it is a death trap, and she will never get in it again. I own I am nervous about doing so, too."

Hawkhurst instantly divined his half-sister's scheme, and he said pleasantly, "Tell me about the new barouche Cassandra has picked out."

"How did you know about it?" Phoebe asked in guileless surprise. "I assure you, it is the handsomest equipage I have ever seen."

And, knowing Cassandra, undoubtedly the most expensive.

"I will inspect your barouche after it is repaired, but I am certain it will be absolutely safe," he assured Phoebe.

"It will not!" a new voice cried. Cassandra marched angrily into the breakfast parlor. She had the same beaklike nose and dark complexion as Hawkhurst, but there the resemblance to her half-brother ended. Her face was long and thin with a needle-sharp chin now thrust forward in outrage.

Damon thought unhappily that Cassandra had inherited the worst of both her parents—their father's unhandsome face and her mother's disposition. No wonder she had failed to win a single legitimate suitor during her London come-out three years ago. How he had hoped that she would shackle a husband who would take her off his hands, but she had aroused no interest in any man, save one desperate fortune hunter.

"And good morning to you, too, Cassandra," he said, steeling himself for one of those tedious scenes that he had grown accustomed to since his father's death.

She did not disappoint him. Like her mother before her, tears were her chief weapon, and she cried copious amounts of them with such predictable regularity that they had ceased long ago to have any effect on Damon.

When they did not move him to agree to buy the new barouche, she stamped her foot and launched into a diatribe about what an unconscionable pinchpurse he was toward his family.

Hawkhurst was used to this unwarranted abuse. Ever since he had inherited his maternal grandfather's enormous fortune, several of his extravagant relatives had thought they had as much right to his money as he did.

He had learned from unhappy experience that satisfying their demands only led to more outrageous ones. So now he kept his spendthrift relations on a financial leash that was comfortable but not nearly so long as they wanted. In retaliation, Cassandra defamed him to everyone as an unnatural, uncaring muckworm with a heart of stone.

Her gray eyes glittered with rancor as she cried, "You refuse us a new barouche, Hawkhurst, because you hope to see us dead in the wreckage of our old one so that you can be rid of us!"

Had such an egregiously untrue insult come from anyone other than Cassandra, he would have been livid, but by now he was as inured to her unjustified abuse of him as he was to her tears.

He said coolly, "Instead of falsely accusing me of nefarious intents, Cassandra, why don't you tell me why you really want a new barouche."

Phoebe answered helpfully, "Cassandra thinks the old one is not grand enough for us when Amy makes her London debut next spring."

Amy, Cassandra's younger sister, had barely turned sixteen, and Hawkhurst said firmly, "Amy is too young to come out."

That brought another explosion from Cassandra.

"How can you be so cruel! Amy has her heart set on doing so. How can you break it by refusing her?"

"What a clanker, Cassandra! I have told you a hundred times I do not want a come-out next season!" Amy cried as she rushed into the room. Grinning at Damon, she propelled herself into his arms. "Hawk, I am so glad to see you." She hugged him tightly, and he returned her welcome with equal warmth.

Amy was the only one of their father's children who had escaped inheriting his nose and Latin complexion, but she did have his most attractive features, his dark eyes and hair.

Her affectionate greeting to her half-brother brought an icy reprimand from Cassandra that she should not behave in such a vulgar, ramshackle manner.

"I do not think it is vulgar to hug my brother," Amy objected.

"Nor do I, puss," he said. "It is nice to know that one member of my family is happy to see me. So you are not pining for a season next year?"

"No, it is only Cassandra who is pining for London."

"That's a lie!" her sister cried.

"It is not," Amy replied. "Phoebe and I both prefer Bath. You are the only one who wants to go to London."

Cassandra flounced angrily from the room, nearly colliding with the butler coming to announce that the dancing master was waiting to give Lady Amy her lesson.

Amy made a face but dutifully followed the butler. With his sister gone, Damon quickly took his leave of Phoebe. He enjoyed her company no more than she did his.

When he emerged from her house, his groom Sewell was waiting for him with his curricle.

"What did you learn about Mrs. Culhane?" he asked as he climbed up on the seat beside the groom. Hawkhurst had bribed the two chairmen who carried her home from the theatre each night to obtain her address, and he had sent Sewell to make inquiries of her neighbors.

"Her lodgings are on a fashionable street near here," Sewell reported.

"So, Damon thought, either Mr. Culhane or another lover was keeping Lily in style. "Take me there," he told Sewell.

As the curricle rolled forward, the groom said, "Her neighbors say she keeps very much to herself. They could tell me very little about her except that she generally goes for a walk each morning about eleven."

It was almost that time now. Perhaps Damon could catch Lily as she left and pretend that their meeting was accidental. He was startled by how eager he was to see her again. Not in years had a woman excited him as she did, and that disturbed him. He had long ago learned that the secret of controlling a woman was to control himself.

Sewell said, "I could discover nothing about her husband. The neighbors say only her maid lives with her. They've never seen a gent staying there."

"None at all?" Hawkhurst could accept that Mr. Culhane was no longer in Lily's life, but he was surprised that she did not spend her nights entertaining lovers.

"No, my lord."

The curricle turned into a narrow street off Queen's Square. Hawkhurst pulled his gold watch from his waistcoat pocket and checked the time. Three minutes to eleven.

"Which is Mrs. Culhane's lodgings?" he asked.

"Number eighteen on the other side of the street, the third door from the far corner."

Damon studied Lily's door. Painted deep-blue, it was a half dozen steps up from the street and recessed behind a pedimented lintel supported on each side by columns of golden Bath stone.

"Stop in the middle of the block," he said, hoping that Lily had not yet left for her walk. He decided that Pel had done him a favor by not introducing him to her as Hawkhurst. The subdued black evening clothes that were his unique style had fooled her into thinking him a country gentleman with a distaste for greenrooms. What a joke that was!

Yet he had been strangely pleased that those shrewd green eyes had mistaken him for having a nobler nature. It pleased him, too, that she was clearly attracted to him even though she did not know he possessed rank or wealth.

He did not intend to tell her either, and he hoped no one else would enlighten her as to his identity. The challenge of seducing her without her knowing that he was a rich earl was irresistible to him. He had never been certain in any of his many affairs whether his inamorata would have come so willingly to his bed had it not been for his title and money.

The curricle stopped to let him out, then continued on, and turned at the corner. He would wait until Lily's door opened, then stroll casually down the street, meeting her as if by accident.

Hawkhurst hoped that she had been as piqued as he had intended her to be the previous night when he had meekly accepted her edict that he could not escort her home.

He was still perplexed by her true intentions toward Pel. If she had no interest in the puppy, why did she not send him packing? She had evaded answering that, although she had claimed that she did not trap calflings. Hawkhurst wanted to believe her, but his wide experience with actresses made it difficult to do.

As he waited for the neat blue door of Mrs. Culhane's lodgings to open, he recalled how cleverly she had handled her greenroom admirers, and his uneasiness grew. He feared that behind her seeming candor, she was playing a deeper game.

She had managed to disarm him last night, but he swore to himself that today she would find him a more skeptical and challenging opponent.

Lily stood before a wall mirror in the tiny entry of her lodgings, tying the vermilion ribbons of her bonnet so that its wide, white brim folded down to frame her face.

She had slept poorly, lying awake for hours, unable to banish Damon St. Clair from her mind. Lily wondered whether she would see him again. She hoped so.

Had he pressed her last night, she might even have broken her rule about accepting an escort home. She should have been delighted that he had quietly withdrawn like the gentleman he was. Instead she was vexed.

With a sigh, she turned away from the mirror and donned a white pelisse, edged along its front closure, neck, and hem with vermilion that matched the ribbons of her bonnet. Then she set out for her morning walk.

As she stepped into the narrow street, a rich, resonant voice exclaimed, "Why, Mrs. Culhane!"

She stopped dead, her heart skidding as she recognized Mr. St. Clair striding with distinctive, loose-limbed grace toward her.

Surely this meeting could not be accidental. Yet how could he possibly know where she lived? She kept her address a secret from all but a few close friends because she wanted none of the greenroom gallants to learn it.

"What a pleasant surprise," he said. "It is my lucky morning."

Lily rather thought it was *hers*.

Looking up into his dark, hooded eyes, the tempo of her pulse quickened. She was struck again by how tall he was. His attire this morning was again subdued and without ornament: a single-breasted russet coat worn over buckskins. No tassels decorated his boots, but they were polished to a high gloss.

She looked him over approvingly. His clothes might be plain, but they fit his long, lean body superbly.

Her perusal seemed to amuse him, but when he spoke it was only to ask politely, "May I walk with you?"

She wanted that, but she felt compelled to point out, "You don't know where I am going."

He shrugged his powerful shoulders carelessly. "I am quite willing to escort you wherever you wish."

Mr. St. Clair offered her his arm, and she took it, a tremor of excitement running through her. As she had the previous night, she caught the faint, pleasing scent of sandalwood.

He asked lightly, "Have I just condemned myself to taking the waters at the Pump Room?"

She laughed at the wry face he made. "No."

"Where are we going then?"

"*I* am going for a walk along the River Avon."

"The Avon it shall be," he agreed.

He shortened his long stride, matching the length and rhythm of her own step. As he skillfully guided her among other pedestrians, Lily thought how agreeable it was to walk with him.

She remarked, "I would have thought you too occupied by the family duty that brought you to Bath to accompany me."

"I have already dealt with it."

Lily might have known he was a man who would waste no time in doing so. She wished that he would tell her what the problem had been, but instead he said, "Since it is Thursday, I presume the Theatre Royal will be dark tonight."

"Ordinarily it would be," she replied. Plays were not normally presented on Tuesday, Thursday, and Sunday nights. "But there is a benefit tonight for one of our leading men."

It occurred to Lily that Mr. St. Clair, not being familiar with the theatre, might not understand about benefits, and she explained, "We actors supplement our regular pay with benefit performances for which we sell the tickets and are allowed to keep most of the proceeds."

"I have some familiarity with benefits," he said.

Lily wondered why he seemed so amused.

He asked, "Do you appear in tonight's benefit?"

"Yes. Will you come?"

"No, but I will buy a ticket for *your* benefit." His smile no longer reached his eyes, and they darkened, hardened. "What will you charge me, Mrs. Culhane, for a ticket?"

Lily stiffened at the inexplicable change in Mr. St. Clair's manner toward her. She sensed now that he did not like her.

"Your purse is safe, Mr. St. Clair," she said tartly. "I have already had my benefit."

"Was it successful?"

"Yes," she answered noncommittally. Actually, she had been surprised by how successful. She was educating her little sister, Sarah, at a select boarding school that was as expensive as it was exclusive, and Lily's benefit had earned her enough to pay Sarah's considerable school tuition next year.

When they reached the river, Lily paused on the

grassy bank to watch a mallard with a bright-green head skimming across the water.

She asked idly, ''Do you like to walk, sir?''

''Not particularly.''

A little taken aback by his abrupt answer, Lily turned to face him. ''Then why did you ask to walk with me?''

''You said last night you must know me better before you would permit me to escort you home. I am giving you the opportunity to do so.''

''Take care,'' she retorted, ''or I might think that you are trying to fix my interest.''

''I am.''

His harsh face was set in such unconciliatory lines that Lily was not certain that she had understood him correctly. ''What?''

''I *am* trying to fix your interest.''

His expression was at such odds with his words that she blurted, ''Why?'' To soften her startled question, she added with a smile, ''Your cousin would not appreciate your doing so.''

His dark, hooded eyes glittered dangerously at her mention of Pel. Lily was reminded again of a raptor circling his prey.

''My naive young cousin is a fool to think he can win the heart of a sophisticated woman, is he not, Mrs. Culhane?''

Lily sensed the trap he had set for her with this provoking question. If she agreed with him, he undoubtedly would tell Pel what she had said. That would only spur the obstinate lad into redoubling his efforts to capture her.

She said carefully, ''I like your cousin, Mr. St. Clair.''

''Don't deny that you enjoy my company more than Pel's.''

It was true that she did, but his arrogant certainty of it irritated her into replying, ''Don't be so sure!''

Lily looked beyond her provocative escort to the Pulteney Bridge with its trio of graceful arches spanning the river. Sunlight glinted on the windows of the shops lining the bridge, but oddly the day seemed far less bright to Lily now than when she had first taken Mr. St. Clair's arm.

He said coolly, "I have another advantage over my cousin. Unlike Pel, I do not have a pregnant wife who will be devastated by my faithlessness."

Lily's gaze snapped back to her companion. She was too stunned to learn that Pel was married to hide her dismay. He was so young and had assured her so often that he had not known what love was until he met her that she had assumed she was his first infatuation.

"Are you hoaxing me?" she demanded.

Damon was watching her with eyes as hard as black granite. She shivered a little at his harsh scrutiny. She could not blame him for being angry, but his ire should be directed at his cousin, not at her.

"Does it distress you, Mrs. Culhane, to learn that Pel has a wife?"

It did. Lily longed to box the silly boy's ears. Aloud she admitted, "I am surprised."

Hawkhurst studied her in puzzlement. Lily was far more than surprised. She was clearly horrified to learn that Pel had a wife. But why should that matter to her? Greedy lightskirts wasted no sympathy on their target's spouse.

He could think of only one reason that she should care whether Pel was wed, and it profoundly shocked him. Lily had hoped to marry his cousin herself!

Yet she could not do that if she herself were already married as she claimed to be. That meant she was not legally married to Culhane. She merely used his name to give the appearance of respectability to an informal liaison.

Damn her, she was more devious than he had suspected. Hawkhurst did not know whether his anger was hottest at her or at himself for having been duped the previous night by her seeming candor and lack of pretense into thinking her unlike any actress he had ever met. No wonder she had ensnared Pel. If she could hoodwink a man of Hawkhurst's experience, his naive cousin had not had a chance against her.

Keeping a tight rein on his temper, Hawkhurst asked blandly, "Why should you be so upset that my cousin is married, *Mrs.* Culhane, when you yourself have a leg shackle?"

"Your cousin repeatedly told me that I was his first and only love."

"Did he now? Well, when I opposed his marriage to Cecilia, he vehemently insisted that he could never love any woman except her." He raked her with mocking eyes. "I fear that my cousin's everlasting love for a woman is of very short duration."

"Like so many men's! Why did you object to Pel's marriage? Did you not think that he and his bride would suit?"

"To the contrary, I thought they would suit very well had they not both been so young and inexperienced. Neither had been to London for a social season or been permitted to know other possible marital candidates. Cecilia was barely seventeen and still too much of a cosseted child to handle the demands of marriage, while Pel should have been allowed to sow his wild oats before he settled into its confines. A broader experience with women would have made him more content with his wife."

Lily nodded, thinking that Mr. St. Clair was a wise man.

She was bewildered, however, by his anger at her. Surely, he could not think she liked having a foolish calfling like Pel mooning over her? Knowing that he had a pregnant wife only made it all the more disagreeable to her.

"What has gone wrong between Pel and his wife?" she asked.

"You!" he growled.

"I don't believe that!" Lily protested. "Young men like Pel do not come to a greenroom unless they are looking for female—er, diversion."

"And they do not keep coming back unless they have found it."

"Not with me, he hasn't!"

"But he has great expectations, does he not?"

She bridled angrily at this insinuation she had been leading his cousin on.

"You are a very clever woman, Mrs. Culhane. I watched you last night with your disparate admirers. You play the greenroom game very well."

Much stung by his contempt, Lily retorted, "It is not a game I wish to play at all."

He raised one thick black eyebrow in mocking skepticism. "Then why do you?"

"Perhaps you are unaware that an actress's popularity, not her talent, often determines her financial recompense."

"Yes, particularly her popularity in the bedroom."

She gasped in outrage. "That is not what I meant! You clearly hold the common prejudice that all actresses are on the catch for a wealthy lover."

"Or a wealthy *young* husband."

Lily felt as though he had taken a whip to her. How could he possibly think her such a heartless hussy as to want to catch a calfling like Pel in a parson's mousetrap? She was insulted and deeply wounded that he could suspect she had marital designs on his cousin.

The truth was that Lily had no intention of becoming any man's wife—or his convenient. Either position would require her to cede all control over her life to him. She had seen too often what happened when a woman became a man's property, at the mercy of his whims, and she had no intention of putting herself in *that* position. Now her money was her own to spend as she wished and she intended to keep it that way. She might give herself to a man she loved, but she would not become his chattel.

And what right did a country squire like Mr. St. Clair have to judge her like this? Obviously he held actresses in contempt even though he had probably never met one before. She asked with what she hoped was freezing scorn, "Your wide experience with actresses enables you to make such a judgment of me?"

"Yes," he said simply.

His answer added fuel to the fire of her temper. "Well, you are wrong! Indeed, I am surprised, Mr. St. Clair, that you would have deigned to walk with me today. Only consider the damage to your reputation if your friends should see you with me."

Instead of embarrassing him as she had intended, he looked as though he was enjoying some private joke.

"It will survive," he said carelessly, "and perhaps even be enhanced. Furthermore, as I told you last night, I take my responsibility for my young cousin very seriously. I will do anything, *anything*, to protect him and his wife from having their marriage irreparably harmed."

Lily inwardly applauded his concern, but it only added to her anger that he could think her the kind of female who would wreck a marriage. She asked scathingly, "Are you offering yourself as a consolation prize for your cousin, Mr. St. Clair?"

He shrugged. "Why not? I am more eligible."

"Because there is no Mrs. Damon St. Clair?"

Lily saw in his eyes the same amusement that she

had seen the previous night when Pel had introduced him.

"Because I am richer than Pel."

That stung her into snapping, "That is no recommendation!"

He smiled sourly. "Most women would disagree with you."

"How cynical you are."

"Yes," he agreed, "but no more than you, I suspect."

"You suspect wrong!" With frigid hauteur, Lily said, "I do not sell myself for money to you or any man!"

Mr. St. Clair lifted a skeptical eyebrow, clearly unperturbed by her outrage, and queried insolently, "For jewels then?"

She sputtered in anger.

He gave her a wicked predator's smile. "Tell me, Mrs. Culhane, what is it you want from me?"

"I want you to leave me alone!"

She wheeled and rushed away from him.

He did not try to stop her.

Chapter 4

L ily was too agitated after leaving Mr. St. Clair
to enjoy a solitary stroll. She needed to distract
her thoughts from that infuriating man, and she decided upon a visit to Milson Street, Bath's most popular shopping area. Lily headed rapidly in that
direction, hoping that her brisk pace would have the
double benefit of carrying her away as fast as possible from Damon St. Clair and of helping her to
vent her anger at him.

When she reached Milson Street, she stopped at
a linen draper's, intending to pick out a length of
sprig muslin for a summer gown. She wanted her
modiste to make it for her before she left Bath at the
end of the season, now little more than a fortnight
away. Lily was still so angry with Mr. St. Clair,
however, that she could not concentrate on her mission and finally departed from the shop empty-
handed.

As she stepped outside, a man in a high-crowned
beaver hat hailed her. She smiled with genuine pleasure as she recognized her brother's best friend, Sir
Roger Hilton. After Lily had managed to scrape together the money to buy her brother an officer's
commission, he had gone off to serve with Wellington's army where he had met Roger.

Until typhoid had killed Roger's father and elder

brother three months ago, he had been Major Hilton. His unexpected inheritance of the baronetcy had required him to sell his officer's commission, leave the army in France, and come home to England.

As Sir Roger swept off his beaver and bowed in greeting to Lily, several female passersby eyed her enviously. With his curly blond hair, sky-blue eyes, wide smile, and muscular build, he was a remarkably handsome specimen.

So handsome that Lily's brother had cautioned her against losing her heart, for she was not in Sir Roger's style. He preferred clinging blondes and was never so happy as when he had a helpless female to lean upon him.

Her brother's admonition had been quite unnecessary. Although Lily liked Sir Roger as a friend, she felt no attraction to him the way she had to that wretched Mr. St. Clair.

"How is your mama today?" Lily asked.

Roger's mother had also been stricken with the typhoid that had claimed her husband and other son. Her health was still so impaired that Roger had brought her to Bath in the hope that the waters would help her.

"Better. She seems to grow a little stronger each day," he said. "I am hopeful that we shall be able to leave Bath in another month or so. May I walk with you?"

Lily nodded, and he fell into step beside her as she started up the hill.

Sir Roger complained, "I know so few people here that it shall be very boring for me after you leave. Do you still mean to go to Weymouth as soon as the Theatre Royal's season ends?"

"Yes," Lily replied. She planned to treat herself to a fortnight's vacation by the sea before fulfilling the reluctant commitment she had made to her Uncle Joseph that she would spend eight weeks performing with his company of strolling players.

He and his troupe had fallen on hard times, and he had asked her to help them out. Lily, who had won much acclaim in the provincial theatre, was certain to attract larger audiences for his company. She regarded her familial duties as seriously as Mr. St. Clair did his, and she could not turn down poor Uncle Joseph's request, much as she wanted to.

Lily told Roger, "I am eager for Weymouth, but I confess I do not look forward to eight weeks of trudging through Dorset and Devon on foot, performing in any country village that will have us."

It would be her first taste of the rigors of a strolling player's lot. She had been talented—and lucky—enough to have escaped performing in that milieu, the lowliest in the British theatre. Her parents had traveled briefly with such a company before she was born, and they had recalled it with loathing.

Roger smiled sympathetically. "But think of what awaits you in the autumn—Covent Garden."

"I hope it awaits me, but I shall not go to London without a contract, and so far I have been offered only a tryout performance."

Lily's goal, like that of every other British actor, was to play at one or the other of London's two great theatres, Drury Lane and Covent Garden. But she had seen the fate of those who rushed to accept the offer of a tryout with either, only to be savaged by the critics and cast adrift without being offered a contract. They never won a second chance to tread the boards in London.

Lily was determined that would not happen to her. That was why she had spurned all tryout offers and was insisting upon a contract. She would not have her years of hard work to hone her talent and perfect her craft go for naught because of a cynical

critic who preferred cruel witticisms at her expense
to honesty.

"I am certain you will be offered a contract," Sir
Roger said. "I saw your Lady Macbeth last night,
and you were brilliant. I predict a triumphant London debut for you. Perhaps your brother will be
home from France by then to share that night with
you."

They paused to inspect the offerings in the window of Mr. Duffield's circulating library that included, in addition to books, gloves, brooches, and
rings.

A young woman in a lavender pelisse and a
plumed hat of the same color came out of the pastry
shop next door. Lily recognized her as the shrewish
female that she had seen several times in the Pump
Room in the company of three other young ladies of
quality. Today, however, she was alone except for
her abigail.

Suddenly, the girl's haughty frown dissolved into
a simpering smile at the sight of a fashionably attired man of perhaps five and thirty approaching
from the opposite direction. Lily couldn't help over-
hearing her speak.

"Lord Waymore, what a delightful surprise."

The sudden warmth in her normally cold eyes betrayed a *tendre* for him, and Lily glanced curiously
at the object of the young woman's gaze.

The well-dressed man did not look as though he
shared the girl's sentiment, but he stopped and
greeted her politely, then asked, "Lady Cassandra,
is the rumor true? Has your brother arrived in
Bath?"

"Please, Lord Waymore," she replied waspishly,
"Lord Hawkhurst is my *half*-brother. Pray, do not
make him any closer a relative than he is."

Lily's attention was immediately captured by the
mention of that notorious rake.

"Yes, he arrived last night, although why he bothered to come, I cannot understand." Lady Cassandra's tone was shrill and grating. "He is such a disobliging pinch-purse. His cruel, clutch-fisted behavior toward me and the rest of his family is not to be believed."

Lord Waymore's eyes took on an icy glaze, and he said with sharp reproach, "Lady Cassandra, I cannot listen to you abuse your brother like this. I could not ask for a better or more dependable friend than Hawk."

Lily watched as Lady Cassandra struggled to hide her anger at his reply. "I declare, Lord Waymore, I do not understand how you can defend him!"

"Easily! Ask any man of the *ton*, and he will tell you that Hawk is esteemed as a man of integrity whose word is his bond."

Hawkhurst's integrity might be unquestioned in dealing with members of his own sex and class, but Lily had heard enough about him to doubt that he applied the same standard of conduct to females.

Lord Waymore quickly parted from Lady Cassandra, resuming his walk at a rapid pace that bespoke his eagerness to escape her. Two spots of high color rose on the girl's thin cheeks as she found herself summarily abandoned, and she went hastily into the circulating library.

"What a thoroughly unpleasant young woman," Roger said as the door shut behind her. "From all I know of Lord Hawkhurst, he does not deserve such abuse."

"Are you acquainted with him?" Lily asked.

"No, but my late brother was, and he was rather in awe of him. He said Hawkhurst was the most trustworthy of friends and the most dangerous of enemies. Men are careful not to get on the wrong side of him."

''With good reason,'' she remarked. ''His skill with both pistols and fists is famous.''

If Roger had heard as much as Lily had about the man they called the king of the greenroom, she doubted he would defend him. His sister had called him a pinch-purse, and Lily could believe that. It was said that he never made a woman his convenient unless she agreed to the famous Hawkhurst Ultimatum that she would not present him with outrageous modiste bills, would not ask him to buy her costly jewels, and would not hurl recriminations at him when their affair ended.

Lily supposed that it would be too much to hope that Hawkhurst, given his fondness for actresses and greenrooms, would not turn up at the Theatre Royal that night. That was all she needed on top of the cousins St. Clair.

Damon had replayed his walk with Lily over and over in his mind. Her outrage when he had suggested that she would be willing to become his for a price would have pleased him if only he had been able to believe that it was unfeigned. But he could not forget that she was an actress.

Was the provoking creature giving a performance or was she sincere? She intrigued him as much as she confused him.

He should have told her that he was Lord Hawkhurst, he thought scornfully. That would have settled the issue instantly.

It always did.

Damon decided to pay a call on Pel and his wife, hoping to catch both of them at home so that he could observe them together.

When he reached their lodgings, Hawkhurst got his wish. They were both in the drawing room, Pel leafing restlessly through a newly delivered London newspaper and Cecilia staring without interest at the cloth stretched taut in her embroidery hoop. The tension between the couple was palpable.

Pel glared at Damon over the top of his newspaper before reluctantly putting it aside and rising. He asked stiffly, "What brings you here, Lord Hawkhurst?"

"So we are back to that, are we?" Damon said sardonically. "I have come to pay my respects to your wife."

Cecilia pulled herself clumsily to her feet. Her slumped shoulders thrust the burden of her belly out even farther, and she came forward with dragging step to greet him.

Never had Damon seen her look so poorly. Normally, she was a sprightly creature with sparkling hazel eyes, clear skin, and a sweet smile. Today, however, her eyes were dull, her face was marred by ugly red splotches, and her mouth was pinched in a sullen, unhappy line.

The change in her was nothing short of shocking, and Damon asked in genuine concern, "Ceci, what is wrong?"

Her mouth trembled. "Nothing," she said, her resigned sigh giving lie to her answer.

"Are you ill?" Damon persisted anxiously.

"No," she said with another long, exaggerated sigh.

"At least, I beg of you, sit down."

She did so, sinking down heavily upon the cushion of her chair as though her weight—and life itself—was too heavy to be borne.

Pel watched his wife with a jaundiced eye that held no sympathy. Hawkhurst wondered how the puppy could be so hard-hearted when the poor girl was clearly miserable, but he reminded himself that he had not been the one who had lived with her the past few months. He remembered his cousin's baf-

fled complaint that she had become a stranger to
him since she had been increasing.

Damon studied her. Whenever he had seen her
regard Pel, it had been with a shy, adoring look, but
now he saw pain in her eyes. He wondered whether
she had heard rumors of her husband's infatuation
with Lily Culhane.

He was certain, though, that the trouble between
the young couple ran deeper than that. Lily had been
right when she had claimed to be a symptom, not
the cause, of it.

Damon spent the next several minutes trying to
cheer Cecilia by recounting amusing tales about
members of the *ton*, but his efforts were in vain. Her
face was fixed in a martyred expression, as though
she was determined to be unhappy. He could see
why Pel would prefer Lily's livelier, more pleasant
company.

What the devil was wrong with Cecilia?

Pel said, "I am expecting Mama to arrive in Bath
within the next few days. She wants to be here for
my birthday."

That reminded Hawkhurst his cousin was only
several days short of attaining his majority, when he
would come into control of his inheritance. While
Damon would welcome relinquishing his duties as its
trustee, he hoped that Pel would not foolishly squander it trying to buy Lily's, or some other woman's,
intimacy.

When Damon took his leave, his cousin accompanied him to the door. Once they were out of Cecilia's hearing, Pel said bitterly, "You see how she
is! She acts like that all the time, and she won't tell
me what is wrong!"

"You must try harder to get her to do so," Damon
replied. Were she his wife, he would get it out of her
quick enough. "I am shocked at how poorly Cecilia

looks. She is clearly having a difficult pregnancy, and you must make allowances for that.''

''I am tired of making allowances!'' Pel cried petulantly. ''It has gotten so that I hate to come home.''

The unattractive pout on his round young face reminded Hawkhurst of a spoiled brat. How he longed to shake some sense into both husband and wife. They had been no more ready for marriage than two children in leading strings.

He silently castigated Pel's overly protective mother, Margaret St. Clair, for having kept her only child safely at her side in the country, away from nubile females, until she had succeeded in marrying him off to the sweet, well-bred heiress she had selected for him.

''Furthermore,'' Pel was saying, ''I am very angry with you for trying to cut me out with Lily last night.''

Damon shrugged. ''I cannot help it if she found me interesting.''

''If you win her, it will be because of your title,'' Pel complained. ''It gives you an unfair advantage over me.''

''Only if Mrs. Culhane learns that I have one. I have no intention of telling her, and I sincerely hope that no one else does either. I confess I am surprised that you could be so enamored of a woman you fear would forsake you at the first prospect of a titled admirer.''

Pel had no answer to that, and Damon continued, ''Perhaps what is wrong with Cecilia is that she has heard gossip about your chasing a lightskirt.''

''Lily is not a lightskirt!''

''Most actresses are; no one knows that better than I,'' Hawkhurst said. ''It would be especially depressing for a girl in Cecilia's condition to hear her husband is straying.''

''I don't know which I feel more guilty about—

hurting Cecilia or not being able to make Lily an honorable offer," Pel cried. "It is hell to be in love with a woman who is not your wife!"

"I would not know since I do not have a wife, and I have never been in love. I don't believe in it. Perhaps if you attended more to Cecilia instead of the greenroom—"

His cousin bridled at that. "Who are you to lecture me on fidelity, with all the convenients you have had?"

"But I did not have a pregnant wife—or any wife at all—that I was hurting. It is very easy to marry, but very difficult to make a marriage work."

As Lily walked reluctantly toward the greenroom that night, the thought that she might have to contend with Lord Hawkhurst there as well as Damon and Pelham St. Clair was more than she could face. Her composure slipped and her steps faltered. What cutting remarks would Mr. St. Clair address to her tonight?

Needing a moment to recover and steel herself for what lay ahead, she stepped among the machinery and props stored backstage. She was so preoccupied that she did not notice the big, burly figure hiding behind a scenery flat.

When she felt sufficiently in control of herself to handle the forthcoming ordeal in the greenroom, she resumed walking. As she passed the flat that concealed the man, he stepped out, grabbing her arm in a punishing grip. "Ah ha, my pretty one."

She looked up into a pair of vacant gray eyes set in a face of surly belligerence. Lily's heart sank as she recognized Hugo Broome, the son of the powerful Lord Olen. He had the build of an overgrown bull, and the manners of one, too.

It was rumored that his father, aware of his son's social shortcomings, had sent him to Bath in the hope he would acquire enough town bronze to make him presentable to London society. Laudable as this aim might have been, it was not likely to be realized because the young noddy had been placed in the care of an ailing aunt who exerted no control over him. She had allowed him to fall under the corrupting influence of Irwin Yarpole, another wealthy ne'er-do-well, who easily maneuvered Broome into doing his bidding.

Lily looked around nervously for Yarpole, since the two were virtually inseparable, but apparently Hugo was alone.

Both Broome's breath, reeking of alcohol, and his slurred speech told Lily he was badly foxed—and it was well known that he could not be reasoned with when he was drunk.

Although Lily was no coward, a shiver of alarm ran through her as she realized that she was alone with him in the narrow passage.

Nevertheless, she refused to let him see her apprehension. Affecting the hauteur of a duchess, she ordered, "Take your hands off me."

He laughed drunkenly, tightening his bruising grip on her arm. "Oh, no, 'tis time to perform for *my* benefit."

She tried to break his brutal grasp on her arm, but he was far too strong for her. He merely laughed at her effort. With his other hand, he grabbed her breast and kneaded it roughly.

Suddenly Broome's hold on her breast was broken by a hand that descended like a hatchet's edge upon his wrist. He let out a yelp of surprise and pain, then clutched at his injured joint with his other hand.

Lily, quite as astonished as her assailant by this unexpected deliverance, looked up at Damon St. Clair's harsh face. There was murderous anger in his dark, glittering eyes as they regarded Hugo Broome.

Relief and an odd exhilaration washed over Lily at the sight of Mr. St. Clair. After her quarrel with him this morning, she would never have expected him to have come to her rescue like this.

"The lady said no." Damon's voice was quiet, but it had the lethal edge of a well-sharpened knife. A wise man would have been alarmed, but Hugo Broome had never been wise.

He cried rashly, "She's no lady! She's a bloody actress."

"I repeat, the *lady* said no."

Damon's long, lean hand slapped Broome's face with such force that his head snapped to the left. Then the hand struck again, snapping it in the other direction. "Dare to contradict me again, and I will break that wooden stump you call a head."

Lily was amazed that Mr. St. Clair would defend her so vehemently when he himself thought so little of her.

For a moment Broome was too stunned by the blows to react to the grievous insult of being slapped. Then his beefy face turned nearly purple. "Damn you," he screamed, "no man does that to me and lives!"

Lily was terrified for Mr. St. Clair, her earlier anger at him forgotten in her concern for him. He might have a two-inch advantage in height, but he was much leaner and older than his thick-set young adversary.

Broome threw the first punch at Damon's face, but the older man easily deflected the blow, then delivered one of his own to Broome's chin that sent him staggering back.

Regaining his balance, Broome roared back at Damon like an enraged bull and swung first one, than the other of his fists at him. Again, Mr. St. Clair dodged him as gracefully as a hawk, then swooped in with a blow to Broome's stomach that sent him crashing against the wall. Broome slid slowly to the floor.

Propped against the wall in a half-sitting position, he looked at his opponent in dazed astonishment.

Lily was equally amazed. Hugo had failed to land a single blow before Mr. St. Clair subdued him. Perhaps in the future, she would model Mr. Culhane on Damon St. Clair instead of Lord Hawkhurst.

Broome touched his jaw and winced in pain.

"Get up," Damon ordered tersely, "so that I can give you the thrashing you deserve."

Broome was not that much of a fool. He stayed where he had fallen, clearly shocked and unnerved by the novel experience of being matched against an opponent who was not intimidated by his size.

Lily would have been amused by the bully's reaction to having the tables turned on him had she not feared she had involved her rescuer in an affair that would have serious repercussions for him. Broome's father, Lord Olen, was a powerful political figure and a perilous enemy for an obscure country gentleman such as Mr. St. Clair to make.

Hugo, unwilling to try his fists again against a clearly superior opponent, blustered, "You bastard, I will call you out."

"Please do," Damon said calmly. "In general, I refuse to duel half-wits. But in your case, I shall make an exception." He gave Broome a smile so full of menace that the young bully stared slack-jawed. "And I promise you, whelp, that you will not live to see another sun set."

Damon's dark glittering eyes, full of scorn and calm self-assurance, stared into Broome's pale-gray ones, which had grown round with fear.

"My father will have your head for this," Hugo

threatened, retreating to his second line of defense, family influence.

Damon sneered. "You terrify me, whelp."

But, Lily thought miserably, he did not know who Broome's father was. She shuddered at what vengeance Lord Olen might extract for this contemptuous treatment of his son. He had a reputation for being hot-tempered and proud—and quick to challenge men to duels. He had twice killed his opponents on the field of honor. She was desperately afraid that Mr. St. Clair would soon rue having come to her defense.

"My father is Lord Olen." Broome spoke the name in the triumphant tone of one smugly certain that it would strike terror in the heart of his adversary.

To both Hugo's and Lily's surprise, Mr. St. Clair only laughed derisively. "Is he now? When next you see him, offer him my sympathy for having such a despicable coward as you for a son."

Broome's face darkened with impotent rage at his opponent's goading, but he made no effort to get up from the floor and again subject himself to those iron fists.

Damon looked at him as though he was inspecting a particularly reprehensible toad. "You must be Olen's brat Hugo, the one he dares not permit in London. I had heard it was because you were a stupid, mannerless boor, which is true, but I suspect he must also have known what a cowardly disgrace you would be to your family."

Lily wished that Mr. St. Clair would not continue to antagonize Hugo, fearing that in the end he would pay dearly for it.

Broome, his face livid with anger, promised, "When I tell my father about you, you will curse this day."

Damon's eyes glittered maliciously. "Tell your father that instead of permitting you to run free in Bath, he should have kept you locked up with the other animals in his menagerie at Olen Hall."

Hugo choked in fury. "My papa will avenge my honor."

"He cannot avenge what does not exist," Damon said calmly.

"I promise you he will call you out and kill you for your insults to me!"

"Trying to hide behind your father now, are you? My quarrel is not with him, you craven coward, but with you."

Hugo apparently interpreted this response as apprehension on Damon's part about facing Lord Olen. "Ah ha, you have heard of my father's successes on the field of honor and are afraid of him."

"I have no fear of him. Nor will your father call me out."

Mr. St. Clair spoke with such quiet conviction that Broome gaped at him for a moment before blustering, "You are a sapskull if you think that."

"No, it is you who is the sapskull. Your father has twice challenged men who were even more abysmal shots than he." Contempt permeated Damon's voice. "He will not be so foolhardy as to call me out."

"Yes, he will," Broome whined, although his confidence was clearly faltering before his adversary's certainty.

"Very well, if you are fool enough to think that, then tell your father that Damon St. Clair awaits his pleasure. Should he wish to pursue this matter as you think he will, I shall be happy to meet him whenever and wherever he wishes. But before I do so, I promise you that I shall have the great pleasure of ridding the world of scum like you."

Mr. St. Clair gave Broome a smile so deadly that Lily's blood ran cold. Apparently it had the same effect on Broome, for he began edging along the hall floor toward the exit. Damon put out his leg to block Hugo's way.

"First, whelp, you will apologize to the lady."

Broome glared at Lily. "Damned if I will."

"You'll be damned sore if you don't," Damon promised him quietly. "Now be quick about it. My patience is at an end."

"Beg pardon," Hugo mumbled sullenly, refusing to look at Lily

Damon grabbed Broome's cravat and yanked it to choking tightness around his neck. He held it for a moment before instructing, "You will tell her, 'I beg your pardon, ma'am,' and you will look her in the eye as you do so."

He loosened his grip on the cravat, and Broome, once he could again speak, hastily repeated what he had been told.

"Good," Damon said crisply. "If ever I hear that you have dared to come near this lady again, you may say your final prayers. Now, get out of my sight, young Broome, or I will sweep the floor with you."

Hugo scrambled to his feet and fled.

Chapter 5

As Hugo Broome slunk from sight, Lily tried to thank Mr. St. Clair for rescuing her, but he interrupted her, saying curtly, "I am taking you home."

Her eyes widened in shock, then narrowed indignantly. "Great as my gratitude to you is, you are very much mistaken to think that I would . . ." Her voice trailed off.

Amusement softened the stern set of his mouth. "You would what?"

"You know what—and I won't."

" 'Tis shocking how little a lady's gratitude earns a man these days." His mournful tone was belied by the teasing light in his dark eyes. "Nonetheless, I am still taking you home because I am concerned about your safety. You are in considerably more danger from Broome tonight than me. Despite my warnings to that dim-witted bully, he may follow you when you leave here. And unlike him, I accept when a lady says no."

Lily had to admit to herself that Mr. St. Clair was probably right. As she had no desire for a second surprise meeting with Hugo, his protection would be most welcome until she was home. Indeed, it would be positively churlish to refuse it when he had rescued her at what would be considerable cost

61

to himself. Although Broome had richly deserved the punishment he had gotten, the young bully's powerful father would cause Mr. St. Clair trouble aplenty.

As Lily took the arm that he offered her, the harsh lines of his face relaxed, and he smiled at her in a way that lifted her depressed spirits and made her a little giddy.

As they stepped outside into Beaufort Square, she was surprised at how much she suddenly looked forward to the ride to her lodgings.

His groom was waiting in the square with his curricle. The servant was not in livery, and Lily took this as another sign that Mr. St. Clair, for all his talk of being richer than Pel, was a man of relatively modest fortune.

He settled on the driver's seat beside Lily while the groom jumped up behind.

As Mr. St. Clair guided his pair of bays out of the square, Lily said, "You were very brave to confront Broome as you did. I pray he and his father will not cause you trouble."

He gave her a searching look, then said with magnificent unconcern, "Olen is not the imbecile that Hugo is."

She hoped that was true, but still she worried. "I must warn you that Hugo has a friend named Yarpole who is also dangerous."

"Irwin Yarpole?"

"You know him?" Lily asked in surprise.

"We have met." An odd little smile danced upon his lips.

"I fear the pair might attack you."

"They may try, but I am not overly concerned about them. Indeed, I would rather look forward to meeting Yarpole again."

Lily admired his fearlessness even as she worried for his safety.

When they were a block beyond the square, Mr. St. Clair turned the curricle down a dark, narrow street that led in the opposite direction from her lodgings.

Alarmed, Lily demanded, "Where are you taking me?"

"Why, I am abducting you, of course!"

"What!" she squeaked in shock.

He laughed. "Don't fly into the boughs! I am quizzing you. This circuitous route is to make certain that Broome is not following us."

They rode on in silence with only the clatter of the horses' hooves and the curricle's wheels on the paving stones breaking the quiet of the night. The faint odor of sandalwood drifted over Lily, and she was acutely conscious of how close Mr. St. Clair's powerful body was to her own on the seat.

They rounded another corner at a rapid clip, sending Lily sliding against him. His arm automatically went around her to steady her, and she felt a slow warmth curl deep within her at his touch.

Lily was a quick study when it came to reading a man, but Mr. St. Clair baffled her. That he was dangerous, she was certain—her heartbeat did not race with other men the way it was doing now with him—but beyond that she was confused.

Terribly confused.

After the harsh words they had exchanged that morning, she could scarcely believe that he could be so intent on protecting her tonight.

She said candidly, "I did not expect to see you at the theatre after this morning."

"Did you think I came to see you tonight?" he queried in a tone that implied she was a fool if she did.

Lily bristled at his mocking inflection. "I am astonished that you forced Broome to apologize to me when you clearly think so little of me yourself."

"In all honesty, I was a little astonished myself," Damon admitted. And that was the truth. He could not remember when he had been filled with such rage as when he had seen Hugo Broome's hands on Lily. Though Hawkhurst despised drunken sots who had not the wit to win a woman willingly but must use force, his reaction to Broome had gone far beyond that.

The pea-brain was lucky to still be drawing breath.

Damon was equally surprised by how collected Lily remained. Under the circumstances, she could have been forgiven for dissolving into strong hysterics. But she had not done so. She had not even shed a tear.

After his helpless, weeping female relatives, she was a blessed relief.

He complimented her on her composure, and Lily replied with conviction, "I despise tears. They accomplish nothing."

"I wish you might convince the women of my family of that," he said wryly. After his own mother had died, tears had always secured for Olivia, his father's manipulative second wife, what she wanted from her husband. Her daughter Cassandra quickly learned to emulate her, causing Damon to observe sarcastically that the rain of tears that fell within their home was greater than the precipitation produced outside by the wet English climate.

He often wondered what quirk in his father had made him so partial to watering pots like Olivia and Phoebe.

Whatever it was, his son had not inherited it.

The curricle turned down Lily's narrow street. It was silent and dark, with only an occasional light in an upper-story window, but Hawkhurst could see no sign of anyone lurking in the shadows. He was satisfied that Broome had not followed them.

Damon escorted Lily to the door. She unlocked it

and turned to bid him good night. But he would not allow her to be rid of him so easily this night. At the very least, he intended to have some answers about the mysterious Mr. Culhane—who, he was convinced, was not her husband.

He brushed past her into the tiny entry dimly lit by a single candle flickering on a small pier table beneath a looking glass. A lamp burned in a drawing room to the left of the entry.

"Mr. St. Clair, I did not invite you in!"

He ignored Lily's protest. "Is Mr. Culhane here?"

"That is none of your business."

"It is tonight. Broome did not follow us here, but I want to be certain that he did not precede us either." Hawkhurst did not for an instant think Hugo could have done so, but he intended to use the possibility to find out more about the missing Culhane.

Damon looked at Lily's indignant reflection in the looking glass on the wall. The green eyes were fiery, and her full, tempting mouth slightly open. She looked lovely even when she was angry. He ruthlessly suppressed his sudden desire to turn and kiss away her displeasure.

Instead, he said, "If Mr. Culhane is here, I can be comfortable that Broome is not hiding in wait for your return."

"Young Mr. Broome does not even know where I live."

"Don't be so certain of that. He might bully your address out of one of your other admirers."

"I do not permit any of my so-called admirers to know my address."

That meshed with what Sewell had learned earlier in the day, yet Damon could not help raising an eyebrow in skepticism. "None of them?"

"None of them," she said firmly.

Either she set a very high price on her favors or

she meant to hold out for marriage to a young fool like Pel. He said blandly, "If Mr. Culhane is not here, I must make certain nothing is amiss before I leave."

She said evasively, "He is away . . . but my maid Trude is here."

"She would be no match for Hugo. Neither are you."

A large-boned young woman in nightclothes appeared in the doorway. A surprised gasp escaped her lips when she saw Hawkhurst, and she hastily drew her wrapper more tightly around her. Her shocked expression told him that her finding a man with Mrs. Culhane like this was indeed a rare occurrence.

Hawkhurst did not reflect on why that should please him so much. "Trude, I presume," he said politely.

"Yes, sir," the maid replied.

Lily asked, "Has anyone come here tonight, Trude?"

"No, ma'am. 'Tis been quiet as a church."

Lily gave Damon an I-told-you-so look. "Thank you, Trude. I am sorry we disturbed you. Go back to bed."

Knowing that Lily would try to dismiss him now, Hawkhurst deliberately strode into the drawing room. Its furnishings were of the indifferent variety common to rented lodgings, but the sofa and chairs had been brightened by draping them in chintz brightly patterned with roses.

Other items had been added to relieve the room's impersonal drabness. In one corner, a chess set rested on a small mahogany table. An intricately wrought gilt-bronze clock graced the mantel. A round tripod table held a vase filled with spring flowers and a miniature portrait in a silver frame.

The result was a surprisingly inviting room. And

a very feminine one. Except for the chess set, it had no accoutrements that bespoke a male presence. Yet the rooms were large and the address expensive. Some discreet gentleman must be paying for them. Was it Culhane?

Lily was watching him warily, her lips slightly parted in an unwitting invitation that made Hawkhurst yearn to taste her mouth.

In a bid to extend his stay, he asked, "Do you have any brandy?"

"No."

"None?" Every actress he had ever known kept a supply on hand for her male visitors, but Lily, apparently, had none of those either. "A pity. I suspect after what happened tonight a sip or two of it would be good for you."

And for him, too, as he kissed its residue from those full, beguiling lips of hers.

Damon tore his fascinated gaze away from Lily's mouth and forced himself to move to the circular table that held the flowers and the miniature.

He picked up the little portrait, studying it intently. So this was Culhane. The artist had captured the likeness of an exceedingly handsome young man. Women would find that face and the laughter in his gray-green eyes, fringed by thick dark lashes, irresistible.

Hawkhurst glanced at Lily. The glow in her eyes as she looked at the miniature was like a claw in his gut. This wave of intense emotion was as alien to him as it was puzzling. Surely, it could not be jealousy, could it? He had never been jealous in his life. Yet he irrationally longed to wrap his hands around the young man's neck and strangle him.

He said harshly, "Mr. Culhane, I presume."

"No," Lily answered.

"No?" he echoed in surprise. "Then who is he?"

"No one you would know."

Damon's eyes narrowed assessingly. "If I were Mr. Culhane, I think I would be jealous of him. Would I be justified?"

"But you are not Mr. Culhane," she parried.

He knew he would not get the man's identity out of her, so he put the little portrait down and wandered over to the chess set in the corner. It was a costly one, with delicate porcelain pieces that were exquisitely painted. He wondered what lover had given it to her.

Behind him, Lily said sarcastically, "*Do* make yourself at home, Mr. St. Clair."

"Thank you, I will," he replied cordially, picking up a porcelain queen with a gold crown upon her head. He preferred chess to all other games, but he had difficulty finding an opponent worthy of him. "Do you play?"

"Yes, I am very fond of the game," Lily said.

"Does that mean you play it well?"

"I'm judged a tolerably good player."

"Indulge me in a game tomorrow afternoon."

"I cannot. I am meeting a friend at the Pump Room for the concert."

His eyes narrowed. "Who is he?"

"*Her* name is Nell Wayne."

Her frankness pleased him. Too many women would have let him continue in his mistaken impression that the friend was a male admirer. "Do you perform tomorrow night?"

"No, the play is *The Country Girl*, and I have no part in it."

"Good, you have the night off, and the Pump Room concert will be over at three-thirty. We will play chess after that."

He thought for a moment she meant to refuse him, but then she capitulated. "Very well. It has been a long time since I have had a challenging opponent."

Suppressing a smile at this unconscious compliment, he asked blandly, "Has Mr. Culhane been away *that* long?"

Irritation flickered in her eyes, and she looked pointedly at the door. "It is getting late. I can't thank you enough for rescuing me from Broome."

"Yes, you can."

She stiffened in suspicion.

He laughed. "No, I am not going to ask you *that*."

Two spots of color rose in her cheeks, and she did not try to deny that his guess was correct.

"You underestimate me as badly as Broome did," he chided.

"Oh, no, definitely not *that* much!" Lily would happily vouch to anyone that Mr. St. Clair was a *very* dangerous man.

"If you wish to thank me, Lily, do so by inviting me to sit down and honestly answering two simple questions. Will you do that?"

It would be a mistake to let him sit down. Lily knew that. She should have demanded that he depart as soon as Trude told them Hugo had not been there. And she most certainly should insist that he go now.

Except she did not want him to leave. Lily was attracted to Mr. St. Clair as she had never been to another man. The realization shocked her to her toes.

She led him to the chintz-covered sofa. He waited politely until she had seated herself, then he sat beside her—a trifle too close. Yet she could not bring herself to move away.

"What is your first question, Mr. St. Clair?"

His sensual mouth curved into a smile that made her heart skip a beat. Lily found herself wondering what it would be like to be kissed by those lips.

"Where is Mr. Culhane?"

She should have known it would be about her nonexistent husband. Mr. St. Clair deserved a truthful answer, but Lily was afraid to trust him with her secret. She hesitated, then said coolly, "That is no concern of yours."

"No," he agreed affably, "but since I was forced to discharge his duty to protect you tonight, I am curious why he leaves a lady as lovely as you alone and unguarded."

That reminded Lily of her fear that Mr. St. Clair would pay a heavy price for his treatment of Lord Olen's son, no matter how justified it had been. She bit her lip anxiously. "I am terribly afraid Broome's father will cause you enormous trouble. He is very powerful. Why are you looking at me so strangely?"

His mouth twisted in an odd smile. "I am unused to having anyone worry about my welfare." He looked as though her concern had touched him. "You need not worry about me. As you saw tonight, I am quite capable of taking care of myself."

"Yes," she agreed, thinking of how quickly he had disposed of Hugo Broome.

"You still have not answered my question," he reminded her. "Where is Mr. Culhane?"

Lily was torn. "I owe you honesty, but can I trust you to keep my secret?"

He put his hand over hers and squeezed it reassuringly. "Yes," he said simply. "You have my word. Where is he?"

"He isn't."

"What?" Damon asked blankly.

"Mr. Culhane does not exist."

Dumbfounded, Damon pointed to the slender, worn band of gold on her ring finger. "Then what is this?"

"It was my mother's," she confessed.

"Hell's fire, why did you create a phantom husband for yourself?"

Lily's delectable chin rose proudly. "To forestall dishonorable offers."

"Does it work?"

"Oh, yes." Her emerald eyes suddenly danced with mischief.

She looked so enchanting that desire flared with such intensity in Damon that he had to grip the edge of the sofa to keep from taking her in his arms.

"You see, Mr. Culhane is noted for his exploits with his fists and weapons," Lily confided, her eyes still alight. "I modeled him after the notorious Lord Hawkhurst."

Damon burst out laughing. It would seem that he had been jealous of himself!

Looking perturbed, she said, "You would not laugh if you were a woman."

That sobered him. He could not explain the reason for his mirth without betraying that he was Hawkhurst, and he had become obsessed with winning Lily before she learned of his title. Otherwise he would never know whether she accepted him because of that or because she truly cared for him.

"No, I suppose I would not were I a woman," Damon agreed thoughtfully. Although greenroom habitués might be gentlemen with their own class, few of them extended that courtesy to actresses whom they considered beneath them. They were more often rude, leering, arrogant, and condescending.

That *he* did not act like that was one reason for his own success in the greenroom. His good manners and polite demeanor made him stand out from the others as much as his subdued clothing did.

It was also true, as Lily had said, that an actress's earnings depended upon her popularity. Invoking a jealous, dangerous husband would not cause the ill will—and perhaps even the retribution—that an outright rejection would. How clever of her.

Lily was watching him curiously from beneath her long, curling lashes. He loved that quizzical gaze of hers. It made him yearn to kiss her, but he knew better than to try it—yet. Instead he touched her cheek, as soft as pink silk, with his fingertips and promised her, ''The secret of Mr. Culhane is safe with me.''

For a moment, she only stared at him, the longing he felt unconsciously mirrored in her eyes.

Then, abruptly, she caught his hand and brought it down to his lap. He let her, but then imprisoned her own when she would have withdrawn it.

''I have not asked my second question,'' he reminded her. ''What is your interest in my cousin?''

Damon could feel Lily trying to extract her hand from his, but he was reluctant to let it go. He kept it tightly in his own.

''You have it backward,'' she said tartly. ''It is your cousin who is interested in me.''

He looked intently into her eyes as he asked, ''Are you saying you have none in him?''

She hesitated.

''Frankly, Lily, I am convinced you have no romantic inclination toward him. Am I wrong?''

''No,'' she admitted.

''Then I ask you again, why have you not sent him packing? I am trying very hard to understand what game you are playing with him.''

She jerked her hand angrily out of his grasp. ''No game at all!'' she cried. ''Contrary to what you think, Mr. St. Clair, I have no interest in catching Pel in a parson's mousetrap. I detect a strong streak of obstinacy in him.''

Her brilliant eyes met Damon's without evasion or guile. ''I am persuaded that he would regard a blunt rejection as a challenge that would only make him all the more stubbornly determined to win me.''

Damon had to admit that she was most likely right. His opposition to Pel's marrying Cecilia had certainly had that effect.

Hawkhurst was surprised at how jubilant he felt. Lily had not been trying to snare his cousin after all!

"I have no desire to marry Pel—or any man."

Damon's elation faded. He did not for a moment believe that. "But marriage is every woman's goal," he said cynically.

Lily raised her chin proudly. "Men like to think that, but it is not mine."

"I don't believe you," he said flatly. "I have yet to meet a woman who did not want to land the best catch she could. The more impressive his fortune and social standing the better."

"Not every woman is for sale!"

He looked slowly, deliberately around her drawing room. "Who pays for these fashionable lodgings?"

"I do!" she cried angrily. "I am fortunate that I am able to make a comfortable living as an actress. I neither need nor want a man to support me." Her gaze—proud, determined, without subterfuge—met his squarely.

In all his wide experience, Hawkhurst had never met another woman like her, and she fascinated him.

Lily continued, "I doubt that you will believe me, but I have Pel's interests as much at heart as you do. I am convinced that the best way to deal with him is to induce him to become disenchanted with me."

Hawkhurst could scarcely believe the dazzling opportunity she had just given him, but he wasted no time in seizing it. "If you truly want to disillusion Pel, pretend to be enamored of me."

"I thought of that," she admitted, her finger tracing the outline of a chintz rose on the sofa, "but I do not wish to cause a breach between you and him."

Once again her concern took him by surprise. "That is a chance I am willing to take." His breath caught at the thought that he might actually persuade her to choose this course.

"Are you?" Her expression was troubled. "I am not sure I am."

"It would be worth it to me to see Pel and Cecilia work out their difficulties," he assured her. "There is no hope of that until he has recovered from his infatuation with you. Can you think of a more certain way to accomplish that than to make him believe you have a *tendre* for me?"

"No," she admitted, still absently tracing the chintz rose with her finger.

She was wavering, he could tell.

"It's odd," she confessed, "last night I was happy to pretend to be enamored of you as a way of disillusioning Pel, but tonight I find I am loath to be the cause of trouble between you."

Damon was startled by both her candor and her concern. Catching her hand in his again, he tried appealing to her compassion. "Only think of Pel's poor wife. Cecilia is so miserable."

Lily hesitated a long moment before she said reluctantly, "All right, I'll do it."

"Good girl!" he exclaimed. "We will begin our charade immediately. I will not leave your side in the greenroom, and I will take you home afterward. You, in turn, will pretend to be infatuated with me."

Hawkhurst thought craftily that Lily would not have to *pretend* for very long. He would make certain that her passion for him would soon be genuine. Their charade would give him the perfect way of ensuring that. It was a delicious scheme.

Getting her to agree to it was the most he could hope to accomplish tonight. Always a superb tactician in the game of seduction, he decided upon a strategic withdrawal. He rose to his feet, saying politely that it was time for him to go.

Lily looked surprised—and perhaps even a little

disappointed—but she did not attempt to dissuade him from leaving.

In the entry, he paused and turned to her. "We will launch our charade by walking together tomorrow morning."

She frowned. "I don't see what that would accomplish."

He didn't either. It had simply been an excuse to be with her. That realization brought him up short. What the devil was wrong with him? He had never been this eager for a woman's company before except in bed.

He was not about to admit that to her, though, and he improvised hastily, "The more we are seen together, the more tongues will wag."

"A better way to set tongues wagging would be to go to the public breakfast."

She was right, he thought, but it was certain to be attended by people who knew him and would greet him as Lord Hawkhurst.

"No," he said hastily. "I would rather walk with you than breakfast with others."

"I see," she said quietly, hurt in her eyes.

Hell's fire, she believed that he was ashamed to be seen with her at the breakfast, when nothing could be further from the truth!

"No, you do not see," he said gently. "I should be very pleased to have you upon my arm."

Indeed he would. She was a glorious creature, with the bearing of an aristocratic lady of highest quality. Anyone who did not know she was an actress would believe her to be a high-bred woman.

He continued, "But I find the prospect of conversing with the tedious people who attend public breakfasts a dead bore." That much at least was true. "Let me take you walking at eleven."

To his relief, the hurt vanished from her brilliant eyes. As he looked down into their bottomless green depths, Hawkhurst could not resist doing what he had been yearning for almost from the first moment he had seen her.

He bent his head and kissed her, lightly brushing her lips with his own. His hands cupped her face so that she could not pull back from him, and he felt her involuntary little shiver at his touch. Her skin was as soft and velvety as the flower for which she was named.

He teased her lips apart and deepened his kiss. She smelled of wild roses on a warm summer evening. Her mouth was as sweet as honey, and he wanted to taste it all night. He had to fight himself to keep from crushing her soft, tantalizing body to his.

Damon could not remember when he had been so affected by a kiss. When at last he lifted his mouth from hers, he saw that she looked as staggered as he felt.

He marveled at the heat of the attraction that arched between them. It almost melted his good intentions, but then he reminded himself fiercely, *The secret of controlling a woman is to control oneself.* Suddenly it was not as easy as he usually found it.

He took a step back and rubbed his thumbs gently over her cheeks in a caressing farewell. "Good night, my lovely Lily."

Then he forced his reluctant feet to carry him out the door before his passion to have her overwhelmed him.

Lily, still dazed from the effect of Mr. St. Clair's kiss, stared at his retreating back incredulously.

She could not believe that after *that* kiss he could so easily turn and walk away from her.

Fortunately for her, though, Mr. St. Clair was a true gentleman. She felt confident that the secret of Mr. Culhane was safe with him. In the moment before he had given her his word on that, she had seen such sympathy in his eyes, as though he truly understood what it must be like for her in the greenroom.

Lily watched until his curricle disappeared from sight, then shut the door quietly.

She wandered dreamily back into the drawing room and sank down upon the chintz-covered sofa. Her tongue slowly traced her lips, savoring the taste of him that lingered there. The heat that his kiss had stoked deep within her began to simmer again at the memory of his mouth upon hers.

Once again he had easily breached her defenses—defenses that had always held firm before every other man.

Chapter 6

B y the time Hawkhurst called for Lily the next morning, he was in decidedly ill humor. He had stopped by his cousin's home on the way, and that had been a mistake. Both Pel and Cecilia had been in the breakfast parlor, he again buried in a newspaper and she sulking over her tea. Damon accepted the offer of a cup and soon regretted it.

Pel regarded him with deep suspicion, undoubtedly wondering whether he and Lily had been together the previous night since neither had been in the greenroom, but not daring to ask in front of his wife.

Worse, Cecilia's sighing, die-away manner was enough to drive a saint crazy, and Hawkhurst was no saint. He was acquiring more sympathy for his cousin. Couldn't Cecilia see that her sullen behavior would drive Pel away and into another woman's arms?

Hawkhurst was considering how to subtly point this out to her when Phoebe and his sisters arrived. Cassandra immediately initiated another argument, full of tears and reproaches, over the barouche she coveted.

That drove Damon to take his leave, thinking sourly that it was turning into a terrible day.

When he reached Lily's, he was still frowning. He

was surprised to find her waiting for him. The first punctual woman he had ever met!

His breath caught at how lovely she looked in a walking gown of navy sarcenet that accentuated her superb figure and a matching white French hat trimmed with navy ribbons.

Her eyes lingered for a moment on his mouth, and he knew that she was thinking of their kiss the previous night. It had truly been one to remember, and he had a sudden, overpowering urge to take her in his arms and give her another. He knew better, though, than to press his luck.

As he held the door of her lodgings open for her, he suggested, "Shall we try the Crescent field today?"

"Yes," she agreed as they stepped outside.

Strangely, the day suddenly seemed much pleasanter to Damon with Lily on his arm.

She seemed oblivious to the admiring stares of the men they passed, but he was not, and he was proud to be her escort.

"I have just come from Pel's," he told her. "He is suspicious because neither of us was in the greenroom last night, but he could not question me in front of his wife."

"Tell me about her."

He was still exasperated with Cecilia's martyrish behavior and it crept into his voice. "She is a taking little thing when she is happy and animated, but at the moment she is acting very much like her mother." And Damon had no patience with Cecilia's mama. "Whenever Lady Burns wants something, she sulks and sighs until she gets it."

"What does Cecilia want?" Lily asked.

He shrugged. "I don't know, but I fear her strategy is doomed to failure. Subtlety is wasted on a noddy like Pel."

"That's not kind," she protested.

"Not kind," he agreed, "but true."

When they reached the Crescent field, he guided her to a tree-shaded, gravel path that skirted its edge.

For the moment, no other strollers were upon the path, which was one of Lily's favorite places in Bath. She was glad that Mr. St. Clair had suggested coming here, and she smiled warmly at him.

He halted so abruptly that Lily stopped too, and turned to him.

"You have a beautiful smile," he said, gazing at her in a way that made her pulse race. He was a positive menace to female hearts, particularly hers, when he looked like that.

Lily suspected that he was thinking of kissing her again. She was shocked to realize she wanted him to do so, even though they were standing in a public, albeit secluded, spot. Had she taken leave of her senses?

They stared at each other, the moment fraught with promise. Then a movement on the path caught her eye. To her dismay, she recognized Hugo Broome and Irwin Yarpole approaching. She recalled that the home of the ailing aunt with whom Broome lived was in the Crescent. If only Lily had remembered that sooner, she would not have come here with Mr. St. Clair.

Broome advanced on them with a cocky, menacing stride. Clearly, having Yarpole with him gave him courage.

He barked, "Now, Mr. St. Clair, you shall pay for what you did to me yesterday."

Damon said coolly, "I see you are sober today, but no wiser than yesterday."

As Mr. St. Clair turned, Irwin Yarpole saw his face for the first time. To Lily's surprise, Yarpole blanched and began hastily backing away.

"So now, Broome, I collect you want me to sweep

this path with you." The menace was heavy in Damon's voice.

Hugo, although clearly startled by his adversary's unexpected response and his friend's retreat, blustered, "Try it, and my father will take a whip to you."

Behind Broome, Yarpole hissed, "It is you Lord Olen will take a whip to. Don't you know who he is?"

Broome, bewildered by his companion's reaction, stammered, "He is Mr.—"

"You damned fool, Hugo! He is *Hawkhurst*."

Broome stared slack-jawed for a moment, then backed away even more rapidly than his companion had.

Hugo might be stupid, but he was not suicidal.

Lily watched the odious pair's retreat in flabbergasted silence, as shocked as Broome at Yarpole's revelation, and even more incredulous.

She had imagined, in light of Lord Hawkhurst's reputation, that he must be eye-stoppingly handsome, with the face of an Adonis and a peacockish wardrobe so stylish that it would put Sir Oswald Ridley's to shame. Charming compliments, as false as they were polished, would tumble from his golden tongue like water down a mountainside.

No one could be more different from the image she had conceived of him than this blunt-speaking, harsh-faced, soberly dressed man. Surely he could not possibly be Hawkhurst, could he?

But she read the answer in his narrowed eyes and the twitching muscle in his rigid jaw.

Lily was shattered. She had liked him so much. Life in the theatre had taught her to take a man's measure quickly and accurately; until this moment, she had prided herself on how well she could do so. It was a great blow to discover that she had mistaken the king of the greenroom for a gentleman worthy of her affection and her trust. Never had she been so taken in by a man!

He seemed so blunt and honest, not at all what she had expected Hawkhurst to be like. No wonder he had looked so amused when she had warned him that his reputation might suffer were he seen with her.

Damon was no happier over Yarpole's disclosure than Lily was. Now, he thought bitterly, she would fawn over him, and he would never know whether she would become his because she truly cared for him. He turned to her, bracing himself for the disgusting transformation he would see in her manner toward him.

But the change he beheld was not the change he had expected.

Her emerald eyes did not regard him with simpering agreeability, but with hostile fury.

"You are Hawkhurst?" She spat out his name as though it was Satan's himself.

He nodded. No other woman had ever had this kind of outraged reaction when she had learned his identity, and he was bemused by it.

"Why did you lie to me?" she demanded. "Why did you tell me you were Damon St. Clair?"

He studied her appreciatively. God, but she was gorgeous when she was in a rage, her eyes blazing with green fire.

"I did not lie to you. I *am* Damon St. Clair, have been since the day I was born."

"You are the Earl of Hawkhurst!"

Hell's fire, she made his title sound like a crime.

"Yes, that too, since my father's death," he agreed, disconcerted by her reaction, so different from what he had expected. "However, it was Pel who introduced me by my family name rather than my title."

"Why did you not correct him?"

He shrugged. ''For one thing, it would have indicated that I set far more importance upon my title than I do. Secondly, Pel clearly feared that if you knew I was Hawkhurst, you would immediately try to fix my interest.''

She glared at him. ''And you thought so, too!''

''It's possible,'' he said warily, careful not to convict himself when she was so angry. ''Most women would have, you know.''

''I doubt that! In any event, I am not most women!''

''Thank God,'' he muttered fervently.

She turned and walked rapidly away from the Crescent field, heading back in the direction from which they had come.

''Where are we going?'' he asked her, keeping up with her.

''*I* am going home!'' she said haughtily.

She increased her pace in an attempt to leave him behind, but with his long stride, he managed to stay with her. He thought ruefully that this was not at all the way she was supposed to act when she learned he was Hawkhurst.

''Please leave me alone,'' Lily requested icily. ''I have no desire to walk with *the king of the greenroom!*''

He winced. He despised that appellation, although he could not deny that it had its uses. To be singled out by him assured an actress instant celebrity of a sort, and ambitious females vied for his attention because of that. Rarely anymore did he have to exert himself to capture actresses who caught his interest. They dropped into his hands like overripe peaches.

Lily said hotly, ''I can scarcely believe that you are Lord Hawkhurst!''

''Why is it so difficult?''

Sounding goaded, she retorted, ''You are not at

all handsome or charming, and you dress like a parson."

No overripe peach was his Lily!

"How flattering you are," he said wryly. "I am sorry that I am such a disappointment to you."

They were striding across Queen's Square at so rapid a gait that they were actually passing some more leisurely moving curricles.

"Your pace would do credit to an Ascot entry," he teased.

"If it is too fast for you—"

"No woman is too fast for me," he interjected in a self-mocking tone. "Only consider my reputation."

She glared at him. "What a low opinion both you and Pel have of me. How could you think I would be attracted to you because you possess a ridiculous title?"

Hawkhurst's lips twitched. He knew of no other person—male or female—who would apply that particular adjective to the coveted title of earl. "Most women are."

"You conceited jackanapes!"

"Not so conceited, you will notice, that I think it is I, rather than my title, that is the allure. And if my 'ridiculous' title is not enough, there is also my enormous wealth to win their affection."

"I told you before that not every woman is for sale!"

Never had Hawkhurst met a woman who professed to dislike him because of his title and fortune, and he was not entirely convinced that he had now. She was, after all, an actress. If she was pretending, though, what on earth could her motive be?

They were still walking so quickly that other pedestrians were turning to stare at them.

She hissed, "I repeat, I do not wish to walk with you."

"You aren't. *I* am walking with *you*, and you will only waste your breath to tell me to go away. You set out under my protection, and you will return under it."

"I will never be under your protection!"

He raised a taunting eyebrow. "But, Lily, never is such a long time."

That visibly stoked her ire. She turned and abruptly crossed the street, forcing a coachman who had not anticipated such a foolhardy move to rein in his horses hard. The shaken man questioned her intelligence and her sanity in loud, uncomplimentary terms.

Hawkhurst grabbed her arm. "Have a care. Are you trying to kill yourself?"

She ignored his question. "You are insufferably arrogant, my lord. I suppose you think that *no* actress can resist you."

He prudently refrained from pointing out that very few had. Better that he say nothing more to her until they reached her lodgings and he could talk to her in private.

At her door, she turned and said frigidly, "Good day, my lord."

"It is not a good day at all," he retorted ruefully. He forestalled her effort to dismiss him by reaching behind her, opening her door, and stepping round her into the small vestibule.

He turned to face her. "You will not fob me off so easily."

"I do not want you here! Your arrogance is beyond belief."

"I am not arrogant. I am merely determined to discuss with you in private why you are so angry."

"I am angry because you hoaxed me about your identity."

She stepped inside after him. He reached behind

her and pulled the door to the street shut. They faced each other in the tiny space.

"To think I believed you were not a man who played greenroom games!" she cried. "Instead you are the most skilled player of them all."

"Somehow I don't think you are complimenting me," he said dryly. In truth, he had long ago grown weary of those games. It was a rare actress that he wanted anymore. His increasing selectivity only intensified ambitious females' determination to capture him, however briefly.

The smallness of the vestibule forced Lily to stand very close to him, and he caught her scent of wild roses. Her eyes were like emerald lightning. She was glorious, and Hawkhurst ached for her. He swore to himself that she would become his yet.

Lily stared at his harsh face. To think she had thought this man a country gentleman. To think she had trusted him! Suddenly she remembered all that she had confided to him the previous night, and her cheeks burned. Believing him kind and understanding, she had even told him the truth about having no husband. He probably could not wait to tell his greenroom friends of her deception.

Reading her face, Hawkhurst asked, "Now what dreadful sin are you laying at my door?"

She tried to back away from him, but the entry was too small to permit that, and she succeeded only in bumping against the pier table behind her.

He captured her arms in a grip that was firm, yet oddly gentle. "Tell me."

"I trusted you. I confided private matters to you that I have never told another man."

"Yes," he said quietly, "and I was honored that you did."

His dark eyes had softened, and he brushed her cheek gently, comfortingly with his fingertips. His touch sent a sweet shiver through her.

"If you are worried I will reveal that Mr. Culhane does not exist, you need not be. I do not betray confidences."

She looked into his fathomless eyes. "If only I could believe you."

"You can, Lily. I will not lie to you."

She wanted to trust him, but he was Hawkhurst.

As if reading her thoughts, he asked quietly, "Does it not occur to you that you are seeing me as I really am, not as rumors and gossip make me out to be?"

Could that be true? Lily knew how cruel and unjust gossip could be. She herself had occasionally been its victim.

His compelling eyes held hers as he brushed back a wayward tendril of hair from her face.

"I like you very much, Lily," he said simply. "There have been very few women in my life that I can say that about."

"I would say there have been far too many," she retorted tartly.

"No, that is not true," he said gravely. "I may have been guilty of many things in my misspent life, but never of confusing lust with liking."

"How you must have laughed when I said you did not look like a man who frequented greenrooms."

"To the contrary, I was flattered."

And Damon had been, knowing that she had perceived the difference between him and the other men who had surrounded her that night.

"I am mortified that I could have mistaken you for a gentleman of breeding and integrity."

The contempt in her tone wounded him, and he said stiffly, "I have never been accused of lacking either. If you do not believe me, ask any man of the *ton*."

"But the ladies of the *ton* would have a different tale to tell, would they not?"

"The ladies of the *ton* have *no* tale to tell of me!" he snapped. Hell's fire, did she think he was one of those bucks who found it amusing to cuckold a friend? Well, dammit, he was not!

"Ah, I see how it is!" she cried furiously. "Your integrity does not permit you to philander among your friends' wives and daughters. You would not dream of ruining one of them, only actresses, servants, and other unfortunate females from the lower orders." She hissed this last accusation, and the scorn she felt for him was not lost on Damon.

That was too much for his own temper. He did not dally with other men's wives or seduce virgins, no matter what their quality or lack of it. He did not make women promises that he did not intend to keep. He never entered into a liaison without making it very clear to the woman that it would be brief. That, not financial considerations, was the real purpose of the Hawkhurst Ultimatum.

If some women regarded his bluntness in this regard as a challenge to prove him wrong rather than as the simple truth it was, that was their problem. He had not misled them.

"I don't ruin anyone," he retorted. "At least grant me that much."

"I grant you nothing! I cannot conceive how you could have all those females at your feet!"

He could have enlightened her. Unlike other greenroom gallants who looked upon a female merely as a vehicle for their own pleasure, he was determined to bring to ecstasy whatever woman shared his bed. A woman might sleep with him initially because of his title and wealth but, by God, she remembered him, yearned for him afterward for a very different reason!

And so would Lily. He would make certain of

that—if only he could get that far with her. Right now, he didn't rate his chances very high.

"Go away!" she cried in agitation. "If I had known you were Hawkhurst, I would never have had anything to do with you."

He feared that if he left her now, she would refuse to see him again, and he could not let that happen. He wanted her too much.

"Why?" He adopted the most provoking tone he could manage. "Are you *that* afraid I will add you to my long list of conquests?"

"That will never happen!"

"Won't it? Then why are you so afraid to see me again? Truly, you disappoint me," he continued, desperate not to lose her now. "I had not thought you such a pudding-heart."

Pudding-heart, indeed! Lily was incensed. Hawkhurst certainly could not be accused of making pretty speeches to her. Did he think her such an easy mark that he had no need to do so? That thought made her even angrier.

"You do not even think me worthy of wasting your polished addresses on!"

"To the contrary, I paid you the compliment of believing you would send me to Jericho if I tried to fix your interest with flattering, meaningless speeches! Am I wrong?"

"No," she admitted. If only he had done so, she would have been on her guard. How clever he was. No wonder they called him the king of the green-room. "I shall not be one of your brief flings!"

He raised a black, skeptical eyebrow, which added new fuel to Lily's already blazing temper. "Then show that you have the strength to resist me," he dared her, his tone mocking. "Prove you can by continuing to see me. You still want to discourage young Pel, don't you?"

Damn him! Lily's pride and temper would not let

her ignore his challenge. He thought all women, herself included, were a game. Ripples of anger undulated through her.

"Don't turn and run from me like a coward," he continued provocatively.

Lily's jaw tightened in resolve. She would show him there was one woman who could resist him. "Very well," she snapped.

Hawkhurst rewarded her capitulation with a grin that made Lily all the more determined to best him. She would prove to this maddening man that she was not such an easy mark as he clearly thought her.

Let him dance attendance on her for all the good it would do him. She would play his game and she would beat him at it.

If the stories about him were true, no woman had ever been the one to end a flirtation with him, and Lily intended to be the first.

She would teach him what it felt like to be abandoned. That goal would sustain and strengthen her against his seductive skill.

She said sharply, "And now that I have agreed to continue seeing you, please be so kind as to leave or I shall be late meeting Nell at the Pump Room."

He bowed politely and took his leave.

Yes, she told herself as she shut the door behind him, she was going to enjoy besting the king of the greenroom.

Chapter 7

⌒⌒○⌒⌒

The Pump Room was only lightly populated when Lily arrived to meet Nell Wayne. Now that the Bath season was drawing to an end, the ranks of visitors were thinning.

Lily made her way between small groups of patrons scattered about the monumentally proportioned room with its Corinthian columns, long windows, and decorative plasterwork. She had told her friend that she would meet her by the clock at the east end of the room.

Lily reached the designated spot beneath the apse that held a statue of Beau Nash, the late social arbitrator who had guided Bath to its glory days, but Nell was not there yet.

As Lily waited, she entertained herself by watching the room's eclectic clientele milling about, conversing with acquaintances and partaking of the waters. The room was open to the public. No social rank was required for admission, only that the visitor present a clean and decent appearance. The richly dressed ladies of the *ton*, however, carefully avoided contaminating contact with the tradespeople and other patrons from the lower orders.

Lily was amused that some of those same ladies were quite accepting of her, smiling and even greeting her in the mistaken belief that she was one of their own. They would be horrified to learn that they were acknowledging an actress.

A querulous female voice interrupted Lily's thoughts, and she overheard the young woman say angrily, "Phoebe, you *must* insist that Hawkhurst buy us the new barouche."

Lily turned her head and discovered the speaker was Lady Cassandra, Damon's needle-jawed half-sister. She was addressing the demure, angelic girl in mourning black who had drawn Lily's attention on previous visits.

Lily wondered what relation the beautiful Phoebe was to Hawkhurst that she could demand such an expensive item as a barouche from him. With her golden curls, cornflower-blue eyes, and milky complexion, she did not look at all like Cassandra who had the same dark hair and coloring as her brother. Nor did Phoebe look old enough to be out of the schoolroom.

They were standing with two other young ladies, one of whom resembled Cassandra a little. The other, a plump girl of about eighteen, had soft brown hair, big hazel eyes, and would have been very pretty had she not looked so sullen and unhappy. Her white muslin gown was fastened below her swelling bosom with a blue belt. The rounded stomach protruding from beneath the high waist proclaimed that she was several months pregnant.

Lady Cassandra said, "And, Phoebe, you must insist that Hawkhurst allow us to go to London next season."

Phoebe began to cry. "But I don't want to go to London."

A portly young gentleman in a forest-green coat and brown pantaloons came up to them. Lady Cassandra instantly assumed a simpering smile. "Lord Bowen, what a pleasure to see you."

His lordship, however, had eyes only for the lovely Phoebe. He was clearly smitten with her.

"Lady Hawkhurst, what has distressed you so deeply?" he inquired.

Lily could scarcely believe her ears. *Lady Hawkhurst! Phoebe was Hawkhurst's wife!*

For the second time that day, Lily's thinking about Damon St. Clair was turned upside down. *"I have another advantage over my cousin. Unlike Pel, I do not have a pregnant wife."*

Lily had assumed, as she was certain he had intended her to, that this meant he had no wife at all.

He was no better than all the other lying greenroom roués, who would happily say anything that would gain them an advantage. Furthermore, she thought waspishly, his *un*pregnant wife looked young enough to be his daughter.

Instead of answering Lord Bowen, Phoebe buried her face in her handkerchief and wept harder. It boggled Lily that this timid, tearful child could be married to a man of Hawkhurst's sophistication. What on earth could have possessed him? Lovely as she was, he must find her a dead bore.

Lady Cassandra told his lordship, "It is Hawkhurst who has reduced poor dear Lady Hawkhurst to tears. My dreadful brother treats her—and, indeed, all of us—so cruelly. You would have been shocked to hear the things he said to us this morning!"

Even without hearing them, Lord Bowen looked shocked.

Cassandra asked, "Do you know my sister, Lady Amy, and Cecilia, my cousin Pelham's wife?"

So the pregnant girl was Pel's wife. Cecilia looked so young and woebegone that Lily's heart went out to her.

"You look blue-deviled, Lily."

She jumped at Sir Roger Hilton's voice, for she had not noticed him come up beside her.

"Not at all," she replied. "Are you and your mother staying for the concert?"

"No, she is feeling unwell, and I must take her home."

Phoebe, lifting her face from her handkerchief, saw Sir Roger. Her tears promptly ceased. Even after he left Lily's side, she observed that Phoebe's wistful gaze followed him until he and his mother departed from the Pump Room.

"Lily, there you are!" Nell Wayne cried, rushing up. "I have the most shocking piece of news. I ran into Sir Oswald Ridley—that's why I'm late. He says that 'Mr. St. Clair' who was so attentive to you in the greenroom is actually Lord Hawkhurst!"

"Yes, so I learned this morning," Lily said, still seething that he had hoaxed her, first about his identity and then about his wife.

Nell shook her blonde curls. "I can scarcely credit that he is Hawkhurst. Not at all what I expected. I find it hard to believe that Pretty Peg would have killed herself over *him*."

Pretty Peg was the nickname approving theatrical audiences had given to Peggy McKay, a popular provincial actress who had caught Hawkhurst's attention. Later she had taken her own life, reportedly because the earl had ended their affair.

Lily had known Pretty Peg five years ago when they had both spent a season at a theatre in York. Although Peg had not been a particularly talented actress, her effervescent personality charmed audiences. She had moved on to Exeter the next season and had written Lily several letters from there.

In the first, she told of her pursuit of Hawkhurst, whose country estate, Hawkhill, was in Devon, not far from Exeter: *He is ignoring me, but I am persisting.*

Her second letter to Lily indicated that the earl

was still eluding her, but by her third letter, she triumphantly reported, *Hawkhurst is the most superb lover I have ever had.*

And Pretty Peg had had many.

Her final letter, written in London before a tryout at Drury Lane, confided: *Lord Hawkhurst told me if I left Hawkhill and came here, our affair was over. But I know once I become a famous actress and the toast of London, he will come back to me.*

The letter distressed Lily because poor Peg, whose talent was meager, was deluding herself in thinking that she would become the toast of London. And she did not.

Nor did Hawkhurst come back to her, and it was rumored Peggy hanged herself over him.

Nell said, ''Young Pel St. Clair was beside himself when you were not in the greenroom last night. He tried to get me to give him your address.''

''You did not, did you?'' Lily asked in alarm.

''No, I would never do that. Oh, there is Mr. Rathbone. I must talk to him.'' Nell flitted off to greet a wiry, balding man who was one of her wealthy admirers.

Lily noticed Cecilia slip away from her companions and cross the room to the large open vase that poured out the medicinal waters for drinking. Looking very white, she took a glass from the attendant and started to retrace her steps. Then she stopped, swaying a little.

Lily, fearing that the girl was about to swoon, hurried to her side.

''Let me hold your glass.'' Lily took it from Cecilia's shaky grasp before she spilled its hot contents. ''I will help you to a chair.''

Lily settled her in the nearest chair and gave her back the glass of medicinal water. ''Is there anything else I can do for you?''

Cecilia gazed at her with beseeching eyes red from

weeping. "Would you stay with me for a few minutes? I feel so wretched."

"Are you having pains?" Lily asked in alarm, wondering if the girl was about to miscarry.

"No, at least not the kind you mean. Please stay."

Lily glanced over at Nell Wayne, who was still deep in conversation with Mr. Rathbone, then sat down, unable to reject Cecilia's unhappy plea.

She clutched Lily's hand in gratitude. "You are so very kind."

"Tell me about your pain," Lily said.

"It is in my heart! I am so miserable. Everyone ignores me, even my husband, and I love him so much!" She began crying.

Hawkhurst's female relatives did have a maddening propensity for tears, Lily reflected as she pulled a clean handkerchief from her reticule and handed it to Cecilia. "Here, take this. A good cry will do you good."

Lily wished that Pel would walk into the Pump Room. She would enjoy seeing his expression when he discovered the woman he was pursuing comforting his weeping wife. The young noddy deserved the shock that would give him.

Lily suspected that Cecilia needed to unburden herself to a compassionate listener. When the girl's tears subsided, Lily patted her arm consolingly. "There, there, now. Dry your eyes and tell me what has made you so unhappy."

Cecilia turned a tragic face to Lily. "My husband does not love me anymore."

"What makes you think that?" Lily asked, fearing that Cecilia might be right.

"He never pays me the slightest heed. I have grown so fat and ugly since I have been breeding that he can no longer tolerate the sight of me. He is gone every night, and his cousin Cassandra says he is dangling after some dreadful actress with the Theatre Royal.''

Yes, Lily thought angrily, that needle-chinned shrew Cassandra undoubtedly took great pleasure in telling Cecilia that.

''My husband and I were so happy until I became pregnant. I thought he would be pleased about the baby, but he isn't.''

''Did he tell you that?''

''Not in words,'' Cecilia wailed, ''but he has not bought me a single present since I have been increasing.''

''What has that to do with anything?'' Lily asked bluntly.

The girl's red-rimmed eyes widened in surprise. ''When my eldest sister's husband learned that she was breeding, he gave her the beautiful ruby necklace that she coveted. When their son was born, he gave her the handsomest gig.''

Cecilia was as naive as her husband. Hawkhurst had been right when he had said they had been too young to marry.

Lily said tactfully, ''That was very generous of your sister's husband, but I fear he is a rare exception. I do not think most husbands heap expensive gifts upon their pregnant wives.''

''Oh, but they do! Mama says she got some of her nicest jewelry from Papa when she was pregnant.'' An unbecoming pout marred Cecilia's face. ''If Pel loved me, he would have done the same for me.''

Lily suspected that Pel had no inkling of his wife's expectations. ''Have you told your husband how you feel?''

Cecilia's chin rose stubbornly. ''I should not have to—he should know!''

So instead of telling her young husband that she believed herself to be unloved and neglected by him, the foolish girl was treating him to an endless fit of the sullens that no doubt left him baffled and hurt.

"He *should* know," Lily said diplomatically, "but perhaps he does not. You must tell him how you feel."

"He would not care in the slightest!" Cecilia sniffled.

Phoebe came up to them. "Who is your friend, Cecilia?" She asked in her tremulous little voice.

"I am Mrs. Lily Culhane," Lily said, holding her breath in fear that the women would recognize her name as that of the actress Pel was dangling after.

But neither did. Instead Pel's wife said, "This is Lady Hawkhurst, and I am Cecilia St. Clair."

Phoebe asked Lily, "Who was the gentleman you were talking to a few minutes ago? I . . . I believe I met him in London last year, but I . . . I cannot recall his name."

Lady Hawkhurst was a dreadful liar.

"His name is Sir Roger Hilton." Lily could not resist adding, "But he cannot be the man you met last year, for he just returned from three years abroad with Wellington's army."

Amy came over to join Lily, Phoebe, and Cecilia. "Cassandra makes me so angry," she exclaimed. Amy's lively, dark eyes reminded Lily of her brother's. "She is telling Lord Bowen how clutch-fisted Hawk is, and that's not true. My friends envy me the pin money he gives us."

Lord Bowen, discovering himself alone with Lady Cassandra, made his escape with ungentlemanly haste, and she came over to her relatives. She studied Lily critically but apparently could find no fault with her forest-green pelisse with its jet buttons and vertical bands of black velvet. It and Lily's matching bonnet were in the first stare of fashion.

A few feet away, a plump matron, whose dress betrayed her modest means, laughed loudly.

Lady Cassandra gave her a contemptuous look. "It is disgraceful the people they allow in the Pump Room," she complained to Lily. "Poor Beau Nash must be turning over in his grave to see it. No wonder Bath is no longer as fashionable as it was in the days when he presided over it."

Clearly Cassandra had mistaken Lily for a lady of quality. How shocked she would be to discover the truth.

The discordant notes of orchestra members tuning their instruments sounded. The concert was about to begin, and Lily was delighted to have this excuse to escape the St. Clair women and rejoin Nell Wayne.

After the concert, Lily and Nell parted company outside the Pump Room. Earlier clouds had given way to sunshine, and Lily decided to walk home.

A block from her lodgings, she met Sir Roger Hilton with three books tucked beneath his arm. "For my mother from Mr. Godwin's circulating library," he explained.

He insisted on escorting Lily to her door. As they reached her lodgings, she glanced at her windows. To her surprise, Hawkhurst was standing at one of them, watching her with a thunderous expression.

What had he to be angry about? Lily was the one he had deliberately deceived about not having a wife!

After bidding Roger good-bye at the door, Lily swept into her drawing room with fire in her eyes.

Hawkhurst was still standing by the window, his frowning raptor's face and powerful body awash in the afternoon sun that poured through it. The devil bathed in light, Lily thought caustically.

When he saw her expression, he asked warily, "Well now, what new sin have you convicted me of?"

"Your tongue is too clever by half."

"Careful," he retorted in amusement, "I might take that as a compliment. Now tell me what my clever tongue has said to so offend you."

"That unlike Pel, you had no pregnant wife."

"I don't," Damon said calmly, coming toward her with that easy, graceful stride that was uniquely his.

She glared at him. "True, your wife is not pregnant, but you do have one!"

He looked genuinely startled. "Not to my knowledge."

"Don't insult me by denying it. I have met her!"

"Then you must introduce her to me for I have not!"

"What a wretched memory you have! But after so many love affairs, I can see you might forget a wife here or there, even one you forced to marry you!"

Hawkhurst raised that infuriating black eyebrow. "Why would I marry an unwilling woman when I have so many vying to shackle me, thanks to my— er, 'ridiculous' title?"

"Perhaps it was the novelty of having your suit rejected! Do you dare deny to me that you are married to Phoebe?"

He had the effrontery to burst out laughing. "Oh, *that* Lady Hawkhurst."

"I collect you remember her now!" Lily cried indignantly.

He was still chuckling. "My character is not so black as you think. Phoebe is not my wife. She is my stepmother."

"You are quizzing me! What an outrageous clanker!"

"Unfortunately for both Phoebe and myself, it is the truth. She is my father's widow."

"How disgusting!" Indeed it was, so why was Lily so happy?

"Isn't it," he agreed, his face taut. "Don't think I don't know how preposterous it is to have a silly goosecap who looks young enough to be my daughter for a stepmama."

His expression softened as he drew closer to Lily. He laid his hands lightly on her arms, and her heart fluttered at his touch. "Lily, how could you think I should have any interest in such a boring child?" His dark eyes gently rebuked her.

"I wondered," Lily admitted. "The poor thing must have been a child bride."

"Not quite." He sighed and his hands dropped away from Lily's arms. "Phoebe is not as young as she looks and acts."

"How could your father have . . ." Lily broke off. Her curiosity was betraying her into an inappropriate inquiry.

He answered her unfinished query anyway. "You don't know how often I have asked myself that very question. He was inexplicably attracted to weepy young females. His second wife was about my age, and Phoebe is thirteen years my junior—a more fitting companion for his daughters than for him. But at least Phoebe's tears are genuine."

Lily, startled by the bitterness in his tone, asked, "What do you mean by that?"

"There is nothing malicious or manipulative about her."

Lily wondered to whom he was comparing Phoebe.

Before she could ask, he continued, "Despite her beauty, she is a shy, frightened little mouse. One could not blame such a timid girl, barely emerged from the schoolroom, for being terrified of a husband nearly old enough to be her grandfather."

"Then why did she marry him?" Lily asked, unbuttoning the jet buttons of her pelisse.

"Her ambitious mama, who was as iron-willed as her daughter is weak, gave her no choice. Fortunately for Phoebe, my father died a few months after their marriage. I am certain that she was secretly very relieved to be a widow. The marriage brought neither one of them happiness."

Lily had finished unbuttoning her pelisse, and Damon politely helped her out of it.

"Phoebe's mother sounds like a dreadful woman," Lily observed, laying her pelisse over the back of a chair.

Hawkhurst shrugged. "Like many ambitious parents, Lady Effington thought she had done her daughter a great favor by marrying her to an earl. She was determined that Phoebe would make an even more illustrious second marriage and hoped to snag at least a marquess for her."

"I think she would have had far better luck doing that in London instead of Bath," Lily said.

"Lady Effington brought Phoebe and my sisters here last fall because she was ailing and hoped the waters would help her. By the time the London season began, she was too ill to leave, and they remained here. She died two months ago."

So that was why Phoebe was wearing mourning black.

"I confess I miss the old dragon," Damon said. "She came to live with Phoebe after my father died. She kept both her daughter and my sisters in line. I never had to worry about their conduct or their welfare with that dragon guarding the door. Fortune hunters and would-be seducers did not stand a chance."

He smiled as Lily removed her velvet-trimmed bonnet. "Very pretty," he said approvingly.

His compliment pleased her more than it ought.

"You must have also met my sisters today since they were with Phoebe." Hawkhurst's mouth curled sardonically. "No doubt, Cassandra gave you a reading of my character that happily coincided with your own."

"Oh, no, even I do not believe you can be *that* bad."

"Could anyone?" he asked dryly.

He seemed so undisturbed by his sister's abuse of him that Lily asked, "Don't you care what Cassandra says about you?"

"No. Those who know me don't believe it."

She remembered the shock on Lord Bowen's face. "How can you be sure?"

He shrugged with magnificent unconcern. "If they do believe her, then I do not care to know them."

Lily admired his careless disdain of others' opinion of him.

"I met Pel's wife, too," Lily volunteered. "She has heard rumors about me, but fortunately neither she nor your sisters recognized my name."

"Not surprising. They have no interest in the theatre. By the way, I hold you to your promise to cure Pel's infatuation by pretending a *tendre* for me."

"That was before I knew you were the king of the greenroom!" Lily's pride revolted at the prospect of everyone thinking she was another one of Hawkhurst's easy conquests.

"You promised," he reminded her. "I did not think you one of those faithless women who goes back on her word."

She bridled at that. "I'm not!"

"Then prove it," he shot back.

Lily could think of no way out. Her word was as important to her as his to him. And there was poor Cecilia to think of too, although Lily wondered how much the charade would help her. It might rid Lily of Pel, but it would not solve the problems between him and his wife.

Unless the unhappy young couple could learn to communicate their feelings to each other, Pel would only chase another petticoat—one who, unlike Lily, would be more concerned about lightening his purse than about his happiness. His relationship with Cecilia would continue to deteriorate into hopelessness.

Damon's eyes suddenly narrowed, reminding Lily again of a raptor about to swoop upon its prey. "I thought you were meeting Nell Wayne at the Pump Room."

"I did."

"Then who was the fribble who brought you home? You told me you did not permit your admirers to know your address."

"I don't, and Sir Roger is not a fribble. Nor is he an admirer of mine. I am not at all in his style. He is a family friend, nothing more. Why do you look so incredulous?"

"What, pray tell, is Handsome Roger's style?"

"He has a weakness for beautiful, helpless females whom he can protect. So you can see, we would not suit at all."

Damon smiled wryly. "Perhaps I should introduce Handsome Roger to my stepmother."

Lily suspected Phoebe would like nothing better, but she kept that thought to herself. Instead she asked, "Why are you here?"

"For our chess game. You promised me."

"I would never have agreed had I known you were Hawkhurst."

He gave her a provocative, challenging look. "So you *are* afraid that I will add you to my long list of conquests?"

"That day will never come," she retorted angrily.

"But you are so afraid that it will you dare not even indulge me in a game of chess?"

She glared at him, then led him to the chessboard in the corner. She would prove to him that at least one actress could resist him.

As he seated himself across the board from her,

she said coldly, "You think that you have only to beckon to an actress and she is yours, do you not?"

His mouth curled cynically. "These days I rarely have to expend that much energy. They generally do the beckoning."

She sputtered, "You arrogant, conceited, insufferable . . . You think yourself utterly irresistible to women!"

"No, not at all! I am not such a cloth-head. It is not me they find irresistible, but the celebrity that attaches to an actress who captures the king of the greenroom's interest."

Lily did not know which shocked her more, the bleak cynicism of his words or his scornful, self-mocking tone.

A muscle in his jaw twitched. "That is why when Pel introduced us I did not tell you I was Hawkhurst. I wanted to see whether for once a woman could like me for myself, not for the attention a liaison with me might bring her."

Lily saw with sudden clarity how it must be from his point of view, and her anger died away. She even felt a tinge of sympathy for him, seeing in his situation an unexpected parallel to her own in which men sought her as an ornament whose acquisition would enhance their own consequence.

Hawkhurst and Lily turned out to be well matched in the chess game. It was long and hard-fought. He won, but it was a near thing.

Lily's skill at the game surprised Damon, a master of it. Only rarely did he find a worthy opponent, and never before one in petticoats.

He leaned back in his chair and studied her appreciatively as her quick, slender fingers placed the porcelain chess pieces in position for another game. A tendril of claret-colored hair drifted across her cheek, and he longed to brush it away, then kiss that wide, provocative mouth.

She was full of surprises. Her conversation, punctuated by flashes of wit, betrayed not only a quick mind, but an education that one would not expect in a provincial actress.

Again she was dressed simply but elegantly in a white muslin dress trimmed with green ruching around its square-cut neck and the hemline of its skirt. Even the most discerning eye would mistake her for a lady of the highest quality. He suspected she had been born and reared in gentler circumstances than her present station would indicate.

She finished arranging the pieces and stood up, saying pointedly, "You have had your chess game."

He did not want to leave her or the cheerful comfort of her drawing room. He thought of challenging her to a second game but decided that tactical retreat was in order.

He followed her to the door, admiring her queenly carriage. Her hair had been coiled up on top of her head, revealing the sweep of her long swanlike neck. He longed to cover it with kisses.

Restraining himself with an effort, he asked, "How long have you been an actress?"

They had reached the door to the drawing room, and she turned to face him. "Much of my life. My parents were actors, and I made my first appearance on a stage when I was four. Why do you look so surprised?"

"You have too much breeding for a woman raised in the theatre," he said bluntly.

Hawkhurst meant that as a compliment, Lily knew, but it angered her, and she would not tell him that her parents had come from good families who had refused to permit them to marry, forcing them to elope and then disowning them for doing so. When her parents had turned to acting to support themselves, Lily's paternal grandfather had even forbidden them to use the family name when they appeared onstage.

Hawkhurst asked, "Where are your parents now?"

"They were killed when I was seventeen," she answered, a catch in her voice. Lily still remembered vividly the terrible shock and grief, the overwhelming sense of despair and abandonment that had gripped her then. Theirs had been such a happy family. Then without warning her parents were gone.

Hawkhurst laid a gentle hand on her arm, his comforting touch somehow banishing the melancholy that threatened her.

Lily looked up at him. When he was angry, his eyes were as black as a cloudless night, but now, softened by sympathy, they had lightened to a deep, rich chocolate.

"How terrible for you to lose both parents at once."

"Yes," Lily agreed, "although it was a blessing for them that they died together. They were inseparable in life, the happiest couple I have ever known."

"How were they killed?"

"The roof of an inn where they were staying collapsed on them in the night. When they found them, my father had thrown himself over Mama to try to protect her with his body, and they were clinging to each other even in death."

His eyes darkened, hardened. "So for all your talk of never wishing to marry, you are a romantic. You believe in love and marriage and happy-ever-after." His tone made it clear that he believed in none of them.

No, the king of the greenroom would not, Lily thought sadly.

"I believe that a love like my parents' is rare. I do not expect to be so fortunate. Mama said she was lucky to have found Papa because he was the only man she could ever have loved."

Lily fell wistfully silent at the memory of her parents' singular relationship. Their love for each other had been so strong and enduring that none of life's travails had weakened it.

Damon put his arms around her and gently drew her to him. She felt the hard strength of his body through the superfine of his coat. His hand came up to smooth her hair consolingly, and she relaxed against him, feeling strangely safe in his arms.

Lily looked up at him. He smiled and dipped his mouth. She did not try to evade his lips as they claimed hers in a long, surprisingly tender kiss. He did not let it deepen into passion, but it shook her to her soul, leaving her breathless, yet soothed and comforted.

He stroked her cheek with his fingertips. "I must go now," he said gently. "Promise not to paint me any blacker than I am."

He dropped another kiss, light as a butterfly's touch, on her temple and was gone.

Chapter 8

T he following night, Hawkhurst insisted upon escorting Lily to the greenroom after her performance.

"It will make a statement to Pel," he argued. "Believe me, it may well forestall an unpleasant scene with him."

She knew he was right, but still she resisted. It galled her pride to make an entrance upon the king of the greenroom's arm.

He raised that maddening, mocking eyebrow. "Are you afraid you will discourage your other admirers?"

"I would love to do that, but I detest having everyone think that I am another one of your easy conquests."

His mouth curved in a wry smile. "You are hardly that! And what does it matter what they think?"

"But it is not the truth."

He smiled at her. "*You* know the truth, and that is all that counts."

"I fear I do not fully share your unconcern about others holding erroneous opinions of me," she confessed as she took his arm and let him lead her to the greenroom.

At its green baize door, he checked their pace, pausing on the threshold.

The room suddenly became as silent as a tomb.

Their appearance together had made a statement to more than Pel.

Lily had never felt more self-conscious in her life. She could feel every eye upon them in the quiet. Hawkhurst's hand tightened over hers, offering her mute support.

The silence ended explosively, like a burst of fireworks, with excited voices filling the room.

Damon said softly, "We have created a sensation."

"I prefer to create my sensations onstage!"

Pel, radiating petulance and indignation, rushed up to them. "What is the meaning of this, Lily?"

Hawkhurst interjected calmly, "I would think the meaning is clear."

Pel flushed. "How could you do this to me, Lily?"

Lily thought of Cecilia, pregnant and forlorn, sitting at home alone. She said quietly, "I have never encouraged your suit, Pel."

That reminder seemed to rob him momentarily of speech. Then he turned on Hawkhurst. "You had better beware of Mr. Culhane. Perhaps Lily has not warned you how jealous he is of her. He is not a man to get on the wrong side of." Pel sounded like a little boy invoking a monster to frighten away another child. "You will find you have met more than your match in Mr. Culhane."

The corner of Hawkhurst's mouth turned up in a wry grin. "To the contrary, I have discovered that Mr. Culhane is precisely my match."

Pel stared at him, baffled, then turned and rushed out of the greenroom.

Hawkhurst was the first man that Lily had shown a preference for, and the significance of that clearly was not lost on her other admirers. They complimented her on her performance, then quickly moved on, leaving her to him.

They did not stay long after Pel's departure, and when Lily left on Hawkhurst's arm, the room again fell silent.

At her lodgings, Damon took the key from her hand, unlocked the door, and opened it.

"Good night," she said firmly.

As though he had not heard her, he stepped into the entry, which was illuminated by a candle on the pier table, and held the door for her to follow.

Lily swept past him. "I did not invite you in."

She turned to face him. His hooded raptor's eyes glittered in the pale light of the candle.

Excitement twisted within Lily, making it hard for her to think logically. She stared helplessly at his mouth, remembering what it had been like to be kissed by him.

His arms closed around her, and he gave her a coaxing kiss, his lips brushing hers seductively. Then his tongue teased hers in a tantalizing dance. When his mouth retreated a scant half inch from hers, a little moan of protest escaped her lips.

His mouth returned to hers, urgent and demanding this time as though he could not get enough of her. Desire swelled and coiled within her.

Damon's lips deserted hers to trace the long sweep of her neck with fiery kisses that made her gasp with pleasure.

When he lifted his head, she stared up at him in confusion. Her pride still rebelled at being another one of Hawkhurst's many conquests. She could not allow that to happen. She could not!

Lily had to show him that one actress could resist him.

Yet she could not deny that no man had ever generated such intense yearning within her as Hawkhurst did.

She pulled away from him. "Stop it!" she cried,

knowing that her entreaty was directed as much at herself as at him. "Go home!"

He obeyed her so abruptly that she blinked in surprise—and disappointment. He stepped outside, leaving her to stare after him as he gracefully descended the stairs.

At the bottom, he looked up at her, his raptor smile wicked in the moonlight.

"You liked it as well as I did." His voice was soft, amused.

Yes, God help her, she did.

Hawkhurst looked down in disbelief at the delicate porcelain figures on the chessboard. Lily had defeated him. She had played a particularly brilliant game, and he had not even seen the coup de grace coming until she had delivered it. He looked at her smiling face in admiration.

"So you have humiliated me yet again," he joked. "How my consequence suffers at your hands."

"Pooh," she retorted, beginning to rearrange the chess pieces for a new game. "Your sensibilities are not so delicate."

No, they weren't. He was secretly delighted that he had found such a challenging opponent.

He liked being in Lily's cheerful drawing room, too. He admired how she had managed with a few vivid touches to transform a drab, uninviting room into this bright, welcoming one.

The miniature portrait of the young Adonis that had been displayed on Hawkhurst's first visit had vanished. He did not comment on its disappearance, but took it as a hopeful sign that he had replaced the fribble, whoever he was, in Lily's affections.

During the past week, Damon had spent much of his time with her, playing chess in her drawing room, walking along the River Avon and in the

Crescent field, and riding on the high, green hills surrounding Bath.

At first, she had protested that none of that furthered their charade in the greenroom. He had treated her to his most mocking smile and accused her of trying to avoid him because she feared he would conquer her after all.

She had risen to the bait as he had thought she would.

He watched her rearrange the porcelain chess pieces on the inlaid board. The antique set of hand-painted pieces was very valuable, and Damon wondered who the admirer was that had presented her with this expensive gift. Had she played with him as she played now with Damon?

"Who gave you this set?"

Lily looked up in surprise. "It was Papa's, and it belonged to his maternal grandfather before that."

Papa's grandfather had clearly been wealthy.

She put the final pieces in place. "Do you want to play another game?"

"No, I prefer to talk." He enjoyed his conversations with Lily even more than he did their chess games. He had quickly discovered that she could discuss frivolous and profound matters with equal ease.

The hours passed like minutes in Lily's company.

Indeed, Hawkhurst had begun to wonder who was seducing whom. He had never been so captivated by a woman. Not only was she intelligent and amusing, but she was well-bred and well-mannered as any lady of quality. And she radiated a vitality that made her more enticing than any diamond of the first water he had ever known.

Lily rose from her seat at the chess set and led him to the chintz-covered sofa. "Tell me about the newspaper account of Toulouse."

Damon had arrived late for their chess game because he had become so absorbed in a lengthy article on the battle of Toulouse in the London *Gazette* that he had forgotten the time. Although the battle had occurred more than a month ago, the story had provided much more detail than had previously been available.

He had never before known a woman who had the smallest interest in military matters, but Lily was fascinated with Napoleon's wars in general and Wellington's campaign in particular. Her quick grasp of battle strategies was astonishing in a woman. No wonder she was such a good chess player.

Now, sitting beside him on the sofa, she listened raptly as he told her what the article had said. He was a little chagrined, though, that she seemed more interested in the valorous actions of Major James Raleigh, the acclaimed hero of the battle, than in Wellington's tactics.

Damon wondered uneasily whether Lily was one of those women who had a fatal weakness for uniforms.

The thought of her in the arms of another man—whether he wore epaulets or not—made him grind his teeth. He wondered how many lovers there were in her past and ground his teeth even harder, smitten with jealousy, an emotion heretofore foreign to him.

He asked bluntly, "Who have your protectors been?"

Lily's eyes sparkled with anger, and she lifted her chin proudly. "No man has ever kept me. I will not cede control over my life to a man, either as his mistress or his wife."

"Why do you profess to find wedlock such a dreadful fate for a woman?" She was the only female Damon had known to do so.

"By law, all that a wife has becomes her husband's to squander upon the gaming table or his incognitos as he wishes. He has full and total control over her person, her income, and her children.''

"One would hope they were his children, too,'' Damon said dryly.

"And one would hope that he would be a caring and faithful husband and a good father to his children, but many men are not.''

No, Damon's own father had not been, but he kept that thought to himself.

"If I marry, my earnings belong to my husband. I have seen how actresses' husbands fritter away their wages.''

"Better, then, to be an incognita so that he has no claim upon them.''

"Tell that to Dorothy Jordan.''

Damon could not help flushing a little. Mrs. Jordan had been a famous Drury Lane actress and the mistress of the Duke of Clarence, the Prince Regent's younger brother. It was widely believed that she had helped to support him and the children she had borne him from her stage earnings. After two decades and ten children, he had repaid her generosity by summarily dismissing her.

When Damon said nothing, Lily prodded, "Perhaps you would like to defend the fair prince?''

"I do not defend the indefensible,'' he said quietly. "Not all men are as heartless as our royal princes.''

"Are they not?'' she retorted with withering sarcasm. "Do you not require your convenients to be at your beck and call until you grow tired of them and dismiss them from your life?''

He was offended that she could equate him with Clarence, whose conduct toward Mrs. Jordan he considered reprehensible. "I have always made it very clear going into my affairs that they would be of short duration and what the lady involved could expect when they ended.''

"Ah, yes, the infamous Hawkhurst Ultimatum!"

"But you cannot accuse me of misleading them," he said defensively. "Furthermore, none of them bore me a child. There are ways to prevent that, and I take care to use them." His mouth tightened. "What am I to understand from this discussion? That you have taken a vow of lifelong celibacy?"

Hawkhurst did not for a moment believe that. She had far too much passion.

"No," she admitted, "but if I give myself to a man, it is because I care for him."

He looked at her admiringly. In an age when women were bred to be helpless and dependent upon a man, Lily was a proud and resolute exception.

Hell's fire, but he ached to have her, to explore every inch of that exquisite body. She was still wary of him, however, and instinct warned him not to rush his fences with her. *The secret of controlling a woman was controlling himself.* He would not risk losing such a prize. Besides, he realized to his surprise, he was enjoying the chase.

That was why he was contenting himself with a subtler campaign, one calculated to leave her aching with unrequited desire.

He was certain from the look in her eyes when he would pull away from her that this tactic, so novel for him, was driving her as wild as it was him.

Chapter 9

The greenroom was crowded with performers and male visitors who showered Lily with praise for her performance as Isabella in *The Fatal Marriage*.

Only Hawkhurst did not extol it. Although he had delivered her to the theatre and was now at her side in the greenroom, he had not, in the interim, joined the audience to watch her onstage.

When she asked him why he had not done so, he shrugged carelessly. "I have already seen that play too many times."

This was the sixth time that she had appeared on-stage in the ten days since she had learned that he was Hawkhurst. Yet he had not watched her perform once. After her previous appearances, he had offered her much the same feeble excuse as he did tonight.

Lily was hurt that he did not want to see her act, no matter how often he had seen the play, but she would not let him know that it bothered her in the least.

When she had come into the greenroom tonight, two of the company's comeliest actresses were vying for his attention. They had paid him no heed on his first appearance in the greenroom, but since they had learned he was Hawkhurst, they boldly cast lures for him, even though he made it clear that Lily was his only interest.

When he had greeted her, she had been unable to smother a caustic comment about his popularity with actresses.

"Yes, but recall they ignored me until they discovered my title," he pointed out sardonically.

Lily had cast him as the predator in a heartless game, but she saw now that he was the prey, too. No wonder he was so cynical about women.

Why did he even bother with her when other women threw themselves at him? But, of course, he meant to prove that Lily could not resist him. Well, she still intended to beat him at his own game.

But it would not be easy.

Not only was he witty and charming company, but Lily was too honest to deny the intense physical attraction between them.

Nevertheless, she was determined to leave him before he seduced her. Thus far, he had not even tried to bed her. Initially, she had been astounded, then confused, and now she was actually a little miffed. To her chagrin, she seemed more affected by his passionate kisses and caresses than he did.

Lily had said nothing to him, but she intended to depart from Bath for Weymouth as soon as the Theatre Royal's season ended in less than a week.

She looked around for Pel, but he was nowhere to be seen. This was the first night he had not come to stand across the room and glower silently at her and Hawkhurst.

Lily told Damon, "I hope Pel's absence means our charade has cured his *tendre* for me."

"He's not here because his mama has come to town for his birthday, which is in a few days. She is addicted to whist and requires that Pel play with her every night. I doubt that we shall see him here again until she leaves Bath."

Then, in his absence, there would be no need for Lily and Hawkhurst to continue their greenroom charade.

She was about to point this out, then thought what it would be like without Damon at her side there.

Lily said nothing.

Lily and Hawkhurst strolled up the principal walk through Sydney Gardens toward the semicircular stone pavilion at the top. Their way was lighted by strings of variegated lamps and slowed by boisterous throngs of people on the graveled path.

"I have rarely seen it so crowded here," Damon observed. "Perhaps it is because the Theatre Royal is dark tonight. Let us try another walk."

They turned on to a secondary path that wound through less populated parts of the gardens. Gradually the noise of the crowds faded away.

They came to a canal spanned by a cast-iron bridge, intricately worked in the Chinese style. Stopping midway across the span, they leaned over the railing to look down at the placid water. Two swans glided on its surface, shimmering in the pale light of a three-quarter moon.

How pleasant it was here, Lily thought, especially with Hawkhurst at her side. She stole a glance at him. The moonlight softened the hard planes of his face, and he looked at her with a smile that made her heart turn over.

How different he was from what she had expected the king of the greenroom to be like. She had thought he would be insufferably puffed-up, full of conceit and deceit, with no thought for anyone but himself. Instead his self-mocking humor, his bluntness, his fidelity to family responsibilities had disarmed her. So had the way he listened to her with respect rather than the condescending air of superiority that so many highborn men affected. He treated her like an aristocratic lady to be honored instead of an actress to be patronized.

Lily smiled to herself as she thought of how the men of the greenroom steered clear of her now. She was so relieved to be free of their unwanted attentions that it was almost worth being thought another one of Hawkhurst's convenients, even though she wasn't.

Yet.

Lily had sworn that she would beat him at his own game: she would not become one of his brief flings. She, not he, would be the one to end their relationship. But with each passing day, she grew less confident that she would win this game he played so well.

Her shoe bumped a small stone and it skidded off the bridge and fell into the water with a splash, disturbing the quiet that had settled around them.

Hawkhurst took her arm, and they left the bridge to continue on the path they had been following.

He said abruptly, "I will not be able to take you home from the theatre tomorrow night."

Her heart twisted. It would be the first time in a fortnight that he had not done so. Had he grown tired of her already?

"Why not?" she blurted before she could stop herself.

He gave her arm a reassuring little squeeze. "I would much rather be with you, but it is Pel's birthday, and I am required to attend the party his mama is giving to celebrate it."

A winding path branched off from the one they were following along the canal, and Damon guided her onto it.

"I will drive you to the theatre as usual and send Sewell to take you home," he said.

They walked on in companionable silence. Ahead

of them, Lily could again see the circles of red, green, and blue light cast by the variegated lamps that lit the central walk they had abandoned earlier. The undulating path was taking them back to it. The hubbub of voices grew louder again.

Lily wondered how long Hawkhurst would stay in Bath. He had said nothing about leaving, but he had told her once that he considered the town a dead bore. The finale of the Theatre Royal's season was only three nights away, and she was a little shocked at how reluctant she had grown to leave Bath while Damon remained.

Hoping to subtly discover his plans, she asked, "Where do you go when you leave Bath?"

"To Hawkhill, my country seat," he replied, volunteering no other information.

"It is in Devon, is it not?" She knew that from Pretty Peg McKay's letters.

He nodded.

Lily would be spending eight weeks this summer in Dorset and Devon, and she wondered whether the troupe's travels would take her near Damon's estate.

Her thoughts turned back to Pretty Peg. Was it true that she had killed herself because Hawkhurst had abandoned her?

"Why are you frowning at me like that?" Damon asked.

"I . . . I was wondering if half the stories they tell about you are true."

He laughed. "If you count Cassandra's tales, probably no more than a quarter are."

They again reached the principal path that led to the pavilion, and a booth selling refreshments was at hand. Damon asked her whether she would like anything, but she declined.

They continued along the meandering track that they had been following, leaving behind the crowds that congregated along the main walk. An orchestra began playing in the distance, and the music drifted on the sweet nocturnal air, perfumed by flowering trees and shrubs.

The night was warmer than Lily had expected, and she half-wished now that she had not worn her forest-green pelisse. She unbuttoned it, revealing the patterned muslin gown beneath it. The green-and-white gown had a wide, square neck and was tied beneath her breasts with a green silk sash.

It was the fashion for the bodice of evening gowns to be a narrow band between a low neck and high waist, and her gown, she thought with a flash of humor, was deeply fashionable.

Damon's eyes glittered as they caught sight of her décolletage. His gaze held there for a long moment, and his breathing quickened.

His hand tightened on her arm, and he suddenly increased his pace. He turned down an even more secluded path between tall box hedges that was lit only by the moon. They reached a private little alcove formed by one of the hedges. Damon pulled her into it and faced her.

"That gown is more than any sane man can resist!" He sounded harassed, angry, and even a little desperate. "Did you wear it deliberately to torment me?"

"No!" Distressed by his accusation, she unconsciously bit her lip, drawing his attention to it. By the meager light of the moon, she saw a flame leap in his eyes.

He pulled her roughly into his arms, and his mouth descended on hers in a hard, demanding kiss as though he expected her to resist him. She was helpless to do so.

When she did not, he softened his attack, and his tongue teased hers, sending tiny shivers through her.

He loosened his embrace, and his hands parted her pelisse.

The night air washed over her suddenly fevered skin. His mouth deserted hers to leave a trail of kisses down her neck and the curve of her breast before returning to her lips. Lily closed her eyes, reveling in the exciting sensations he was stoking within her.

Then, without lifting his mouth from hers, one of his hands slid beneath her pelisse and lightly cupped the weight of her breast in his hand. She could feel the warmth of his palm through the thin muslin of her gown.

Lily tried desperately to conquer the magnetic appeal that he held for her, but it was like fighting the ocean tide that swept all before it.

He fondled her gently, as though he held in his hand a very delicate, very precious object. Her nipple grew hard. His thumb, moving in a tiny circle, rhythmically rubbed the taut peak, and the aching tension of desire built deep within her.

She told herself she must stop this, but she could not bring herself to do so quite yet. Her pleasure was too intense.

Somewhere in the distance, the orchestra played a soft, dreamy tune.

Then, all too soon, his thumb stopped, and his hand relinquished its sweet burden. An involuntary little moan of protest escaped her lips.

He chuckled, lifting his head a little. He gazed down into her eyes with an odd, pleased look in his own. Then he murmured in an unmistakably satisfied voice, "You like that, don't you, my sweet flower?"

Awash in pleasure, Lily was powerless to deny it.

She gasped as his long, slender fingers slid gently beneath the muslin of her bodice and played with the rosy crest hidden there. Tremors of delight coursed through her, and she moaned again, this time in bliss, but the sound was lost in the warmth of his mouth that once more closed over hers.

His skillful fingers moved again, slipping beneath her breast and lightly pushing it up from its muslin nest. His mouth left hers to claim this prize. He licked its hardened peak lightly, teasingly, and she cried out from the exquisite pleasure of it.

Loud voices pierced the quiet of the night, drowning out the faraway music. A group of men—young and half in their cups from the sound of them—was walking down the path, approaching the hedged alcove where she and Damon stood.

Hearing them, he reluctantly raised his head and removed his hand from her gown. His lean face, agonized in the pale moonlight, mirrored what it cost him to do so.

Hastily, he pulled her with him into the darkest corner of the recess. He whispered to her to lower her head onto his chest. When she did so, he wrapped his arms around her, drawing her against him, so that his long, hard body hid her from the revelers' view as they passed by.

Lily felt utterly safe and protected. His silent strength reassured her in ways that no words could have.

She held her breath as the group reached the alcove, but they continued on, apparently without noticing the figure dressed in black in the corner.

When they were gone, the magic of the moment they had disturbed was lost. Damon said, amazement in his voice, "I have never before been reduced to making love in a hedge."

His face was set in disgusted lines, but whether at her, himself, or both of them Lily was not certain.

With a jerky motion, he pulled her pelisse together and quickly fastened it. She had to bite her lips together to keep from protesting, and that shocked her.

The skill his long tapering fingers displayed in manipulating the buttons of the pelisse reminded her of how often he must have done so for other women. She swallowed hard.

Silently, he guided her to the garden entrance at a pace that told her he could not wait to be gone.

Hawkhurst's curricle was parked by the entrance under Sewell's watchful eye. Damon's silence continued during the ride back to her lodgings in the open equipage.

As he helped Lily down from the curricle, she shivered with nervousness. She had promised him and herself that she would never become one of his brief flings, but she was not at all certain that she would have the power to resist him tonight.

Excitement surged through her as she remembered his mouth upon her breast, and an unrequited ache throbbed again deep within her.

He unlocked and opened the door, then stepped back so that she could enter. In the vestibule, she turned and discovered that he had not followed her inside.

She asked in surprise, "Are you not coming in?"

His face was shadowed and unreadable.

"I think not," he said coolly. "We both know what would happen if I did."

He turned abruptly, without giving her so much as a good-night kiss, and, with the easy grace that was so peculiarly his own, strode to his curricle.

Lily should have been relieved. Instead she was disappointed and hurt.

And mortified, too, at how easily he could control his desire for her.

It was still a game to him, but it no longer was to her.

She yearned for relief from the aching longing he

fired in her. Clearly, he did not have the same problem.

So much for her determination to beat Hawkhurst at his own game!

Chapter 10

Pel's mother, as wide as a frigate and as determined, bore down on Hawkhurst. He thought of taking evasive action, slipping away between the guests attending her son's birthday party, but that would only be postponing the inevitable. He was too tall a target to escape.

When she reached him, he said politely, "A splendid party, Margaret." That was a lie. It was boring, and made all the more unpleasant by Pel's pointed hostility toward him.

"Yes, isn't it," Margaret answered smugly. "My son turns twenty-one only once, and I have spared no expense."

Her idea of no expense was three musicians, inferior champagne, and a meager supper buffet. But at least she had not asked Hawkhurst to pay for it. He wished now that he had offered. He was always more eager to dispense largess when it was his idea and not the recipient's.

Damon caught sight of Cecilia, her martyred expression firmly in place, standing by herself against the near wall.

Thank God, Lily did not treat him to such petulant displays. In fact, she had made no demands at all on him; she was the first woman he could remember who had not tried to manipulate him in one way or another.

Did she truly want nothing from him? He would find out when he offered her a carte blanche. With a sudden flash of painful insight, Damon realized he had been procrastinating doing so because he feared that for all her talk of independence, she would disillusion him by instantly accepting it and then trying to extract more gain for herself as actresses were wont to do.

He would have to act soon, though. The Theatre Royal's season ended in two nights, and Lily would be free to leave Bath.

Damon turned to Pel's mother. "What ails Cecilia?"

Margaret snorted impatiently. "My guess is she wants something. I know that look from her mother. But when I ask her, she denies anything is wrong."

Yes, Damon thought, Cecilia was too afraid of her mother-in-law to confide in her.

"Hawkhurst, would you try to find out what is bothering her?" Margaret gave him a vinegary smile. "You might as well put your vaunted way with women to work on behalf of your family."

Cecilia was no more likely to tell him than she was her mother-in-law, and for the same reason. Before he could voice this opinion, a white-haired dowager, almost as wide as Margaret, came up to offer her effusive praise for the party.

Seizing the opportunity, Hawkhurst drifted away toward a deserted corner. He missed Lily. He had been required to spend the day on various matters pertaining to ending his trusteeship of Pel's inheritance. That had left him with only enough time to drive her to the theatre before her performance.

Maybe he would attend the season finale of the Theatre Royal in which Lily would play Lady Macbeth. Damon knew that she was hurt he had not yet watched one of her performances, yet he feared her acting would disappoint him. Not for a minute did he believe the compliments that were paid her in the greenroom. The gallants there would happily indulge in egregious hyperbole to the most execrable actress in the hope of gaining an advantage with her.

Damon respected Lily's dedication to her craft, but that would not make up for a lack of talent. Had she been the fine performer her admirers all said she was, surely she would not at her age still be appearing in a provincial theatre. She would be in London at Covent Garden or Drury Lane.

If he watched her perform, she would insist on knowing what he thought. He had promised her that he would not lie to her, and he was a man who kept his promises. But neither did he want to hurt her feelings by telling her the truth.

He had done that once under similar circumstances. It had set in motion a tragedy, and he would not make that mistake again. No, better to refrain from watching her on stage.

"Lord Haw'hurt!" a belligerent young voice called.

Hawkhurst turned. Pel in his blue-velvet evening coat was making his way unsteadily toward his cousin. Clearly, the young man had imbibed too much of his mama's inferior champagne, and it had given him false courage.

Pel glowered at Damon. "I never thought you'd serve me such a backhanded turn as you have!" "How could you do this to me? How could you try to steal the woman I love from me?"

"Lily is free to choose whomever she wishes for company," Damon said calmly. "If she prefers mine to yours, your quarrel is with her."

"I swear I shall win her back from you!"

"Keep your voice down," Damon cautioned. "Do

you want your mother and your wife and all your guests to hear you?''

Pel gave Damon a look of burning anger and jealousy, but he dropped his voice to a near-whisper.

''I'm warning you, now that I'm of age and control my inheritance, you will find me a much more formidable rival for Lily's affections.''

Damon looked at the absurd puppy with real pity. ''Do you really believe that you can buy Lily's favors? You would be a fool to try.''

''You only say that because you are terrified that I will succeed!''

Damon was hanging on to his temper by a thread now.

''Your title and fortune, *Lord Hawkhurst*, are the only reasons you were able to seduce Lily.''

The thread holding Hawkhurst's temper snapped. He had never taken credit for a conquest he had not made, and he growled, ''I have not seduced her at all, you impudent puppy!''

He knew the instant the words left his tongue that they had been a terrible mistake, knew it even before he saw the hope and elation in his cousin's eyes.

The young man cried jubilantly, ''I knew my Lily would not be such an easy conquest for you!''

Pel had that much right.

He turned and rushed out of the room.

Hawkhurst, watching him go, wondered uneasily whether the young fool meant to desert his guests and rush to Lily in the greenroom. If he did, he would have to hurry. The enameled hands of the tall pendulum clock by the drawing-room door told Damon that Sewell would be taking Lily home in ten minutes.

Lily sipped tea in her little dining parlor and read again the message from Pel. It had been delivered to her last night by a breathless footman who had run up just as she had been leaving the theatre with Sewell.

Pel's note began querulously, complaining that he had to send it to the theatre because he did not know where she lived. Then he begged her to meet him somewhere away from the greenroom so that they could talk privately.

Lily would grant him his meeting, but their discussion would be very different from what he expected. An idea had just come to her as to how she might bring about a reconciliation between him and Cecilia and, in the process, show them the importance of discussing their problems with each other instead of sulking in silence.

First, though, she must talk to Cecilia. Lily hoped that she would find her in the Pump Room this afternoon. If she was there, no doubt Phoebe would be as well. Lily smiled slyly. Perhaps she would invite Sir Roger Hilton to meet her there.

The door knocker sounded, and Lily's heart thudded. Hawkhurst! Then her excitement faded as she remembered he had said he would not be able to call until this evening.

Last night was the first since Damon had rescued her from Hugo Broome that he had not been at her side in the greenroom, and she was astonished at how much she had missed him.

Strange how time seemed to evaporate in the wink of an eye when she was with him and dragged like a recalcitrant mule when she was not. Lily did not want to think of what it would be like when he was gone from her life forever.

Trude came into the dining parlor. "That was the post at the door with a letter for you."

Lily held out her hand eagerly, thinking that it must be from her brother, who was still in France with Wellington's army.

But it was from the Covent Garden Theatre in

London. Lily hastily scanned its contents. She was being offered a two-year contract without a tryout first. At long last, the theatre had capitulated. Lily let out an exuberant whoop. Her daring gamble in holding out had paid off, and now she would be appearing in London, the pinnacle of the British stage, without having to expose herself to the cruelty of the reviewers in tryouts.

She would have to tell the manager of the Bath Theatre Royal immediately that she would not be returning in the fall.

Lily hastily wrote a note to Sir Roger asking him to meet her in the Pump Room, and paid a young neighbor lad who was always anxious to earn a few coins to deliver it for her.

Then she set out for the theatre to tell its manager, Mr. Steeple, her good news.

She found him, a short, portly man with a luxurious beard, in his crowded little office in the bowels of the theatre.

Lily quickly discovered he did not share her happiness at her offer from Covent Garden. Instead of congratulating her, he loudly vented his anger that she would not be returning to his company the following season.

In his pique, he told her that she could not perform in the season's finale the following night as she had been scheduled to do. Since the theatre was dark tonight, Lily's performance the previous night, although she had not known it at the time, was her last in Bath.

She refrained from telling Mr. Steeple that he was being foolishly petty and said instead, ''I am sorry you feel that way. I should have liked our parting to be on a pleasanter note.''

As Lily walked out of the theatre, several chairmen on the square called to her, offering their services, but she declined. She preferred to walk to the Pump Room.

The afternoon concert had just ended as she stepped inside the vast room. She hastily scanned the sparse crowd. To her relief, Sir Roger was waiting for her near the door. More than a few pair of female eyes were attracted to his fine form, displayed to perfection in a well-cut brown jacket and buff pantaloons.

Lily was delighted to see that one pair of those eyes belonged to Phoebe, who was with Cecilia and Hawkhurst's sisters. Phoebe was watching Roger with the same wistful expression that she had the day Lily met her.

Roger greeted Lily warmly. "It has been so long since I have seen you here that I began to think you had already fled Bath for Weymouth."

"I have been busy," she murmured. Hawkhurst had danced such constant attention on her that she had had little time for anything else.

Nor did she now. It was already late afternoon, and he would be calling on her in an hour. That did not leave her much time to accomplish what she had set out to do with Cecilia, Phoebe, and Roger.

He asked, "Have you heard from Covent Garden yet?"

"Yes, today, and it is wonderful news. I am being given a two-year contract."

Roger's face lit up in a smile that would have caused many female hearts to race, but had no effect on Lily's. "I am so pleased for you," he said.

Cecilia, looking, if possible, more woebegone than she had the first time Lily met her, started toward the marble vase of medicinal waters.

"Excuse me a moment," Lily told Roger. "I must speak to someone."

She hurried to intercept Pel's wife.

Cecilia's eyes brightened when she saw Lily. "I so hoped I would see you here again."

"There is someone I want you to meet." Lily took her arm and guided her to Sir Roger. When Phoebe saw Cecilia being introduced to him, she hurried up too.

Lily watched Roger to gauge his reaction to Phoebe. He looked positively dazed. Infatuation at first sight! Lily took care to introduce her as the Dowager Countess of Hawkhurst so there would be no mistaking her for Damon's wife.

Sir Roger blurted, "Have you been widowed long? No, of course, you cannot have been."

"Nearly seven years," Phoebe confessed.

"The devil!" he exclaimed. From his horrified look, he clearly thought she had been married when she was scarcely out of leading strings.

"It was an arranged marriage," Phoebe explained in a suffocated voice.

"How dreadful for you," he said sympathetically.

Phoebe promptly dissolved into tears. Sir Roger was immediately all concern and solicitude.

Lily, remembering what her brother had written her about Roger's penchant for weeping, helpless females, had to smother a smile. Phoebe could not have picked a more effective tactic for capturing his interest.

Leaving him to comfort the young dowager, Lily took Pel's wife aside to ask whether there was some piece of jewelry that she would particularly like her husband to give her.

"Oh, yes!" Cecilia answered instantly. "There is the most beautiful diamond ring that I long for at a jeweler's on Bath Street. If only Pel would buy me that, I would be the happiest girl in the world."

The change in her as she described the ring amazed Lily. For the first time, she could appreciate what Hawkhurst had meant when he had said Cecilia could be a taking little thing when she was animated.

If Lily's scheme worked, the girl would soon have much to be animated about.

"The ring sounds so lovely that I should like to see it," Lily said. "Perhaps you could show it to me."

"Oh, yes!" Cecilia cried, obviously eager to look at it again. "Could we go now? It is at Forney and Son Jewelers, which is very near here."

"Of course," Lily agreed, even though doing so meant that Hawkhurst would most likely arrive at her lodgings before she did. It could not be helped, though.

As she and Cecilia left the Pump Room, Lily glanced back at Phoebe and Sir Roger. They were so deeply engrossed in conversation that Lily doubted an artillery round landing in the Pump Room would have caught their attention.

The ring that Cecilia coveted turned out to be a many-caret diamond in an ornate gold filigree setting. Lily held it in her fingers, examining it under the interested eye of a thin young clerk with wispy hair the color of ripe wheat. She wondered if he might be the son of Forney and Son.

The ring was far too large and gaudy for Lily's taste, but it was clear that her companion had her heart set upon it.

When Lily learned its price, she pointed out, "It is shockingly expensive. Your husband must be a very rich man."

Cecilia's eyes remained fastened enviously on the ring. "No," she admitted, "but I want it more than anything. If only I could have it, I swear I will not want another thing!"

Lily doubted that, but she asked, "If your husband gave you this ring, you would be satisfied that he loves you?"

"Oh, yes," Cecilia assured her.

As they left Forney and Son, Lily said, "I am certain that your husband does not know how important gifts are to you. He does not understand that you regard them as an assurance of his love. Promise me that the next time he gives you a gift, you will tell him how much it means to you and why."

Lily's request clearly surprised Pel's wife, but she agreed to it.

The two women parted outside the shop. Cecilia went back to the Pump Room to rejoin her companions while Lily paused to consider the next step in her scheme. She must send Pel a note agreeing to meet him, but she would have no chance to do so once she returned home because Hawkhurst would undoubtedly be waiting for her.

Lily decided to pen her message to Pel at the nearby York House. Going into one of its lounges, she sat down at a writing desk equipped with pen, ink, paper, and sealing wafers.

She wrote Pel that she would meet him at 10 A.M. the next day at the corner of the Bath Street colonnade nearest the Pump Room.

After sealing the note with one of the wafers, she hurried over to the handsome stone portico in Stall Street where the sedan chairmen waited for prospective fares to leave the Pump Room. There, she hired one of the idle men to deliver the message to Pel.

That done, she hurried toward her lodgings. Hawkhurst would want to know what had made her late, but she would not tell him about her plan to reconcile Cecilia and Pel quite yet. Tomorrow, after she had succeeded, she would tell Damon. He would be proud of her.

When Hawkhurst arrived at Lily's, he was surprised to be told by her maid that she had gone out on an errand and not returned. Pressing Trude for more specifics, he learned that Lily's destination had been the Pump Room. An odd place for an errand.

It was not easy for Damon to trust a woman, and he could not entirely quiet a nagging concern that Lily might be playing some deeper game with him than he comprehended.

As he waited in her drawing room, he thought of the pleasant hours he had spent here with her. The restlessness and boredom that had increasingly plagued him had been in abeyance since he had met Lily. She did not play a role or silly, coquettish games with him. Lily was herself—and that was why he could be himself with her.

Hawkhurst frowned at the gilt-bronze clock on the fireplace mantel. It was nearly a half hour past the time he had told Lily he would call. She had never before kept him waiting like this.

He wondered whether she had any inkling how hard it had been for him to leave her after Sydney Gardens. Never had he found it so difficult to adhere to his guiding principle that the way to control a woman was to control himself. He had wanted nothing more than to finish here what he had started there.

But he appreciated how proud and spirited she was. She had been so determined that she would not become his mistress that he wanted to give her plenty of time to think about the step she would be taking.

He wanted her pride to have time to accept what her body ached for.

But he would wait no longer.

Chapter 11

The door flew open, and Lily rushed into the drawing room, looking delectable in a white, wide-brimmed French bonnet, trimmed with lilac satin ribbons, and a white muslin walking dress. Below the ornamental knotted work that decorated the hem of its skirt, Hawkhurst caught a glimpse of lilac half-boots.

"I am sorry I am late," she apologized, stripping off her lilac kid gloves. "My errand took me longer than I thought."

His delight at seeing her gave way to suspicion. "What errand took you to the Pump Room? Had I known you were going there, I would have accompanied you."

She tossed her gloves upon the tripod table. "I know," she said, smiling. "But my errand was private."

Why this sudden secrecy? Lily was usually so candid with him. Jealousy pricked at him.

"Whom did you meet there?" he asked brusquely.

She stiffened, and anger flashed in her eyes. "A friend, and you have no right to ask who."

Her infernal independence! To pursue the subject would be futile. It would only make her angrier, and she would not tell him. He did not want to argue with this irresistible creature, he wanted to make love to her. This was not the time to wage a battle that would lose him the war.

"No, I have no right at all," he agreed soothingly.

She visibly relaxed, mollified by his conciliatory response, and rewarded him with a smile as warm as refracted sunshine.

It sent a shaft of acute desire through him. Hell's fire, he wanted her more than he wanted breath. "You look especially lovely today."

"You approve of my dress?"

"Yes, but I approve even more of what is in it."

"You did not two nights ago."

"But you are wrong, my sweet. I approved *too* much."

She had neglected to remove her bonnet, and its wide brim shadowed her eyes, preventing him from gauging her reaction to his admission.

Slowly, deliberately, he untied the lilac ribbons beneath her chin, and removed the bonnet, laying it on the table beside the sofa. Smiling, he said, "Pretty as this hat is, your face is lovelier, and I prefer to gaze upon it."

But he did not gaze long. His lips descended on hers, lightly teasing them until they parted willingly for his invasion. Their kiss was long and hot and consuming, and the reaction of his body to it was so powerful as to be painful.

His fingers brushed her face gently, then her hair. Suddenly he buried them in its coils. The scent of wild roses wafted over him. "You hair is like silk," he breathed. "I have never seen it free. May I?"

She nodded slowly, and his fingers gently removed the pins, letting it fall in a fiery cascade about her shoulders. His breath caught at the shimmering beauty of it. Dazzled by its brilliance, he could not keep his hands from stroking it. It was like touching a sunset.

She purred a little and her eyes closed. He bent

his head and lightly brushed the tip of her nose with his lips, then her eyelids. They fluttered open.

Beneath her long, thick lashes, desire that mirrored his own smoldered in the green depths of her eyes.

Suppressing a groan, he wrapped an arm around her and bent his head to lay a path of kisses down her elegant neck. Her gown was cut much more modestly than the one she had worn at Sydney Gardens, and his lips soon encountered fabric where he would have preferred skin. Tightening his hold on her, he slipped his hand around her breast and fondled it. He felt the hardening response of its tip through the light cloth.

His mouth found hers again as his other hand sought her belly, caressing it in slow, rhythmic circles. She moaned.

His own passion spiraled, becoming as intense and uncontrollable as if he were a calfling with his first woman. He had to have her.

Years of ingrained habit penetrated the haze of his ardor. It was time to deliver his famous ultimatum. Hawkhurst had not bedded a woman in years until he had done so, and she had agreed to it. *The secret of controlling a woman is to control yourself.*

Now, however, he could not bring himself to mention it. He told himself there was no need to. Lily was so different from all the others.

And what he felt for her was different, too.

Besides, he thought ruefully, knowing Lily, she would likely throw his ultimatum back in his teeth.

Then where would he be?

In truth, he was so damn wild for her that he would give her anything she asked. His patience and his vaunted self-control had been reduced to ashes by the fire of his desire for her. He had to have her, no matter what the cost.

His mouth recaptured hers in a passionate, distracting kiss.

Lily was so lost in its rapture that she was oblivious to his skillful hands busy with the buttons at the back of her gown. He eased its small cap sleeves and the straps of her chemise down her arms. Gasping in surprise, she stared up at him.

A marveling glow on his dark face softened its harsh lines and made him breathtakingly handsome.

"You are so lovely, Lily," he murmured almost reverently as he looked at her breasts that he had bared to his hungry gaze.

She blushed and tried to pull her gown up, but he caught her hands.

"No, please, my darling, let me look at you." His voice was husky and pleading and utterly irresistible.

Her blush faded. How could she be embarrassed when he looked at her with such admiration and desire in his eyes? It made her feel like the most beautiful of women.

His mouth came down to claim the rosy peak of her breast. He cherished it with a tenderness that made her shiver, and she was helpless to protest, to move, even to utter an intelligible syllable.

Then his lips moved to the other crest and suckled it, sending new waves of sensation through her. Still she was powerless to stop him, caught as she was in the throes of desire so intense that she thought she would die of it.

His fingers were again busy behind her, and suddenly her gown lay about her feet. His mouth increased its titillating pressure on her breast as his hand caught the skirt of her lawn chemise, glided beneath it, and stroked her thighs. His warm hand moved higher and caressed her belly, so exquisitely sensitive to his touch that she gasped. Her knees seemed to turn to liquid, and she sagged against him.

He caught her weight with one arm and supported her. His other hand ceased its tantalizing movements. When he removed it from beneath her chemise, she wanted to protest its loss.

He guided her to the sofa. She sank down upon it, and he lifted her legs onto its cushions so that she was reclining.

That movement restored her, at least for a moment, to some semblance of sanity. She belatedly summoned the will to object. "I won't—"

He put his finger gently over her lips. "Hush, my sweet. I will not take you unless you want me. Only let me pleasure you a little now." His eyes were like brown velvet, softer than she had ever seen them. "It is what you want."

Yes, God help her, it was.

He dropped to his knees beside the sofa, and his lips replaced his finger on her mouth. His tongue explored it in a way that made coherent thought impossible.

His hand slipped the skirt of her chemise up about her waist, and his fingers drew feathery circles up the inside of her thighs. She shivered helplessly, then forgot all else as one long finger lightly touched her most private place.

It caressed her there slowly, skillfully, concentrating on one special spot. She moaned aloud at the sensations twisting through her body.

What was it about Hawkhurst that made her respond to him with such a flaming passion that she cared about naught else? Caught up as she was now in an intense tide of longing for him, she could not understand how any woman could resist him.

And she no longer wanted to.

No other man had made her feel as though she would die if she could not have him, if only for a moment. No other man had set her blood afire as he did. Before she met him, she had been convinced that no man ever could.

She did not want to go through life wondering what it would have been like to have been Hawkhurst's lover, wondering what she had missed. She did not want to regret never discovering what ecstasy he could bring her.

Once she had regarded Hawkhurst's conquests with icy scorn. How could they have been such fools to give themselves for a brief moment to a man like him?

Now Lily knew that it was she who had been the fool.

She had thought to teach him a lesson. Instead he had taught her.

Hawkhurst, kneeling beside her, kissed her long and deeply as once again his magical fingers continued to excite the nub of her pleasure.

His mouth left her lips, and his tongue slowly licked the crest of her breast, tracing tiny circles on it that sent uncontrollable shivers through her.

Lily buried her hands in his thick black hair that was surprisingly soft. She writhed in sweet agony beneath the onslaught of his mouth and his talented hands. Caught in the grip of an unbearable ache that must be eased, she knew instinctively that only he could do so.

"Help me, Damon," she begged.

He raised his head from her breast and said gently, "There is only one way I can do that, my sweet. Do you want that?"

Caught in the intolerable ache that had to be assuaged, she could give him only one answer. "Yes," she whispered.

His face betrayed nothing. "Are you certain?"

He was not making her surrender easy for her,

and she hesitated. Would she see victory in those hooded, unreadable eyes when she capitulated?

A second passed, then another. As Hawkhurst waited for her reply, he felt as though he had been stretched upon a rack. If she denied him now, he did not think that he could stand it. He was on fire for her.

Her eyes fluttered shut. "Yes."

Hawkhurst knew that her eyes had closed because she feared she would see triumph in his. She was wrong. What he felt was elation—and profound relief. He needed her desperately.

He dropped a light kiss on the forehead. "Then I think, my lovely Lily, that we would be more comfortable in your bed."

Hawkhurst helped her up. She was a little unsteady, and he kept his arm tightly around her as she led him into her bedroom.

It was perfumed by that scent of wild roses that was uniquely Lily's. He was relieved to see that the bed was sturdily constructed and more than large enough to accommodate them both easily—not some spindly, narrow affair that like as not would collapse beneath the ferocity of his passion.

Like Lily's drawing room, her bedroom's indifferent furnishings had been disguised. A quilt in a pattern of green and white diamonds covered the bed. Another patchwork quilt, this one in a colorful starburst design, hung on the wall. An embroidered cloth disguised the scarred top of a chest of drawers, and he was certain the handsome gilt-framed mirror above it was Lily's addition.

When they reached the bed, she faltered.

He recognized how hard it was for a woman of her pride and independence to capitulate to him. Nuzzling her temple with his mouth, he asked softly, "Second thoughts, my sweet flower?"

"Yes . . . no . . ."

"You are free to change your mind." And if she did, he thought in agony, he did not know what he would do.

She looked up at him with eyes half-veiled by her long, thick lashes. "But I want you so desperately." Some of the frustration he was feeling echoed in her voice.

She would not regret it. He would see to that.

Hawkhurst was determined to make it better for her than it had ever been or ever would be with another man. He gathered her in his arms and gave her a kiss that was designed to drive all else from her mind.

As he slid her chemise off, she blushed a little under his appraisal. It startled him that she was unused to a man seeing her naked. "Don't be embarrassed," he said gently. "You are even lovelier without clothes than with. Few women are."

When they were between the pristine white sheets, he laid siege to her body, tantalizing and pleasuring it with all the skill at his command.

His finger glided into her, eased by the slick, abundant honey of her response, but he was surprised at how tightly it hugged him. Clearly it had been a long time since she had been with a man, and he would have to be very careful at first. He wanted it to be perfect for her, and he was suddenly as nervous as a youth with his first woman.

He blazed a trail of hot kisses down her body. When his mouth reached its destination, she gasped in shock and twisted in pleasure.

He lifted his head and knew by her startled expression that no man had kissed her like that before. She puzzled him. His finger returned again to explore her more deeply. Suddenly he was no longer puzzled, only dumbfounded.

"Lily," he asked softly, "have you ever given yourself to a man before?"

"No," she admitted.

"Why didn't you tell me?" he demanded hoarsely, stunned by the realization that he was the first. Hell's fire, he might have hurt her even more than was necessary.

"You would not have believed me."

She was right about that, he thought guiltily. Even if she were not an actress, she was such a passionate woman that it never occurred to him that she had not had other lovers. He was deeply moved—both honored and humbled—that he would be her first.

Now, even more than before, he was determined to make it perfect for her. His own need receded before his desire to give her a magnificent initiation into the rites of love.

He said huskily, "I want it to be wonderful for you, but I cannot prevent the hurt that occurs at first. I promise you, though, I will do my best to make it as painless as I can for you."

He lifted himself over her and kissed her mouth deeply as he began a slow penetration into her tight but welcomingly wet sheath. He moved carefully. Sweat beaded on his forehead and back from the strain of keeping himself in check. The muscles in his arms and back began to ache from holding his weight so carefully.

When he judged it time, he broke the barrier with one quick surge. His mouth closed over hers, swallowing her gasp of pain, then remained still, giving her body a chance to adjust to his invasion, while he murmured tenderly, encouragingly.

Then he began to move. She stiffened, but after a minute her body relaxed, and she joined him in a sensual cadence. As its tempo accelerated, Lily's breath grew rapid and ragged. She moaned and her fingers dug convulsively into Damon's back. He exulted in her growing passion.

Lily could not believe the gathering storm within

her. A strange torment, demanding relief, and an exquisite pleasure were building simultaneously within her.

Suddenly her body convulsed around Damon in shuddering tremors of passion. He arched, stiffened, and shuddered, too, then lay gasping.

In the aftermath of her intense, shattering release, Lily was dazed with pleasure and wonder. She looked up at him, astonishment in her eyes.

His own gleamed in response, and he laughed. "Surprised, are we?"

"Very," she admitted.

Apparently mindful of his weight upon her, Damon started to roll away, but she hugged him fiercely to her.

"No, don't leave me," she pleaded. "I like having you a part of me."

"Not as much as I like being a part, my lovely Lily." His voice had the deep timbre of a well-satisfied man.

They remained joined in a silent, utterly satisfying communion. Lily could not remember when she had felt so content and languidly happy. He had been so tender and patient with her, more concerned for her pleasure than for his own. She might be inexperienced in lovemaking, but she knew instinctively that she had been initiated by a master.

No wonder, despite his reputed parsimony, he cut such a wide swathe through theatrical greenrooms. However close he might be with his purse, he was both skilled and generous as a lover. She belatedly understood why women might be so willing to accept the Hawkhurst Ultimatum.

Except he had not delivered it to her. That puzzled her, but she was too happy to ask him about this omission.

When she felt him growing small within her, she sighed in regret. He lifted himself away and lay on his back beside her. She saw his hands move quickly beneath the sheet, removing something that he dropped on the floor beside the bed. She guessed what it was, and was pleased that he had protected her.

He looked around her room curiously. His gaze stopped abruptly on a dagger suspended on the wall near the door. Its handle had been set with three jewels of remarkable size: an emerald, a ruby, and in the middle a pearl.

"Why do you display that in your bedroom?"

"I like it. I enjoy the way light from the window plays upon the jewels in the morning."

"A gift from an admirer?"

"Yes, but not the kind you mean." Its giver had been an elderly theatre-lover in his waning days with no amorous intentions and no heirs. Lily's portrayal of Lady Macbeth in the sleepwalking scene had so moved him that he had presented the jeweled dagger to her. He had maintained that she was better in the role of Lady Macbeth than even the great Sarah Siddons had been, but she did not tell Damon that. "He was an old gentleman who appreciated my acting."

"Among other things," Hawkhurst said sardonically.

Lily's happiness and contentment faded. His cynicism wounded her deeply. For him, seducing her had been nothing but a game that he had won yet again. It made her feel tawdry and weak and defeated.

In a choked voice, she said, "How pleased you must be with yourself. Once more, the king of the greenroom has triumphed over another foolish actress who could not resist him."

She tried to turn away from him, but he grabbed her and would not let her.

"Believe me, I do not feel in the least triumphant,

only euphorically happy. No one knows better than I, my lovely flower, that you are as different from other actresses as the lily is from a nettle.''

That made her feel better, and she did not resist him when he pulled her tightly against him. ''You cannot conceive how I have ached for you, Lily.''

She was not convinced. ''So much so that you were not the least bothered by leaving me on my doorstep after Sydney Gardens.''

He laughed. ''I was so unbothered I had to take a midnight swim in the Avon after I left here.'' He dropped a kiss on the tip of her nose. ''I wanted you to distraction. Still do,'' he added ruefully, looking down.

Although he had just found glorious release in her depths—or perhaps because of it—his staff was already magnificently erect, demanding an encore. He could scarcely believe his quick, urgent arousal.

She looked down and murmured, ''Amazing.''

Amazing, hell! At his age, bloody miraculous was what it was. ''You have turned me into a calfling again.''

This time, they made love to each other slowly. Lily explored and tantalized his body as eagerly as he did hers. He gloried in the honesty and depth of her response to him. She was even more passionate than he had suspected.

They soared to rapturous heights that few lovers were privileged to reach. He was experienced enough to know that, even if Lily did not.

Afterward, she lay nestled in the circle of his arm. Outside the long twilight of May had given way to darkness.

Lily said thoughtfully, ''Now I understand why you are the king of the greenroom. But you forgot something tonight—the Hawkhurst Ultimatum.''

Damon tensed. Had that been a mistake? He did not tell her that he had deliberately refrained from issuing it. Instead, he inquired warily, "Since I did not, what will you ask me for tomorrow?"

"To give me another night like tonight," she answered promptly.

"What, no request for jewels?" he asked, trying to sound as though he were teasing her, but his tone betrayed his deep-seated suspicion of women that he could not fully conquer even with Lily.

Anger flashed in her eyes. "Do not insult me, Damon. I do not sell myself for jewels."

"What would you sell yourself to me for?"

"Nothing! What I give you, I give freely, not out of necessity or avarice. Can you not accept that I want nothing from you but the pleasure you give me?"

The truth was that he could not, and he said, "I have never before met a woman who was willing to settle for so little."

"So little!" she sputtered.

That pleased him enormously, and he reached for her, saying, "Let me give you more."

Chapter 12

L ily awoke the following morning in the shelter of Damon's warmth. She was on her side with him pressed against her back, his arm thrown protectively over her. His deep, even breathing told her he was still asleep.

As she lay there, she was assailed by morning-after doubts. She should have sent him away as soon as she learned he was Hawkhurst. Lily had known that she was playing with fire by continuing to see him, but she had been unable to resist his challenge. She had been determined to show him that there was one woman who could resist him, one woman who could beat him at his own game.

What a pea-brain she had been to think that she could. Instead of besting him, he had spun a gossamer web that had entrapped her heart.

The bright light seeping in around the edges of the window hangings told her it was late. She wanted nothing so much as to remain with Damon, but she had to meet Pel in Bath Street.

Taking care not to disturb Damon, she eased her way, inch by slow inch, out of his arms and got up. His thick black hair was tousled boyishly, and sleep had softened the harsh lines of his face, making him unbearably handsome to her. She could have watched him for hours, but she forced herself to

151

gather clothes from the wardrobe and glide silently out of the bedroom.

Lily went into Trude's room to dress. The maid was sitting by the window, mending a tear in one of her mistress's gowns. They had been together for four years, and Lily had come to regard Trude as her friend as well as her maid. So when she read the silent question in Trude's eyes, Lily admitted frankly, "I fear I have lost my heart."

Lily had been so certain that would never happen. But pride goeth before a fall she thought ruefully, and she had fallen hard—into love with Hawkhurst. And she was very much afraid she would turn out to be like her mama, a woman who could love but one man.

Trude said hesitantly, "But, ma'am, he is a lord. He won't . . ." She broke off, looking worried and embarrassed.

"Yes, I know." Lily was not such a fool that she thought Hawkhurst would marry her. Even if he believed in love—and she knew that he did not—he understood what was due his station. He would never marry a woman who made her living upon the stage.

But she hoped that he would not insult her love for him by offering her a carte blanche. No matter how much she loved a man, she would never let him make her his convenient, dependent upon him. She would be Hawkhurst's lover, but not his mistress.

He would not understand the difference, but it did not matter. Lily did.

She smiled at her maid. "Be happy for me, Trude. It is better to enjoy love for as long as I can rather than never to know it at all."

Damon was still asleep when Lily departed to meet Pel. She left a brief note for him with Trude in case he awoke, but he was sleeping so soundly that, with any luck, he would continue to do so until she returned.

In Bath Street, Pel was waiting for Lily at the corner of a colonnade. His round, earnest face broke into a wide smile at the sight of her.

Before she could speak, he cried passionately, "Lily, I am determined to save you from a terrible mistake that you will regret all the rest of your life!" He sounded as though he had rehearsed the line carefully. "Hawk is not the man for you! He is too old!"

Lily said coolly, "I prefer mature men. They know how to make a woman feel loved, which is what every woman wants."

"Hawk never loved a woman in his life!" Pel protested.

No doubt that was true, Lily thought sadly, but she continued smoothly, "Every woman wants to feel loved and cherished by the special man she chooses to be her husband."

"Hawk will never marry you!"

Ignoring that, Lily began to lead Pel along the colonnade. "A woman wants a husband who tells her that she is beautiful and that he loves her, even when she is pregnant and feeling fat and ugly and unloved—*especially* when she's pregnant."

"You will always be lovely to me," Pel insisted.

"You say that now, but what kind of husband would you truly be?" she asked slyly as she edged them both toward Forney and Son's shop. "A woman is often moody and tearful and sullen when she is bearing the fruit of her love for her husband, and she counts upon him to lift her spirits. Are you mature enough to be that kind of husband, Pel?"

He flushed guiltily.

They were only a few steps now from the jeweler's and Lily closed her trap. "Would you buy your pregnant wife presents to show her in deeds as well as words how much you care for her?''

"What sort of presents?" he asked eagerly.

She smiled. "Women always love jewels."

They had reached Forney and Son's door, and Lily stopped in front of it. "Perhaps this shop has something suitable to reassure a wife of her husband's love."

Pel dutifully followed Lily inside where the same thin young man who had helped her and Cecilia the previous day came forward. He was not much older than Pel. It was clear from the gleam in his eye that he remembered Lily. She prayed that he would not betray that she had been here before.

"I believe we should look at rings," she said, smiling at Pel. "I think a woman particularly likes rings as a pledge of her husband's love."

The clerk, a knowing smirk upon his face, presented to them the velvet tray that contained the ring Cecilia wanted.

Lily pretended to consider various other rings—an emerald, a ruby, a sapphire—before picking up the diamond that was Cecilia's choice.

"Oh, this is it!" she exclaimed, holding it up for Pel's inspection. "This is perfect! Any wife would be thrilled to have this from her husband."

The odious clerk snickered as she displayed her choice, and she longed to box the impudent little toad's ears. Fortunately, Pel was staring in such shock at the size of the many-caret diamond that he did not notice the clerk's peculiar reaction.

When Pel asked the price, he blanched at the reply. He said dubiously, "It is frightfully expensive."

"Yes, but I suspect you would be astonished at the warmth of your wife's response were you to present her with this ring," Lily said.

She wished that the wretched clerk was not listening to her with the liveliest interest, but it could not be helped. She had to convince Pel to buy the ring for Cecilia. "Why, I wager a wife would throw herself into your arms and do everything that she could to make you the happiest man alive."

Pel looked at Lily with an inspired light in his eyes. "Do you truly mean that?" he asked.

"Yes, I do," she assured him, returning the ring to its niche upon the tray.

She had pushed him as far as she could, and she turned to leave. "I must go. I am late for an appointment with my modiste." She had no such appointment, but she was hoping to get back to her lodgings before Hawkhurst awakened.

When she stepped outside the shop, she glanced back at Pel. He was still agonizing over whether to buy the ring, but Lily was certain that he was about to do so.

She smiled happily, wishing that she could be a fly on the wall to witness Cecilia's reaction when she received it.

Hawkhurst, more asleep than awake, realized that Lily was no longer in his arms. Without opening his eyes, he reached out to pull her back to him, but she was not there. Coming instantly awake, he was incredulous and much displeased to discover that he was alone in Lily's bed and she was gone from the room.

Cursing angrily, he jumped out of the bed and jerked on his pantaloons. He went storming out of the bedroom to look for her, only to be informed by her maid that she had gone out a minute or two earlier.

"She hoped to be back before you awoke, but she left a note for you in case she weren't."

Trude handed him a folded sheet of paper with the single word "Hawkhurst" written across the back in a bold hand.

He unfolded it and read hastily: *You were sleeping so soundly I did not like to disturb you, and I have an errand that I must take care of. I will be back soon. L.*

He admired her bold, graceful handwriting that was as distinctive as she was, but he frowned at the note's contents. He could not believe after the night they had spent together that she would have slipped away like this on another mysterious errand. He wondered grimly whether it, like the one the previous day, was also at the Pump Room.

He decided to find out. Going back to the bedroom, he dressed quickly, then left. It was starting to drizzle, and he had not had the foresight the previous day to equip himself with an umbrella. Resigned to getting wet, he walked toward the Pump Room.

He thought of Lily's protestations that she wanted nothing from him except another night like the last. He wanted to believe her, but in all his affairs, the lady had inevitably grown greedy. That was always fatal to his interest, not because he was clutch-fisted as Cassandra claimed but because he disliked discovering that a woman cared more for his purse than for him.

His distrust of women was so ingrained by now he could not shake the apprehension that in the end Lily would disillusion him like every other woman had.

The streets were half-deserted. The Bath season was coming to an end, and most of the town's visitors had already left. Tonight would be the final performance of the season at the Theatre Royal, and Lily would be free to leave Bath. Damon decided that he would take her to Hawkhill.

When he reached the Pump Room, it was emptier than he had ever seen it, another sign that the Bath season was ending. It did not take him more than a few minutes to ascertain that Lily was not there.

When he came outside again, the clouds had parted a little and the drizzle had stopped. Looking around him, he caught sight of Lily coming out of one of the shops along the Bath Street colonnade. She strode rapidly away from him in the direction of her lodgings. So she had merely been shopping. Then he frowned. Surely she could have waited to do so until he awakened.

He started after her. As he passed the shop of Forney and Son, he hesitated. He never purchased a woman expensive jewels. But perversely, because Lily had rejected them, he wished to buy her something that was both as extraordinary as the night had been and as tasteful as she was. He would stop in the jeweler's to see what he could find.

When he entered the shop, he was surprised to discover Pel there, admiring his new purchase, a large, showy diamond ring in a gold filigree setting. Hawkhurst uneasily recalled the puppy's impassioned threat to win Lily's affections by buying her expensive gifts. Damon hoped that was not what he was up to now.

His cousin's face turned instantly hostile when he saw Hawkhurst. "Why are you here?" he demanded.

"And a good day to you, too, Pel," Damon said with a sardonic grin. "I believe I am allowed to shop where I choose."

He nodded toward the ring in Pel's hand. "I hope that is for Cecilia."

His cousin's lip curled. "I am certain you do, but you know better than that, don't you, Lord Hawkhurst? It is for Lily."

If Pel thought to buy his way into her heart, he was in for a well-deserved surprise. Damon could not help but blame himself for this unfortunate situation. His admission at the party that Lily was not yet his lover had given his cousin renewed hope.

Pel handed his purchase to the young clerk with instructions to wrap it.

As the man went off to do as he was bid, Damon said quietly, "Pel, your inheritance is not so large that it can bear many such extravagant expenditures as this."

"I control my money now. You can no longer tell me how to spend it!"

"No, I cannot," Damon said patiently, "but you are about to become a father, and you have a responsibility to preserve and increase your inheritance for your own heirs, just as your father did for you."

His cousin's face hardened in recalcitrant lines.

"If you must give such a gift as this to anyone, Pel, give it to your wife, who is bearing your child. She has a greater claim on your generosity, and the ring will remain in your family. It is far too expensive a gift to give to a passing infatuation."

"Lily is not a passing infatuation!"

"It is still too expensive a gift for a man of your means."

Pel sneered. "Perhaps it is far too expensive for a notorious muckworm like you! I, however, am more generous."

"No, just more naive," Damon said in exasperation. "Revealing yourself to be a rich pigeon ready for the plucking!"

Pel flushed angrily and his face was set in mulish obstinancy. "You are trying to stop me from giving it to Lily because you know it will carry the day over you. You cannot bear to be bested by me!"

Damon almost laughed aloud at that.

"All is fair in love and war, Lord Hawkhurst."

"This is not love, Pel. You are merely infatuated with her," Damon said quietly. And so too, God help him, was he. "Do you truly think you can buy Lily's affections?"

"I don't think, I know!" Pel said triumphantly. "Lily promised me that if I gave her this ring, she would do everything in her power to make me happy."

Damon stared at him in shocked disbelief. "What?"

"Lily picked this ring out herself."

"I cannot believe that!"

"It's true. She sent for me." Pel pulled a thin sheet of paper from his pocket and thrust it at him. "Here is her note."

Hawkhurst scanned the message hastily. He had no doubt that the bold, distinctive handwriting was Lily's. The note dropped from his fingers as though it had burned him.

Pel retrieved it as the clerk returned with the wrapped package.

"Remember the woman who showed me this ring a few minutes ago?" Pel said to the clerk.

Damon was thunderstruck. *A few minutes ago! Hell's fire, this was the shop that he had seen Lily coming out of!*

"Aye, I'm not likely to forget her," the clerk said with lecherous appreciation. "Today was not her first visit here. She has been in before to inspect this very ring."

"Do you recollect what she said would happen if I bought this ring for her?" Pel asked.

The clerk leered. "Something about your becoming the happiest man alive."

Damon could not doubt that the clerk was telling the truth. He felt as though Lily had stabbed him through the heart with that damned jeweled dagger that decorated her bedroom. After the night they had spent together, the deceiving wanton had been so greedy that she had risen from the bed she had shared with him to bargain with his cousin for her favors in exchange for that damned ring.

"I do not sell myself for jewels."

And Damon, fool that he was, had believed her. Never, in all his thirty-six years, had he felt so hoaxed and betrayed by a woman. She had known that he would not give her them, and so she had not asked him. Instead, she had told him exactly what he wanted to hear. *"Can you not accept that I want nothing from you but the pleasure you give me?"*

His lips curled in cynical contempt as he contemplated what he was certain was the full magnitude—and cruel cunning—of Lily's clever machinations. She was playing the cousins against each other. Now that she had coerced this extravagant ring out of Pel, she would no doubt use it to try to wheedle out of his cousin a very expensive carte blanche.

He was beset by disillusionment and humiliation that he could have been so blinded to her true nature. Hawkhurst's rage at Lily was growing as rapidly as his rage at himself for having been such a fool. There had never been a woman that he could not walk away from. By God, he would walk away from this one!

Pel said, "I am going to take this to Lily now." He started for the door with the package containing the ring in his hand, then stopped, looking stymied. "I do not know Lily's address."

Damon gave it to him.

As Pel rushed off, he called triumphantly back over his shoulder. "I have bested you! Lily will be mine now!"

"You are welcome to her!" Damon exclaimed savagely. The young sapskull would soon learn a very expensive lesson.

Hawkhurst hoped that Pel's disillusionment at Lily's hands would be as painful as his own was.

Chapter 13

Pel swaggered toward Lily's, convinced that he was a very fine fellow. Her promise that she would make him the happiest of men had gone directly to his head, swelling to amazing proportions his estimation of his own consequence.

He had never before appreciated what a remarkable figure he must cut among the fair sex that Lily should prefer him to Hawk.

Pel had always been in awe of his sophisticated cousin and his reputation for being irresistible to actresses. Yet now he, Pelham St. Clair, had actually succeeded in winning a most sought-after and desirable woman away from the king of the greenroom. He felt like a young princeling who had dethroned a powerful ruler.

Even though Hawk, when faced with humiliating defeat at his cousin's hands, had told him he was welcome to Lily, Pel could not imagine that he meant it.

Hawk had been right about one thing, though. The ring had cost Pel far more than he could afford. He was deeply impressed by what he saw as his unparalleled generosity.

An unhappy thought struck him. What if his cousin should decide to buy Lily even more impressive gems? He could certainly afford to do so.

Suddenly Pel was racked by jealousy and doubt. The first thing he must do before he put the ring in Lily's hand was to extract from her a promise that she would have nothing more to do with Hawk.

How thrilled Lily would be when she saw the ring. Pel entertained himself for the remainder of his walk by imagining various exotic forms her gratitude might take.

When he located the address Hawkhurst had given him, he exhibited his newfound self-confidence by banging loudly upon her door.

Lily herself answered it. "Oh, Da—" She broke off, clearly shocked, when she saw Pel.

"Good God," she blurted, "how did *you* discover my address?"

Had Pel, smug in his newly inflated conceit, not known better, he might have thought she was unhappy to see him. Ignoring her question, he held up the small box containing the ring.

"I have it for you!" he cried proudly, his voice squeaking with excitement. He sounded sadly unsophisticated even to his own ears.

He was surprised at how Lily was staring at the box. She looked as though she could not believe her eyes.

Pel affected what he hoped was the amused, indulgent air of a debonair man of the world. "Could it be, my darling, that you thought I would not buy it for you?"

She closed her eyes for a moment. He took this as a sign that she was so overwhelmed by his enormous generosity that she was rendered speechless.

A more astute man might have thought she was praying for patience.

When she opened her eyes again, she said in a voice that sounded more resigned than grateful. "No, I did not think you would buy it for *me*. You had better come into the drawing room."

He followed her, disappointed by her odd, unenthusiastic reaction. He had expected her to throw herself upon his neck in gratitude. Would she have been so subdued had Hawk presented her with such a gift? Jealousy gripped Pel, and he held up the small box, careful to keep it just out of her reach like a man teasing his dog with a bone.

"This is a very expensive ring," he said in a voice that betrayed how impressed he was by his own largesse. "Before I give it to you, you must swear to tell Hawkhurst that you are mine now and that you will have nothing more to do with him."

He had meant to sound stern and masterful, but his voice was querulous and jealous. Lily looked at him so keenly he felt his cheeks redden.

He tried to recover with what he hoped was a suave, assured smile.

She said in a tone of petulant reluctance, "Well, I suppose since you mean to marry me, I might be persuaded to tell him that."

His masterful smile vanished. *"Ma—marry you?"* he squeaked in consternation.

"In truth, though, I would much prefer to marry Hawkhurst," she confessed candidly. "But since he will not wed me, I suppose I shall settle for you."

It was hardly the profession of undying love and gratitude that Pel had expected to hear from her, and he stared at her aghast, his high opinion of himself fraying.

Before he realized what she was about, she snatched the box from his hand. He demanded angrily, "What do you think you are doing?"

"You said that you bought it for me. It is mine now."

He made a grab to retrieve the box from her, but she was too quick for him and hid it behind her back.

He glared at her. "You told me at the jeweler's

that if I gave you this ring you would do everything you can to make me the happiest man alive."

"I very clearly said *your wife* would. So as soon as we are married . . ."

Pel thought she had said that merely as an euphemism for the benefit of the clerk's ears. Did she actually not know he was already married?

"Of course, I must have a trousseau. I shall have the bills sent to you."

"You . . . I . . ."

"I am thinking about Hawkhurst again." Lily's expression was suddenly dreamy. "Surely you would not mind if I continued my affair with him after we are married?"

"Continued?" Pel stammered, infatuation rapidly giving way to darker emotions.

"I understand it is all the crack to have a titled lover, and you surely want your wife to be fashionable, do you not?" She smiled sweetly. "You must procure a special license so we can be married immediately."

Sweat had broken out on Pel's forehead. "I cannot marry you," he blurted. "I thought Hawk would have told you that I am already married."

His announcement touched off an emotional volcano the likes of which he had never seen. Tears, recriminations, and threats rained down upon him like hot lava.

He was dazed and horrified. Could she truly bring suit against him for breach of promise? Even more daunting was the thought of what his mama would say if Lily wrote her a letter about his shocking behavior as she threatened. That was enough to make him tremble in his shiny new Hessian boots. God only knew what Lily might say about him in it, given the state she was in.

Pel stared dumbly at her as though she had suddenly turned into the mythical Medusa, complete with a head full of snakes, before his very eyes. Sweating profusely, he beat a hasty retreat from her lodgings.

He was a block away before he realized that in his hurry to escape, he had forgotten the ring. He should go back for it, but he refused to subject himself again to her fury.

His first inclination, as it had been for years whenever he was in trouble, was to seek Hawk's help in extracting him from it. His cousin could always be counted upon to know what to do in times of difficulty.

Except that after swearing to Hawk that he would win Lily away from him, Pel found it extremely awkward to ask him now for assistance in escaping her clutches and in retrieving a ring that Hawk had warned him not to buy her.

When Pel was gone, Lily could only shake her head in disbelief that the young dunce could have so thoroughly misinterpreted what she had told him at the jeweler's. She had emphasized the word *wife* over and over. She recalled what Hawkhurst had said about subtlety being wasted on Pel. She must tell him how right he was!

Lily looked at the ring box, still in its wrappings. When she had first seen it, she had wanted nothing so much as to blister Pel's ears with a scathing set-down and send him on his way. But while that would have soothed her own exasperation, it would not have gotten Cecilia the ring she coveted.

So Lily had decided to teach Pel a lesson that he would not soon forget. She had played her share of wronged women during her years on the stage, and she had drawn upon that extensive repertoire for inspiration. All in all, she thought she had given an excellent improvised performance. Had young Pel been more knowledgeable about the theatre, he might have recognized many of the lines she had hurled at his head.

She flicked open the card attached to the box and read what Pel had written in his childish hand:

> To my one and only love,
>   I give you this small token of my affection.
> Know by it that I shall worship you forever.
>   Eternally yours, Pel.

Lily's eyes gleamed with mischief as she finished reading the card, a new scheme rapidly taking shape in her mind.

She called Trude, then handed the box and card to the maid with instructions to deliver it at once to Cecilia St. Clair.

"If anyone else at her house tries to take it from you, refuse to give it to them. Insist you must put it into Mrs. Pelham St. Clair's hands yourself."

Lily was certain that the much-shaken Pel would need some time to collect himself before he went home and that, if Trude hurried, the ring would be in Cecilia's hands before he returned.

Lily watched from the window as Trude set off for Pel's at a rapid pace. When the maid was out of sight, she sank down upon the sofa and massaged her aching temples. It was turning out to be a perfectly horrid day.

After leaving Pel at the jeweler's, she had hurried home, hoping to reach it before Hawkhurst awakened. She had been terribly disappointed to discover that not only was he no longer asleep, he was not even there.

Trude had told her, "Went dashing off in a flame, he did, when he discovered you weren't here."

Hawkhurst was still in a flame an hour after parting from Pel. He had never before been much affected by a woman's perfidy, but he had never before trusted and cared for a woman as he had Lily. He could contain his anger no longer, and he decided to confront her whether Pel was still with her or not.

When he reached her lodgings, he doubted that he would be able to keep from wringing her bloody neck if she greeted him wearing Pel's ostentatious diamond ring on her finger.

He banged on the door.

"Who is it?" Lily's voice on the other side of the door sounded apprehensive.

"Hawkhurst," he growled.

She immediately flung open the door. "Oh, Damon, I am so happy to see you!" she cried.

Lily sounded so sincere that had he not known her real game he would have thought she truly cared about him.

She was looking exceptionally lovely in a green silk gown that brought out the brilliance of her eyes and the milky whiteness of her skin. The sight of that beautiful body and the memory of how soft and exciting it had been in his arms the previous night had an instant impact on his own anatomy.

He could not believe the effect this woman had on him, even knowing what she was. She lifted her face toward his, expecting him to kiss her.

And it was all he could do to resist. Hell's fire, but this creature had bewitched him.

He asked gruffly, "Why are you answering your own door? Where is your maid?"

"I sent her on an errand."

"I never met a woman with so many errands," he observed sarcastically.

He caught both her hands and swept them up to observe whether she wore Pel's ring. Only the worn gold band that had been her mother's wedding ring adorned her fingers.

She regarded him with such a quizzical smile that, despite his best intentions, he could no longer withstand the lure of her mouth. He dropped her hands and pulled her in his arms, kissing her sweet, lying lips with a passion that even his anger at her could not curb.

The secret of controlling a woman is controlling yourself.

Utterly baffled and disgusted by his sudden inability to do so, he pulled back a little from her and gazed down into her brilliant eyes.

She smiled at him. "I missed you." She hugged him and sought his lips again.

God help him, he could not resist her! That he could still want her so desperately, even knowing what she was and what she had done, ate at his soul like lye. He despised himself for his weakness even as he accepted her kiss. Its fervor brought him to hot arousal.

Damn her, had she kissed Pel like this when he had given her the ring?

It didn't matter; Damon had to have her. And he would not share her with any man, especially not his greenling cousin. He would hie her off to Hawkhill where he would keep her for a week or two or however long it took until his maddening hunger for her was sated. Then he would send her packing with nothing to show for the interlude except the pleasure she claimed he gave her.

She was looking up at him with a question in her brilliant eyes, her lips still half-parted. He bent his head, and his kiss this time was rough, part passion and part anger.

She pulled away, a puzzled frown on her face. "What is wrong?"

He was too damned furious at her for her perfidy and at himself for his weakness to make pretty speeches to her. He growled, "I am taking you to Hawkhill."

The color drained from her face. "What are you saying?" Her smoky voice was suddenly reduced to a croak. "Are you offering me a carte blanche?"

"No, why should I?" he responded with cool malice. "Have you forgotten that only hours ago you told me you wanted nothing from me but the pleasure I give you?"

Damn her, she had told him, too, that she would not sell herself for jewels, and she had promptly left him to do just that. "Have you changed your mind?"

Lily could not find her voice, could only stare silently up at him, too stunned by the scorn in his eyes to answer him. What had happened to the tender, loving man of last night? She had given herself freely to him because she loved him, and now he seemed to have nothing but contempt for her.

The front door opened, and Trude came in, nearly bumping into Lily and Hawkhurst who were still standing in the small entry.

Lily struggled to make her voice sound normal as she inquired of her maid, "Was your errand successful, Trude?"

"Aye, I delivered it into her very own hands as you instructed me," she answered, sliding past them toward the back of the house.

Lily whispered to Hawkhurst, "Let us finish this discussion in the privacy of the drawing room."

As she shut its door behind them, she asked, "Why do you want to take me to Hawkhill?"

He gave her a look that curdled her blood. "To assure that you will never again leave our bed, as you did this morning, to bargain with my cousin for your charms."

"What!" she cried, aghast.

"Don't deny that you were at Forney and Son

with him this morning. I saw you leave there with my own eyes. Don't deny you promised to make my cousin the happiest man alive if he gave you that gaudy ring.''

"I *do* deny it!" Lily cried. How could he believe her guilty of such a thing? Surely, after the past fortnight and especially last night, he knew her better than that. "That was not what I told Pel! How can you think that I would—"

"I could not initially," he interrupted bitterly, "but then the clerk confirmed to me that was indeed what you had said."

Lily could scarcely believe her ears. How could Damon believe that she was so treacherous? How could he falsely convict her on the word of that leering fool of a clerk? Her anger flared at the injustice of it all, and she exclaimed indignantly, "That clerk is as much a cork-brain as your cousin!"

"No, *I* am the cork-brain," Damon ground out, "for ever believing that you had a decent bone in that cruel, deceiving body of yours."

Lily stared with agonized eyes at this man who had made such sublime love to her only hours before. She could not believe he could be saying such terrible things to her. They wounded her as she had never before been wounded.

He sneered at her. "How you fooled me with your protestations of wanting nothing but me. You are like every other greedy actress!"

Lily felt suddenly ill. Damon was the first man she had ever given herself to, and now, instead of appreciating that, he was accusing her of being an avaricious liar.

He grabbed her arms with bruising force.

"You're hurting me!" she cried, trying in vain to twist out of the cruel grip of hands that had caressed her so tenderly last night. Hands that had taught her things she had never suspected about herself—and about passion.

Her heart seemed to implode from his explosive contempt for her.

Suddenly, he released his hold on her arms. Before she realized what he was about, he seized the back of her neck with one hand while the other tightened around her chin, capturing her head in a hard grip. She struggled to escape him, but he was too strong.

His mouth that had given her such pleasure the previous night came down on hers in a merciless, plundering kiss that had nothing to do with passion, but was meant to punish and degrade her.

And it succeeded.

She was humiliated. Lily had to fight to keep from bursting into tears of pain and rising fury. No man had ever dared treat her like this! And he would not go unpunished for it. No, indeed, he would not!

He let her go. Lily stared into his face, which was full of scorn for her. How could she have been such a fool as to have given herself to this man?

"Tell me what price you set upon your favors," he taunted.

She gasped. Why, he regarded her as no better than a whore who sold herself for whatever the market would bear! Lily was so incensed that for a moment she did not trust herself to speak.

How she longed to teach this arrogant, contemptuous, infuriating man a lesson he would never forget. Suddenly an idea of how she could do that sprang into her head.

She would pretend to be as vulgar and avaricious as he clearly thought her to be.

She would pretend to be everything *she* most despised.

Her acting talent was getting considerable exercise today.

Lily managed a cunning smile. "What will you give me to become your convenient?"

The disgust in his eyes was almost more than Lily could bear. She was, however, too good an actress to let him see how affected she was. "I must tell you that your cousin—"

He interrupted her. "Do not think you will start a bidding contest between Pel and me for your favors."

"So you are as much a muckworm as you are reputed to be."

"Be careful," he warned. "Do not push me too far."

Lily recklessly disregarded his advice. "Frankly, I prefer generous men like your cousin. I believe I will cast my lot with him." She had no intention of doing so, but she knew that it would enrage Damon.

She succeeded beyond her most optimistic expectation. She could not remember when she had ever seen a man so infuriated.

"How you fooled me, you mercenary jade!" Hawkhurst snarled.

She had indeed, he thought bitterly. He could not believe any woman could have gulled him as completely as she had. Even after the damning note in her own handwriting to his cousin, even after everything that Pel and the clerk had said, Damon had clung to a hope, as weak as the light of a guttering candle, that somehow she was not as bad as she appeared. Actually, she wasn't.

She was worse!

He demanded icily, "Does it give you pleasure to destroy the marriage of a couple that might be very happy otherwise?"

When she did not answer, he said, "You have sadly overestimated the size of Pel's estate. He can afford no more grand gestures like that bauble he gave you."

She shrugged carelessly. "When I have gone through his fortune, I will move on to another man."

"Damn you! So now the real Lily Culhane stands revealed." It was all Hawkhurst could do to keep from throttling the greedy, conniving bitch!

Lily smiled provocatively up at him. "Since you are so concerned for the poor calfling's welfare, what would *you* pay me to drop Pel?"

Damon was well and truly shocked. So it had come to that, had it? "A thousand pounds," he snapped.

She looked insulted. "You are as clutch-fisted as you are reputed to be! You will have to do much better than that."

"Two thousand."

"Pinch-purse! Twenty thousand!"

"Five thousand!"

After more angry haggling, Lily agreed to ten thousand pounds.

Damon insisted that she bring pen and paper and write out an agreement stating that in consideration of the payment of ten thousand pounds, she would never see or attempt to contact Pel again.

Not until she had signed it did he make out a draft on his bank. As he handed it over to her, he asked for Pel's ring back.

Lily looked suddenly uneasy, but then she gave him a crafty smile. "Oh, no, I want something to remember the dear boy by."

"I don't believe that! You have as much sentiment as a paving stone."

"No, you should not believe it," she confessed with a twitter, "the truth is it will bring a handsome price from a pawnshop."

Hawkhurst uttered a blunt expletive.

She waved his bank draft at him. "I suggest you leave before I decide this is not enough!"

Hawkhurst gave a low, angry growl. "Don't press

your luck! My cousin will not be so enamored of you after he learns you are one of my castoffs!''

He slammed from the house without another word.

Hawkhurst's parting words stung Lily like the lash of a whip, even though she had given him excellent reason to believe himself right in his dreadful summation of her character.

She sank down upon the chintz-covered sofa, fighting back tears, a weakness she despised. Lily told herself fiercely that she had no time for them now. She had too much to do.

She rose resolutely and summoned Trude to tell her that they would be leaving Bath that very afternoon. There was no longer any reason to stay. Lily had no more performances, and she never wanted to see either Hawkhurst or his cousin again.

She would go immediately to Weymouth and spend the next two weeks there as she had originally planned. It would mean missing the farewell party at the Theatre Royal after the season finale tonight, but it could not be helped.

While Trude began packing their belongings, Lily set out to hire a post chaise to carry them and their baggage to Weymouth.

Chapter 14

Hawkhurst was not a man to put off discharging unpleasant tasks, and after leaving Lily's, he went immediately to Pel's. He would show his foolish cousin the agreement she had signed, promising never to see him again.

Damon would also tell Pel that she planned to pawn the ring he had given her. If that did not open the young fool's eyes to what she was, Pel was beyond hope and should be confined to a lunatic asylum for his own protection.

The earl thought of what that diamond ring had cost his cousin. It was an expensive lesson that the boy could ill afford.

It had been an even more expensive lesson for Hawkhurst. Ten thousand pounds! And that was the cheapest part of it. Far more costly to him was the intolerable sense of betrayal, as bitter as bile, that ate at him. He was humiliated that he had been so taken in by her. That was what came of trusting a woman! No female had ever made such a fool of him before and, by God, none would again.

Even Olivia's treachery all those years ago, although it had cost him dearly, had not hurt him as much as Lily's did now. Indeed, he had not thought any woman would have the power to wound him so deeply.

The young footman who answered Pel's door tried to turn Hawkhurst away with word that neither Mr. or Mrs. St. Clair was at home to company.

"They are to me," he said, stepping past the footman into the hall. "Where is Pel?"

The footman's eyes darted toward a small withdrawing room, and Damon strode into it, then stopped dead in astonishment.

Pel and Cecilia were locked in a passionate embrace.

After what had transpired that morning, it was the last thing the earl had expected to see. He knew that he should back out of the room, but the tableau was too astonishing for him to leave without some explanation.

Their kiss continued for so long that Hawkhurst finally cleared his throat loudly.

Pel's head jerked up. Seeing his visitor, he demanded indignantly, "What the devil do you mean by bursting in on us like this, Hawk?"

Hawkhurst paid him no heed for Cecilia had turned toward him. The transformation in her was so dramatic that he could scarcely believe his eyes. Gone was her sulking pout and unhappy eyes. She was regarding her husband adoringly.

And Pel was looking at her as though he had fallen in love with her all over again.

Clearly they were enjoying a reconciliation. Hawkhurst found that as difficult to comprehend as the change in Cecilia.

In his usual blunt fashion, he asked her why she looked so exultant.

Blushing, she replied, "I know now that Pel truly loves me!"

Hell's fire, the poor girl wouldn't feel that way if she learned about the ring that Pel had given Lily.

"You see," Cecilia explained earnestly, "I thought

that Pel had stopped loving me because I had grown so fat and awkward and ugly with the baby."

Hawkhurst wondered whether anything would be gained by telling her that it was her martyrish sulking, not her pregnancy, that made her ugly.

Pel confessed, "And I thought you hated being pregnant and hated me for making you that way."

"Oh, darling, I have been the most miserable creature, thinking I had lost your love. If only you had given me this sooner."

"Given you what?" Damon interjected. Had Pel bought her a gift too?

Cecilia held out her left hand for Hawkhurst's inspection. There, next to her gold wedding band, glittered the big diamond ring that the young fool had bought for Lily.

Damon was so flummoxed he blurted, "Where the devil did that come from?"

His question drained the color from Pel's face.

"My husband gave it to me!" Cecilia cried jubilantly.

Pel gave Hawkhurst a desperate look that pleaded for his silence on the true circumstances of the ring's acquisition.

She thrust a white card at Damon. "Read his message that came with it."

To my one and only love,
 I give you this small token of my affection.
 Know by it that I shall worship you forever.
  Eternally yours, Pel.

How fortunate that Pel had not identified his one and only love by name!

"Isn't that the most beautiful message you have ever read?" Cecilia asked, beaming with pleasure. "I shall treasure it forever, even as much as this gorgeous ring itself."

No wonder Pel had such a dazed look—like he had been hit by a load of quarried Bath stone.

Hawkhurst felt like he had been hit by *two* loads of quarried stone.

Lily had to have sent that damned ring to Cecilia before he had called at her lodgings. She could not have given it to him when he had demanded it because she did not have it.

"Was your errand successful, Trude?"

"Aye, I delivered it into her very own hands as you instructed me."

Why had Lily not told him the truth about what she had done with the ring? For a moment, Damon could think of no answer. Then, determined to think the worst of her, he decided that she had seen it as a way to extort a large amount of money from him.

And damn her, she had succeeded! Ten thousand pounds! He was shocked by just how Byzantine Lily's plot had been. She had known how much he wanted to protect Pel and save his marriage. Clever creature that she was, she had guessed how he would react to learning about that accursed ring.

"My darling," Cecilia was saying lovingly to her husband, "I have been so miserable thinking that you no longer cared for me."

"I thought it was something that I had done."

"It was what you had *not* done," Cecilia replied. She explained how she had expected him to express his happiness at her giving him an heir with gifts as her brother-in-law had.

"I had no idea," Pel said. "I would have bought you anything you wanted had I known."

"But, darling, what is amazing is that you have bought me the very thing that I most coveted. I have been admiring this ring for days."

Hawkhurst looked at her with sudden suspicion. Could Lily have known . . . No, that was impossible.

"I—I thought you would like it," Pel said weakly. He had enough conscience to blush as he met his cousin's eye.

When Damon took his leave, Pel said hastily, "Before you go, Hawk, I have a question about one of the investments you made for me. Please come into the library so we can discuss it."

Damon knew that the question would have nothing to do with investments. And he had a few questions of his own.

They left Cecilia in the withdrawing room, gazing proudly at her new ring.

In the privacy of the library, Pel said in a voice trembling on the edge of panic, "Hawk, you must take Lily off my hands. I beg of you."

Damon raised a questioning eyebrow. "Why, when only this morning you were afraid I might do just that?"

"That was before!"

"Before you discovered that Cecilia still loved you?"

"Before Lily got a maggot in her brain that I was proposing marriage to her." He gave Damon a look of burning reproach. "I thought surely you must have told her I was married!"

Damon did not betray that he had done just that.

"If only you had told her." Pel shuddered. "You cannot conceive the peal she rang over me today when she learned I was married."

"What did she say?" Hawkhurst asked, much interested.

Her words seemed to have engraved themselves on Pel's memory, and he repeated them in great detail.

Unlike his cousin, Hawkhurst recognized the source of many of Lily's lines, and he had to smother a smile. She must have given a marvelous performance to have poor Pel in such a quake.

"If you can persuade her to leave me alone, Hawk, I swear I will never look at another woman except my Cecilia again."

Hawkhurst wondered whether that might have been exactly what Lily had intended.

He said casually, "I do not understand how she got the idea that you meant to marry her."

"Because of what she said when she showed me that ring."

"I thought she promised to make you the happiest man alive."

"Actually she said that my wife would," Pel admitted.

From the look on his cousin's face when Hawkhurst had found him with Cecilia, Lily had been right.

"But I thought that was a euphemism," Pel continued, "what with the clerk listening to us and all. But then, when I gave her the ring and reminded her of her promise, she said she would keep it as soon as I made her my wife. That's when I had to tell her I was married."

The memory of what had followed so agitated Pel that he began to pace the tiny confines of the room, like a distressed puppy on a very short tether.

Damon wished that he had been privileged to see that scene.

Pel, still pacing, said bitterly, "Frankly, I think the woman is mad. First, she refuses to give me back my ring, then she sends it to Cecilia."

"With very happy results," Hawkhurst pointed out.

"Only because Cecilia did not understand!" Pel stopped pacing and faced his cousin. "I know that Lily sent it to cause trouble between us."

Damon was less certain of that, but was every bit as confused as to what Lily's real motive had been. If her purpose had been to reconcile the couple, why had she not told Hawkhurst that instead of . . . He stiffened in anger. Instead of extorting ten thousand pounds from him.

There was his answer. She had realized Pel's resources were far too modest. His cousin was a much fatter pigeon.

And she had been right.

Granted, Lily had taught Pel a much-needed lesson, but the price to himself had been high, ten thousand pounds and a disillusionment more painful than he had ever before known.

When Hawkhurst left Pel's, he strode through the streets of Bath with a quick, angry stride, trying to work off the worst of his rage. He had no conscious destination.

Slowly the fury that burned within him cooled a little and with it his conviction that Lily had merely been out to swindle him.

Belatedly it occurred to him that perhaps Pel was not the only St. Clair that Lily had taught a lesson that day.

As he walked, there seemed to be nowhere in Bath that he had not strolled with her. Every street he took was haunted by some memory of her: Lily on the North Parade, drinking in the beauty of a sunny morning when the air was as clean and sweet as spring itself; Lily on Milsom Street, pointing out some amusing oddity in a shop window; Lily on Queen's Square, her head thrown back and her eyes gleaming up at him, laughing at one of his jokes.

Less than two hours ago, he had sworn he never wanted to see her again. Now he could not bear not to. He started toward her lodgings.

He was a block away when he realized that the long sunlight of mid-May had lulled him into thinking it was earlier than it was. By now, Lily would already be at the theatre, preparing for her final appearance of the season.

His previous reluctance to watch her perform vanished and he bought a ticket for a seat as close to the stage as he could get. He settled into it, waiting impatiently for the curtain to go up. As that was about to happen, a portly, bearded man appeared at the corner of the stage to announce that an understudy would be playing Lady Macbeth in Lily's place. Moans and hisses rang out from the disappointed audience.

Hastily Damon got up to leave before the curtain rose. To his surprise, several dozen other people did the same thing.

He went into the greenroom, hoping to find her there, but she was not. No one there could tell him why she was not appearing tonight.

Much alarmed by now, Hawkhurst hurried through the twilight to her lodgings. There his knock went unanswered.

He tried the door. Finding it unlocked, he stepped through the tiny vestibule, flung open the door to the drawing room, and stopped abruptly in disbelief.

All hint of Lily had vanished as though she had never been there.

The colorful chintz had been removed from the sofa and chairs, revealing their worn, stained upholstery. Gone were the gilt-bronze clock from the mantel and the chess set from the corner.

Just as Lily herself was gone from his life. The thought settled like a crushing boulder on Hawkhurst's heart.

What a dreary, uninviting place this room was. Until now he had always found it so cheerful and welcoming.

Damon had no idea where Lily might have gone. He tried to rekindle his bitterness toward her, telling himself that with his ten thousand pounds, she could travel anywhere in great luxury. But he felt only desolation and loss.

He made his way back to York House, where the desk clerk presented him with a carefully sealed note that had been delivered for him.

His heart gave a leap of joy as he recognized Lily's bold handwriting on it. He offered up a silent prayer of thanks. She had not left after all without letting him know where she was going.

He ran up the stairs, taking them two at a time, so that he could read her message in the privacy of his own suite.

As soon as he gained it, he ripped open the note. The torn pieces of paper that once had been a ten-thousand-pound bank draft fluttered to the floor.

No message accompanied the fragments.

None was necessary.

Hawkhurst felt as though his heart was in as many pieces as the paper that littered the floor of his lonely room.

Part Two

Hawkhill, Devon

Chapter 15

Hawkhurst looked out over the rolling hills of Hawkhill's park, which spread lushly green as far as the eye could see. Until he had returned here from Bath ten weeks ago, this view had never failed to fill him with pride and delight, but now he scarcely noticed it.

He was standing on the portico of his sprawling Georgian mansion, built on the highest hill in the area, waiting for Sewell to bring up his curricle. The sky was gray, promising rain. It matched his mood that had grown darker with each day that passed with no word of Lily.

Never in his life had Damon been so haunted by the memory of a woman. The two and a half months since she had vanished from Bath had been the longest of his life. He had tried frantically to find her, but in vain.

No one in Bath, except perhaps Nell Wayne, had known where Lily had gone. Nell had laughed at him when he had asked her where her friend was. He had been reduced to trying to bribe her, but she had scornfully refused his offer.

The bearded manager of the Bath Theatre Royal had been no help either. Sounding rather like a spurned lover, he had told Hawkhurst acidly that he did not know where Lily had gone and did not care. Nor would she be returning there next season. He would not have her back!

So Damon had gone home to Hawkhill, hoping against hope that when Lily's justifiable fury at him burned out, she would miss him as much as he missed her and would contact him there. But as the weeks crawled by with no word from her, he knew that she would not do so.

Why should she, he thought unhappily. She had given him a gift she had given no other man—herself—and he had repaid her by thinking her a conniving, manipulating extortionist.

He desperately wanted at least the chance to tell her how sorry he was for having doubted her.

She would most likely tell him that he should have known better, and she was right. He would try to make her understand how hard it was for him to trust a woman—even her.

The memory of the night they had shared made his body ache for her. Worse, he could not even consider taking another woman into his bed to ease his need. After Lily, it would be like drinking vinegar following an exquisite French wine. Hell's fire, he *had* to find her. But how the devil was he to do that when he had no clue where to look?

His curricle rolled around the curve of the drive. The matched grays harnessed to it were the latest additions to his stables at Hawkhill. Yet even these prime bits of blood failed to elicit the excitement and enthusiasm in Damon that such a prize acquisition would have done in the past.

It was yet another sign of the disinterest bordering on apathy that had gripped him since Lily had vanished from Bath. He still oversaw Hawkhill with his keen, experienced eye, but he did so more out of duty than out of the love and pride that he bore for his Devon estate.

Even the arrival a week ago of Phoebe and his

sisters had failed to stir him from his strange leth-
argy. Now his young stepmama was beginning to
tax his patience almost as much as Cassandra did.
She was clearly afraid of him, but he did not understand why. He had never been unkind to her, although he could not hide his exasperation with her
endless tears.

Phoebe had always been a watering pot, but since
her return from Bath, she could not seem to look at
Damon without bursting into tears. When he would
ask her what was wrong, she would deny anything
was the matter and continue to weep. When he
would inquire why, if nothing was amiss, she was
crying, she would only sob the harder.

Given Phoebe's odd behavior, he could only be
thankful that she had suddenly decided at the end
of the Bath season to stay on there for an additional
two months instead of coming immediately to Hawkhill.

As Hawkhurst took the reins of the grays, Cassandra and Phoebe came around the corner of the
house.

"Where are you going?" his sister called.

"To exercise my grays." It was only an excuse for
another one of those aimless excursions, long and
solitary, that he had been taking since his return
from Bath in a vain attempt to find relief from his
unhappy thoughts.

"Take us with you," Cassandra demanded, hurrying up to his equipage.

The last thing he wanted was her company—or
Phoebe's.

"But *you* invited guests for dinner," he reminded
Cassandra. She had taken it upon herself to ask Lady
Portman, an elderly widow whose estate was on the
other side of Lowhampton, and her two sisters who
were visiting her. Only after they had accepted had
she told Hawkhurst that he was having guests. He

found this trio of ladies particularly tedious. While politeness dictated he would have to suffer through dinner with them, he intended to disappear immediately afterward and leave the women to their hen chatter. "What if your guests arrive before you return?"

But Cassandra was already climbing into the curricle. "We shall be back in time," she said airily. "Come, Phoebe, get in."

As the two women settled beside him, he pointed out politely, "This seat is not built for three."

"Oh, pooh, we can fit," Cassandra insisted. "Phoebe is so tiny, she hardly takes up any room."

So much for his solitary ride, Hawkhurst thought. He told Sewell that he would not need him. The groom's relief was obvious. Sewell disliked being within earshot of Cassandra as much as Damon did.

As they drove through the park, even the complaints Cassandra showered upon Damon did not fully distract him from the problem of finding Lily. He could scarcely think of anything else. She was driving him mad. Hell's fire, no woman had ever obsessed him like this.

The curricle reached the gates of Hawkhill's park, and he guided it onto the narrow Wolverdale road that cut through his land.

The new grays were very fresh, and Hawkhurst loosened the reins. The pair surged forward, racing along the narrow road that snaked among the rolling green hills.

Hawkhurst was coming up fast on a post chaise. Ahead of it, the road began to climb a hill, curving around its shoulder. He would have to pass the slower equipage now or be stuck behind it all the while they ascended the winding grade. Urging his team forward, he calmly passed the yellow bounder with no more than four inches to spare between the wheels of the two vehicles.

His sister shrieked. "Why are you driving as though you are trying to kill us all, Hawkhurst? Is this your scheme to rid the world of me?"

Leave it to Cassandra to believe everything he did was directed against her personally. He said sardonically, "I know you will not be able to comprehend this, but I am not trying to do away with you. You know how I drive. If it unnerves you, you should not have asked to come."

"Perhaps we should go back now," Phoebe stammered, clutching the edge of the seat as though it were her anchor to the world. Tears began to run down her cheeks.

Hawkhurst had not meant to frighten her, and he said soothingly, "Yes, of course, we will go back, but I cannot turn around here." They were already on the hill, and the road curved along it, with the terrain dropping away at its edge. Below them, a small creek meandered along the bottom of the dell. "There will be a place to turn on the other side of this hill."

A company of strolling players came into sight around the curve ahead of them, trudging toward them. They were walking two abreast, hugging the far side of the narrow road. Some of them were pushing painted handcarts loaded with costumes and props. Hawkhurst could not tell how many there were, for the last of them was hidden from his view by the sharp curve. He would not have much room to pass them safely, and he slowed his grays.

The players' clothes were shabby, and the paint on their handcarts was faded and chipped. Clearly, it was not a prosperous troupe, but that was not surprising. Strolling players, who walked from town to town giving performances wherever they were permitted to do so, rarely collected much money for their efforts. They were the lowliest practitioners of a lowly profession. Most of them possessed more stubborn determination than talent, although a few actually managed to make it to the London stage.

As Damon reached them, one of the actresses caught his eye, mostly because she was so tall. He could not see her face for it was hidden by a heavy veil attached to a large, wide-brimmed straw hat decorated with yellow roses around the crown. Her height reminded him of Lily, but this woman was thinner than she. Too thin, he thought critically, and she lacked Lily's proud carriage and queenly gait.

Instead, she shuffled along in a utilitarian walking dress of brown cotton, her head down and her shoulders rounded. He had the impression of an aging actress, worn and weary from her hard life as a strolling player. The woman paid Hawkhurst no heed, not even glancing in his direction.

She walked beside a wiry, white-haired man who was probably her husband. He pushed a cart decorated with harlequins, whose once-bright colors had faded to pastels.

Phoebe's frightened scream drew Hawkhurst's attention from the actress back to the road.

The curricle had reached the blind curve, and he saw to his horror that a farmer had stupidly chosen that spot to pull his wagon, filled with produce and drawn by a plodding horse, over to Damon's side of the narrow road to go around the players. The fool had been so impatient that he had not waited to reach a stretch with better visibility for passing them.

Now the farmer could only gape at the equipage rushing toward him, and he made no attempt to avoid it.

To the side of him, a young actress with a red-and-green kerchief tied over her hair stared at Hawkhurst in frozen horror. The look on her face told him that she thought she was about to die.

He had only two choices to keep from hitting the horse and wagon head-on. Neither was a happy one, and he had only an instant in which to decide. Either he could pull over to the wrong side, plowing through the thespians walking there, severely injuring and perhaps killing some of them, or he could run his curricle off the road and down the side of the hill, using his skill with the reins to try to keep it from overturning in the process and killing its occupants.

The latter was the only possible choice, for it gave him a faint hope of avoiding disaster while the other gave him none.

Keeping a tight rein on the scared grays, Hawkhurst forced them off the road, cursing his luck under his breath. If he had met the wagon a hundred feet later on the road, there would have been a wide spot where he could have pulled off, but here there was nothing.

The curricle teetered precariously as it careened across uneven, grassy terrain, jolting its occupants mercilessly.

His task was made all the more difficult by the dissonant, ear-splitting shrieks of his terrified female companions that further frightened his horses. But he managed to guide them adroitly at a diagonal slant over the rough hillside, avoiding rocks and other obstructions, until he could bring them to a stop.

Damon breathed a great sigh of relief that he had succeeded in his audacious gamble and no one had been injured.

Even though Phoebe and Cassandra were no longer in danger, they continued to weep in fright. For once, he thought a little grimly, he had given them justifiable cause for tears.

He glanced up the slope toward the road. The players had stopped beside their handcarts. The young actress with the bright kerchief over her head had dropped to her knees by the side of the road and was offering prayful thanks for her narrow escape.

The farmer, apparently realizing he had nearly caused a tragedy, was frantically whipping his poor nag down the road, trying to escape the scene. Most likely he had recognized Hawkhurst. Indeed, his face had seemed vaguely familiar, and Damon suspected he might even be one of his tenants. No wonder he was so eager to flee the earl's ire.

Hawkhurst jumped down and helped the two women to the ground, then hurried forward to try to pacify his nervous grays. That, he thought wryly, was likely to be an easier job than quieting his companions. His hope that the feel of terra firma beneath their feet would reassure them that they were safe and stem the flow of tears had been a vain one.

Noise on the road drew his attention again. The post chaise that he had passed earlier was slowing, apparently intending to pull off at the wide spot. A horse and rider coming from the opposite direction left the road and raced toward the curricle. Hawkhurst recognized his neighbor and friend, Lord Waymore, on the unruly, ill-tempered black that he had aptly named Devil.

As Waymore brought his horse to a stop, Cassandra, who her brother knew had long cherished an unreciprocated *tendre* for his lordship, rushed forward, eager to capture his attention.

"Oh, Lord Waymore!" she screeched as she ran up to him. Her voice, shrill enough to shatter glass, spooked his already skittish horse. The big black reared on his hind legs.

Hawkhurst, knowing that he had only a split second to save Cassandra from being struck down and pummeled by the black's cruel front hooves, hurled himself at her, grabbing her by the waist. Still holding her, he threw himself—and her—toward the downward slope of the hill and as far away from the bucking black as he could manage. As they fell, he twisted so that he would be beneath her when they hit the ground and his body would absorb the punishing brunt of their hard landing.

He was successful, but he struck the ground violently with Cassandra—who was no lightweight—atop him.

On the road above, Lily stifled a horrified scream as she saw Hawkhurst's desperate, courageous effort to rescue Cassandra from the pummeling hooves. Both man and woman fell heavily to the ground beyond reach of the rearing horse. As Waymore struggled to retain his seat and bring his mount under control, Cassandra rolled off her brother and sat upright, but Hawkhurst did not move.

Lily's heart seemed to stop. She was so terrified for him that she had to bite her lips together to keep from crying out. Heedless of what she was doing, she rushed down the hill toward him. As she ran, she tore frantically at the veil of her straw hat. It obscured her view of the man lying so still on the grass.

She had chosen to wear this hat and heavy veil after she had learned that the road they would be taking that day passed through Hawkhurst's vast holdings. Lily had not expected to see him as they traversed his land, but if by some contrary quirk of fate she did, her pride revolted at having him recognize her as part of her uncle's sorry, bedraggled troupe. Hawkhurst would pity her, and she could not bear that.

She had told herself over and over the past two and a half months that she hated a man who could misjudge her so shamefully and that she never wanted to see him again. Yet she had found herself eagerly scanning the few vehicles that had passed them that day, looking for Damon's face.

When she had seen the curricle approaching on
the hill, she had instantly recognized that tall, com-
manding figure tooling the ribbons so expertly. Her
heart had pounded like a wild thing trying to break
free from the cage of her chest. Only then had she
admitted to herself how much she had wanted to
see him again.

And how much she still cared. Fool that she was!

Fearing that he might recognize her despite her
veiled face, she had hastily assumed the slump and
shuffling walk of a weary old woman. Lily kept her
face bent earthward as the curricle approached her,
but her peripheral vision had marked its passing.
She felt Hawkhurst's gaze upon her, but she was
certain that he did not recognize her.

She should have been delighted that he did not,
but instead she felt as though her heart was an aching wound.

Now, as Lily approached him, lying inert on the
ground, she was consumed by fear that he might be
dead. She had managed to throw the heavy veil back
from her face so that she could see him better.

With terror in her heart, she dropped to her knees
beside him.

Chapter 16

⟨───⟩⟨✦⟩⟨───⟩

Hawkhurst lay stunned and motionless, his eyes closed, his body aching. He was getting too old to take this kind of fall, but at least he had saved his foolish sister from serious injury or even death beneath the hooves of the panicked horse.

Hawkhurst heard Phoebe and his sister sobbing. He was the one who hurt, and they were the ones who were crying!

He kept his eyes closed and longed for the peaceful oblivion of unconsciousness. Since it was not forthcoming, he would feign it for another minute or two before he opened his eyes and had to deal with two hysterical females.

He heard the rustle of skirts approaching him and sensed that their wearer was dropping to her knees beside him. It could not be one of his relatives because she was not—thank God—crying. He wondered without much interest who she was.

Gentle but determined fingers pulled impatiently at the cuff of his shirt, seeking his pulse, and an unforgettable scent of wild roses wafted over him.

An equally unforgettable voice, weighted with concern, demanded, "Lord Hawkhurst, can you hear me?"

For an instant, he thought that he must be hallucinating. He had feared that he would never hear that rich, throaty voice again. Her fingers found the pulse in his wrist, and he opened his eyes. He stared up into Lily's face; it was full of alarm for him.

Exhilaration surged through him. Suddenly, he felt happier than he could remember having been for some time—two and one-half months, to be precise.

The look of profound relief on her face when she saw that he was conscious told him far more than she would have wanted him to know. Whatever she might try to say, he knew now that she still cared about him. He was elated.

Phoebe and Cassandra were still weeping, and Lily looked up at them in disgust as her fingers worked swiftly to untie his neckcloth. "What are you crying about? He is the one who is hurt! Stop your wailing and do something to aid him."

That shamed them into blessed silence, but it was clear from their perplexed faces that they had not the smallest notion of what to do to help.

Lily pulled his neckcloth off and held it up to them. "Here, dip this in the creek so I may make a cold compress for his head."

They did as she ordered.

"Peace at last," Hawkhurst muttered, reaching for her hand. He clasped it tightly in his own, determined that she should not get away from him this time.

His sudden move startled her. She looked at him questioningly but did not try to remove her hand from his.

Smiling up at her, he said softly, "Behold me at your feet, begging your forgiveness, my lovely lady, for having so grievously misjudged you." His thumb lightly caressed the back of her hand.

Her mouth formed a silent O of surprise. Whatever she might have expected from him, it clearly had not been that. A faint rosy tint of pleasure brightened her cheeks.

He had been so busy drinking in the sight of her face that only now, belatedly, did he notice her large, wide-brimmed hat, trimmed with yellow roses. The heavy veil that had concealed her face from him earlier had been thrown back.

"So it *was* you!" He felt suddenly weak at the realization of how near he had come to passing her without knowing it. Maybe he ought to reward that fool farmer.

Delighted as he was to see her, he was distressed by how much thinner she was than she had been in Bath. He tried to force himself to a sitting position, but Lily held him down. "Do not move, please, until we can determine how badly you are hurt."

He smiled up at her, unable to keep the mischief from his eyes, and said in a voice so low that she alone could hear him, "Only if you promise me that you will make that determination yourself."

This brought another blush to her cheeks, and she said a little testily, "Must you tease me even when you are hurt?"

He fiercely resisted the temptation to let her continue to think him injured so that her lovely, competent hands would examine him; but he had sustained no serious damage, only bruises and abrasions. He would not mislead her to the contrary.

Besides, he could not bear to have her hands explore his body without being able to reciprocate.

Smiling, he told her, "Much as I would love to have you minister to me, honesty compels me to tell you that I am fine. I was merely dazed."

A voice above them asked, "I say, Hawk, are you certain? Perhaps I should summon a doctor."

Damon dragged his gaze away from Lily's concerned face and saw that Waymore had dismounted and was standing beside her kneeling figure, looking down at him anxiously.

"Yes, I am certain. I merely have a headache and a few bruises. I need no doctor. Only let me rest a bit."

Phoebe and Cassandra returned with the wet neckcloth. Lily took it from them and wiped his face tenderly with it before folding it into a cold compress for his head.

He lay with it on for a few minutes, then asked Waymore for his hand to help him to his feet.

Lily stood up and stepped back to allow Waymore to do as Hawkhurst asked.

Now that he was upright, Cassandra, who had been uncharacteristically silent, renewed her attack. "Only look at what you did to me, Hawkhurst. My dress is ruined. 'Tis covered with dirt, and the skirt is torn!"

To Damon's surprise, Lily turned on his sister, her green eyes full of anger.

"What he did was save your life, you ungrateful pea-goose!"

For a moment the startled Cassandra could only stare at Lily slack-jawed. Then she opened her mouth to protest.

But Lily cut her off, saying coldly, "You should be thanking your brother instead of haranguing him. Stop making such a cake of yourself."

No one had ever addressed Cassandra in such blunt terms before, and she gaped at Lily's blazing eyes in openmouthed astonishment, her tears forgotten.

"Yes, Lady Cassandra," Lord Waymore interjected. "I am appalled that you can show so little gratitude to your brother for risking his life to rescue you from serious injury or worse."

It was all Damon could do to keep from laughing aloud at Cassandra's dismayed reaction.

"But, Lord Waymore," she said defensively, "it was all Hawkhurst's fault—"

The look of disgust on his lordship's face silenced her. "Nonsense, it was all *your* fault. Whatever possessed you to run at Devil and frighten him like that?"

Cassandra promptly fell back upon her favorite weapon, tears, but they seemed to have no more effect upon Waymore than they did upon her brother. He merely turned away impatiently.

When his back was to her, she stamped her foot angrily. Her weeping grew louder, but failed in its intent to win back his attention.

He told Hawkhurst ruefully, "I thought to be of help to you when I rode up. Instead I nearly got you killed."

"No harm done." Little did Waymore know what a blessing in disguise the mishap had been, bringing Lily back into Damon's life.

Hawkhurst looked up at the road. The strolling players had resumed trudging toward Lowhampton. The post chaise that he had passed earlier was still stopped by the road. Its occupant, a stocky, middle-aged gentleman unknown to Damon, was standing beside it, watching them.

Cassandra stopped crying and said peevishly, "We must get back to Hawkhill. Our guests will be arriving, and we will not be there to greet them."

Lily said quietly, "I must go now, too."

Damon had no intention of letting her walk out of his life again. Yet he was frustrated by circumstances. He had to return to Hawkhill to meet the guests, and he could not fit Lily into the curricle. He had no choice but to leave her now and catch up with her later.

Hawkhurst asked Waymore to help Phoebe and Cassandra into his curricle. His lordship shepherded the women off to the equipage, providing Damon and Lily a modicum of privacy.

He looked down at her reproachfully. "You would have let me drive by you today, never knowing it was you."

"Yes," Lily admitted.

In a voice too low to be heard by the trio at the curricle, he asked, "Why did you not tell me the truth that day in Bath instead of pretending to extort money from me?"

"You were so determined to think the worst of me, I did not wish to deny you that pleasure," Lily said frostily.

"I deserve that," he conceded ruefully.

That elicited a smile from her. "How are Cecilia and Pel?"

"Happily reconciled, thanks to you, and the parents of a son born last week. You taught them both a lesson, and their marriage is the stronger for it." He touched her arm. "Lily, I must talk to you."

"We have nothing to talk about." She pulled away from him and started up the hill toward the road.

He fell into step beside her. "You are wrong. Where do you perform next?"

She sighed. "I wish I knew. The magistrate at Wolverdale where we planned to play tonight refused to allow us to do so." The law required traveling troupes of actors to obtain permission from the local magistrate before they could perform.

"We are on our way now to Lowhampton," Lily continued, "but I understand that the magistrate there is even less likely to grant us permission than the last was."

Damon was certain she was right. Magistrate Rawson was a pompous, straitlaced little man who felt it his duty to protect the townspeople from all frivolous or corrupting influences, including plays.

The earl asked casually, "But you plan to try there anyhow?"

Lily nodded. "We have no choice but to petition the magistrate, even though he will undoubtedly refuse us. The next town beyond Lowhampton is too far away for us to reach in time to put on a performance today."

Hawkhurst guessed how it must be for this impoverished troupe. "And if you do not perform today, there will be no money for supper or a roof over your heads tonight."

She did not reply but he took the embarrassed flush that rose in her cheeks as answer enough.

Hell's fire, no wonder she was thinner than she had been in Bath. He had never imagined that when he found her it would be in such deplorable circumstances. Damon had not seen her act, but he had thought she was at least competent. Now he realized he must have been mistaken. No competent actress would have been reduced to joining this shabby company of strolling players, living each day from hand to mouth.

It was a great comedown from even a provincial theatre, especially the Bath Theatre Royal that was considered one of the best outside of London. Clearly, she had been fired from it and could find no position with a more respectable and profitable company. Hawkhurst was happy now he had not watched her perform. He would have been even more disappointed than he had feared he would be.

He wondered how many nights during the past weeks she had gone hungry. Surely, she must have known what a precarious existence lay ahead of her when she had torn up his bank draft for ten thousand pounds. Had she not done so, she could have been living in luxury the past weeks. His admiration for her proud determination soared.

He wanted to offer her money—no strings attached—to ensure that she was fed and sheltered, but he knew that he would only insult her and that she would indignantly refuse it.

There was one thing at least that he could do for her without her even being aware of it. And it would serve the added purpose of keeping her in Lowhampton until he could escape from his guests at Hawkhill and talk to her. The village was part of the earl's estate, and his was the final word there. Even if it were not, Magistrate Rawson stood in too much fear and awe of Hawkhurst to oppose him in anything.

Intent on carrying out his plan, he parted from Lily halfway up the hill and hurried to his curricle.

As he climbed into the driver's seat, Phoebe said, "That must be Mrs. Culhane's uncle."

Startled, he glanced up the hill. The man in the post chaise was offering Lily his hand to help her up a steep stretch of the hill.

As Damon's curricle regained the road, he asked Phoebe, "What do you know of Mrs. Culhane?"

"She is a widow that we met in Bath."

Had Lily told them she was a widow? He could not believe that she would have lied. "Why do you think the man in the post chaise is her uncle?"

"Because that is who she was to travel with this summer."

Lily had never mentioned an uncle, and she had been quite explicit about having been on her own after her parents' death.

As Hawkhurst's curricle rounded the curve, he cast one final glance back and was relieved to see that Lily was walking rapidly down the road to catch up with the troupe while the stranger was climbing into his post chaise alone.

"What else did she tell you about her summer plans?"

"Actually she told us nothing about them," Phoebe said. "It was a mutual friend."

"Was it that friend who told you she was a widow?"

Phoebe nodded, suddenly looking oddly nervous.

When Hawkhurst reached home, he ordered Sewell to saddle up the fastest horse in his stable while he went into his library to scrawl a few lines on a sheet of writing paper.

He gave the note himself to Sewell with instructions to take the shortcut to Lowhampton and deliver the message posthaste to Magistrate Rawson.

Damon watched as Sewell galloped off. He should reach the town before the strolling players.

Chapter 17

Lily, having caught up with her uncle's company, walked along the road toward Lowhampton with her mind in turmoil.

She had no doubt that Hawkhurst had been happy to see her again. She would never forget the look of wonder and delight in his eyes when they had at last opened. Then he had immediately apologized so sincerely to her. She had not expected that. But he had puzzled her, too. First, he had said they must talk, but then he had taken his leave of her rather abruptly, clearly in a hurry to return to Hawkhill.

Her thoughts of him were bittersweet. He had given her a magnificent night that she would never forget, and then he had broken her heart. Much as she longed to see him again, she knew that it would only bring her more misery.

She had fallen in love with him, imbecile that she was. He did not even believe in love, only in the passion of the moment, and that was all she was to him. Even if he could come to love her, he was an earl, and she was an actress. Never could their worlds meet.

"You would be a fool to let him back into your life," she told herself fiercely. "He will only break your heart again."

The troupe was approaching the neat cottages of

Lowhampton with their whitewashed walls and thatched roofs.

Lily's white-haired uncle, Joseph Drew, fell into step beside her, saying glumly, "First I must find the magistrate and see whether he will permit us to perform here. Come with me while I look for him. Perhaps you can persuade him."

Lily nodded. On several occasions since she had been with her uncle's company, she had been able to win approval from a reluctant magistrate after Drew had failed.

"I fear in this case, however, it will be futile," her uncle grumbled. "Rawson is infamous for refusing permission to every company that has sought to appear. But we must try. It is a four-hour walk to Marshton."

"If we cannot perform here, then you will have to go on without me," Lily said. "I must wait for Sarah's stage to arrive."

Lily's fifteen-year-old sister, who had been visiting with a school friend, was coming to join her. Thinking that their uncle's company would be performing in Wolverdale for three days, Lily had written Sarah to take the stagecoach there.

When the troupe had unexpectedly been refused permission to perform and had to move on, Lily had left word for Sarah at the Wolverdale coach stop that she should remain aboard until it reached Lowhampton. The stage did not go to Marshton, so Sarah would have to get off in Lowhampton.

Lily's painfully shy little sister would be terrified if she found herself alone on her own in a strange town.

Uncle Joseph started to protest Lily's leaving him, but she said firmly, "No, I must stay here until Sarah arrives."

"You coddle your sister too much," he complained. "She will be fine here. After all, she is only a year or two younger than you were when your parents died, and you—'' He broke off abruptly at the flash of anger in Lily's eyes.

''Sarah is not me! She is timid and easily frightened. Furthermore, she is my ward, and I will care for her as I believe right.''

Her uncle scowled. ''You owe me a performance tonight.''

''Only if you present one, and you know that we cannot possibly reach Marshton in time to do so.''

''Then you must give it tomorrow.''

''No, Uncle,'' she said resolutely. ''Tonight is the final night of the eight weeks that I promised you.''

When Lily had agreed to join his troupe, she had thought that her sister would accompany her. But within a week of joining the group, it became apparent that the hard, peripatetic life was too much for the delicate Sarah. Lily had been forced to let her sister accept an invitation from a school friend in Dorset who wanted her to visit her for several weeks.

Uncle Joseph said peevishly, ''Surely, you could stay with us for at least another week.''

Lily, who had been looking forward to spending Sarah's vacation with her, had hated being separated from her, but she could not go back on her word. She had no intention, however, of giving up any more of her precious time with her sister.

''No!'' Lily told him flatly. Besides, her uncle would never be satisfied. If she promised him another week, he would try to wheedle a fortnight out of her and do his best to make her feel guilty if she did not give it to him. She had come to regret that she had agreed to join him at all.

''But how will I manage without you?'' he asked irritably.

''The same way you managed before I joined you.'' It would not be easy, though, for the company was small. In plays requiring a large cast, the performers often had to assume two or more roles.

She knew, however, that was not what was bothering her uncle. In the weeks she had been with him, Lily had proven to be the best drawing card he had ever had. Her uncle was making the most of this, even casting her occasionally in male roles like Hamlet.

While Lily enjoyed the challenge of playing many different parts, she was weary of tramping from town to town where their lot was invariably uncomfortable lodgings and meager food.

As they walked toward the center of Lowhampton, past neat cottages brightened by begonias and hollyhocks, an elderly little man dressed in an outmoded many-buttoned coat and breeches hurried toward them.

Lily said, "Perhaps he can tell us where to find the magistrate."

It turned out he was the magistrate. Lily had the distinct impression that he had come expressly to meet them.

To their amazement, he wanted them to perform not merely for one night as they had hoped, but for three. He even offered them an empty storage barn at the edge of town in which to do so.

As Rawson left them, Uncle Joseph said wonderingly, "When I sought permission here last year, he refused even to see me."

Puzzled, Lily observed, "It is very odd. He was so conciliatory and eager to oblige us, yet it seemed to me that he hated doing so."

They proved to be less lucky in the lodging that they were able to secure for the night. The town's posting house would not deign to shelter a disreputable troupe of strolling players. That left only a small, dilapidated inn, hardly worthy of the name, which had but two rooms to let. Lily, the troupe's three other actresses, and Sarah, when she arrived, would be forced to share one cramped, dingy chamber while the male players took the other.

Lily had hoped that she and Sarah would at least have a room to themselves.

When Lily saw the accommodation, she suppressed a shudder of revulsion. The room smelled of mildew and cried out for a good cleaning. It lacked such luxuries as a mirror or a fireplace. From the number of containers scattered about the floor, waiting to trip the unwary, its roof apparently leaked badly.

Worse, it had only two beds for five females. Lily did not know how they would manage. The beds were narrow and lumpy with linen badly in need of washing. Poor Sarah would be as appalled as Lily when she saw it, but it was the only lodging to be had.

Damon made his escape from Hawkhill and his unwelcome female visitors as soon after dinner as he could contrive. He had ordered up his carriage for the ride into Lowhampton because the sky was growing increasingly dark and forbidding. The rain that had been threatening was certain to start before long. He hoped that he could convince Lily to return to Hawkhill with him, and he wanted to offer her the protection of a closed conveyance.

Although he knew he had little chance of succeeding in that goal, he substituted the close-mouthed Sewell on the box for his coachman. The latter loved to gossip, and his groom could be trusted to say nothing to the other servants or anyone else about Lily.

By the time Damon arrived at his barn that was serving as the strolling players' temporary theatre, they had finished their evening's performance, and the audience had drifted away.

As the carriage rattled to a stop, drops of rain began to fall. Opening the window, Hawkhurst hailed an actor standing by a side door and asked where he would find Lily.

"Not here," the man said. He gestured with a stubby finger toward the center of the village. "There she is."

Hawkhurst leaned out the window. In the gloom of the long summer twilight, he saw a graceful figure receding in the distance. As he watched, she unfurled an umbrella to protect herself from the drizzle. He nodded at Sewell, and the carriage moved on.

When it reached Lily, who was walking at a brisk pace, Hawkhurst offered her a ride. She hesitated and for a moment he feared that she would refuse his invitation, but the rain was coming down hard now, and she nodded. Closing the umbrella, she allowed Sewell, who had scrambled down from the box, to assist her into the carriage.

"I am going to the posting house to meet the night stage," Lily told them. "I understand it is due at any moment."

As she settled herself on the seat beside Damon, he asked in alarm, "Are you fleeing Lowhampton on the stage?" He had thought that by telling Rawson to permit the strolling players a three-day run, he had ensured that he would have at least that long to convince her to remain with him.

"No, I am meeting my little sister, Sarah," she answered, a note of anxiety in her voice.

He had not even known that she had a sister. He asked gently, "What has made you so concerned about her?"

"I am worried that she may not be on it. You see, I was to meet her in Wolverdale, but when we could not perform there, I left word for her to continue on and meet me here."

The wind was rising, driving the rain against the carriage, and distant thunder rumbled. Damon closed the curtains over the carriage windows, enveloping him and Lily in privacy.

She said, "I pray that Sarah got my message and did not leave the stage in Wolverdale. She is only fifteen, and she would be terrified to find herself alone in a strange town. If she is not on this stage, I shall have to find some way to get to Wolverdale tonight."

"I will take you there," he said promptly.

"But I will be detaining you from the business that brought you here."

"Surely you must know *you* are the business that brought me."

"What business could you have with me?"

"This." He turned, pulled her to him, and kissed her. She stiffened and tried to push him away, but he tightened his arms around her and deepened his kiss until her resistance vanished. Suddenly, she was clinging to him, returning his kiss hungrily.

Not until the carriage stopped in the courtyard of the posting house did Lily break the kiss. "This is madness!"

"No, this is happiness!" Damon corrected.

She moved to get out, but he would not let her.

"No, not yet. The stage is generally late, and there is nowhere for you to wait out of the rain except the taproom. It is not a place for a lady. You will be far more comfortable here." He grinned at her. "And so will I."

The rain was coming down in sheets now, and the temperature was dropping rapidly.

"When your sister arrives, I will drive you to your lodgings," he promised. "You will both be soaked if you attempt to walk there."

This last argument seemed to decide the issue in his favor, and she relaxed against him.

He called to Sewell on the box. "We will wait here for the stage. Go into the taproom where it is dry and enjoy a pint while we do so."

"Aye, my lord," he answered, scampering off.

With his arm still around Lily, Hawkhurst bent his head and laid his cheek against her hair, breathing deeply of the scent of wild roses. He confessed softly, "I have dreamed of holding you like this since you vanished from Bath. I have been so afraid that I would never again have the opportunity."

"You should have trusted me." Her voice quavered, betraying how painfully he had hurt her.

His fingertips stroked her soft cheek comfortingly. "Yes, I should have, but you don't know how hard that is for me. I have not met many women worthy of trust. And when I was faced with seemingly certain evidence that you were deceiving me, I went a little crazy."

"I could not believe it when Pel appeared on my doorstep with that wretched ring," Lily said.

Damon laughed. "The poor boy quaked in terror for days that you would write his mama."

The stagecoach thundered into the courtyard, and the ostlers rushed out to change the horses.

Sewell came out of the taproom and ran to help Lily down from the carriage. The rain had momentarily slackened a little as she hurried toward the coach with Hawkhurst in her wake.

A pale, delicate girl carrying a large portmanteau stepped unsteadily down from the stage. She was dressed in a thin muslin dress with only a light paisley shawl over her shoulders for protection against the weather.

"Sarah," Lily called to her.

Hawkhurst saw the fragile girl sway alarmingly in the pelting rain. The portmanteau fell from her hand. He rushed past Lily to catch her sister as she fainted.

"Sarah!" Lily cried in distress.

Damon swept the girl up into his arms. She weighed no more than a feather, he thought as he carried her to his equipage. Looking back, he observed that Sewell had retrieved her fallen portmanteau.

Hawkhurst deposited Sarah's motionless form across the seat and pulled the wet paisley shawl from her shoulders. Grabbing a heavy carriage robe from a corner, he draped it over her as Lily scrambled into the carriage.

"Do you have a vinaigrette?" he asked Lily.

"No, I have never needed one," she said, looking down with a stricken expression at her sister lying unconscious on the seat.

Hawkhurst, noting how hot and flushed Sarah's cheeks were, felt her forehead.

"She is burning with fever. Direct Sewell to your lodgings and tell him to hurry," he told Lily.

As the carriage left the courtyard at a gallop, Lily huddled beside her little sister's still form. The look on her face, so full of love and fear, told Damon more clearly than words that the relationship between the pair was more nearly that of mother and daughter, rather than sisters.

"You did not tell me you had a sister," he said quietly. "She was not with you in Bath."

"She was away at school."

No more than two minutes had passed when the carriage pulled to a stop in front of the dismal little inn. Hawkhurst wrapped Sarah in the carriage robe to protect her from the cold, wind-blown rain that was coming down in a torrent.

As he emerged from his equipage with Sarah in his arms, he ordered Sewell to go for Dr. Lasham at once.

Lily led him up the uncarpeted stairs to the chamber that had been assigned to her and the other actresses. Sarah had always had a delicate constitution, and Lily was terrified for her. She was thankful that Hawkhurst was with her. He was so strong and calm and competent that she was confident he would know what to do.

When she reached the room, she saw to her dismay that the pots spread about it were not numerous enough to catch all the leaks in the roof. Water was dripping onto the floor and one of the two narrow beds.

Hawkhurst looked about the damp, cold little chamber with undisguised disgust. After he removed the carriage robe from Sarah and laid her on the one dry bed, he told Lily bluntly, "You cannot stay here. Your sister is too ill. She needs a warm, dry place, and this is neither. Let me take you to Hawkhill."

"No!" Lily cried in alarm. "I cannot—"

"Don't be a ninnyhammer!"

Lily looked at him uncertainly, torn between her concern for her sister and distrust of what the outcome of accepting his hospitality would be.

"Don't worry," he assured her. "I will ask nothing of you in return, I swear."

Lily looked down at Sarah. She knew that he was right when he said they could not remain here. Her sister was sicker than she had ever seen her, and the poor thing would not even have a bed of her own in this dirty, wretched little inn.

Furthermore, when the other actresses returned from their late dinner, they would most likely fly into the boughs at the prospect of sharing their room with someone as ill—and perhaps contagious—as Sarah was.

Lily warned Damon, "You cannot want us at Hawkhill. Whatever she has may be catching."

"What if it is?" he said with a shrug. "Surely you do not think I am such a faint-heart that I would turn my back upon you at such a moment."

Sarah moaned and her eyes fluttered open. "Lily," she muttered so weakly her sister could barely hear her, "I feel dreadful."

"Yes, my dearest, I know," Lily said soothingly, gripping one of her thin little hands in her own.

"My throat is so sore."

"Let me see it," Hawkhurst ordered.

Sarah obediently opened her mouth. He studied it for a long moment, then said, "Yes, I can see how painful it is."

She murmured, "I am so hot and thirsty. Could I have a sip of water?"

"Yes, of course," Lily said automatically, rising from the bed to get it. When she looked around the room, however, she saw that the only water in it came from the leaking roof.

"You must come to Hawkhill." Damon laid his hand lightly on her arm. "You will have everything you need to nurse her there."

Still she hesitated.

"Let me help you, Lily. I owe you that much."

"You don't owe me anything," she protested.

He drew her away from the bed and whispered, "Listen to me for your sister's sake. I believe that she has a malignant sore throat. She will require vigilant care in a well-equipped sickroom if she is to survive this."

Lily knew that he was being honest with her, and his words hit her like a physical blow. She swayed a little at their impact. Sarah could not die!

Damon's hands were instantly about Lily's arms to steady her, and she was thankful for their comforting strength.

"Then she will need days, more likely weeks of recuperation," he continued. "It is not possible in this miserable hovel."

Lily fought the panic that nibbled at her.

Further discussion was cut off by the arrival of

Sewell with word that Dr. Lasham had gone to Wolverdale to treat a man badly injured in a fall.

A dismayed groan escaped Lily.

"That settles it," Hawkhurst announced. "As you know, Wolverdale is on the other side of Hawkhill. We shall take Sarah to Hawkhill now, and Sewell will ride on to get the doctor. That way she will have medical attention considerably sooner than if we must wait for Sewell to bring the doctor all the way back here."

His argument made such good sense that Lily could not object. She was too terrified for her sister.

Her only thought now was to do what was best for Sarah by getting her out of this dank, dreadful room to Hawkhill as quickly as possible.

Lily dared not think what the consequences of this decision might be for herself.

Chapter 18

On the ride to Hawkhill, Sarah moaned so piteously at each bump of the carriage that Lily looked at Hawkhurst in alarm.

"I know it is very painful for you, Sarah," he said soothingly, "and I am very sorry, but it is crucial that we get you into a warm, dry bed as soon as possible. That is why we must go at such an uncomfortable pace, but we will soon be there."

Lily was touched by his understanding and sympathy for her sister. His long tapering fingers lightly brushed away a lock of brown hair from Sarah's wan face. Lily remembered with a little shiver of pleasure what it had been like to be touched by those skillful, gentle hands.

When the equipage reached Hawkhill, he quickly lifted Sarah out and carried her himself up the broad steps to the mansion while Sewell went on for the doctor. As he reached the top step, the double entry doors opened. Without breaking stride, Hawkhurst swept inside with Lily behind him.

She was much too worried about her sister to spare more than a quick glance around the impressively large marble hall.

Two footmen in scarlet and silver livery sprang forward to relieve the earl of his burden, but he refused to relinquish it to them. Instead he said to the elderly butler who had opened the door, "I trust that the guest suite is ready. I will take her there."

"Take who?" a young girl's voice called from a door off the great hall. A second later Amy came through it, followed by Cassandra and Phoebe.

"Damn!" Hawkhurst muttered under his breath as he started for the wide staircase.

Amy's eyes widened at the sight of her brother carrying a strange girl. "Who is she?"

"Mrs. Culhane's sister, Sarah," he replied. "She is very ill, and I am going to put her to bed here. Sewell has gone for Dr. Lasham."

Had Lily not been so worried about Sarah, she would have been amused by how closely the reaction of Hawkhill's female residents to this news matched their characters. Phoebe burst into tears, murmuring, "The poor little thing." Amy begged to be allowed to help nurse Sarah. Cassandra launched into a tirade on how uncaring her brother was to expose his innocent family to a disease that would surely prove to be as contagious as it was deadly.

He ignored them all and said instead to one of the footmen, "Tell Mrs. Nesmith to send me the most dependable maid she has immediately. Tell her, too, that after she has done that, I wish to speak to her."

The man hurried off toward the back of the house. Hawkhurst proceeded up the stairs with Sarah in his arms and Lily in his wake.

The second footman ran ahead of this strange party along a long corridor lighted at intervals by candles in polished brass sconces. Near the far end of the hall, he stopped, plucked a candle from a sconce, threw open a door, and disappeared through it with Hawkhurst after him.

Following them, Lily found herself in a dark room lit only by the flickering candle in the servant's hand. After pulling back the covers of a high tester bed so that his master could lay Sarah upon it, the footman moved hastily around the room lighting candles.

As the darkness receded, Lily saw that she was in a spacious bedchamber. The hangings on the tester bed and the windows were of an airy white fabric sprigged with pink that gave the room a light, cheerful air for which Lily was thankful. A somber, formal room would have further depressed her already low spirits. Furthermore, it would delight Sarah once she began to get well.

If she got well.

Clenching her hands into fists, Lily resolutely pushed that dire thought from her mind.

Hawkhurst told the footman, "Sewell left two portmanteaux on the steps outside. Bring them here at once."

"Yes, my lord," the servant said, hurrying out of the room.

Damon asked Lily, "Shall I hire a nurse for your sister?"

"No!" she exclaimed. She would not permit anyone but herself to care for Sarah. Lily was not without experience in the sickroom, and that, coupled with her love for her sister, would serve the girl better than the ministrations of a stranger.

He did not argue with her, saying instead, "This apartment has two connecting bedrooms. The other is for your use."

"Thank you, but I shall not need it." Lily gestured toward a single-ended chaise longue by one of the room's long windows. "I will use that when I wish to rest. I would not feel comfortable being away from Sarah."

He looked as though he wanted to protest, but he held his tongue.

A maid in a crisply starched white apron rushed into the room. "You sent for me, my lord?"

"Yes, Molly. This is Mrs. Culhane, and I want

you to help her remove her sick sister's clothes and give her whatever other assistance she might need.''

Then he went out, shutting the door behind him.

Molly's broad, freckled face puckered in concern when she saw Sarah lying on the bed. ''Poor little mite,'' she exclaimed.

She and Lily worked swiftly and gently to strip Sarah. They were not yet done when a knock at the door signaled the arrival of the sisters' portmanteaux. Molly retrieved them, and Lily pulled a night rail from Sarah's case to put on her.

When she was settled beneath the covers, Sarah murmured happily, ''This is so comfortable.''

If she slept fitfully in the big, soft featherbed, it would be because of her illness, not a lumpy, uncomfortable mattress. Despite Lily's earlier misgivings about coming to Hawkhill, she was deeply grateful now to Damon for rescuing Sarah and her from that wretched inn.

She pulled up a chair for herself beside the bed. Molly unpacked Sarah's portmanteau and put away the garments, then took Lily's into the adjoining bedroom.

Lily did not see her host again until Dr. Lasham arrived. Hawkhurst brought the physician, a thin man with a short, well-trimmed beard, into the room and withdrew while the doctor examined Sarah.

When he was done, he set out several vials of medicines on the bedside table and gave her doses from two. Then he picked up his bag and motioned for Lily to accompany him into the hall.

Hawkhurst was waiting there, and the doctor told him, ''I fear it is what you thought, my lord, a malignant sore throat. Her illness is very dangerous. She must be kept absolutely quiet and not permitted out of bed.''

''For how long?'' Lily asked.

''Perhaps weeks.''

"Weeks!" Lily cried in dismay.

"Yes," the doctor confirmed, stroking his beard. "Otherwise, she could suffer serious, even fatal, complications."

He began delivering precise, detailed instructions to Lily for what must be done in nursing Sarah.

When he finished, Damon accompanied him downstairs, and Lily went back to her sister's bedside. Clearly one of the medications had been intended to make Sarah sleep, and she was already drifting off.

Lily quietly seated herself in the chair beside her sister's bed. Outside, the angry wind pounded rain against the windowpanes, and she shuddered at what this night would have been like beneath the leaking roof of that dreadful inn.

Yet she and Sarah could not possibly remain here for weeks. She would be so enormously in Hawkhurst's debt.

When he returned twenty minutes later, Sarah was asleep. He was accompanied by a footman carrying a heavily loaded tray. The servant set it down on a Pembroke table before vanishing into the hall.

As soon as the door closed after him, Lily told Damon with considerable agitation, "You have been very kind to us tonight, but we cannot presume upon your hospitality by remaining here for weeks."

"But of course you can," he replied smoothly. "You are welcome to stay as long as you wish or—" He smiled wryly. "—even longer."

"I cannot be beholden to you like this."

"You aren't," he said, amusement in his dark eyes. "It is your sister who is."

"That is worse!" she cried, much shocked.

The humor vanished from his eyes. "Believe me, I have absolutely no interest in shy, innocent girls who are young enough to be my daughter. I neither expect nor want any repayment for my hospitality from you or your sister *in any currency*. I trust I make myself clear.''

Lily was torn between relief and puzzlement. ''Yes, but why then are you putting yourself to so much trouble for us?''

His hooded eyes were unreadable. ''Certainly not to make you beholden to me.''

''I am afraid our presence here will subject you to dreadful harangues by Cassandra. She will object vehemently to having an actress here.''

''No doubt she would if she knew you are one.'' Hawkhurst gave Lily a searching look. ''But she and Phoebe are under the impression that you are a young widow traveling in the company of your uncle since you left Bath.''

''I never told them I was a widow! How on earth could they have gotten that idea?''

''It seems some mutual friend told them.''

Lily wondered whether it could have been Sir Roger Hilton. Had he and Phoebe seen more of each other after Lily had introduced them at the Pump Room? She had frequently wondered since leaving Bath whether her sly matchmaking had borne fruit.

''Lady Hawkhurst is so lovely,'' Lily remarked with feigned innocence. ''Does she have any admirers?''

''None that interests her, unfortunately.''

So Lily's efforts had not succeeded. ''Unfortunately?''

''Frankly, I would be delighted to be relieved of her.'' Damon looked almost desperate. ''She has always been a watering pot, but since she returned from Bath, I have only to glance at her, and she begins to weep.''

''Have you asked her—''

''Of course I have,'' he interjected impatiently. ''She insists that nothing is wrong and then cries all the harder. It is driving me mad. But enough of Phoebe. You must eat.''

Hawkhurst drew her attention to the tray that the footman had left. It contained barley water and a saline solution that Dr. Lasham had ordered for Sarah and food for Lily.

''But I could not possibly eat,'' Lily exclaimed, feeling no hunger even though she had not had time for dinner.

''Yes, you could,'' he said calmly, pulling a chair over to the Pembroke table. ''Now, come here and sit.''

She did so, and he removed the cover from a bowl of thick soup. It was accompanied by several generous slices of bread, a mound of freshly churned butter, and a plate of assorted cheeses and fruit. The aroma arising from the soup was so delicious that it awakened Lily's dormant appetite, and she discovered that Damon was right.

As she ate, Lily read the sheet of paper on which Dr. Lasham had written out the most important of his directions for Sarah's care, including the times she must be given the various medications.

After consuming all of the soup and much of the bread and cheese, Lily smiled a little sheepishly. ''And I did not think I was hungry. Thank you.''

Damon smiled approvingly, then asked, ''Are you certain you would not like me to hire a nurse to help you?''

''No,'' Lily said firmly, ''but . . .'' She hesitated.

''Tell me what you want,'' he commanded.

''I should like to send for Trude.'' Her maid had gone to visit her family while Lily was traveling with her uncle's troupe. ''She is with relatives in Hampshire.''

''Summon her. I will frank the letter for you—and any others that you might wish to send.'' He nodded toward a delicate, kidney-shaped writing table against the wall opposite the bed. "You will find pen, ink, and writing paper there."

She went to the writing table and dashed off a quick letter to Trude. When she was finished, Damon promised it would be posted first thing in the morning.

Lily went back to the bed to check on her sister. Sarah was still sleeping, but when Lily laid a hand on her forehead it seemed warmer to her than the last time she had done so. She settled into the chair, trying to quiet her apprehensions.

Hawkhurst brought a second chair over and sat beside her. "Where was Sarah coming from tonight?"

"She has been visiting a school friend who lives in Dorset."

"How long have you been responsible for her?"

"Since my parents died."

His thick, dark brows rose in surprise. "But you were only seventeen when they were killed. Did they leave you well fixed?"

"No." Although Lily's parents had done well in the theatre, they had lived even better. They had let a handsome house and had been determined that their children should have the education that would have been their right had their parents not been cast out by their disapproving families.

The boarding school they sent Lily to had been expensive. So had her brother's school. Having been ostracized by the society into which they were born, they had tried hard to return their children to it. When they were killed, they left behind only debts.

Lily had immediately left school and returned to the stage in a desperate attempt to pay the bills and keep her family together.

"How did you manage?" Damon asked.

"I was very fortunate that I could earn enough by acting to support the three of us."

"Three?"

"I have a younger brother, too."

He frowned. "But it must have been very difficult for a girl of seventeen."

"At first, it was a struggle," she admitted.

"I suspect you are guilty of gross understatement."

The unmistakable admiration on his face pleased her enormously. He looked over at Sarah's feverish form.

"Does she wish to follow in her big sister's footsteps and pursue a career on the stage?"

"No, that is the last thing Sarah would want. She is very shy and trembles with fright at the thought of stepping on a stage."

A movement from the bed drew Lily's attention back to her sister. Sarah was growing more restless.

A few minutes later, her eyes opened. They were dull and glazed with pain and fever. It was so unlike Sarah to complain that when she began fussing with increasing frequency that she ached terribly all over, Lily's anxiety soared.

"Do you wish me to send for Dr. Lasham?" Hawkhurst asked.

The doctor had warned Lily that her sister might well get worse before she got better, and she hesitated to disturb him if the illness was only following its normal course. Nor was it likely that he could do anything more for her than he had already done. "No, not yet," she decided.

Sarah sank back into a restless, fevered sleep, and it seemed to Lily that her breathing had become more labored.

After another hour, Lily knew that her sister was much sicker. Her fever had grown hotter and her pulse more tumultuous.

When Lily told Damon that her sister was worse, he went at once to the bed. After checking both her forehead and her pulse, he nodded gravely. "Yes, she is. I fear we have a long night ahead of us."

Lily was startled that he apparently intended to remain with her. She knew that she should protest. He had already done so much for them, and sitting up with a sick stranger went far beyond the dictates of hospitality. Yet she was so frightened for her sister and so comforted by his presence that she could not force herself to say a word.

As the night wore on, Sarah grew progressively more fevered, tossing and moaning in such pain that it tore at her sister's heart.

"I could bear it better if the pain were my own," Lily confessed as she bathed Sarah's burning face with lavender water.

Lily did not know what she would have done without Hawkhurst's comforting presence. Only his imperturbable calm held at bay the demons of fear and panic that ate at her control and threatened to overwhelm her. He was such a solace to her that had he tried to leave her, she would have begged him to stay.

But he did not try.

As the morning light grew bright around the closed curtains, Sarah became quiet, her fever dropped, and she fell into a more restful slumber.

Hawkhurst insisted that Lily try to sleep, preferably in the other bedroom rather than upon the chaise longue.

"You must take care not to become ill yourself," he cautioned her. "I will have Molly stay with Sarah until you wake. If there is a change for the worse, she will call you immediately."

Lily was too exhausted to argue. "I am very grateful to you for staying up with me."

He smiled at her, an odd smile that made her breath catch.

After giving Molly careful instructions, Lily went

into the other bedroom and fell asleep almost as soon as her head touched the pillow.

When she awoke, she was horrified to see by the brass bracket clock on the mantel that it was already afternoon. She jumped up and hurried into the other bedroom.

Sarah was sleeping. Molly, who was sitting attentively beside her, rose at Lily's entrance and told her, "His lordship was by about a half hour ago and was concerned about her fever."

So Damon had not slept as long as she herself had, Lily thought guiltily.

"He has sent for Dr. Lasham again," Molly said.

The physician arrived forty-five minutes later, but this time Hawkhurst did not escort him to Sarah's room. Dr. Lasham promptly dashed her weak hope that her sister might be out of danger.

"I won't wrap it in clean linen; it will be a near thing," he told her, stroking his beard. "There's no way of knowing whether she will pull through. It depends upon whether the fever breaks soon."

That so depressed Lily's spirits that she was hard-pressed not to weep after he left.

As the long summer twilight waned, Sarah's fever waxed. The minutes passed as slowly as hours for Lily. A footman brought her dinner on a tray, but there was no word from Hawkhurst. She wondered where he was.

She wanted him with her desperately, but when the clock struck ten, she abandoned any hope of seeing him again until the morrow.

By the time another hour passed, she knew that Sarah was even sicker than she had been the previous night.

Lily hovered on the brink of despair. She did not know how she would get through the interminable night ahead without Damon beside her.

Chapter 19

When Hawkhurst had left Lily, he had intended to soak his aching body, still sore from the fall he had taken the previous day, in a hot tub, then go immediately to sleep.

But other matters intervened. First, he was called upon to resolve an acrimonious dispute between two of his tenants, then to deal with other problems on the estate requiring immediate decisions.

Then he checked on his guests and found that Lily was still asleep. Sarah's fever seemed slightly higher to him, and he decided to send for the doctor.

By the time he finally eased himself into a soothing tub, it was nearly two. After a long soak, he climbed into bed. As he fell asleep, he reflected on the irony that a perverse fate had forced the proud, self-reliant Lily to accept his help. She would never have done so had it been for herself, but her beloved little sister was another matter entirely.

He awoke at ten, and it was eleven by the time he dressed and ate and made his way to the guest suite. He had not meant to be so late. As he knocked lightly, he expected Lily's recriminations for his tardiness.

When the door opened, his breath caught at the sight of her relieved expression. She did not try to disguise her joy at seeing him.

"I thought that you would not come and that I would have to face the night alone." Lily cast an anxious glance toward Sarah. "Oh, Damon, I am so afraid for her."

He would have given anything to spare Lily the ordeal that he was certain lay ahead. He drew her into his arms and held her close. There was nothing sexual in his embrace. He wanted only to offer her comfort and the assurance that he understood and shared her fear. He longed to protect her as he had never before wanted to protect a woman.

Sarah moaned, "Lily, Lily, where are you?"

Lily broke away from him and hurried back to the bed.

"I am so hot, and I hurt," Sarah complained piteously, her voice so weak it could scarcely be heard.

"Yes, my dearest, I know." Lily poured lavender water on a cloth. "Here, let me bathe your face. It will help a little."

The room was scented with lavender. Damon watched as she lovingly sponged her sister's face. He was much moved by how tenderly she cared for Sarah.

The thought came unbidden to him that Lily would make a wonderful mother. He tried to imagine what it would have been like to have such a loving, caring mother. His own had been a remarkable woman, noted for her keen managerial talent and her impartial fairness to everyone, but she had not been blessed with maternal inclinations. She had paid her son little heed for the first decade of his life. Indeed, he sometimes wondered whether she had not been as uncomfortable with small children as his father had been, only more skilled at concealing it.

It had been Mrs. Nesmith—then Damon's nurse, now Hawkhill's housekeeper—who had nursed him through his childhood illnesses.

When Lily finished bathing Sarah's face, she

moved away from the bed and gestured to him to come to her.

She whispered, "I did not think it was possible for her fever to rise any higher, but I am certain it has."

He went to the bed and laid his hand on Sarah's forehead. "I fear you are right," he said.

Lily swallowed hard. "What are we to do?"

Hawkhurst took her hand and squeezed it sympathetically. "There is nothing that we can do beyond what we already are," he said gently.

She sank down into the chair beside the bed, and he sat beside her again.

By one A.M., Sarah was racked by delirium. She thrashed about in the throes of hallucinations and babbled incoherently. It required Hawkhurst's strength to restrain her in her wildest moments and his ruthless determination to get the medicines the doctor had prescribed down her at the appointed times.

"I do not know what I would have done without you tonight," Lily told him gratefully toward dawn. "I have nursed her through other bad illnesses, but none like this."

Trying to distract Lily from her sister's deteriorating condition, he asked, "What was her worst illness before this?"

"An ague eight years ago. Her fever was so high for three days that I dared not leave her side, but she was not out of her head with delirium and unable to recognize me as she is now."

Damon frowned. "Eight years ago? You could not have been much older at the time than she is now."

"I was seventeen. It was shortly after our parents died."

"How difficult it must have been for you," Damon said admiringly. "Was your brother able to help you?"

"He tried, but he was only sixteen at the time."

"Yes, a whole year younger than you, which I suppose you will tell me made all the difference!"

"I think men in general are a disaster in the sickroom. Except," she amended, "for you."

"At last, you recognize I have some limited value," he teased. 'Where is your brother now?"

"In Wellington's army."

Poor bastard, Damon thought. The life of a common soldier was miserable at best. The Duke of Wellington, the commander-in-chief of these lowly troops, dismissed them as cannon fodder. It must be a great worry to Lily to have a brother in those ranks. Nor was any advancement to officer's status possible, because only the wealthy could afford to buy commissions.

Perhaps he ought to think about doing that for her brother. The idea appealed to Damon as a way to relieve Lily of whatever worries he could. Besides, he suspected that the way to her heart might be through her siblings.

"Did your soldier brother serve with Wellington in the Peninsular War?"

"Yes. How thankful I am that is over. The day I learned of Napoleon's abdication was one of the happiest of my life. The army is not what I would have chosen for my brother, but it was what he wanted."

Hawkhurst would have asked her more about her brother, but she seemed oddly reluctant to talk about him and changed the subject. Had the young man's insistence upon joining the army caused an estrangement between them? Hawkhurst wondered.

Sarah suddenly screamed. "No, no! Do not hurt me! Lily, help!" she cried, flailing about on the bed in terror.

Both her sister and Damon were at her side in an

instant. Her wild, panicked eyes stared at them without recognition.

He took her pulse and found it was racing.

Lily looked up at him, her green eyes bright with unshed tears. "I am so afraid for her."

He gathered Lily in his arms comfortingly. "I have faith that she will come through this."

Finally, about seven A.M., he sent for Sewell and asked him to go again for Dr. Lasham.

Hawkhurst watched from the window as his groom rode out at a gallop and disappeared in the distance.

When Sewell was out of sight, Damon turned away from the window and looked at the bed. Cold terror seized him as he realized that Sarah's delirious thrashing and feverish moaning had ceased.

Lily was bending over her sister. She looked up at Hawkhurst, a frightened, urgent query on her face.

A half dozen long strides brought him to the bed. One hand went to Sarah's forehead, the other to her wrist. Her forehead was cool. To his intense relief, her pulse was still beating—and at a much more normal pace.

Hawkhurst smiled at Lily. "The fever was broken. I am certain that she will make it now."

He opened his arms to Lily. She stepped into their protective circle and wept in relief and exhaustion against his shoulder.

He held her to him, stroking her hair comfortingly. When her crying subsided, he lifted her chin and gently wiped away her tears with his handkerchief.

Damon longed to kiss her, but he was too acutely aware of his promise that he would ask nothing of her. He wanted to give her no possible reason to suspect that he would not keep it.

He did not intend to botch this opportunity fate had given him to redeem himself in Lily's eyes.

Sarah continued to improve at a snail's pace; she was shockingly wan and weak. On the afternoon of the third day after her fever broke, Trude arrived at Hawkhill, relieving Lily of some of the sickroom burden.

Now that Sarah was better and Trude had come, Hawkhurst was adamant that Lily must have exercise and fresh air to protect her own health. He coaxed her into leaving her sister in her trusted maid's care for an hour and took her off for a walk in Hawkhill's gardens. Lily was secretly touched by the concern he showed for both her and her sister.

That night, he insisted that Lily join him and his family in the dining room instead of eating her dinner on a tray in Sarah's room. Although the food was superb, Lily could not help feeling sorry for her host. Cassandra did nothing but complain, mostly about him, and with such venom that he was moved to remark dryly, "I do not know how I would get on without you, Cassandra, to disparage me and keep my consequence in check."

Phoebe seemed to dissolve into tears every other minute. Damon had not exaggerated when he had said that she could scarcely look at him without crying. The attraction between her and Sir Roger Hilton clearly had not flourished after Lily left Bath. Phoebe was far too unhappy. Lily wondered whether, despite Roger's weakness for delicate, helpless blondes, even he had found her tears trying.

Over dessert of Bavarian cream with walnuts and gooseberry pastries, Cassandra badgered Hawkhurst to allow her and Phoebe to go to London for the season next spring.

When Phoebe joined her voice to this plea, he

frowned. "But you told me in Bath that you wished to return *there* next season."

She looked frightened, and tears welled up in her eyes. "I . . . I have grown tired of Bath."

Damon's frown deepened. "I am astonished to hear that after you stayed on an additional two months this summer because you liked it so well. Why this sudden change of heart?"

His question seemed to confound Phoebe, and her only answer was to cry in earnest.

"You are so cruel, Hawkhurst," Cassandra complained, beginning to sniffle in unison with Phoebe. "You intend to keep us from London next season because you know how much we want to go there. That is why you would not let me go this year."

"Bath was the choice of your chaperone, Lady Effington," he reminded her. "It made no difference to me whether she took you there or to London."

Cassandra glared at him. "I don't believe you!"

As soon as dinner was finished, Lily went back to Sarah's bedside, thankful for an excuse to escape Phoebe's tears and Cassandra's complaints.

The next day, Hawkhurst insisted that Lily have another outing with him. As they strolled along a graveled path between the parterres and box borders of Hawkhill's formal garden, the sweet perfume of summer flowers hung heavy on the air.

Lily asked whether he opposed Cassandra and Phoebe's desire to go to London next season as his sister claimed.

"No. I would have been happy to send Cassandra to London last season as she wanted, but the truth is I could not find a single female relative who would agree to chaperone her. I had no choice but to send her to Bath with Lady Effington."

"I gather she is unaware of your reason for doing so."

''I am not so cruel I could tell her that no one wanted her.''

He had a kinder heart than Lily had suspected. Since she had been at Hawkhill, she had seen a very different man than his reputation made him out to be. He had been so good to her and Sarah, and she marveled at his patience with Cassandra and Phoebe.

A blackcap rose up from a boxwood hedge, startling Lily from her thoughts, and flew off.

''Next season is an even greater dilemma for me,'' Damon confessed. ''In theory, Phoebe could serve as Cassandra's chaperone, but in reality that widgeon needs a chaperone even more than my sister. I felt fairly safe letting them stay in Bath after Lady Effington died, but London is a very different situation. They must have someone there. I would have no trouble providing Phoebe with a companion, but no one will take on Cassandra. Until I find someone, I cannot let them go to London.''

''You were right about Lady Hawkhurst,'' Lily observed. ''She can scarcely look at you without crying.''

Hawkhurst ran his fingers through his thick, black hair in an unconscious gesture of frustration. ''It has been much worse since she returned from Bath. I have no notion what is upsetting her so. Do you think that you might be able to discover what it is?''

Lily was determined to try. It was the least she could do for Hawkhurst in return for his kindness to her and her sister. There was something else she could do for him, too, she decided, and that was to make dinner more pleasant for him.

So that night she ruthlessly took control of the conversation at the table, keeping it lively and amusing and giving Cassandra little opportunity to complain. Damon and Amy—who, Lily discovered, had a quick mind and sharp sense of humor—responded to her efforts like parched plants to water, and their laughter echoed through the dining room.

The following afternoon when Lily returned from what had become her daily walk with Damon, she found Amy at Sarah's bedside. Lily's sister was well enough now to sit up in bed and to eat solid foods, although her appetite was still not what it ought to be. Once Sarah had begun to improve, Amy had begged to be allowed to sit with her, and Lily had given her permission. The two girls took to each other immediately and were becoming fast friends.

It occurred to Lily that Damon's sister might be able to shed some light on why Phoebe's tears had become so frequent.

"Amy, do you have any idea why Lady Hawkhurst is unhappy?" Lily asked. "She did not cry so much when I met her in Bath."

"And after you introduced her to Sir Roger Hilton, she did not cry at all. Indeed, she positively glowed all the rest of the time we were there. You cannot imagine how pleasant it was."

"Are you saying that she has a *tendre* for Sir Roger?"

"Oh, much more than that," Amy assured her. "She's madly in love with him. That is why we stayed in Bath so much longer than we had planned. If Sir Roger had not had to return home, I think we would be there still."

"But why then is Phoebe so woeful? Does Sir Roger not return her affection?" Had Lily succeeded only in making matters worse for Damon with her attempt to match his stepmother with Roger?

"Phoebe says he wants very much to marry her."

"But she acts as though she is sinking into a decline!"

"She is convinced Hawk will not let her marry Sir Roger."

Lily's eyes widened. "Has your brother told her so?"

"No, she is afraid to tell him about Sir Roger, and she has made me swear I will not do so either."

The ridiculous goosecap! It was time for a talk with her.

Lily found Phoebe in the sitting room of the suite she occupied in a wing at the other end of the great house.

Lily said bluntly, "Please tell me, Lady Hawkhurst, what your feelings are for the gentleman I introduced you to in Bath, Sir Roger Hilton."

At the mention of Roger's name, Phoebe burst into tears. It was several minutes before Lily could draw out of the incoherent girl that she was, indeed, wildly in love with Sir Roger and he with her.

"But that is wonderful!" Lily exclaimed. "Why are you crying about it?"

"Because . . . we want so much to marry . . . and it will never . . . *never* . . . be possible!" Phoebe gasped out between sobs. "Hawkhurst will not permit such a match!" She buried her face in her white linen handkerchief edged with lace.

"Why should Lord Hawkhurst have any say in the matter? You are of age. Indeed, you are a widow of six years' standing and free to make your own choice."

"No, I am not! I do not fully understand it, but it has to do with the terms of my marriage settlement to the late earl." The memory of that gentleman sent Phoebe into a fresh paroxysm of weeping, and it was a minute before she could continue. "His successor's permission is required for me to remarry. Mama said so."

"I do not see how that is legally possible," Lily said doubtfully. "But even if it is, I do not think Lord Hawkhurst would withhold permission if it is truly what you want." In fact, she suspected that once he met Roger, he would be pleased. He could entrust his stepmama to the young baronet in good conscience.

Phoebe lifted her tearful face from her handkerchief. "If only that were true! Hawkhurst is vastly particular about whom I may marry. Several men have sought my hand, but he rejected them all because their titles were not lofty enough."

Lily frowned. That was at odds with what Damon had said about Phoebe having no admirer that interested her. "Did you wish to marry one of these suitors? Did he prevent you from doing so?"

"No!" Phoebe dabbed ineffectually at the tears running down her cheeks. "I did not like any of them! Indeed, I was quite thankful that he refused them, but he would have done so even if I had wished to wed one of them."

"Perhaps Lord Hawkhurst will also feel differently about Sir Roger."

"No, he won't! Hawkhurst told both Mama and Cassandra that he would not permit me to wed any man below the rank of marquess. He said he would not let the Earl of Hawkhurst's widow demean herself and his father's memory by marrying anyone of lesser stature."

"What nonsense!" Lily exclaimed. "At least ask him about Sir Roger. He might surprise you."

"I dare not," Phoebe wailed. "This way, Cassandra and I have some hope of persuading Hawkhurst to let us go to London for the next season, and I will be able to see Roger there."

So that was why she was suddenly so anxious to go to London instead of returning to Bath.

"But if Hawkhurst learns of Roger, he will make certain that I never see him again!" Phoebe cried. "He is a cruel man."

Lily strongly suspected that Phoebe was merely

parroting Cassandra, and she said impatiently, "Tell me specifically what cruelty he has inflicted upon you."

Phoebe's tongue flailed inarticulately for several moments, but in the end she could come up with no specifics.

Lily decided it was time the pea-goose heard a few home truths. "Lady Hawkhurst, you—"

"Please, do not call me that!" Phoebe cried in real distress. "You cannot know how much I hated being Lady Hawkhurst, married to that dreadful old man!" She shuddered. "I was terrified of him. Mama said that he conferred a great honor upon me by making me his wife and I must do whatever he wished, but hard as I tried, I could not . . . ever suffer him to touch me without revulsion. And then I would cry, and he would get very, very angry."

Lily could well imagine.

Phoebe shuddered again. "Indeed, it is a terrible thing to say, but I could not mourn for him after he died."

"I trust that you feel differently about Roger."

"Oh, yes, I love him so much! But Hawkhurst will never allow us to marry."

"Ask him!" Lily said in exasperation.

"I cannot! Cassandra says that if he finds out about Roger, he will lock me in the dower house and never permit me to leave or even to have visitors."

Lily stared incredulously at Phoebe. How could she believe anything the spiteful Cassandra said about her brother?

Phoebe was sobbing hard now.

Even given Roger's weakness for delicate, help-less blondes, Lily began to wonder whether he could truly have lost his heart to such a lachrymose ninnyhammer. Perhaps it would be wise to ascertain that his interest in Phoebe was as passionate as she believed it before Lily broached the subject to Damon.

After leaving her, Lily went to Sarah's room and sat down at the writing table to tactfully seek more information about the state of Sir Roger's heart.

When she finished, she went to Hawkhurst to ask him if he would mind franking the letter for her. He replied with a smile, "If I minded, I would not have offered."

He took it from her, his smile fading as he saw the name and address. "Is this perchance Handsome Roger that I saw you with in Bath?"

"Yes," she said, surprised that Damon remembered him.

"Why are you writing him?" he asked bluntly.

Lily did not want to explain until she had ascertained Roger's true feelings about Phoebe. "He is a family friend who will want to know about Sarah's illness." That much was true, but that was not the real reason for her letter to him.

Hawkhurst's eyes narrowed suspiciously. "A very good family friend, it would appear!"

Chapter 20

T he connecting door between Lily's and her sister's bedrooms was open, and Lily could hear Mrs. Nesmith, the elderly Scottish housekeeper who presided over Hawkhill, in Sarah's room.

"Now, Lady Amy, dinna you be wearin' out Miss Sarah," the motherly housekeeper was cautioning.

Lily went to the connecting door. Amy was at Sarah's bedside in the armchair where Lily had spent so many apprehensive hours. The two girls, so near in age, were talking like bosom bows.

"Do you know where Hawk is?" Amy asked the housekeeper.

It was the very question that Lily wanted to ask. This was the first morning since Sarah's fever had broken that Damon had not come by to check on her.

"One of the tenants had an accident," Mrs. Nesmith replied. "I dinna know when he'll be back."

Lily felt a pang of disappointment at his absence. In the twelve days that she had been at Hawkhill, she had come to cherish the time she spent with him: his morning visits, their afternoon walks, the chess games and charades after dinner.

Lily reflected on how obliging he had been to her during her stay. No man had treated her with such solicitude before. Yet he had made no attempt to coax her into his bed.

Despite his promise to her that he would ask for no repayment in any currency for his kindness to her and her sister, Lily had been wary, but his behavior was impeccable. He acted toward Lily like she imagined a gentleman would to a lady of quality who was his platonic friend. Indeed, that was what all his servants mistook her for.

Lily should have been delighted by his gentlemanly behavior, but perversely she was a little hurt that he had not made any overture to her by now.

She stepped into her sister's room and greeted its occupants cheerfully. When she had first arrived at Hawkhill, the housekeeper had acknowledged her with frigid politeness and unmistakable suspicion in her eyes. But since then Lily had been able to thaw the woman to the point that now she greeted her with a friendly smile.

"Was the accident serious?" Lily asked.

"I dinna know."

It was unusual for an estate owner to take such an interest in his tenants. When Lily remarked upon this to Mrs. Nesmith, the housekeeper replied, "Aye, a good man is the young master, fair and nononsense. He is his mother's son." Her tone made clear her respect for the old earl's first wife. "She trained him well."

"What of his father?" Lily asked curiously.

The housekeeper's eyes narrowed coldly. "His papa didna like children—his or anyone else's." Mrs. Nesmith apparently had not respected Hawkhurst's father nearly as much as his mother.

The sickroom was stuffy, and Lily crossed over to the window farthest from her sister's bed to open it wide. The housekeeper followed her. The day was warm and a soft breeze was stirring.

"Aye, the fresh air will be good for the little lassie," Mrs. Nesmith said approvingly. "We at Hawk-hill are most fortunate to have the young master as the lord. He takes his duty to his family and to his people very seriously, although Lady Cassandra wouldna agree with me."

"She is most unfair to her brother."

The look on Mrs. Nesmith's wide, lined face told Lily that her defense of Hawkhurst had raised her several notches in the housekeeper's estimation.

"Aye, she is. She makes him out to be a cruel pinch-purse when he is not."

The housekeeper glanced toward Sarah and Amy. They were deeply engrossed in their own conversation, but Mrs. Nesmith still lowered her voice to barely above a whisper. "It distresses me, it does, to hear Lady Cassandra talk about the young master so hatefully. She is *her* mother's daughter, and almost as great a mischief-maker. That woman was so different from the late earl's first countess, who loved Hawkhill as though it were her own inheritance instead of her husband's."

Lily looked out over the rolling hills of Hawkhill's park. "I can see why she would love it."

"It prospered under her. We all mourned her when she died—and mourned the old lord's choice for a second wife. I dinna know how the earl could have married that woman—and with his first lady not dead a week. A terrible thing it was for us all when he shackled himself to Lady Olivia, but especially for the young master."

The housekeeper offered no explanation of why it had been so terrible for Damon. Lily, unable to contain her curiosity, asked, "Why do you say that?"

"He was only a laddie of fifteen or sixteen then, and that evil woman did everything she could to turn his father against him. Succeeded, too. Even managed to get the poor laddie banished from here and sent to live with his mama's father. I've always wondered what lies she told to accomplish that.''

Lily wondered, too. In her short time at Hawkhill, she had come to appreciate how much Damon loved it. How painful it must have been for him to be exiled.

"A cunning creature was the Lady Olivia," Mrs. Nesmith continued. "For years, she could twist the old earl around her finger with her tears, but he finally came to see her for what she was."

"What happened then?"

"By the time she died, he couldna stand the sight of her. He knew by then what she had cost him with her lies.''

When Hawkhurst reached Sarah's room, the door was open, and he paused for a moment on the threshold, unnoticed by the room's occupants. His eyes sought first, as they always did, Lily. She was standing by one of the long windows deep in conversation with his formidable housekeeper.

He remembered with amusement the frigid disapproval with which Mrs. Nesmith had greeted the arrival of Lily and her sister at Hawkhill. The housekeeper had been his nurse when he was small, and she did not scruple to let "the young master," as she still called him, know her mind.

She had made clear that she considered his unexpected guests an imposition on herself and her staff. But somehow Lily had managed to melt the redoubtable woman.

Indeed, he thought wryly, Lily had all his servants falling over each other trying to serve her. It reminded him of how cleverly she had handled her diverse admirers in the greenroom at Bath.

She had even managed to work her magic on his family. He was amazed at the difference her presence made at dinner. Now he could actually look forward to a meal without tears and reproaches.

The bright light streaming through the open window behind Lily gave her rich auburn hair the brilliant glow of a red sunset. Standing there so tall and regal, she looked rather like a pagan goddess. Hawkhurst's desire for her burned hotter than ever.

But he was bound by his oath to her in that wretched little room beneath the leaking roof. *"Let me take you to Hawkhill . . . I will ask nothing of you in return, I swear."*

He would keep that promise if it killed him. And it well might! If they became lovers again, she would have to be the one to come to him.

But what if she did not?

His body ached in frustrated longing for her, and he studied the tantalizing curves of her body hungrily. She was wearing a clinging gown of canary-yellow muslin that must have been in her trunk that had arrived two days ago from storage in Bath.

A sudden burst of laughter from the bed drew Hawkhurst's attention to Sarah, lying there propped up on pillows. She still looked pale and weak, but she continued to improve.

Amy was laughing with Sarah. Watching his sister, Damon decided that he had rarely seen her so happy as she had been since Lily and her sister had come to Hawkhill.

Lily glanced toward the door and saw Hawkhurst there. The glow of pleasure in her eyes at the sight of him delighted him.

"My lord, do come in," she exclaimed. She was always careful to address him as "Lord Hawkhurst" or "my lord" when others were around.

"I have come to bear you away for some fresh air," he told her. "It is a rare day outside, far too beautiful to be missed."

After a hug and kiss for Sarah, Lily allowed him to lead her downstairs. "How is your tenant?"

"A broken arm is all. He was very lucky. He fell from his roof, but fortunately, a hawthorn bush helped break his fall."

The man had been unconscious after the fall, and Hawkhurst had feared he had suffered head or internal injuries, but later he ascertained that the man apparently had fainted from fright.

Once Damon and Lily were outside, he guided her away from the broad lawns and formal gardens surrounding the house.

"Now that Sarah is well on the road to recovery, can I steal you away one day for a ride in my curricle if I promise not to run you off the road in it?"

"Amy mentioned that you had a racing curricle. Would you take me in that?" Lily asked eagerly.

Her request surprised him, for most women would have shrunk from the prospect of a ride in it. "Yes, if you are certain you want it."

"Very certain. It would be great fun!"

They reached a wooded dell with a rill flowing lazily through it. At first glance, the glen appeared to be nature's work, but closer inspection revealed that its laurel, rhododendron, yew, copper beech, and sycamore marched in too orderly and eye-pleasing a fashion for it to be anything other than an artful, carefully planned creation of man.

"What a glorious spot," Lily murmured appreciatively.

He smiled at her, delighted that she liked what was one of his favorite places at Hawkhill.

The creek's banks were formed by large flat stones. Looking at them, Lily said in a puzzled tone, "Surely the current is not so strong that it could have deposited them here."

"No, this entire dell was created by man's—actually I should say woman's—hand."

"Who was she?"

"My mother."

"She knew how to create great beauty," Lily said admiringly.

"Yes, she did," he agreed. Hawkhill had flourished under his mother, declined under her successors, and been restored by her son. It would have broken her heart to have seen its condition when his father died, but he suspected that she would be pleased if she could see it now.

"Did your mother play with you here?"

"No, she would never have dreamed of wasting her time in such frivolity." He could not keep a bitter edge from his voice. "She was far too busy creating a great and profitable estate to waste time with a son."

Lily touched his arm, and he saw the compassion in her face.

"In my mother's defense, I look like my father, whom she hated, and that did not help. She feared that I would grow up to be weak and irresponsible like him too, and she was determined that would not happen. Mama never let me forget the duties and responsibilities that I would inherit along with my title, and my obligation to meet them."

"Your mama would be proud of you now."

"Perhaps," he said skeptically. "She was a very difficult woman to please. When I was a child, I tried very hard, but I doubt I ever succeeded."

"How terrible for you." Lily touched his arm comfortingly, her eyes warm with sympathy.

"It was unfortunate my mother was not born a man, for she inherited her father's great talent for finance and management, and his strength of will, too." He gestured toward a large flat-topped boulder with wild daisies growing around it. "Shall we sit?"

When they were settled on the stone, its surface

pleasantly warmed by the sun, Lily said, "I collect your parents did not like each other very much."

"No." He summed them up bluntly. "My father was weak and my mother strong."

He reached down to pluck one of the wild daisies growing around the rock. "Like many weak men, he wanted a woman who would make him feel strong, a woman who would gaze adoringly at him as though he could do no wrong."

Damon thought about Cassandra's mother Olivia, his father's second wife. That was a look that she had perfected, and his father had lapped it up. She had been careful never to use her waspish tongue on him. Instead, when Olivia had not gotten her own way, she had wept until she did. She had been the most cunning and deceitful woman Damon had ever known.

Lily asked, "Your mother did not gaze at your father that way?"

"My mother had no patience with weakness. She did not hesitate to point his faults out to him. Mama ran his estate far more capably than he ever could. His people looked to her for guidance, rather than to him. He hated her for that."

"Why did two such ill-suited people marry?"

"My mother wanted to be a countess and the mistress of Hawkhill." Hawkhurst twirled the daisy absently in his fingers. "My father wanted her money. Her father was immensely wealthy; she was his only child and sole heir. The St. Clair fortune had been dissipated, and my father saw her inheritance as a way to refill his depleted pockets."

"So they married and lived unhappily ever after."

"Unhappily, but not ever after. The irony is that the vast fortune for which my father married eluded him. Mama died before my grandfather, and he left it all to me."

"Did that cause a problem between you and your father?"

"It was one of several," he said. The worst had been Olivia. Once she had married his father, she had done everything she could to widen the gulf between him and his son. Soon the boy had not been welcome at Hawkhill. It was no consolation to him that in the end Cassandra's mother had caused his father even more grief than she had caused him. He said quietly, "For a time, my father hated me."

"How could he hate his own son?" Lily cried, clearly shocked.

"Oh, he thought he had good reason to." Even after all these years, the lacerating memories tore at Damon's soul.

"But not a valid reason," Lily said, making it a simple statement of fact, not an inquiry.

Damon was pleased that she divined he had been innocent of his father's dark accusations.

"No, but for years he believed it was. How did you know it was not?"

Her smile made his breath catch. "Because I know you. In the end, though, your father finally realized the truth?"

"Yes, but by then . . ." Damon shrugged. He ached to take Lily in his arms, but he feared she would think he was going back on his word to her. He did not want to see the admiration in her eyes turn to disillusionment.

"What were his invalid reasons for hating you?"

He could not bring himself to tell her the sordid story. He shook his head, then levered himself gracefully to his feet. "I have told you more than I have told any other human being, but I insist upon keeping one or two family skeletons in the closet."

He held out his hand to her and helped her up. They resumed their companionable walk along the path beside the creek.

Chapter 21

Hawkhurst's racing curricle streaked along a narrow ribbon of road that wound through Hawkhill's neat, green fields spread across rolling hills. Lily watched admiringly as Damon skillfully guided his new prize pair of grays.

"Would you like me to slow down?" he asked her.

"Oh, no!" she exclaimed. "I should like to go faster if that is possible."

He cast her a quick look of undisguised astonishment. "It is, but are you quite certain that you want to?"

"Yes!" she cried, smiling at him. He looked so handsome in his plain, but perfectly tailored Devonshire-brown riding coat. As usual, his waistcoat, neckcloth, and shirt were all an immaculate white.

Their pace increased until it seemed to Lily that they were flying. The green Devon countryside was rushing past in a blur.

The wind generated by their speed stung her face and tore at her hat. She untied its ribbons from beneath her chin and pulled it off. The wind soon yanked her hair from its pinnings, and she could feel it streaming out behind her.

Never before had she ridden at such a pace in a

vehicle, and she loved the thrill, the sense of wild freedom that it gave her. She laughed aloud in sheer, joyous exuberance.

That brought another quick, sharp look from Hawkhurst, and then the hard lines of his face relaxed into a pleased smile. "Enjoying ourselves, are we?"

"Oh, yes!" she cried. With another driver she might have been frightened, but Hawkhurst was tooling the ribbons so expertly that she was not even nervous.

The curricle swept up a hill. As they topped its crest, a blast of wind hit them, carrying on it agitated, unintelligible shouts.

A little valley lay before them, with a narrow river meandering through it. The slopes leading down to the water were cultivated. Two men who had been laboring in the field on this side of the river threw down their hoes and ran toward a trio of children screaming on the near bank. Two other laborers on the opposite slope had also abandoned their implements and were nearing the water at a run.

"What is it?" Lily shouted at Hawkhurst.

His answer was lost on the wind. The racing curricle closed rapidly on a stone bridge across the river. About twenty yards to the right of it, the three children were standing on the grassy bank. The two laborers on the other side of the water were now directly across from them.

Damon was checking his grays' speed, and he yelled at Lily, "Hold on!" He brought the curricle to an abrupt halt just short of the stone bridge and jumped down.

Instead of running toward the group gathered on the bank, however, he went in the opposite direction, shedding his brown coat, white waistcoat, neckcloth, and shirt as he ran.

Lily scrambled down from the curricle. Grabbing

her discarded hat from the seat, she ran to the bridge.

As she reached it, Hawkhurst was at the water's edge, ten yards downstream, yanking off his boots. Looking upstream, Lily glimpsed a little boy caught in a patch of crowfoot and pond weeds about fifteen feet from shore. Even as she watched, the water swept the child free and into the middle of the channel where the current was strongest. He flailed frantically in the water, clearly unable to swim.

The helpless groans and curses from the agitated onlookers told Lily that none of them could either. She lost sight of the boy as he was swept under the arch of the stone bridge.

Hawkhurst dived into the river. With powerful strokes he cut through the water. A cry of hope went up from the onlookers gathered on the bank.

Lily's long, fiery hair, freed by the wind from its restraints, tumbled about her and the breeze blew stray strands across her face. She gathered the long tresses up and ruthlessly stuffed them under the crown of her hat to hold them.

The little boy, barely struggling now, emerged from beneath the bridge. She saw that Hawkhurst had gauged the speed of the river's current so accurately that the child very nearly floated into his arms. Grabbing the boy beneath the arms, he pushed back toward shore.

But the current was powerful and the panicked child began to struggle against him. Burdened as he was, he could seem to make no progress against the swift water.

As he and the child were carried farther downstream, Lily's heart seemed to stop. She was so terrified that both man and child would be swept away that she had to stuff her fist into her mouth to keep from crying aloud. She could not bear to have anything happen to Damon.

In that moment, she realized with shattering clarity how desperately she loved him. She had thought that she had loved him in Bath, but it was nothing compared to what she felt for him now.

She watched, hardly daring to breathe, as he struggled against the current for what seemed like an eternity.

At last, however, he escaped the worst of it and was able to swim steadily toward shore.

Relief surged through Lily with such intensity that for a moment she could not move. Then she ran from the bridge toward the spot where he would emerge. As she went, she gathered up the clothes that he had shed willy-nilly during his sprint to the river.

Reaching shallow water, Hawkhurst found his footing, stood up, lifted the child out of the water, and carried him up the bank where he deposited him.

The boy, a thin lad of perhaps six years, with hair that was wispy and coppery in color, was sneezing and choking and coughing out water, then wheezing and gulping air.

Hawkhurst called to Lily, "Give me my neckcloth."

She complied. He knelt beside the boy and used it to dry his mouth, face, and body.

As Damon worked, Lily stared in helpless admiration at the sight of his powerful bronzed chest with its glistening black hair curling wetly in abstract patterns.

The children who had been on the bank ran to them. One boy looked to be the same age as the victim, while the other boy and a little girl were younger. The younger boy had hair that was the same copper shade as the child Damon had rescued, and Lily guessed that he was his brother. They gaped silently at the earl as he worked.

The laborers rushed up, staring in amazement at the tableau before them. Lily heard one of the men whisper wonderingly to the others, "Snatched the nipperkin from the jaws of death, he did, and now look at him. Most high-and-mighty swells like himself would not bother with the brat."

The man was right, and her heart swelled with love for Damon. After a fortnight beneath his roof, seeing his patience with his exasperating relatives, his concern for his retainers, and his kindness to her and her sister, Lily knew that her first impression of him in Bath had been correct. He was not at all like other greenroom gallants.

The boy was shivering, and when Damon finished drying him, he told Lily, "Now my coat."

Quickly he wrapped the child in the expensive Devonshire-brown coat to warm him, heedless of the damage to it from the boy's wet clothes.

The boy began to cry. Damon gathered the forlorn little creature in his arms and comforted him with soft, reassuring words.

Lily's heart turned over at how kind and gentle Damon was with him. She suspected he would make a fine father. His children would not suffer at his hands as he had at his parents'.

Her heart ached for Damon as she thought of his boyhood: an unloved, lonely child, rebuffed by one parent and trying desperately to measure up to the demands of the other, who only criticized and did not praise. How different her own childhood had been, and she felt blessed to have had parents who had lavished love and accolades on their children.

Lily began to understand why Damon did not believe in love. How could he when he had never known it?

Much later, as they rode back to Hawkhill, Lily repeated the laborer's remark to him.

"I could not let a child die if I had the smallest

hope of preventing it," he said. "Especially not when he is the son of one of my dependents. They are my responsibility."

Yes, his unloving mother had trained him well. Lily cast a covert, sidelong glance at him, at his mouth and at the long tapering hands that had brought her such exquisite pleasure that night in Bath. The memory of it warmed her like fine brandy.

But not once since she had been at Hawkhill had he sought an encore of that night. Yearning rippled through her for his kiss, his embrace.

And for more.

After Trude left Lily that night, she was far too wide awake to consider sleep. She stood at one of the windows of her bedroom, looking out. The moon, a bright crescent in the clear sky surrounded by a million sparkling stars, illuminated the peaceful, rolling grounds of Hawkhill. It was not the estate, however, but its owner that occupied Lily's mind.

As she contemplated the night sky, she heard Hawkhurst's footsteps in the hall on his way to his apartment.

His firm tread paused outside her door.

She held her breath in hopeful anticipation and aching desire. If he sought her now, she would not, could not deny him. She loved him too much.

A long minute passed, and then she heard his steps again, moving on to his apartment at the end of the hall.

He would not come to her. *"I will ask nothing of you in return, I swear."* He was bound by his promise to her in that dank little room in Lowhampton.

She smiled a little sadly to herself. She had doubted him then, but she had been too desperate for Sarah's sake to turn down his offer of shelter. Now she knew that Damon would never go back on his word, no matter how much he might like to. *"If I am to be judged, let it be on my integrity."*

If they were to make love again, she would have to take the first step.

But did she want to do that?

Lily swallowed hard at the choice facing her. She loved him so much, but he did not believe in love between a man and a woman.

Who could blame him for that, or for his suspicion of women? His mother had not loved him, his stepmother had hated him. He was the prey of ambitious women who he believed sought him for his title or wealth or the celebrity he could bring them.

Lily wanted to teach Damon the joy of love as he had taught her the joy of passion that night in Bath.

But even if she succeeded and he could come to love her, he still could offer her no more than a temporary liaison. It was perfectly acceptable for him to enjoy elastic connections with as many actresses as he wished, but he could not wed one. His title and his station in life precluded him from marrying someone so far beneath him.

His unloving mama had so carefully inculcated in him all the duties and responsibilities that went with his title. Lily had no doubt that one of them was that he must wed a lady of quality worthy of bearing the Earl of Hawkhurst's heir.

Even if Damon were willing to flaunt convention by marrying an actress, society would ostracize him and most likely his offspring as well. Lily could not do that to him.

It was what had happened to her own parents when they had defied their families to wed. She remembered how painful it had been for them, especially her father when former friends had given him the cut direct. Had her parents' love not been so strong, it would not have withstood the strain.

Lily loved Hawkhurst too much to cause him to

become a pariah. She sighed. If only he were not an earl, perhaps they would have found happiness together—but his title made that impossible.

So where did that leave her? The cautious, sensible, realistic part of her warned that she was a fool to chase a love that could only end unhappily for her.

But her heart wanted more than anything for Hawkhurst to know that for once in his life he was truly loved by a woman for himself alone.

They would only have a few short weeks together before she must leave for her engagement at Covent Garden, but she would make the most of them. When she left him, she would ask nothing of him, accept nothing from him.

Until she had fallen in love with Damon, she had thought a woman a fool to become a man's mistress for then she had not even the meager protection that a wife enjoyed. But now Lily understood why a woman would accept less than marriage with the man she loved. When she loved him as much as Lily loved Damon, and marriage was impossible, what else was she to do?

He had no wife who would be hurt by their affair. No, only Lily would be hurt.

She put on her green silk wrapper over her sheer lawn night rail, secured it around her, and waited by her door.

Lily heard Damon's valet leave his master's chamber. After his steps had faded down the hall, a profound silence settled over the house. The only sound was that of a night bird somewhere beyond her open window. Still, she waited, wanting to be certain that everyone had retired for the night.

Finally, tightening her wrapper about her, she opened her door a little and peeked out. Only two candles had been left burning in the sconces along the hall, but it was enough light for her to ascertain that no one was about.

Damon's door was at the end of the hall. Only one room lay between it and hers.

Yet suddenly it seemed so far away. What if someone were to come into the hall? The thought made her face grow hot.

It was not that possibility, however, but the question of what Damon's reaction would be that brought a hot flush of embarrassment to her cheeks. Lily had never before in her life sought a man's attentions, and she felt awkward and uncertain.

What would she say to him?

What if she had misinterpreted the message in his hooded eyes?

What if he rejected her overture?

Knowing that she would lose her nerve if she hesitated another instant, she nudged her slippers off and walked silently in her bare feet to his door. She tapped lightly.

After an agonizing moment in which she very nearly fled back to her room, Damon opened the door.

His dark eyes widened in surprise when he saw her there, and her courage failed her.

She would have turned and fled, but he was too quick for her. He caught her in his arms and whirled her into the room, shutting the door behind her.

Lily would remember the look he gave her for the rest of her days. It vanquished all her doubts.

Nor had she needed to worry about what she would say to him for he gave her no chance to say anything.

Instead he claimed her mouth in a long kiss, so full of passion and hunger that she melted in his arms. She buried her fingers in his thick, dark hair, and returned his kiss as torridly as he gave it.

When at last he lifted his head, his smile took her

breath away. "You don't know how I have longed for you to come to me like this." His voice was rich and husky with emotion. "I thought I would go mad I wanted it so much."

He lifted her hair, swirling loose and unbound around her shoulders, and appreciation gleamed in his dark eyes. "How lovely it is—like a fire fall."

He was wearing a banyan of figured silk fastened with a wide belt at the waist. The open V of its neck gave her a tantalizing glimpse of the midnight-black hair that curled on his chest.

He kissed her again while his quick fingers undid the buttons of her night rail. He dropped his mouth to her neck, nibbling provocatively at it.

Desire flared deep within her, and he stoked its flames, sliding his hand beneath her wrapper and night rail to caress her breast as he teased its crest with his thumb.

She slipped her fingers beneath the silk of his banyan and ran them lovingly over his chest, delighting in the contrasting textures of his curling hair and warm skin. He groaned with pleasure, his hands moving urgently down to the tie of her wrapper.

Her fingers, suddenly clumsy, fumbled unsuccessfully with the two buttons that fastened the belt of his banyan.

He untied her wrapper and pushed both it and her night rail from her shoulders. They fell about her feet.

His eyes glittered with a strange wildness as she stood naked before him. She blushed beneath his gaze and instinctively started to wrap her arms protectively around her, but he caught her wrists and brought them up around his neck. He held her against his hard body, and she felt the swell of his passion through the silk of his banyan.

Suddenly she wanted to feel his warm skin against

her own. She drew back to seek again the buttons that held his banyan.

He misunderstood the reason for her movement. "Did I frighten you?" he asked in concern. "I cannot hide my desire for you."

"No, I want nothing between us," she said, finally managing to undo the belt.

He drew in his breath sharply. "Nor do I, my lovely Lily." He shucked the banyan away and held her tightly against him. His hands caressed her hair and her back and her derriere.

"Why did you come to me tonight?" His breath as he spoke was soft and warm against her cheek. "Much as I want you, I do not wish you to give yourself to me out of gratitude."

She laughed shakily. "Gratitude has nothing to do with it." She wanted to tell him the real reason: that she loved him desperately.

But he did not believe in love, and she was afraid he might mock her with one of his sardonic comments.

No, she could not tell him of her love. Not yet. She would have to teach him what love was before she could speak of hers for him.

Smiling up at him, she said softly, "Oh, Damon, can't you tell that I want you as much as you want me?"

Hawkhurst gently touched her secret place, and he found in the nectar profusely bathing it confirmation of her words. The discovery of how lushly her body welcomed him was too much for his own self-control. It was all he could do to get her to his bed.

When she lay on it, he wanted to make it slow and marvelous for her, but she reached out for him with a hunger that matched his own. He could withstand the temptation of her lovely body no longer.

When he parted her thighs and entered her, she

surged to meet him. They moved together in the timeless rhythm of love. She felt so good, so warm and tight around him that he could no longer forestall his satisfaction.

As he gave in to it, he felt her body stiffen and convulse around him, responding to him with a fiery passion that matched his own and heightening his own exquisite pleasure.

After the tremors that shook them subsided, Damon remained joined with her. She stroked his back lovingly, and languid contentment stole over him.

The unbidden thought came to him that this was where he belonged always, in Lily's arms.

After a while, though, they separated, and he rolled on his side, facing her. She raised her head a little from the pillows and curiously inspected his room, lit by a silver candelabra on his bedside table. He had given her no chance to look around it earlier. His need for her had been too intense.

He had furnished the room for comfort rather than elegance. From the massive tester bed in which they lay to the large chairs, it was clearly a man's room, without any feminine frills to soften it.

"It is very masculine," she whispered, "just like you."

Hawkhurst's breath caught as she ran her fingers appreciatively over the muscles of his shoulders.

He took her in his arms and pressed the full length of his body to hers, loving the feel of her silken skin against his own. His mouth nuzzled her temple. "I am so happy you came to me tonight."

She pulled her head back a little to look at him. "So am I." The smile she gave him was dazzling.

"I dreamed of how it would be if only I could have you in my bed again," he confessed ruefully. "I promised myself that I would make such slow and tender love to you that you would be begging me. Then at last you came to me, and I was so wild for you I could not contain myself. I had to have you at once. I am sorry."

"I'm not." Her emerald eyes were dancing with pure mischief. "But you might show me now what I missed."

And he did. He used his mouth and his tongue and his hands to pleasure her everywhere until she was writhing in aching need. "Please, Hawkhurst, please," she begged.

He took her, and they rode a wave of passion cresting higher, ever higher, until they were left gasping and spent by its stunning force.

Afterward Hawkhurst sighed in supreme contentment. Lily was as honest and open in her passion as she was about everything else.

Yes, he thought again, he did belong in Lily's arms.

For the rest of his life.

This thought caused him to blink in surprise. For the first time, he understood why a man would propose marriage to a woman for any reason other than the dynastic and financial advantages of the union.

But he could not marry Lily.

One of the inescapable responsibilities that accompanied his title was contracting a suitable marriage with a high-bred lady to bear him an heir of impeccable bloodlines.

The thought cast a dark shadow over his happiness. He swallowed hard, and tightened his grip on Lily. She had fallen asleep.

Hawkhurst lay there, much troubled, listening to her deep and even breathing. He would keep her with him tonight, but he would return her to her own bed before anyone could notice her missing from it. And to prevent chance of discovery, he would take her through the room that lay between his and hers rather than use the hall.

Lily had won the liking and respect of his servants, and he did not want to cost her that. He could not give her his name, but he did not want her to suffer any hint of unpleasantness or disapproval because he could not. He would protect her in every way he could, but it was so much less than he wanted to give her.

It was a long time before he fell asleep.

Chapter 22

Damon, dressed in buckskin breeches and chocolate riding coat, strode briskly down Hawk-hill's marble staircase with the smile of a man well-satisfied with life.

And why shouldn't he be? Waking up in Lily's bed each morning the past week could not fail to make him feel right with the world.

The day's post, a half dozen letters, had arrived and lay in the hall on an elegant tulipwood table inset with marquetry. He leafed through them idly. His ebullient mood ended abruptly when he reached the final letter in the pile. It was addressed to Mrs. Lily Culhane and carried Sir Roger Hilton's name as sender.

Jealousy stabbed at Hawkhurst. He told himself sternly that he was a fool to be upset when he did not even know the letter's contents. He went into the breakfast parlor, but the letter seemed to have wrecked his appetite, and he walked out again.

Lily was still in her room, and he decided to take the letter up to her himself.

When she answered his knock, he handed it to her, saying curtly, "Your 'family friend' has written." Would Lily use the same term to describe Damon to another gentleman admirer?

She took the letter from him eagerly.

Too eagerly, Hawkhurst thought sourly. He stepped inside her room and closed the door behind him.

She broke the wafer and scanned the letter's contents. By the time she finished reading it, she was glowing.

Hiding his trepidation, Hawkhurst asked tonelessly, "What is on Handsome Roger's mind?"

Lily's face was radiant. "Marriage."

Whatever answer he had expected that was not it. And damn her, she seemed so overjoyed about it.

"Oh, Damon," she assured him eagerly, "he will make such a wonderful husband! I know he will. He is strong and dependable and kind. His wife will be a most fortunate woman indeed to have such a fine man."

Hawkhurst was numbed by shock. So Lily would consider herself fortunate to leg-shackle the man, would she? Well, Handsome Roger would soon consider himself fortunate if Hawkhurst did not kill him.

"I am persuaded that when you meet him, Damon, you will heartily approve of him."

Not bloody likely! Hawkhurst's shock gave way to a volatile mixture of fury, jealousy, and incredulity. Lily was acting as though she wanted him to give his blessing to her marrying Roger. Damon rarely had difficulty keeping his temper in check except when Lily was involved, and then it seemed to ignite like tinder, destroying his normally rational mental processes.

He said scornfully, "But Handsome Roger is a lowly baronet."

Lily looked at Damon in alarm and dismay. She had not for an instant believed Phoebe's protestation that he would not permit her to wed a man of lesser rank than a marquess, but now it appeared that might be the case.

Damon's expression when she told him that marriage was Sir Roger's purpose had warned her he did not like the idea, and she had rushed to add her own glowing recommendation that the baronet would make an excellent husband for Phoebe or any other woman.

Lily had thought her endorsement would help sway Damon in Roger's favor, but clearly it had not impressed him at all. Somehow she had to persuade him that marriage to Roger, lowly baronet or not, would be the best thing for Phoebe.

"I am disappointed that you would look down upon Sir Roger because he is only a baronet," Lily said quietly. "You should not. His fortune is very comfortable, and he has a handsome estate. His wife will be well taken care of. Her future will be very secure."

"And what of our future together?"

His question was so far removed from the subject they were discussing that she said, "I do not understand why you ask that. If we are honest with ourselves, we both know that we can have no future together."

"Unless I marry you?"

Lily was confounded by this turn in their conversation. "But marriage is out of the question for us, Damon; an earl cannot possibly marry an actress," she said earnestly. "I neither want nor expect that of you."

He frowned. "Then what do you propose we do?"

"What we've been doing. What else can we do?"

Lily sounded so sincere and accepting of this unhappy fact that Hawkhurst could not doubt she meant it. He suddenly felt ashamed. When he himself could not offer her marriage, what right did he have to deny her a respectable union if that was what she truly wanted? Yet the thought of it made him want to grind his teeth in rage, and he demanded through clenched jaw, "What will Sir Roger think of our affair?"

"It is none of his concern."

"None of your husband's concern! Are you mad?"

Hawkhurst saw dawning comprehension brighten Lily's face. "No, you are! Roger does not want to marry me!"

He frowned. "But—"

Lily interrupted, "Oh, Damon, what a ninnyhammer I am. I was so eager to convince you what a fine husband Roger would make that I neglected to tell you it is Phoebe he wants to marry."

"Phoebe?" he asked, nonplussed. "Why would he want to do that?"

Lily looked exasperated. "Honestly, Damon, you act as though she were an antidote, but she is lovely little thing, even though she may not be in your style."

Damon grinned. "Yes, a beautiful, tearful, boring pea-goose." His relief was so intense that he felt light-headed. He did not give a damn who Sir Roger married so long as it was not Lily.

She chuckled. "I told you in Bath that Sir Roger has a marked taste for helpless, clinging females."

"Like my father."

"From all I have heard of him, Roger is far superior," Lily retorted. "I am sorry, I did not mean to insult your father, but I think you will find Roger quite different. I am persuaded that he is precisely the sort of man Phoebe needs, and she is wildly in love with him."

"Is she now?" Hawkhurst asked in amusement. "Tell me, my sweet, how did she come to meet this 'lowly baronet'? Matchmaking were we?"

Her color heightened a little. "Well, yes," she admitted, "but it was you who gave me the idea. Remember that day you saw me with him? You said that I should introduce him to Phoebe.''

''So you took me at my word and did so.''

''Although you oppose her marrying a lowly baronet, Sir Roger is—''

He interrupted, ''Why would you think I would oppose her marrying a respectable man of good character who would make her happy?''

''Because you said you would not permit her to marry anyone of lesser rank than a marquess.''

''I said nothing of the sort! As if that were any measure of a man's worth as a husband!''

Lily looked utterly confused. ''Did you not reject several petitions for her hand?''

''Yes, but only because she clearly disliked all of them except for Lord Raynes. I was less certain about him, but when I asked her whether she wanted to marry him, she assured me she did not. That is why I rejected his suit, not because he lacked a lofty title.''

''But her mother told her that you would not permit—''

''Ah, the mystery is solved. I told you that Lady Effington was determined that Phoebe should marry even higher the second time. She favored the old Marquess of Leishmore, a sorry libertine even older than my father and sinking into his dotage, but very rich. It was clear that poor Phoebe was even more frightened of him than she was of my father, and I secretly put an end to his attentions.'' He grinned. ''Fortunately, her mama never discovered my role in the matter.''

''You truly do not object to Sir Roger?''

''I cannot say for certain until I have met him. What I do not understand is why, if he wants to marry her, he has not come to me himself.''

''Phoebe convinced him that you would never agree to it.''

"It would not matter if I did not. I have no control over her."

"But Phoebe and Roger think you do. Her mama insisted that under the terms of the marriage settlement with your father, your permission is required for her to remarry. Roger calls it a barbaric stipulation in his letter."

"And it would be were it true. I will write and ask him to call on me."

Lily smiled happily. "Phoebe was convinced you would not permit her to marry him. That is why she has been so tearful around you since she returned from Bath. She will be ecstatic."

"In the unlikely event I do not approve of Handsome Roger, I would prefer you say nothing to her about this until I have met him."

Lily agreed, but she frowned a little anxiously.

Hawkhurst gently brushed her cheek with his fingertips. "Do not look so distressed. If Handsome Roger is what you say, I shall be delighted to have him take Phoebe off my hands. The poor child deserves some happiness. She had none with my father."

Lily caught Damon's hand and squeezed it. "Phoebe seriously misjudged you." She gave him an arch look. "As you once again misjudged me. How could you think that I wanted to marry Roger?"

"Oh, I did not think you *wanted* to marry him."

She looked puzzled. "I don't understand."

"I thought you must be trying to manipulate me into marrying you by threatening to wed him if I did not."

Her eyes were suddenly blazing green fire. "How could you think such a thing of me?"

"Because you drive me mad," he said simply, "and I am no longer rational."

He then did the most rational thing he could think of. He kissed her long and hard to smother any further recriminations on her part.

* * *

Sir Roger Hilton arrived at Hawkhill five days later in response to Damon's summons. As luck would have it, Phoebe had left on a round of afternoon calls with Cassandra and Amy only minutes before he appeared at the door.

The two men closeted themselves in the library while Lily waited upstairs with Sarah.

Lily decided that it was just as well Phoebe was away. Were she aware that Damon and Roger were meeting, she would most likely work herself into strong hysterics.

As the afternoon faded away, Lily began to fear that the two men had not hit it off and that Damon would not agree to the match. If that were the case, she hoped Roger would be gone before Phoebe returned.

Finally, after nearly two hours, Hawkhurst came to Sarah's door. He laughed when he saw Lily's apprehensive face.

"Don't look so worried. I like Handsome Roger, and I have no objections to the match. It is all Phoebe's decision now. I will talk to her as soon as she returns."

"Where is Sir Roger?"

"Changing out of his traveling clothes so that he will be more presentable when he sees Phoebe. Come for a walk with me."

They got only as far as the hall when Lady Hawkhurst and her stepdaughters returned.

"Come into the library with me, Phoebe," Damon said. "You too, Lily, since this is partly your doing."

Phoebe followed him into the library, her expression terrified and her eyes filling with tears.

Damon told her, "I have had an offer for your hand, Phoebe, and you must tell me whether you wish to accept it."

Her face crumpled, and she began to sob into her handkerchief. "From . . . Lord . . . Leishmore."

"Good God, no," Damon said in exasperation. "I sent that old goat packing months ago. I knew he would be unacceptable to you."

That surprised her into raising her head. "You . . . did?" she stammered, tears still running down her cheeks. "But Mama said . . ."

"Mama was wrong," he said briskly. "What I want to discover now, Phoebe, is whether you wish to accept an offer from Sir Roger Hilton."

She gaped at him. "But you would never permit me—"

"Phoebe, it is your decision, not mine. I would be well pleased by the match, but only if it is what you want."

Her face reminded Lily of the sun emerging from behind black storm clouds. "Oh, yes, it is what I want more than anything on earth! How could you think it would not be?"

"You must forgive my lamentable obtuseness," Damon said with a grin, "but let me be the first to wish you happy, Phoebe."

"Thank you!" she cried, throwing her arms around him and hugging him to her, her face luminescent with joy. "Oh, thank you!"

She floated out of the room with Lily in her wake.

Cassandra was waiting in the hall. "What did Hawkhurst want with—"

The rest of her question was drowned out by Phoebe's elated shriek as Sir Roger appeared at the top of the staircase.

Seeing her, he bounded down the steps. As he reached the bottom, he asked, "Are we betrothed, my pet?"

"Yes, oh, yes!" she cried.

He opened his arms to her, and she propelled herself into them.

"Phoebe, you are a fool!" Cassandra screeched. "Hawkhurst will never permit you to marry him."

"To the contrary," her brother said, appearing in the doorway of the library, "she has my blessing."

Cassandra turned on him in a rage. "How can you, Hawkhurst? How can you let her marry him?"

Four pairs of astonished eyes stared at her.

"You are doing so merely to disoblige me, aren't you, you hateful man?" she shrieked at her brother.

"What other reason could I possibly have?" he asked ironically.

"It wasn't enough that you robbed me of my inheritance," she screamed. "It wasn't enough that you drove away a wonderful man who adored me and wanted to marry me, but now you have done *this* to me!"

Cassandra turned, pushed past Phoebe and Roger, and fled up the stairs. Hawkhurst, his face grim, stepped back into the library, shutting the door hard.

"That female is demented," Roger muttered as he turned back to Phoebe.

Lily was inclined to agree with him.

Mrs. Nesmith, who had come into the hall during Cassandra's tirade, bustled up to Lily. "What was that about? Who is the man with Lady Hawkhurst?"

Lily drew the housekeeper into a small withdrawing room to give Phoebe and Roger a few moments of privacy.

"He is the man Lady Hawkhurst loves. Lord Hawkhurst gave his permission for them to wed, but Lady Cassandra has the silly notion that he did so simply to disoblige her. She also accused Lord Hawkhurst of stealing her inheritance."

"She didna have an inheritance to steal. Her papa cut her out of his will—not that there was much left to inherit. The young master's wealth came from his grandfather, his mama's father, not from his own."

"Why did the old earl disinherit Lady Cassandra?"

"I dinna know for sure, but I think she reminded the old earl too much of her mama who had caused him so much misery. She was separated from the old earl when she died. Lady Cassandra had been living with her, and he wouldna let the lass come back here. Instead he paid her mama's sister in Lancashire to keep her. She hated it there. They didna get on, although the aunt was willing to keep her so long as she was paid. After the old earl died, Cassandra begged the young master to allow her to come back to Hawkhill. He talked to Lady Effington, and she agreed to let Cassandra live at the dower house with her and her daughter and Lady Amy."

"It seems to me that Lady Cassandra should be grateful to Lord Hawkhurst."

"Aye, she ought, but that dinna mean she is," Mrs. Nesmith replied sourly. "Were it not for the young master, she would have been forced to seek employment as a governess or paid companion instead of enjoying a London come-out."

When Hawkhurst came to Lily's room that night after the rest of the household had retired, he kissed her long and hard, then said with a smile, "Well, my lovely matchmaker, you should be proud of your latest success. I believe Phoebe and Roger will suit very well. I hardly recognized her at dinner."

"That is because you have never seen her happy before."

Lily had brushed out her hair, and it swirled around her in a fiery fall. Damon combed his fingers through it, and she shivered with pleasure.

"I love your hair when it is down like this," he murmured. Then a teasing light gleamed in his dark eyes. "Now that you have rid me of Phoebe, perhaps you could do the same with Cassandra."

"That will be considerably more difficult. Such an unpleasant creature. I confess I was delighted she refused to come down to dinner tonight. Is it true that you rejected the suit of a man who loved her?"

Damon's hands stilled in Lily's hair. "No, that allegation is wrong on two counts: I did not reject Vernon Manchester, and he did not love her."

Lily gasped at the name. Even she had heard of Vernon Manchester. "But he was one of London's most infamous fortune hunters, and I understood Cassandra has none."

"She does not." Damon absently twisted a lock of Lily's hair around his finger. "In fact, she has nothing. My father disinherited her, but Manchester was unaware of that until he came to me, seeking to know the extent of her fortune. I am afraid Cassandra was guilty of leading him on in that regard."

"What a fool she is!" Lily exclaimed.

"Once Manchester learned the truth, he never brought up the subject of marriage, for which I was thankful. Much as I would like to be rid of Cassandra, I could not let her wed such a man."

"I heard he married last year."

"Yes, to a sweet innocent whose fortune met his expectations. He has banished her to the country, and he now lives in her London house with his mistress, a very expensive bird of paradise." He smiled wryly at her. "When I see a scoundrel like Manchester, I can understand your distaste for ceding control of your life to a man." Damon smoothed Lily's hair gently.

She smiled at him. "Surely, Cassandra can see—"

"No," he said wearily, "she has convinced herself that Manchester only married the girl because he was so distraught over my denying him her hand. If he had only been permitted to marry her, they would be living happily."

If Hawkhurst had been talking of anyone but his

sister, Lily would have been incredulous that she could have so deluded herself; but Lily had never met anyone who was as determined as Cassandra to see only what she wanted to see.

"Why does she accuse you of robbing her of her inheritance when it was your father who cut her off?"

Damon's hands dropped away from Lily's hair, and he sighed. "She is convinced that I persuaded him to do so. I did not. The truth is he was so badly under the hatches when he died that there was very little to leave her even if he had not cut her off."

"Then why did he bother to do so?"

He shrugged. "I think partly because she reminded him so much of her mother and partly because he was trying to make up for his injustice to me by leaving me what little was left."

Lily observed, "Without a dowry, it will be very difficult for a girl of Cassandra's limited charms to find a husband."

"If a suitable man presents himself, I shall provide for her, but so far that has not happened."

Lily brushed his cheek comfortingly. "What a trial she must be for you."

"Yes," he admitted. "If only she did not remind me so much of her mother. Sometimes I swear I hear Olivia speaking through Cassandra's mouth."

The hatred in his eyes as he spoke of Olivia was so intense that Lily asked, "What was she like?"

His thick brows knit in a scowl. "The devil born as a woman. She was very clever. My mother scorned my father for his ineptitude, and Olivia was very careful to make him feel superior. She convinced him to marry her less than a week after my mother died."

"I heard that she persuaded your father to send you to your grandfather."

"Yes, she did." His mouth hardened at the memory. "I was devastated at the time because Father did not want me."

Lily's heart ached for the young Damon, the neglected, unloved child of a loveless marriage who became the victim of a cruel, manipulative woman. She took his hand in hers and pressed it against her cheek in a gesture of comfort.

His mouth twisted in a sad little smile. "Actually Olivia did me a great favor. Although my father had never shown any interest in me, my grandfather doted on me, and I adored him. The years I spent with him were the happiest of my youth."

"You said your father hated you for a time. Was that the period you were talking about?"

She felt him stiffen at her question, and he pulled his hand from hers. "No," he said bleakly, "that came later when I was twenty-one, although it was still Olivia who was responsible."

"How?" Lily asked. He had refused to tell her before and, for a moment, she thought he would not do so now either.

But he said through clenched jaw, "She told him that I had tried to rape her."

"How horrible!" Lily cried, aghast. "How could she?"

"What was horrible was that my father believed her."

"How could *he*?"

"Aren't you even going to ask me if it is true?"

"I don't need to!" Lily exclaimed, putting her arms around him and giving him a quick, fierce hug. "I know you."

That drove some of the terrible bleakness from his eyes. "Thank you."

"What really happened?"

"After my grandfather died, she tried to seduce me. Her sudden interest in me coincided with my inheritance of Grandpapa's vast fortune." The cynicism in his voice made Lily wince. "I ordered her out of my house."

"And in retaliation, she told your father that you had attacked her."

He held Lily to him, resting his cheek against her temple. "Perhaps revenge was part of it, but I suspect Olivia feared that I might tell him what she had done. I would not have. I saw no point in causing him pain. But it was precisely what she would have done in my place. She no doubt thought that if she could tell him first, he would be more likely to believe her version. And she was right."

Lily was nauseated by the woman's behavior. No wonder Damon had such contempt for women and so much difficulty trusting them. She was amazed that he could be so patient with Olivia's daughter.

Damon lifted his head, and Lily looked up into his tormented eyes, as black now as a stormy night.

"It was a long time before Father would believe the truth." The muscle in Damon's jaw, always a barometer of his anger, twitched. "By then, she had had so many lovers that he could no longer deny what she was. Also, unknown to her, Waymore was staying with me the night she came to my house to seduce me. He overheard it all. When he judged my father was finally willing to listen to the truth, he told him."

"Did he believe Waymore?"

"Yes, my father never permitted her in his presence again." He gave a distasteful grimace. "I despise talking about her."

He took Lily's face gently in his hands. "In fact, my sweet, I do not wish to talk at all. I yearn for another form of communication."

"So do I," she admitted, as his hands dropped down to remove her wrapper.

Chapter 23

Amy came to Lily the next day and begged her to talk to Cassandra. "She is carrying on so and saying such dreadful things about Hawk that I cannot bear it. Perhaps you can reason with her."

Lily would have preferred not to try, but she was very fond of Amy and could not deny her request.

Going up to Cassandra's room, Lily found her angry and defiant and still clinging to the nonsensical conviction that Hawkhurst had approved of Phoebe's marriage to Roger merely to prevent his sister from having a London season.

"He is determined to keep me from marrying," she complained in her querulous voice that so grated on Lily's ear.

"Why would he want to do that?"

"Because he hates me! He wants to deny me what I want most: a husband and family of my own. Mama warned me it is what he would do. He poisoned Papa against her and me." Cassandra's needle-chin jutted angrily. "It was because of the lies he told about Mama that Papa would have nothing more to do with us and sent us away. That is why he would not let me live with him after Mama died."

Lily knew that it was her mama who had done the

poisoning, but unfortunately she had poisoned her daughter as well.

Cassandra was sprawled on a yellow damask sofa and Lily sat down beside her.

"Hawkhurst robbed me of my portion," Cassandra whined. "Because of his lies, Papa left me with nothing."

It infuriated Lily to hear the girl, who should have been grateful to Damon for what he had done for her, disparage him so unfairly. Nevertheless, she kept her voice calm as she asked, "What makes you think Lord Hawkhurst was responsible for that?"

"Mama told me. She warned me before she died that he was determined to ruin me as he had her."

Lily, looking at Cassandra's expensive brocade wrapper and the elegant furnishings of her bedchamber, pointed out, "You are hardly living in poverty and deprivation. For a man who is required to give you nothing, your brother is very generous to you."

Cassandra sniffed. "It is the least he can do."

Was the girl grateful for nothing?

"I know that he wants nothing more than to be rid of me."

"And who could blame him," Lily retorted acidly, "given the way you act toward him?" The provoking creature was long overdue for a healthy dose of truth, and Lily decided to give it to her.

"Furthermore, you contradict yourself, Lady Cassandra. First, you accuse your brother of wanting to keep you a spinster, then you accuse him of wanting nothing so much as to be rid of you. What better way to be rid of you than to marry you off? You cannot have it both ways. Which is it?"

It was clear from the girl's surprised expression that she herself had never considered the inconsistencies in her allegations against her brother.

"It is time that you faced up to the reality of your

situation, Lady Cassandra. Your father cut you off with nothing. Nor did he ask his son to care for you. Were it not for your brother's kindness in taking you in, you would be forced to earn your own way, and you would not find it pleasant."

Cassandra looked at Lily as though she were a coiled snake.

"The truth is that you are entirely dependent on your brother, and he is under no obligation to do anything for you. Quite frankly, the way you talk about him he would be justified in turning you out tomorrow."

The girl's bravado crumbled, and she began crying. For once her tears were genuine and not artifice. As her sobs subsided, Lily slowly, patiently drew from her various admissions that unconsciously revealed considerably more than she suspected.

Cassandra was truly terrified that she would end up a spinster, and she regarded a London season the next spring as her last chance to shackle a husband. Now, without Phoebe to chaperone her, she was certain that her brother would not allow her it.

That she was not married yet was, in her mind, all his fault. Cassandra preferred to blame her brother for all that was wrong in her life rather than to face her own inadequacies.

But Lily discovered that her unhappiness went deeper than that of an unattractive girl yearning for a husband and family of her own. She harbored a deep-seated fear that Hawkhurst would send her back to her aunt's austere home in Lancashire. Yet by acting as she did, she seemed hell-bent on driving him to do what she most feared.

She wailed, "You do not know how dreadful it is to be thrown upon the mercy of someone who hates you."

"That day Lord Waymore's horse reared, I saw

Lord Hawkhurst save your life at the risk of his own," Lily reminded her. "Is that the act of a man who hates you?"

The question clearly nonplussed Cassandra.

"Is it?" Lily pressed.

Instead of answering, Cassandra challenged, "If Hawkhurst doesn't hate me, why would he not let me marry Vernon Manchester?"

"Vernon Manchester! You would consider marrying Vernon Manchester?" Lily inquired in feigned horror. "I am shocked. Do you not know that he was the most infamous fortune hunter in the kingdom? Your brother would have been negligent indeed to permit such a match, although I cannot believe that once Manchester learned you had no fortune, he would have married you."

The look on Cassandra's face told Lily that the girl, in her heart of hearts, had suspected the truth.

Still she insisted sullenly, "Hawkhurst does hate me. I can cry my eyes out, and he pays me no heed."

"Why should he when you shed them only to manipulate him?"

"Mama said tears were the most effective weapon a woman has against a man. They always worked for her."

"Did they now?" Lily asked. "They worked so well that your papa would have nothing more to do with her—or you."

The girl could only stare at Lily in astonishment. Clearly that had not occurred to her before.

"Your brother is no fool, Lady Cassandra, and tears are not an effective weapon against him."

"What is?"

"Why do you think you need one?" Lily countered.

"Mama said every woman must . . ." She broke off, looking stricken.

She would no longer accept her mama's word as gospel, Lily thought with satisfaction.

"Instead of looking for a weapon against Lord Hawkhurst, you would be better advised to try civility." Lily got up to leave. She had given Cassandra enough to think about for one day.

At the door, Lily delivered her final piece of advice. "You might also make some effort to appreciate what Lord Hawkhurst does do for you rather than wail about what you think he does not. Everyone, not just your brother, will like you the better for it."

Cassandra did not emerge from her room until dinner the next night. When she came down to the dining room, her eyes were swollen and red with weeping. She was subdued and quiet and so polite to Damon that he was startled into inquiring whether she was ill.

Lily had not told him of her talk with Cassandra, fearing that it would not affect the girl's behavior, but now she began to hope that it was bearing fruit.

As they were leaving the dining room, Cassandra said quietly to Damon, "I . . . I am sorry I have been so hateful to you. I shall try to be better in the future."

He seemed to appreciate how hard it was for Cassandra to apologize to him, and he said with an encouraging smile, "I should like that. I truly do not wish you any ill, you know."

She looked as though she might at last believe that.

Hawkhurst awoke to the apprehension that something was wrong. It came to him in an instant what it was. He had gone to sleep with Lily in his arms, and she was no longer there. Even as his eyes opened, his mind flashed back to that awful day in Bath.

His eyes flew open. By the pale-gray light of the dawn, he saw to his intense relief that Lily had merely rolled away from him in her sleep. He took a long deep breath and let it slowly out, expelling the panic that had gripped him when he had thought she was gone.

She was lying on her side with her back to him, and he gathered her into his arms. Lily murmured in her sleep and wriggled closer to his warmth. He held her tightly against him, reflecting that he had never known such contentment as when he was with her.

No woman had ever excited him as much as she did. Her passion matched his own. Her response to him was as honest as Lily herself, without artifice or calculation. She was one of the very few females he had known who made no attempt to manipulate him.

Nor had she asked him for anything. Because she had not, he wanted to give her the world. But when he inquired what she would like, she would give him that sensual smile of hers and say, "You, only you." Every other woman he had bedded had always been ready with a long list.

The light was growing brighter. He raised himself on his elbow and looked down at her, admiring the provocative face, the fiery hair fanned across the pillow, and the tempting curves of her body. He could not resist dropping a kiss on her smooth shoulder. She was a remarkable woman, and he wanted to keep her in his bed forever. His desire for her grew more intense each time he took her.

With any other woman, he would have been seeking a way to end the affair by now, but with Lily he was scheming how to keep her.

If only he could marry her. It amazed him to discover how much he wanted that, but it was impossible. It was the Earl of Hawkhurst's duty to make an illustrious marriage, and he had never shirked his familial responsibility. Fortunately, Lily realized as clearly as he did that he could not wed her, and had even told him so.

Smiling down at her, he thought that there was one thing he could do for her, though. She would never again have to perform with an impoverished company of strolling players. Clearly her acting talent was inferior. No actress of any real ability would have been reduced to joining such a ragtag group. Indeed, it surprised him that she had persisted in pursuing an acting career, but then she had a younger sister and brother to support.

Well, she would no longer have to worry. He did not doubt that for all her talk of independence, she would be grateful for that. But knowing her pride, he would have to be diplomatic.

The wisest course would be to say nothing at all to her, to continue on as they were, and he would do everything in his power to make her so happy at Hawkhill that she would be loath to leave it—and him.

They would continue together by unspoken agreement, and he would make Lily his wife in everything but name. He would happily give her everything else that she wanted—and a good deal that she did not. She would be as well taken care of as the most cosseted of wives. It was the only way he knew to assuage his own guilt and pain over not being able to marry her.

But what of children? Lily would make a fine mother. Suddenly he was overcome by a longing to be surrounded by strong sons of Lily's making and fiery-haired daughters with brilliant green eyes.

Fiercely, he banished the image, telling himself harshly that it simply could not be. He wanted no child of his to grow up with the stigma of bastard.

She rolled over and bumped against him. Her eyes

fluttered open, and his heart stopped at her radiant smile when she saw him. Her arms came up, encircled his neck, and pulled him down to her.

Their passion flared, and he sank into her warm, moist, welcoming depths, forgetting all else.

Chapter 24

L ily stood by the window of her room, watching sadly as the darkness settled over the green hills of Devon. The days were growing shorter now, and so was her time at Hawkhill.

Sarah was well. Indeed, she had been sufficiently recovered from her fever for them to have departed days ago, but neither of them wanted to leave. They had both grown to love Hawkhill.

Now they could put off their parting no longer. Sarah's new term at Milton's Academy for Young Ladies would begin in two days, and Lily's contract with Covent Garden called for her to be in London for rehearsals shortly after that.

Lily had said nothing to Damon about leaving or about her future plans because she had not wanted to argue with him during the precious little time they had together. Although he had not told her that he wanted her to stay, Lily was certain that he expected her to do so and would object strenuously to her leaving.

She could put off telling him no longer. But she did not find it easy. When he came to her room, she rationalized that it would be better to wait until after they had made love, and she went willingly into his arms.

Afterward, as they lay joined while their breathing calmed, she hated to disturb the serene peace that enveloped them. She was not normally such a pudding-heart, but she loved Damon so much, and she feared that he would be furious. They would undoubtedly quarrel, and she hated to think of that after they had been so happy together.

She hoped that when his anger cooled, he would agree to join her in London, but she knew from Mrs. Nesmith that he always remained at Hawkhill until well after Christmas.

As Lily struggled to find the words to tell him, he said, "I have an early meeting in Lowhampton tomorrow with Magistrate Rawson. I will try not to awaken you."

It was all the excuse she needed, flimsy as it was, to keep from telling him tonight. He needed his sleep. If she told him now, they might be up half the night arguing. But she would have to do so in the morning before he left for his meeting.

He cuddled her to him. Lily swallowed hard as she contemplated how lonely she would be if she could no longer sleep with his arms about her. His breathing deepened, telling her that he had already fallen asleep.

At least, she thought sadly, she would be leaving Hawkhill a happier house than she had found it. A glowing Phoebe had not cried since the day she was betrothed to Roger, and soon she would be leaving Hawkhill to marry him.

Cassandra had at last accepted that her brother was not her enemy, out to destroy her. She finally understood that her own behavior was responsible for many of the problems she had blamed on him. While it was hard for her to change patterns of thought and conduct instilled in her by her mother, she was trying. Some days she was more successful than others.

When Lily awoke, Damon was already up and

slipping quietly into his banyan for the short walk back to his apartment.

He smiled down at her, that lazy smile that she had come to love so much. "Awake, are we? Good, now I can claim my morning kiss before I leave." He sat down on the bed beside her and his mouth explored hers in leisurely, expert fashion.

Finally he lifted his head reluctantly. "If I do not go at once, Magistrate Rawson will find himself waiting in vain for me."

As he rose from the bed, Lily tugged at his hand. "Please, Damon, before you go, there is something I must tell you."

He was standing now, and she felt at a helpless disadvantage with his tall frame towering above her. She got up, his eyes watching her appreciatively as she grabbed her green silk wrapper and put it on to cover her nakedness.

"I like you better without it," he said huskily.

The warmth in his eyes made her tingle. It also made telling him all the more difficult, but she could postpone it no longer. "Sarah is recovered now," she began, "and the new term at her school is about to start."

He looked unperturbed. "So Sarah will be leaving us?"

"*We* will be leaving you. I must go back to work."

He smiled at her, that glittering, irresistible smile, and his hands gently cupped her face. "No, you don't, my sweet flower. I want you to stay here with me."

Lily wanted that too; wanted it so much that she felt as though she were being torn on a rack. But she could not weaken now.

"Much as I would like that," she said wistfully, "I cannot afford to do so. I have a sister to support as well as myself."

His thumb caressed her lips, making it hard for

her to think. This was going to be even harder than she had feared.

"Don't worry, my sweet. I am not the muckworm Cassandra made me out to be. I will take care of you both."

Lily looked at him in dismay. He sincerely believed that what he was offering her as his mistress was so much better than anything she could achieve on her own. She had hoped that he had gained some understanding of how important her career was to her and some appreciation of how she felt about becoming a kept woman at the mercy of a man's whim.

But clearly he had not understood her at all.

Her voice quavered. "That is not enough."

It was an unfortunate choice of words, she realized when she saw the sudden wariness in his eyes. His hand dropped away from her face.

"What do you want from me, Lily?"

"Nothing!" she cried in frustration. "I am much obliged to you for your kind offer, but I must decline it. I intend to continue to support myself as an actress."

"Don't be a fool, Lily!"

She was dismayed by how clearly affronted he was that she should want to continue acting. It took great effort to keep her voice calm. "Please, Damon, try to understand that I cannot jeopardize my career, which I have worked so hard to establish, for a romantic interlude."

Sudden anger blazed in his eyes. "Your career," he scoffed. "What a sorry thing that is!"

"I am an excellent actress!" she cried, deeply wounded.

"Of course you are," he retorted sarcastically. "That is why you were trudging about the countryside with a destitute troupe of strolling players who could not even afford decent food or lodging."

His scorn raked Lily like the lash of a cat-o'-nine.

So that was what he thought of her acting. Well, he was wrong!

"I am not going back to that!" she told him proudly. "I am going to London. I have an offer from Covent Garden."

His reaction dumbfounded her. She had expected him to be suitably impressed. Instead, he looked horror-struck.

"No!" he exclaimed in great consternation. "You cannot go to London! I forbid it!"

This was a view of Damon that Lily had not seen before: the Lord of Hawkhill at his most autocratic. It fired her own temper, and she cried, "You cannot stop me! I am not your wife!"

His face darkened angrily at her defiance. "You are my mistress."

"No, I am your lover. There is a difference!"

"To you perhaps, but not to me or the rest of the world." The muscle in his jaw twitched furiously. "I will not have you appearing on the London stage while you are living under my protection."

No, Lily thought angrily, he expected her to be always available for him whenever he desired! "Don't worry, I shall not be living under it. Can you not understand? I will not abandon a career I have worked hard for and the independence that I cherish to become a man's toy—not even when that man is you!"

Not even when she loved him so much.

Hawkhurst thought frantically that Lily was the one who did not understand. She was being lured to London with the empty promise of a tryout that would come to naught. She had no idea of the pain and disillusionment that lay ahead of her.

Provincial performers receiving such a bid always thought it meant their great break, their ticket to fame and fortune on the London stage. But for many of them, it meant not elevation to the loftiest heights of the British theatre but a fast slide to oblivion.

The London critics loved to unsheathe their poisoned pens upon these provincial innocents in their tryouts. Even those who gave credible performances were often mocked in the most scathing and viciously funny terms.

The London readers laughed at these malicious comments, the provincial theatregoers and managers believed them, and the poor actor was not only routed from London in humiliation, he was lucky after that to find another position in the provincial theatre. Only an occasional actor of enormous talent managed to survive this critical mayhem to later win a permanent spot with one of those two London theatres.

It would be even worse for Lily. She was clearly a mediocre performer or she would not have been reduced to traveling with that pathetic company of strolling players. Damon could not bear to have her subjected to such cruelty.

He was so desperate to save her from her own folly that he cried, "For God's sake, give it up, Lily! Covent Garden will not have you. You are a fool to think that it will."

She looked as though he had flayed her. He realized that in his eagerness to protect her from ridicule and misery, he had not been as tactful as he should have and had wounded her. He said more gently, "Lily, please, stay here with me. I am offering you so much more!"

"Are you?" There was hurt and antagonism in her tone.

"Yes, Lily, I am." Had she ever lived in such elegant comfort as she had at Hawkhill? Did she not appreciate what they had together? "You will want for nothing."

"Except my freedom!"

"You have been happy here, have you not?"

"Very," she admitted, "but—"

"Then remain here with me. It will be just as it has been."

He was taken aback by the fury in her eyes.

"Oh, but it won't be!" she cried. "Because now you will own me. I will be one more of your possessions. You will think as all men do that you have total control over your chattel for so long as you wish to possess her. Once you tire of me, you will toss me aside as you have all your other mistresses!"

So *that* was what she was really afraid of—that he might someday abandon her. To his agitated mind, it sounded as though she were trying to maneuver him into a permanent union. His deep distrust of women resurfaced.

"What is it you want from me, Lily? Marriage and protestations of everlasting love? I am sorry but, as you yourself have said, I cannot give you the former, and I do not believe in the latter."

"No, you do not believe in love because you do not even know what it is. You are right, I *am* a fool! You do not want a woman who loves you—you want a lapdog obedient to your every command! I will never be that."

She swiped angrily at her eyes that were bright with unshed tears. "Go away before I disgrace myself and cry in front of you."

He was so used to women using tears as a weapon to try to control him that he was touched by her valiant effort to hold hers back. Seeking to lighten the tension between them, he smiled and invited, "Go ahead, cry on my shoulder. I am quite used to tears being shed upon it."

He meant to be humorous, but Lily's expression told him that she had taken it as an insult. Dismayed, he tried to take her in his arms to comfort her, but she pushed him away, reminding him sharply, "You are keeping Magistrate Rawson waiting."

He had forgotten his meeting. He must go. Cursing softly, he turned to leave. "We will discuss this further when I return."

After Hawkhurst left, Lily felt more bereft and alone than she had since the death of her parents. It was one thing to be Damon's lover, but it was quite another to give up her freedom and the security of her career to become his convenient, utterly dependent upon him emotionally and financially. She had seen the fate of all too many women who had followed that path, and she had sworn that she would never walk it.

Yet she was so wildly in love with him that it would take every ounce of determination she possessed to keep from breaking that vow to herself. If she did not get away from Damon immediately, he would persuade her to do as he wanted, and she could not let that happen.

Lily rose from the bed, resolute. She and her sister must leave Hawkhill that very morning. She intended to be packed and ready to go by the time Damon returned. Lily summoned Trude and sent her to ask Mrs. Nesmith to have her trunk brought up.

Within five minutes, the housekeeper herself was at Lily's door, clearly distressed.

"Please, dinna go," she begged. "This house has been a different place since you came. Even Lady Cassandra has improved. And I have never seen the young master so happy as he has been since you have been here. Not to wrap it in clean linen, I was hoping that you and he . . ." The housekeeper's boldness failed her. Her ruddy cheeks grew ruddier still, and she mumbled, "You know what I was hoping."

Lily managed a forlorn smile. "That can never be. He is an earl. He must marry a high-bred lady, and I am not of noble birth."

"There're two kinds of nobility to my thinking, that of birth and that of the heart. The young master needs the latter."

"But he does not think he does," Lily said sadly.

"What is it you want from me, Lily? Marriage and protestations of everlasting love? I cannot give you the former, and I do not believe in the latter."

When Phoebe heard about the departure, she burst into tears, the first time she had done so since her betrothal to Roger. Amy begged Lily and Sarah to stay. Even Cassandra urged them to do so.

But Lily was not to be dissuaded. They were packed and their baggage was strapped to Hawkhurst's carriage, which would transport them into Lowhampton to await the afternoon stage. All that remained was for Damon to return so that she could bid him good-bye.

It would not be easy for her to do. She loved him so much that she was terrified her will would fail her and she would give in to him. She had never understood before how weak love could make a woman. So Lily waited for him by the carriage, determined to stage as public a farewell as possible. She feared that if he managed to get her alone and tried to persuade her with more than words, she would succumb to him.

As Damon rode home from Lowhampton, he cursed himself roundly for having handled the confrontation with Lily so badly. Hell's fire, but she could make him lose his temper and his iron control over himself as no other woman ever had.

Of course, she could not know what terrible memories her announcement that she wanted to try out at Covent Garden had resurrected for him. He had been caught off guard and thrown badly off balance. His usual imperturbable coolness had deserted him. He had felt as though he had been suddenly plunged into the same nightmare a second time.

Damon had been so desperate to stop her from making a fatal mistake that he had seriously overreacted. He had succeeded only in insulting her and making her all the more determined to go.

Hawkhurst reminded himself that Lily was a strong woman. Even if she went to London and was savaged by the critics, it would not destroy her. Still, he wanted to spare her that pain—any pain.

Maybe if he explained to her what was at the heart of his concern, she would forgive him his heavy-handed response. But that would require dredging up a tragic incident he had never discussed with another living soul, and he was loath to do that.

Perhaps it would not be necessary. Surely once Lily's own anger had faded, she would accept what he offered her and remain at Hawkhill.

This hope was shattered when he arrived home and saw his carriage, loaded with baggage, standing in front with Lily beside it. She looked so distressed when she saw him that he could only assume she had hoped to be gone before he returned. This realization wounded him grievously.

Damn her, she had meant to run away from him again as she had in Bath without even so much as a good-bye! How could she be so quick to give up the wonderful reality of what they had together to chase after a cruel, unattainable mirage of fame and fortune on the London stage?

For the second time that day, Damon's iron self-control evaporated, this time in the heat of a wild, consuming fury. After all the happiness that they had shared here, she would—could—still do this to him!

He felt utterly betrayed by the one woman he had

truly trusted, but he would be damned if he would give her the satisfaction of knowing how much she had hurt him. Instead he looked pointedly at the equipage. "I was not aware that I was going on a journey."

Lily's eyes did not quite meet his. "No, you are not, my lord."

"My lord?" He raised a mocking eyebrow. "Really, Lily, such formality between us is unwarranted, don't you think? If I am not going anywhere, why is my carriage here?"

"It is taking Sarah and Trude and me to Lowhampton. We shall catch the stage for London there."

Curse her, how could she have been so willing to walk out of his life without even a farewell? He felt as though she had ambushed him from behind. For the first time in his life, he had found a woman that he believed truly cared for him, not his rank and money, and now she was so eager to abandon him for a cruel illusion that she had not even wanted to wait to say good-bye.

He stepped very close to her and said in a low, withering voice, "How unfortunate that I returned home before you were able to sneak away as you did in Bath. Although I told you I wanted no repayment for my hospitality to you and your sister, a simple thank you and good-bye would have been both courteous and appreciated."

"I was not sneaking away," she protested. "I have been waiting for you to return so that I might bid you farewell."

A slight movement at one of Hawkhill's long windows caused Damon to glance up toward its stately Georgian facade. Draperies suddenly dropped at several windows and faces vanished from others. Every bloody servant in the house must have found himself a spot from which to view this very interesting scene!

That realization made Hawkhurst livid. What did Lily hope to gain by staging this very public farewell? He could feel the muscle in his jaw twitching wildly. What game was she playing with him? What did she want him to do? Beg her on bent knee in front of all his servants not to leave?

The thought that she was as manipulative as every other damn woman made him want to throttle her.

He would be damned if he would gratify his curious servants and every gossip in the shire by being a party to such a scene! It was the kind of public spectacle that Olivia at her most devious and malevolent would have staged.

How could Lily do this to him?

If she wanted to leave, let her leave. She would soon be sorry that she had.

Lily said in a stubborn, defiant voice, ''I shall not be talked out of going.''

''Nor shall I try to do so,'' Damon said icily. ''You will regret leaving soon enough. When you do, come to me, and *perhaps* I will take you back.''

He turned and stomped into the house, telling himself that she would return when her London try-out ended in disaster.

But what if she did not?

Part Three

London

Chapter 25

Hawkhurst's restless gaze swept the elegantly dressed throng gathered in Lady Morton's ornate London ballroom. Jewels sparkled like multicolored stars in the light of three massive crystal chandeliers.

He recognized everyone save a muscular young major, with reddish-brown hair resplendent in dress regimentals. The officer was almost as tall as Hawkhurst. His handsome face with its nobly sculpted brow, nose, and jaw looked vaguely familiar, but Damon could not place it.

A dozen nubile young ladies crowded around the major, gazing adoringly into his gray-green eyes. Although he was smiling politely and chatting amiably with his admirers, Hawkhurst suspected from the set of his jaw that he was uncomfortable. The earl sympathized with him. When he had first been on the town all those years ago, he had been just such a magnet for simpering young ladies of quality, and he had hated it.

"Hawk, it is you!" Lord Waymore said at Damon's elbow. "For a moment I could not believe my eyes. I've never known you to come to London in early November before."

It was true Damon had always preferred to remain at Hawkhill until February, but this year had been

different. Without Lily there, Hawkhill had seemed
strangely cold and empty—yet far too full of memories of her. He could not eat in the dining room
without recalling her laughter, could not sit in the
drawing room without seeing her in a charades skit,
could not pass her bedchamber or enter his own
without remembering the passion and ecstasy that
they had shared in both.

Yes, Hawkhill was haunted by Lily's ghost. Able
to bear it no longer, he had fled to London.

But he had no intention of telling Waymore that.
Instead, he asked, "Who is the young officer over
there who is the center of so much attention?"

"Ah, that is the Duke of Wellington's protegé,
Major James Raleigh. A handsome devil, is he not?
He is the most sought-after man in London these
days. All the young ladies have fallen wildly in love
with him and besiege him at every squeeze."

"James Raleigh," Damon mused. "Why is the
name familiar?"

"Probably because he was the hero of Toulouse.
Much was written about his bravery in that battle. He
is also the grandson of that retired old war-horse, General Sir Francis Raleigh."

Hawkhurst recalled now reading about the major
after Toulouse, but he had not realized that he was
the grandson of one of the foremost British military
tacticians of an earlier age. "So young Raleigh is following in his grandfather's footsteps. That old mar-
tinet must be very proud of him."

"Fairly bursting his buttons," Waymore replied.
"Wants to show him off everywhere."

A new dance was about to begin, and Waymore
excused himself to go in search of the lady he was
to partner for it.

Hawkhurst did not remain long at the ball. The
restlessness and discontent that had afflicted him the
past two months drove him to stop at two other

squeezes that proved to be no more interesting than Lady Morton's ball. Then he set off for White's, his club on St. James's Street.

As he rode there, he wondered whether Lily was still in London. He doubted it. The critics most likely had had their cruel fun with her by now, and she would have left London—but to go where? Hawkhurst's heart ached to think of her reduced to working yet again with a lowly company of traveling players.

He had always followed the dramatic reviews in the London papers that he received at Hawkhill, but he purposely avoided reading them this fall. He feared that if he ran across one in which a caustic critic made fun of Lily, he would not be able to stop himself from killing the man.

Hawkhurst had hoped that Lily would relent and come back to Hawkhill, if not to him, at least for Phoebe's wedding, but she had not. Phoebe had been a glowing bride and was now living happily with Sir Roger in Dorset.

Damon sighed. Lily had left Hawkhill much changed for the better. Phoebe was off his hands, and Cassandra now tried hard to treat him like her brother instead of her enemy. Despite the improved atmosphere at Hawkhill, he missed Lily so much that he could not bear to remain there.

He castigated himself endlessly for letting his anger and his ingrained distrust of women overwhelm him that day she had left Hawkhill. He had been so furious and hurt that he had actually been stupid enough to let her walk away from him.

Hawkhurst still cringed when he remembered his parting jibe at her. *"Come to me, and perhaps I will take you back."*

Perhaps? Hell's fire, he'd give everything he owned to do so. But with that cruel taunt he had ensured that his proud, spirited Lily would not return to him no matter how much she wanted to.

No other woman had ever penetrated his determined self-control and made him lose his temper the way Lily did. Why was it that she could make him so wild and irrational? The answer, when it belatedly came to him, was blinding in its simplicity.

Because I love her so much.

Until now, he had believed that love was no more than another name for passion between a man and a woman, but he had been wrong all these years. Lily had taught him to love.

If only he could find her to tell her that.

But would she listen? He had acted so imperiously with her when she had told him about going to London. His goal had been to save her from pain. Instead he had unintentionally insulted her. Once again, Damon simultaneously cursed and admired her stubborn, proud independence.

Even the familiar confines of White's did not relieve Hawkhurst's boredom or soothe his restlessness. He greeted friends but had no inclination to stop to talk to them. He did not want to go home, however, for that would mean facing another night of fitful sleep in a bed without Lily

He intended to begin looking for her in the morning. First he would inquire at Covent Garden in the hope that someone there would know where she had gone after her tryout. When he found her again, he swore that he would let her dictate to him whatever she wanted in their relationship.

Lord Rudolph Oldfield planted himself in Damon's path. "Well, well, what brings you to London at this time of year, Hawkhurst?"

Damon smothered an expletive. Oldfield was the most malicious gossip in London, and Damon did everything he could to avoid the man. But he had been so lost in his thoughts of Lily that he had not even noticed his approach.

"I wager I know why you are here," Oldfield said with an insinuating smile. "You have come to look over the new Siddons at Covent Garden."

"I don't know whom you are talking about," Damon said coldly.

"I cannot believe that you have not heard of her. She has taken the town by storm. Everyone is abuzz over her splendid acting. Surely, you—"

Hawkhurst impatiently cut him off. "I only arrived in London this afternoon."

"Ah, that explains it," Oldfield said, unruffled by Damon's curtness. "Everyone concedes she is a worthy successor to the great Siddons. Some contend her Lady Macbeth is even better than the divine Sarah's was. By the way, she is appearing in that role tomorrow night. You must try to catch it, but I warn you tickets are as hard to come by as hen's teeth."

"What is her name?" Damon asked without much interest.

"Lily Culhane."

It was all Damon could do to keep from betraying his shock. Managing a tone of indifference, he said, "If she is as good as you say she is, perhaps I could be induced to attend one of her performances sometime."

He would be there tomorrow night without fail.

Hawkhurst took the chair beside his white-haired aunt, Lady Edith Purcell, in his box at Covent Garden. She was a woman of ample proportions, and it took considerable shifting and squirming to arrange herself comfortably in her seat.

When she succeeded, she said to her nephew, "You are in for a rare treat tonight. Even a man as jaded as you about actresses will have to admit that Lily Culhane is an extraordinary performer.''

''From the crowd outside vying to get in, I think all London must agree with you.''

Lady Purcell gave Damon a shrewd look. ''I understand the greenroom is equally crowded with smitten gentlemen eager to woo her.''

Damon stiffened. That news did not please him at all, but remembering Bath, he was not surprised.

His aunt continued, ''I doubt that she is in your style, however. She is said to be every inch a lady. There is speculation that she must be of respectable birth, although if that is the case one cannot imagine why her parents would have permitted her to go on the stage.''

Damon could have told his aunt that far from being respectable, Lily's parents had been actors, too, but he held his tongue. Her ladyship assumed he did not know Lily, and he was not yet ready to tell her otherwise. Besides, he had something else to discuss with his aunt.

''I have a favor to ask of you.''

''You do?'' He had never before asked her for one, and she was clearly startled. ''Well then, I shall be happy to oblige you, Damon.''

''Better hear what it is before you agree,'' he warned. ''You won't like doing it, but would you chaperone Cassandra next season?''

He hated asking it of his aunt, knowing how much she disliked his sister, but Cassandra wanted a London season so desperately.

Lady Purcell frowned. ''You're right, I don't like it. You know I cannot abide that creature. She reminds me so much of her dreadful mother. How my brother could have married that female is beyond me. But then he always was a fool when it came to women—and to his son.''

During the years his father had cut himself off

from his son and heir, his aunt had steadfastly taken
Damon's part, and he had always been welcome in
her home even when he was not at Hawkhill.

"I marvel that you put up with Cassandra, Damon."

"It is getting easier. She has finally grasped what
her conduct costs her, and she is trying hard to
change."

"I cannot imagine she often succeeds," Lady Purcell said sourly, "but I own that even to see her try
would be diverting. Very well, I will do it, but only
as a favor to you."

Damon almost sighed aloud with relief that Cassandra would get her season.

As the curtain went up, he felt a rush of excitement over seeing Lily again.

The first scenes before she took the stage seemed
to drag on endlessly. But at last the moment approached when she would appear. Hawkhurst
leaned forward in anticipation. God, he had missed
her. He had not thought it possible for him to miss
anyone as much as he had her.

At last, she appeared onstage, and Damon's heart
leapt at the sight of her, standing so proud and regal. She paid no heed to the applause that rang out
for her, but began to speak. Instantly, the audience
fell silent.

Damon watched her performance in growing
amazement. No wonder she was the toast of London. She was brilliant. He flinched when he recalled
how he had scorned her acting talent. No wonder
she had been so insulted and outraged. Would she
ever forgive him?

Would he ever forgive himself?

After the play was over, Hawkhurst escorted his
aunt to her waiting carriage. Then, calling himself
every kind of fool, he headed for the greenroom.

He paused on the threshold of the crowded room

with its green baize carpet and walls. Lily was easy enough to pick out for she was the center of attention.

Damon looked at her in the way a famished man stares at a lavish feast. How lovely she was in a gown of cream lace and silk that clung to her alluring body. Her fiery hair was piled high on her head, revealing the long elegant sweep of her neck. Pride and desire in equal measure rose up in him. The restlessness that had plagued him vanished as if by magic.

He wished that she would notice him. Damon wanted to see her reaction, before she had time to remember how displeased she was with him. He prayed that when her emerald eyes alighted on him for the first time, he would see an involuntary flash of pleasure before it was replaced by anger.

He willed her to look at him, but she did not. It stung him that she could be so oblivious to him.

It did not take him long to discern that she handled her London admirers with the same detached skill that she had the men in Bath. Damon was breathing a little easier when one of the men, Sir Harvey Thornton, noticed him and came over.

"So, Hawkhurst, are you here to look over Lily Culhane?" asked Thornton, a burly man of forty with a thin, sneering mouth. "I wager you will not meet with your customary success with her. Major James Raleigh, the dashing young hero of Toulouse, is the fair Lily's favorite."

The image of Raleigh's noble face surrounded by eager females at Lady Morton's ball rose up in Damon's mind, and jealousy stabbed at him. He looked at the men surrounding Lily but the handsome major was not among them.

"My money is on Raleigh should you challenge

him for her favors,'' Thornton said, his voice full of malice. ''Indeed, Hawkhurst, I believe that you are about to find yourself dethroned as the king of the greenroom.''

Chapter 26

Lily sensed Hawkhurst's presence in the green-room, felt his eyes upon her even before she stole a quick, covert glance at the door. She told herself she did not care that he had come, but her heart turned over at the sight of him, standing so tall and straight. He was dressed, as he had been that night she had first seen him in Bath, in black tailcoat and pantaloons.

His dark eyes were appraising the men around her, and he did not see her fleeting peek at him as she conversed with Lord Alvanley. Although she returned her gaze immediately to Alvanley, she managed to keep Damon in her peripheral vision without looking directly at him again.

Much as she longed to drink in the sight of him, she had no intention of betraying herself like that to him. She would not let him know that she cared in the slightest that he was here, even though her heart seemed to be beating as loud as a drum and she no longer heard a word that Alvanley was saying.

She had told herself over and over since she left Hawkhill that she did not want to see its master again.

What a liar she was!

Still chafing from his belittling of her talent, Lily wondered whether he had finally watched her perform. If he had, would he admit he had wronged her in his estimation of her talent?

Would he come up to her at all?

Her heart fluttered, than sank. No, of course he would not. *"You will regret leaving soon enough. When you do, come to me, and* perhaps *I will take you back."* Her cheeks grew hot at the memory. Even though he had been in a towering fury when he had told her that, it would keep him from coming to her now, just as it kept her from going to him.

So why was he here?

Because he is the king of the greenroom, you fool! This is his realm.

He would seek out some other actress to lavish his attention upon while ignoring Lily. Well, if he thought to use that tactic to pique her into approaching him, he would find it did not work.

Damon was making his way slowly across the room. Lily had no difficulty following his progress. Not only was there his height, but he was the only man in the room wearing a black coat and it stood out in sharp contrast to the assorted colors of the other men's.

He was coming toward her. Her heart beat wildly.

Damon was very near now. Although she was finding it increasingly difficult to breathe, she still pretended not to have noticed him. She realized to her dismay that everyone was watching them curiously. Could it be that they knew about her and him?

He was only three steps away, and Lily could no longer avoid looking at him. Steeling herself to show no emotion, she gazed up at him at last. His face was sober.

She heard one of the men near her whisper to another, "The Hawk is after a new conquest."

His companion snickered suggestively. "Care to wager how long before the Lily succumbs to him?"

She froze. Would Hawkhurst humiliate her by

telling them that he had already conquered her? She was not certain at first whether he had heard the men, but then she saw that telltale muscle in his jaw twitch, and knew that he had. Knew, too, that for some reason, the remarks had angered him.

He was in front of her now, so close that his distinctive scent of sandalwood drifted over her. His hooded eyes held hers, yet gave her no hint of his intentions. The tension within her was unbearable.

"You gave a magnificent performance tonight as Lady Macbeth, one of the best I have ever seen."

The quiet sincerity of his tone thrilled and pleased Lily as much as his praise did. Suddenly, she was happier than she had been since she had left Hawk-hill.

He smiled a little sadly at her. "Tonight was the first time I have been privileged to see you onstage. Now I understand why you are the toast of London. I confess that until I saw you tonight I was skeptical of reports of your extraordinary talent. You proved me so wrong that I feel compelled to offer you my profound apologies for having been a doubter."

Lily stared dumbfounded at him. She had not expected such a graceful and public apology from him. And he had couched it so carefully that it would give no rise to gossip about a prior relationship between them.

She found her defenses against him crumbling, and she could not let that happen. It took every bit of acting ability she possessed to present a cool face to their interested audience and to say with just the right touch of detachment, "How very kind of you. I thank you."

One corner of his mouth turned upward as it did when he was teasing her. "Your talents are so remarkable that I hope I may be privileged to enjoy them often in the future."

Lily knew the talents he was talking about were

not confined to the stage, and she could feel the warmth rising in her cheeks.

Instead of pressing home his advantage, he said politely, "I have interrupted you. Pray excuse me, but I wanted you to know how brilliant I thought your performance was."

He left her then. As he moved slowly across the room, the company's loveliest actresses vied shamelessly for his attention.

Lily watched Iona Lawson, widely acknowledged as the most beautiful woman on the London stage, try to entice him into her orbit. No wonder they called him the king of the greenroom, Lily thought waspishly.

"You think you have only to beckon to an actress and she will fall into your bed."

"They generally do the beckoning."

Wasn't that the truth! By now, Lily appreciated Hawkhurst's cynical view of actresses. To her surprise, he ignored the various females' enticements and began talking to Blandon Jerome, the actor who had played Macbeth.

Damon had skillfully put the ball in Lily's court, and now the next move would be up to her.

What did she want to do? No, that was not the question. She knew what she wanted. She loved him, and she yearned to have him hold her in his arms.

But she longed now for more than a few brief moments in his bed. She who had scorned being a man's wife and chattel thought wistfully of the enduring love and companionship that her parents had enjoyed. What she truly *wanted* was to be Damon's wife and to bear him the fruit of her love, his children.

But that was impossible.

He could never marry her, could never give their children the protection of his name. Hers was a love without hope and without future, a love that could only end in misery for her. She was realist enough to recognize that.

So the question was, what *should* she do? She had been so wretched after she had left Hawkhill, but she had forced herself to go on with her life. If she resumed their affair now, she would only have to go through the agony of parting all over again. She did not have the strength to go through that a third time.

Hawkhurst conversed mechanically with Blandon Jerome, scarcely knowing what he said. His thoughts were entirely on Lily. He had deliberately chosen this corner of the room in the hope that she would break away from her other admirers and come to him. He knew that he was asking more than he ought of her. If she joined him, she would be advertising her interest in him, but if she cared half as much about him as he did about her, she would do it.

Suddenly, a new figure, splendid in his regimental uniform and boots polished to a high gloss, strode briskly into the room. Every eye in it was drawn to Major James Raleigh.

Hawkhurst, remembering what Sir Harvey Thornton had said, glanced hastily at Lily. The love and pride in her eyes as she looked at the major shriveled Damon's heart. He could not deny that Raleigh was a prime specimen of manhood, young and virile with a smile that would melt iron.

The major cast such a fierce, disapproving eye at her admirers that two or three of them backed off a step. He told her, "Come, my dear, I am taking you home."

Damon prayed that Lily would give Raleigh a setdown for his presumption. Instead she meekly took his arm and let him lead her from the room. Not once as she made her exit did she glance toward Hawkhurst.

So it was true! The conquering hero of Toulouse had conquered Lily as well. *Damn!* Damon had suspected in Bath that Lily had a weakness for officers.

He waited a full minute after their departure, then sauntered toward the door of the greenroom.

A smirking Sir Harvey Thornton stepped into his path. "I told you Raleigh was Lily's favorite."

"So you did," Damon said carelessly. "He is welcome to her."

Like bloody hell he was!

Once Hawkhurst was beyond the curious eyes of the greenroom, he abandoned his easy gait and moved quickly outside. The crowds that had thronged outside the theatre to see Lily were long gone now. So were their vehicles, and Damon was relieved to see Sewell guiding his curricle into a spot almost in front of him.

He hurried to it. Before he could rap out a command, Sewell, his face impassive, said, "I believe you wish me to follow the hack just turning the corner. Mrs. Culhane is in it."

"Your astuteness is one of the things I particularly prize about you, Sewell," Damon remarked dryly. "Go, and I will see you back at Hawkhurst House."

As his curricle disappeared around the corner, Damon turned to hail a hackney.

Almost an hour passed before Sewell joined Hawkhurst in his library. The groom gave him the address of the lodgings on a quiet, respectable street where the hack had deposited both of its passengers, then drove on.

Hawkhurst's hands involuntarily clenched into fists at this. Clearly the Hero had not planned to leave Lily's soon or he would have had the hack wait.

Damon spent a mostly sleepless night, tormented

by thoughts of Raleigh's handsome face and of Lily in his arms. Hell's fire, the thought of her with another man made him want to commit mayhem. What disturbed him most was the certainty that she would not give herself lightly to a man. Nor could he forget the look in her eyes when the Hero had walked into the greenroom.

Damon reminded himself that when she had been at Hawkhill, Lily's eyes had shone even more brilliantly at the sight of him. He intended to make them light up like that for him again. He would win her back before the Hero managed to claim her irrevocably for his own.

With that aim in mind, he set out early the next morning for the address that Sewell had given him. His sharp, authoritative knock was answered by a startled Lily herself.

"Hawkhurst, what on earth?" she exclaimed as she opened the door. A narrow hall with doors only on the right side stretched behind her. Her green silk wrapper looked to have been hastily donned, and the white embroidered collar of her night rail peeked above the green collar.

Clearly he had awakened her. Her green eyes were still dull with sleep. Her long, fiery hair fell about her shoulders, loose and disheveled—and seductive. His longing to sweep her back into bed and make love to her was so intense that it almost undid his control.

"Sleeping in this morning, are we?" he asked.

She looked as though she had slept quite as badly as he had, and he wondered how long Major Raleigh had stayed. He could not stop himself from inquiring sardonically, "A late night?"

A man, clad only in breeches that he was still buttoning, burst into the hall behind her. With his noble face framed by thick, tousled red-brown hair and a bronzed chest corded with muscles, Major James Raleigh looked like a young Greek god.

Hawkhurst felt as though the blade of an ax had been thrust into his heart.

"Lily, what the blazes . . ." Major Raleigh's voice trailed off as he saw the caller. "Who is he?"

"Her *other* lover," Hawkhurst answered for her.

The major's jaw dropped.

Well, dammit, Raleigh was no more shocked than Hawkhurst himself was. How could Lily have so quickly forgotten what they had shared together? How could she have gone immediately from him into the Hero's arms?

Lily's eyes, glittering with wrath, raked Hawkhurst. "How dare you say that!"

He cocked a cynical eyebrow. "How dare I speak the truth?"

"It is not the truth!"

"Is it not?" he asked. He looked curiously at the embroidered collar of her night rail. She had never worn a night rail when she had slept with him.

Lily glared at Damon. "You are my *former* lover."

His faint hope that she would deny that the Hero was her lover gave way to a pain so intense that he flinched. To think that he had come here intent on declaring his love for her. She most likely would have laughed in his face.

The major belatedly recovered his power of speech. "Lily is not—"

She interrupted him angrily, "Go back to bed."

"But—"

"Honor your promise to me, James, and go back to bed."

The Hero looked as though he were torn between two unhappy alternatives. He hesitated, then reluctantly disappeared back into the room he had come out of.

Hawkhurst said scornfully, "This very much involves him!"

"I have no intention of arguing that point or any other with you," Lily said, at her most remote and majestic.

He looked down at her. Only the quick rise and fall of her chest beneath the green silk betrayed her agitation. She had pulled the robe tight around her. It outlined the sensual curve of her breasts, and he longed to taste their sweetness again. His gaze dropped lower, to her hips, and he remembered how provocatively they moved when he made love to her.

Hell's fire, he still wanted her desperately, even knowing that her current lover waited for her down the hall. His mind was a seething cauldron of emotions. He hated himself for needing her and hated her for making him do so. He should turn away from the faithless witch.

He should walk out of her life forever.

If she were any other woman, he would.

Instead, he could not resist slipping his hand beneath the silk and cupping one of those tantalizing breasts as his thumb caressed its peak. Passion, hot and unbridled, surged through him. Damn her!

She gasped in surprise and tried to push him away, but he would have none of that. He locked her in a suffocating embrace, and his mouth came down hard on hers in a punishing kiss. She struggled against him, but he held her in a grip that would not permit her to escape either his arms or his lips.

Only when she ceased to struggle against him, and her mouth accepted his kiss, did it soften. His tongue caressed hers, and he felt the shiver of her response. It fueled his own passion.

He pushed open her robe, only to be confronted by a row of tiny buttons that fastened the bodice of her night rail. He was so damned starved for her that he knew he could not manage them. He yanked at the cloth, sending buttons flying and making an opening that allowed his mouth to claim the crest of her breast.

"Stop it," she protested, pushing at him.

Her sudden resistance when he was so damned wild for her infuriated him. He lifted his head. "Why?" he demanded with deliberate malice. "Surely a woman like you, who takes a new lover into her bed while it is still warm from her previous one, would not be adverse to granting her favors to two men at once."

She reeled back as thought he had struck her. Her eyes had the peculiar brightness of unshed tears to them.

"Oh, Hawkhurst." Her voice was trembling with outrage. "Why must you always think the worst of me?"

He was too angry and hurt himself to give rational consideration to her question, and he ground out through clenched jaw, "Because you give me such good reason to do so."

"Do I! Do I indeed!" Her eyes were green lightning. "Surely, the great Hawkhurst, the king of the greenroom, would not deign to share a woman with another man! Now get out of here. I never want to see you again!"

She shoved him so hard that, caught off guard, he stumbled backward over the threshold.

Lily slammed the door in his face. He heard the bolt sliding into place.

The intensity of her anger confused him, but he was every bit as enraged as she was. It was all he could do to keep from breaking the damn door down. Instead he stomped away.

Chapter 27

As soon as the door shut after Hawkhurst, Major Raleigh, still in his breeches, came back into the hall. "Lily, why did you not tell that man the truth?"

Her chin tilted stubbornly. "Because he always insists upon believing the worst of me, so I am going to let him do just that. If he wishes to jump to the conclusion that you are my lover, let him!"

The major looked at her as though she were touched in the upper works. "Well, what the devil else is he to think? He finds me here when I have obviously just tumbled out of bed—and so have you."

"He should have known better!"

"I don't know why. Only the flattest of the flats would believe anything else, and I've never seen a man who looked less like a Johnny Raw than that one. Who is he?"

"Lord Hawkhurst."

Raleigh groaned. "Splendid! Lily, I could throttle you. Do you have any notion how powerful he is? If there is any man in this kingdom that I do not want as my enemy it is the Earl of Hawkhurst. You must tell him the truth."

"No!

"Then I will."

"You cannot. You swore you would tell no one, and I hold you to your oath."

"And I curse the day you extracted it from me. I tell you it will not matter!"

"Yes, it will!" she cried in distress.

He sighed. "Stubborn as always. Tell me about Hawkhurst."

"There's nothing to tell," she said stiffly.

"Isn't there? Sarah is persuaded that you are wildly in love with him."

"I am," she admitted.

He shook his tousled head incredulously. "You bacon-brained ninnyhammer, you could not have done anything more calculated to drive him away than your pretense this morning."

That night Lily approached the greenroom with trepidation, half-fearing, half-hoping that Hawkhurst would be there.

But he was not.

She found herself scarcely listening to the men who quickly gathered around her. Each time a newcomer appeared at the green baize door, she could not stop herself from looking to see whether it was Hawkhurst. But it was not.

Lily told herself it was for the better that he stayed away. No good could come of seeing him again. No good at all.

Except perhaps she would no longer feel as though she had a great gaping hole in her chest where her heart had been.

The night dragged by interminably for her until at last James appeared to take her home. She accused him of being late.

He looked at her oddly. "No, I am twenty minutes early."

Lily did not appear again at Covent Garden until three nights later when she played Isabella in *The*

Fatal Marriage, one of her best roles. The thought that Hawkhurst might possibly be in the audience spurred her to one of her most inspired performances.

She had heard nothing from him since his angry departure from her lodgings. And she told herself that he would not be in the greenroom tonight either. Yet she was disappointed when she discovered that she was right.

Lily was immediately surrounded by men, mostly longtime greenroom habitués with their practiced patter, but she had difficulty suppressing her yawns.

Then Hawkhurst appeared in the doorway. Lily's heart thudded. She held her breath as he strolled into the room, wondering what he would do.

Iona Lawson moved with unseemly haste to intercept him, and he allowed her to lead him to a quiet corner. He scarcely glanced at Lily who was seething at Iona's boldness—and his acquiescence to it.

If Hawkhurst had watched Lily perform that night, he did not compliment her as he had after *Macbeth*. He did not come near her.

She remembered how handsomely he had apologized to her for his doubting of her talent. And she had reciprocated by letting him think that James was her lover.

She should not have let Damon upset her so much that morning at her lodgings. She knew how deeply entrenched his distrust of women was. Instead of putting his suspicions to rest, she had, in her anger, foolishly fed them.

She longed to go up and ask to speak privately with him so that she could explain about James, but her pride would not permit her to do that while he was with Iona.

The way the lovely actress fawned over Hawkhurst was enough to make Lily want to substitute a real asp the next time Iona played Cleopatra.

Now and then, Lily had the feeling that Damon was watching her. Apparently, though, it was only her own wishful thinking for whenever she looked, his eyes were on Iona.

Sir Harvey Thornton suddenly grabbed her arm. "Come, pretty one, I will take you home." He stank of blue ruin, and Lily knew that he was in his cups.

"No!" she said sharply. "Major Raleigh is coming for me."

Thornton sneered. "That young fool is not yet dry behind the ears."

"Take your hand off me," she ordered, a thread of steel in her voice.

"You heard the lady, Thornton." Hawkhurst's voice behind her was as cold and deadly as a knife's edge. "Release her and get out of here."

She felt weak with relief—and with joy that Damon had come to her aid like this. He had seemed so engrossed in Iona that Lily was astonished he would have even noticed Sir Harvey's behavior toward her.

Thornton's hand instantly fell away from Lily's arm. He paled at the look in Damon's eyes. "W-w-why should you care, Hawkhurst? You have not shown her the smallest interest."

"That is beside the point," he snapped. "Do not bother her again or you will answer to me."

Thornton hastily backed away.

Lily said huskily, "Thank you."

But as she spoke, Damon's face hardened. "Your lover has arrived," he hissed.

She turned and saw James hurrying toward them. His timing could not have been worse.

Hawkhurst's voice, so low that only Lily could hear it, was laced with sarcasm and scorn. "You ought to insist that the Hero take better care of you. He is less protection than a phantom husband!"

Damon whirled, and without a backward glance at Lily, left the room.

The following night, Hawkhurst was already in the greenroom, talking to Iona Lawson, when Lily reached it.

Her spirits plummeted. She had promised herself that if he were here tonight she would seek a tête-à-tête with him.

But she would not do that while he was with Iona, who would spread it to the four winds that Lily had tried to steal him from her. Iona would have every tongue in London gossiping about how Lily had brazenly solicited the king of the greenroom's attention after he had pointedly ignored her.

Lily did not lack for male attention, but she paid little heed to what her admirers said and answered them mechanically. She was surreptitiously watching Damon. Iona was using every wile in her extensive repertoire to captivate him.

Clearly she must be succeeding too, because he did not leave her side.

Lily longed to go home, but the red tortoiseshell clock on the mantelpiece told her that James would not be arriving to take her there for another half hour.

The minutes crept by until at last her brother appeared.

Unable to stand the sight of Damon with Iona another moment, Lily hurried up to James as soon as he stepped through the door. "Please, I want to leave at once."

"Why are you in such a hurry tonight?" he asked.

"I have a dreadful headache." And she did. A headache named Iona Lawson.

Hawkhurst watched Lily leave the greenroom with Major Raleigh. Seeing her depart on the Hero's arm drove him crazy with jealousy and frustration.

He wanted to kill them both.

No, he wanted to kill the major; he wanted to kiss Lily.

The humiliating, gut-wrenching truth was that despite her having become another man's mistress, he still wanted her more than he had ever wanted anything in his life.

He, who had always been the one to walk away from a lover, had discovered what it was like to be the one rejected. And he did not like it at all.

Beside him, Iona Lawson was prattling away. He scarcely heard anything she said, but he was thankful for the way she pounced upon him whenever he walked into the greenroom. It kept everyone from guessing the real reason he was there.

Damon shoved his hands, clenched in tight fists, into his pockets. He should never have come to the greenroom tonight.

He would not have, he told himself, except he could not leave Lily unprotected to fend off the likes of Harvey Thornton.

But in his heart he knew that he did not come to the greenroom merely to protect Lily from troublesome reprobates. He came because he wanted desperately to be near her and hoped against hope that she would make some overture that would tell him his cause was not dead.

But she had made none. After his intervention on her behalf with Thornton, Lily might at least have acknowledged him tonight. But she had not deigned to give him so much as a nod of her head. His only reward was the satisfaction of seeing that Thornton did not go near her again.

Iona plucked at his sleeve. "Would you be so kind as to take me home tonight?" she asked with a seductive smile that left no doubt what his reward would be.

He looked down into her lovely face. Here was the most classically beautiful actress in the kingdom offering herself to him while Lily ignored him. He would be a fool not to take Iona up on her offer—an even greater fool than he already was for pining after a woman who preferred another man to him.

He must forget Lily. Damon's jaw clenched in determination. It would not be easy, but there were plenty of beauties like Iona who would help him erase Lily from his heart, and he would begin the task tonight.

"Yes," he told Iona a trifle grimly, "I shall take you home."

Lily made her way to the greenroom feeling every bit as nervous as she did on opening night in a role that she had never played before.

James would not be able to come for her tonight because General Sir Francis Raleigh was giving a dinner for him. As guest of honor, he would be forced to remain until the last of the attendees departed. He had made Lily promise that she would ask Hawkhurst to take her home in his stead.

"It is your own fault that he ignores you," James had told her bluntly. "So do something about it instead of moping over him."

The thought that Damon might agree to take her home was enough to make her heart sing.

But if he refused her, she did not think she could bear it.

When she reached the greenroom, it was buzzing with excited chatter that signaled a particularly delicious tidbit of gossip was making the rounds.

She stopped to ask Blandon James what it was.

The actor looked surprised. "Haven't you heard?

Iona Lawson says Lord Hawkhurst has offered her a carte blanche.''

Lily gasped. "Is it true?" Surely it wasn't! It could not be!

Jerome shrugged. "We should know the answer to that when his lordship appears. I do know that he took her home from the greenroom last night. I saw her get into his carriage with him."

Gertrude Mayer, a character actress, had come up as Jerome was talking, and now interjected, "Iona is boasting that Lord Hawkhurst is an even better lover than he is rumored to be."

"I would not have thought that possible," Jerome remarked dryly.

Lily felt as though the world was disintegrating around her.

At that moment, Damon appeared in the doorway, dressed as always in a black tailcoat that contrasted sharply with the more colorful garb of the other men.

Iona hurried up to him.

Lily watched as the actress put her dainty little hand possessively on the sleeve of his black evening coat and quickly drew him into a quiet corner.

The room had suddenly grown very quiet. Looking around, Lily discovered that everyone else was intently watching the couple, too.

Seeing Iona gaze up at Damon with an adoring smile on her face, Lily knew what it was to be wildly, desperately jealous.

Suddenly, Iona gave Hawkhurst a dazzling smile, threw her arms around him, and kissed him passionately.

A knowing twitter ran through the room.

Jerome said, "It's true."

Lily felt as though her heart had been pulverized. Unable to stand the sight another instant, she turned and fled from the greenroom. As she ran past her dressing room, she grabbed her pelisse but did not take the time to put it on before running out into the cold night.

Thick clouds hid the sky, and the air was heavy with the damp. It would rain, or perhaps even snow before long, but what did Lily care?

What did she care about anything!

She wanted only to escape from the scene she had just witnessed as quickly as she could, even though she knew her effort would be futile. That embrace would be engraved on her memory all the rest of her days.

To her dismay, the only vehicle for hire left in front of the theatre was a shabby hackney that had seen better days—most likely a century or two ago. Its paint had peeled off in great ragged strips, and it was drawn by a broken-down nag that looked as though it might expire at any moment. The elderly coachman on the box did not look to be in much better shape.

Lily was far too upset to wait for a more promising equipage to appear, and she climbed in. The interior of the hack was damp and cold and smelled dreadfully of mildew. How fitting that the dismal coach should match her own emotions so perfectly.

The vehicle plodded forward so slowly that it would likely be morning before she reached home. But Lily did not mind. Perhaps by then she would have gotten over the worst of her misery.

But she doubted it.

Lily began to shiver. She still had not put on her pelisse, and she struggled into it.

She wanted nothing so much as to sob her heart out in the lonely blackness of the evil-smelling coach, but she was determined that she would not weep over the king of the greenroom. She would not!

Still she could not stop a trickle of tears from spilling down her cheeks at the thought of him in Iona's bed.

She wished them both to perdition!

At last the hackney turned the corner to Lily's street and stopped in front of her lodgings amid a row of narrow attached houses. As she got out, she noticed a carriage stopped far down the street. That surprised her, for usually no one else was about when she returned home from the theatre.

She shivered a little at how dark the street was. The clouds blotted out all light from the moon and stars.

She paid off the jarvis and went up the four steps, edged with iron palings, to her lodgings.

As she inserted her key in the ornate brass lock, a large shadow detached itself from the blackness that engulfed the rustic next door. Lily froze.

A footpad had been hiding in wait for her!

Chapter 28

⟨⟡⟩

A s the tall figure glided toward Lily, she realized
that he moved with the peculiar loose-limbed
grace that was uniquely Hawkhurst's.

"Why isn't the Hero with you?" The rich timbre
of Damon's voice confirmed his identity even though
his face was hidden in shadow.

Lily's fear dissolved into wonder. Could he truly
be real? When she had run from the theatre he had
been locked in Iona Lawson's arms, and now he was
waiting outside her door.

"What does the major mean by leaving you to
make your way home by yourself?" Hawkhurst
sounded furious. "I would take better care of you,
Lily Culhane."

She remembered how solicitous he had been of
her during those wonderful weeks at Hawkhill, and
a lump the size of a gull's egg rose in her throat.

The darkness masked his expression. He advanced
on her, stopping on the stairs two steps below her.

He was so close that she caught the scent of sandalwood. Her heart throbbed wildly.

"Where is the Hero?" he persisted.

"At a dinner," she stammered. "What do you
want?"

"You," he said flatly.

For an instant she thought she could not have

330

heard him right, then her temper flared. How dare he tell her that when he had offered Iona Lawson a carte blanche and had just been shamelessly kissing her for all the world to see! How dare he come to her with the taste of Iona still upon his lips!

"Is Iona not enough for you?" Lily demanded, giving him an angry shove just as he lifted his foot to climb the next step.

She caught him off guard and he stumbled back. Lily saw his hand flailing for the palings to catch himself. He half-turned and managed to grab one of the palings just in time to prevent himself from falling back on the pavement below the steps. But as he caught himself, his foot came down hard with his ankle at an awkward angle.

An ejaculation of pain escaped his lips. The leg gave way beneath him, and he fell to his knee, landing on the second lowest step.

A low, anguished cry escaped Lily's lips, and she scrambled down the stairs to kneel beside him.

He tried to stand up but failed.

"Dear God, Hawkhurst!" she cried in an agonized voice. "What have I done to you?"

"Can't . . . stand," he rasped.

Lily put her arm around him. He turned and his face was only an inch from hers, close enough for her to see by its grim set that he was in considerable pain.

And it was her fault. Awash in guilt, she unconsciously tightened her grasp around him.

The corner of his mouth turned up as it always did when he teased her. "Almost worth . . . getting . . . hurt for."

She heard footsteps running toward them, coming from the direction of the carriage that had been stopped down the block.

A man rushed up, and Lily took a deep breath of relief as she recognized Hawkhurst's groom Sewell.

"His lordship is injured!" she cried. "We must get him inside."

Hawkhurst gritted his teeth against the pain in his ankle and leaned heavily on Lily and Sewell as they helped him into a bedroom of her lodgings.

The room was so small that the bed took up most of it. The colorful starburst quilt on the wall and the green-and-white cover on the bed were the same ones that had been in Lily's bedroom in Bath. When Damon saw the jeweled dagger set with the emerald, ruby, and pearl on the wall, he was certain this was Lily's bedroom.

After she and Sewell eased him down on the big, comfortable featherbed, he was convinced of it. He turned his face into the pillow perfumed with Lily's distinctive scent of wild roses and breathed deeply of it.

Despite the pain in his ankle, a wave of sheer happiness washed over him. This room was not the one that he had seen the Hero come out of that morning.

Lily immediately dispatched Sewell for a Dr. Knolton who lived on the next street over.

Damon let her do so, even though he didn't think he was badly hurt. Most likely only a sprain and not a bad one at that, but he might as well use it to his advantage.

She bent over his ankle, turning pale at the sight of his ankle swelling against the constraints imposed by the tight leg of his pantaloons, which was drawn taut by a strap around his foot. Her concern for him fed the hope that had begun growing in him since he had seen her ravaged face as Iona Lawson had kissed him.

Lily might claim she no longer cared for him, but her face had told him differently.

She went to the wall, took down the jeweled dagger, and came back to the bed with it.

He arched an inquiring eyebrow. "Tell me, my flower, do you intend to stab a helpless man?"

"No, only to cut the strap of your pantaloons."

Hawkhurst felt the cold blade of the dagger against his foot as she severed the strap.

"This is your bedroom, is it not?" he asked.

"Yes." Lily laid the dagger down on the bedside table, then pulled his pant leg up and away from his ankle. She glanced at him through her long, thick lashes and said acidly, "Iona Lawson would be most unhappy to find you here."

"Jealous, are we?"

"Yes," she admitted with that honesty he so liked.

"You have no reason to be."

She looked as though she were suddenly tempted to put the dagger through his heart. "No? Even though you were kissing her passionately in the greenroom?"

"I was not kissing her!" he protested indignantly. "*She* was kissing *me*."

"No doubt because she found you such a superlative lover last night!"

He shot bolt-upright at that, sending a shaft of pain through his ankle. "I did not make love to Iona Lawson last night," he growled. "I have never slept with her and I never will!"

Lily's chin was trembling. "And I suppose you did not take her home last night either?"

"Yes, I did do that, but I swear I left her at her door without so much as a good-night kiss. I spent the night in my bedroom at Hawkhurst House—*alone*. Which is the way I have spent every damn night since you left Hawkhill."

Hope and doubt warred in Lily's eyes.

He reached out and took her chin gently in his hand. "I admit that when Iona asked me to take her home, I thought I would spend the night. By the time we got

there, I knew that I had no desire to sleep with her—
or any other woman except you."

"But Iona said you were . . ." Lily's voice cracked
and she could not continue.

He stroked her quivering jaw comfortingly with
his thumb. "No doubt she did," he said dryly, "and
then she hugged me and kissed me publicly to try
to give credence to her lie. She is not the first woman
to claim me as her lover when I was not."

Hawkhurst did not tell Lily that when he had seen
her stricken face he had deliberately removed Iona's
arms from around his neck. Then, without a word
to her or a backward glance, he had walked out of
the greenroom to follow Lily. He had rushed to her
lodgings, only to discover he had reached them
ahead of her.

Damon could withstand the temptation of Lily's
lovely mouth no longer. She made no attempt to
evade him as he captured it with his own in a long,
sweet kiss that confirmed what he had suspected
when she fled the greenroom. She might be living
with the Hero, but she still cared for Damon.

Their kiss was brought to an abrupt and prema-
ture end by the arrival of Sewell with the doctor.
Damon bit back a frustrated curse.

Lily left the room while Dr. Knolton examined
him. Hawkhurst noted that the physician's collar
was frayed, and the elbows of his coat shiny. He did
not appear overly prosperous and was probably delighted to have a paying patient even in the middle
of the night. He was certainly impressed at having
a titled one, managing to insert "milord" in every
sentence.

When Dr. Knolton finished his examination, he
confirmed what Hawkhurst suspected. The ankle
was sprained.

"You must not put weight on it at all for the next
forty-eight hours, keep it elevated, and stay off it for

a couple of weeks. I would prefer you remain here at least for the night, milord, until you can secure a pair of crutches in the morning.''

"No, Doctor," Hawkhurst said in a tone that made the man blink nervously, "you insist upon my remaining here for several days. In fact, it is imperative to my recovery that I do so." He placed a bank note in the doctor's hand. "Otherwise, I may risk permanent damage. I am certain you agree, do you not?''

Dr. Knolton's eyes widened at the size of the bank note. He looked confused for a moment, then he hastened to assure his patient, "Yes, yes, milord, you are absolutely right."

"Good," Hawkhurst said. "Now you must tell my hostess that.''

Let him earn his bank note.

After the door closed behind the physician, Damon smiled slyly up at the ceiling. He had never before been part of a *ménage à trois*. The next few days should prove to be most interesting.

Especially since he intended to very quickly make it a *ménage à deux*, and he would not be the odd man out.

When Lily came into the room, she looked so worried that Damon's conscience pricked him.

"Dr. Knolton says that your injury may be quite serious, and you cannot be moved for several days. I fear you will find it most uncomfortable here.''

Hawkhurst almost laughed aloud. In Lily's bed? Never!

He lied politely, "I am sorry to put you to so much inconvenience, but after all it was you who pushed me." He took her hand in his own.

"But this is not at all what you are used to. These rooms are so small, and I have no retinue of servants to wait upon you.''

She was so worried about him and his comfort

that she wasn't even suspicious. "I shall be very comfortable," he assured her.

Especially if she joined him in her bed.

Lily had not tried to withdraw her hand from his, and he began to caress the back of it with his thumb.

She asked, "Do you need anything before I leave you?"

Where did she intend to sleep? With the Hero?

Over Hawkhurst's dead body!

He gave her a silky smile. "A good-night kiss." He tugged lightly on her hand to draw her down to him. "It will help me to bear the pain."

She sat on the edge of the bed and bent over him, clearly intending to give him a prim little kiss, but he was not about to settle for that. He slipped his hand behind her head and held it while he gave her the kind of kiss he wanted, hot and deep and infinitely exciting.

And she returned it with a fervor that matched his own. The pain in his ankle was joined by another higher on his anatomy.

His hand holding her head slipped lower and his other arm came up around her. She gasped as he suddenly pulled her down beside him on the bed. Her thrusting breasts, pressed hard against his chest, felt wonderful.

She made a halfhearted effort to free herself and sit up, but the fire between them burned too hot and she melted against him. They clung to each other, and time, too, melted away.

The door flew open and in burst Major Raleigh.

Hawkhurst bit back an expletive. He was in no position to defend himself from an irate lover. Damon hoped that the Hero was either unarmed or had too much honor to shoot a bedridden man, even though the bed he occupied belonged to the other man's mistress.

Lily tried to sit up, but Hawkhurst tightened his grip around her.

Raleigh asked, "What is the meaning of this touching scene, Lily?"

It was exactly the question Damon expected from the Hero. His expression, however, was not. He was grinning at Lily as though the sight of her lying on the bed beside Damon pleased him.

The man was daft.

"Aren't you—er, upset?" Hawkhurst asked. He was so startled that he let Lily escape his arms and sit up.

"Why should I be?" Raleigh inquired cheerfully.

Why should he be? Hell's fire, he had just found Hawkhurst in Lily's bed locked in a fierce embrace with her. If it had been Damon, he would have been murderous.

Raleigh's grin widened. "I know how much Lily loves you."

That was the last thing Hawkhurst had expected Lily's lover to tell him.

"James!" Lily cried indignantly. During their tumble on the bed, her fiery hair had escaped its pins and now fell about her shoulders in a glorious veil. "How could you tell him that?"

"Because it is the truth," the Hero replied, unperturbed by her ire, "and you know it."

Raleigh gave a bewildered Damon an engaging smile. It was becoming increasingly difficult to dislike the Hero.

"Lily, introduce me to Lord Hawkhurst."

"I know who you are," Damon said.

"I don't think you do," the major said.

Lily said grudgingly, "Major Raleigh is my brother."

The Hero burst out laughing at Hawkhurst's stupefied expression.

Damon was suddenly so happy that he would

have danced a jig had his ankle permitted it. Then his elation gave way to anger at the misery Lily had caused him by letting him think the major was her lover. "Dammit, if I wasn't so relieved I think I would throttle you. Why didn't you tell me the truth that day I came here?"

"Because you are always so determined to think the worst of me."

Her expression told him how much he had wounded her by immediately assuming she was Raleigh's mistress. "It will not happen again," Damon promised her, bringing her hand to his lips and kissing it. As he lowered it, he said, "Now I know why the major's face looked familiar when I first saw him. The miniature that you had in Bath was of him."

"Yes," Lily admitted. Apprehension clouded her face. "Damon, you must promise to tell no one that James is my brother."

"Why?"

The major answered for her. "Lily is terrified that if it becomes public knowledge that my sister is an actress and I am the son of actors, my prospects for a brilliant military career will be considerably diminished. When she purchased my commission, she made me swear that I would tell no one in England of our relationship, and she has held me to it all these years."

"Hell's fire, Lily, you bought his commission?" Damon exclaimed. "How could you possibly have afforded it?"

"I managed."

Yes, Hawkhurst thought, just as she had managed to keep her family together after her parents' death. Just as she had managed to send her sister to an expensive school. She had managed, but none of it could have been easy. His mouth tightened at the thought of the sacrifices she must have made.

The Hero was saying, "I've never regretted anything so much as my oath to Lily that I would keep our relationship a secret. I am proud that I am her brother."

Lily said, "But if it became known your sister is a common actress—"

"Not a common actress, the toast of London!" James interjected.

"Grandfather would be apoplectic. Only think how proud he is of you."

"He ought to be proud of you, too!" her brother retorted.

Amen, Hawkhurst thought.

"But he is not. He is an old man, and he would be humiliated if his relationship to me became public knowledge. I cannot embarrass him like that."

"What about my embarrassment at being thought your lover?" James inquired.

Lily said stubbornly, "I hold you to your oath, even though you broke it when you told Sir Roger Hilton the truth."

"I did not. I promised I would tell no one in England and Roger was in *Portugal* at the time." He turned to Damon. "I ask one thing of you, my lord, before I take my leave. Do not hurt my sister."

"I assure you that is the last thing I want to do."

The major smiled. "I thought as much."

When he was gone, Lily said to Damon, "You did hurt me dreadfully, you know. You are the only man I have ever given myself to. How could you believe that I would fall into another man's arms as soon as I left you?"

"I could not believe it! That's what made me so angry. But what else was I to think when he had clearly spent the night here?" Lily was still sitting beside him on the bed, and he reached up to smooth her disheveled hair. "Do you know the agony you have put me through?"

"No more than you put me through," she retorted, "trying to fix Iona Lawson's interest in front of me."

"It was she who was trying to fix mine, and I let her because I wanted to be near you. I could hardly stand around the greenroom with my hands in my pockets watching you like a lovelorn calfling. I had to do what everyone expected me to do, which is accept the advances of the most beautiful woman in the room. Only this time," he amended hastily, "I had to settle for the second most beautiful."

He did not think it wise to mention he had also hoped that as Lily watched Iona with him, she would feel a fraction of the jealousy that tormented him when he saw her leave the greenroom on James's arm.

His hand dropped from her hair to caress her thigh on the bed beside him. "Stay with me tonight."

Lily gave him a look that told him she wanted to, but she said, "I should not."

"Is this any way to treat the man you love?" Damon held his breath, fearing that she would try to deny that she loved him.

She did not. Instead, she said, "It would not be good for your ankle."

"It would be wonderful for the rest of me." He took her face gently between his hands. "So you admit you love me?"

"Yes," she said quietly.

"I wish you looked a little happier about it."

Lily wished that she *was* happier about it, but much as she loved him she could not forget that, although he might talk of love, he did not believe in it.

He tugged her down beside him. "I cannot tell you how much I have missed having you beside me in bed," he told her. "I do not think I have had a good night's sleep since you left Hawkhill."

Nor had she. She would awake in the night,

yearning for the heat of his body and the protection
of his arms around her.

Now he was here, and the doctor had said he
could not be moved for a few days. Lily had not
quite understood why. Knolton had murmured
something about "a possible fracture . . . too swollen to tell . . . permanent damage if he were
moved," and Lily had been too guilt-ridden at having caused the injury to question him closely.

Damon brushed his mouth along her lips and her
cheek. His breath tickled her ear as he whispered
huskily. "Let me hold you in my arms tonight, my
love."

My love! But it was only a causal endearment to
him, meaning nothing. Yet Lily could not resist it—
or him.

"Yes," she agreed softly, and rose to change out
of her clothes.

She would have gone behind the screen in the
corner, but he implored, "Let me watch you un-
dress. Your body is so beautiful."

The deep, earnest richness of his voice sent little
shivers of excitement along her spine.

She complied. The air was cool on her skin, but
his eyes warmed her with their appreciation. She
looked questioningly at her night rail.

"No," he said, "I want nothing between us,
nothing at all."

Lily left one candle burning at his request, then
slipped beneath the covers on the side away from
his injured ankle.

He gathered her to him, and his hands made love
to her, stroking, petting, teasing, tantalizing until
she was writhing in her aching need for release.

When his hands suddenly stopped, she groaned
in frustration.

Damon whispered, his breath tickling her ear, "It
is your turn to ride me tonight, love."

He was in full, splendid erection as she straddled him, but her body was as ready for him as his was for her.

After they were joined, she was quiet for a moment, looking down at his powerful chest, all bronze muscle and dark curling hair, in helpless admiration.

He reached up and caressed her breasts. "You are lovely, so lovely," he whispered almost reverently. Smiling up at her, he urged, "Ride me, my beautiful flower. Have your wicked way with me."

She began to move, slowly at first, and then more vigorously.

Suddenly, fierce spasms of pleasure rocked her, even as he gave a muffled shout that signaled his own climax was upon him.

Afterward, he held her tightly against him, as though he feared she might try to escape his arms, and they slept.

Chapter 29

Hawkhurst awoke the next morning with a dull pain in his left ankle, the warmth of Lily beside him, and profound contentment in his heart. Except for the ache in his ankle, this was the way he wanted to awake every morning for the rest of his life.

Lily's eyes fluttered open, she looked at him sleepily for a moment, then her mouth curved in a glowing smile.

"How is your ankle?" Her voice was low and thick with sleep.

"After a smile like that, it is another part of my anatomy that is giving me trouble. Kiss me."

She obeyed, a long, loving melding kiss. Afterward, he said in a voice husky with happiness, "It is heaven to wake up to your smile and your kiss in the morning."

And he intended to continue to reside in that particular heaven. The only question was how best to accomplish it. He had an idea, but first he needed more information about Lily's family. He rolled on his side, facing her.

"I collect your illustrious grandfather, General Sir Francis Raleigh, does not acknowledge you and most likely had nothing to do with your brother either until he became a hero."

Lily raised her brows, no doubt in startlement at his odd choice of pillow talk.

"That's right," she said with uncharacteristic sarcasm. "Then Grandpapa was eager to claim James."

"Did you go to the general after your parents were killed?"

Her mouth tightened. "Yes, but he refused to see me."

Damon thought of how it must have been for Lily then, a penniless girl of seventeen responsible for herself and two younger siblings, and he was furious. How could a man do that to his own descendants?

Hawkhurst intended to have a talk with her grandfather, and the stiff-rumped old tyrant would not like it at all.

"He said he did not consider me one of his grandchildren," Lily explained. "You see, he had disowned Papa when he wed Mama."

"Because she was of lowly birth?"

"No, she was not. Her father was Sir John Drew."

That meant Lily came from two highly respectable families. Sir John had been a distinguished member of the Commons until his death a decade earlier.

Damon gently smoothed back a strand of hair that had fallen across Lily's face. "Why did the general object to your parents' marriage? It would seem to have been a suitable match."

She sighed, rolled onto her back, and stared up at the ceiling. "Both my grandfathers objected. They hated each other, and they had already arranged other marriages for my parents. They would not hear of Mama and Papa marrying. When my parents eloped in desperation, both families disowned them, and they turned to acting to support themselves. Fortunately, they were both talented, and Mama had a brother who'd run away earlier to join a theatrical troupe. He helped them get started."

Damon lifted a lock of Lily's hair from the pillow and rubbed the silken strands absently between his fingers. "The general must have been furious at having his son appear on stage. He is such a high stickler."

"Yes." Lily was still looking up at the ceiling. He even forbade them to use the Raleigh name when they performed, saying he would not have it sullied by actors. That is why my parents and I, too, used Culhane."

Damon said thoughtfully, "I recollect that Sir John had another daughter who married Lord Charing."

"Yes, Lady Charing is my aunt."

"Did she refuse you help, too, when your parents died?"

Lily turned to face him. "No, I did not approach her because I knew she would want to help me, but her husband would not have permitted it. She tried once to aid my parents when they were still alive, and he flew into the boughs. Forbade her to see Mama again."

"That sounds like Lord Charing. He and the general were cut from the same cloth." With men like that in Lily's family, it was no wonder she was so wary of placing herself in a man's control. "Did you know Charing died a few months ago?"

"I heard that."

Damon stroked Lily's cheek lightly, loving the satiny feel of her beneath his fingers. "How difficult it must have been for you after your parents died."

"At first," she admitted. "That is why I am so grateful for my acting talent. It enabled me to buy my brother his commission, send my sister to an excellent school, and live comfortably myself."

Damon looked at her almost in awe. He was so used to clinging, helpless women whose only way of dealing with a crisis was to burst into tears. "You should be very proud of all you have done."

"I am," she said simply.

He was proud of her, too. She had dignity and beauty and talent, and he loved her as he never thought he could love a woman.

"That is why acting is so important to me," Lily said.

Damon could understand why, especially when she was brilliant at it.

When he told her that, she scoffed, "How do you know? You have only seen me in *Macbeth*."

He grinned. "I have seen every performance you have given since I came to London. All of Wellington's army could not have kept me away. Each time I watched, I grew increasingly angry at myself for having so underrated your talent. But in my defense, I was misled by finding you with that ragtag company of strolling players. What possessed you to join them?

"A favor. The company is in dire straits."

"I noticed," Damon said dryly.

"The manager is my uncle, and he begged me to appear for a few weeks with him this summer because I would draw larger audiences. I did not want to, but I could not refuse him."

"Why not?"

"For the same reason that you put up with Cassandra's unpleasantness. He is family, and I have a responsibility to him."

It pleased Damon that they held similar views on this. He was about to gather her in his arms when her face suddenly puckered in an agitated expression.

She pulled away from him and sat up. "Why wouldn't you come to my performances in Bath?"

Damon closed his eyes. He had never discussed with anyone the tragic incident that haunted him, but now he must tell Lily so that she would understand why he had avoided watching her perform and why he had reacted as he had that day she left Hawk-hill.

Opening his eyes, he thrust himself into a sitting position beside her. "For the same reason that I was so desperate to stop you from going to London." Damon pushed the pillows up between his back and the headboard. "Did you ever hear of an actress called Pretty Peg McKay?"

"She was a friend of mine," Lily said gravely.

Her expression told him she already knew the tale that everyone assumed was true. But only he knew the truth, and he had never told anyone. Would Lily believe him?

"Then you know what a charming little minx Peg was. I met her when she was appearing in Exeter She was determined to have me as her lover. Not that she cared much about me personally. Like Iona Lawson, she wanted the celebrity of having captured the king of the greenroom."

Damon's voice was cool and self-mocking, but Lily saw the muscle twitch in his jaw, always a certain sign that he was intensely disturbed.

"I was perfectly willing to indulge Peg. Unfortunately, she was not . . ." Damon paused as though searching for words that would give the least offense. ". . . a very talented actress."

Lily would concede that. Peggy had been perfect in one role, that of Little Pickle, but she had been a disappointment in most others that she had tried. Still, that had not mattered with unsophisticated provincial audiences who had loved her vivacious effervescence. It was that, not her limited acting talent, that had drawn them to the theatre.

Damon said, "I unwittingly betrayed to Peg how little her acting impressed me. I had no desire to hurt her, but when I did not praise her as effusively as she wanted, she kept trying to get me to do so."

Yes, Lily thought, that had been Peg, never satisfied with the compliments she received, but always soliciting more extravagant accolades, then pouting, even sinking into a fit of the sullens if she did not get them.

Poor Peggy's exuberance had had a terrible, dark side to it. When it had failed her, she had been cast into a depression of truly terrifying depths that neither Lily nor anyone else could coax her out of.

Damon continued, "After she realized what I thought of her acting, she became obsessed with proving me wrong. I came to heartily regret ever having seen her perform."

Lily frowned. "So you decided against watching me because you thought I was an inferior performer like her!"

His dark eyes pleaded for understanding. "I had promised you I would not lie to you, and I do not break my promises."

No, he did not, and Lily loved him the more because of it. "But I don't see what Peg has to do with your dictatorial reaction to my going to London."

"To prove me wrong, she was determined to get a tryout at either Drury Lane or Covent Garden and she did not rest until she succeeded." Damon turned his gaze toward the starburst quilt on the wall. "By that time, I was so weary of her and disturbed by the wild oscillations in her moods that I would have been happy to be rid of her. Nevertheless, I tried to stop her from going to London because I knew that the critics would savage her and her career would be over."

The very reason Lily had held out for a contract at Covent Garden instead of accepting a tryout.

Damon's gaze returned to Lily. "I told Peg that if she went to London, I would have nothing more to do with her. I thought that would stop her, but it did not. She was convinced that she would become the toast of London and then I would come crawling back to her. Her London tryout went even worse than I had feared, and the critics were merciless."

"And you kept your word that you would have nothing more to do with her, and she killed herself."

He sighed wearily. "No, she made no attempt to contact me. I think she was too humiliated. I was at Hawkhill, and it was a few days before the London reviews reached me. When I read them, I was deeply worried, knowing how fragile she was."

Lily would have been concerned, too, in view of how desperately Peggy had craved praise and adulation and how despondent she could become over the smallest criticism.

"I went immediately to London, but I was too late. She killed herself over the critics' reviews, not over me." His gaze met Lily's squarely. "She left a note saying so, but its contents were never made public."

Instead gossip had held Damon responsible. Lily touched his arm in a gesture of comfort, and he promptly captured her hand with his own, squeezing it hard.

"When you announced you were going to London," he said sadly, "it was as though I were reliving that scene with Peg again."

"Do you think me such a weakling that I would react as she did to bad reviews?"

"No, but you took me by surprise that day. We had been so happy together at Hawkhill, and I had no idea you were contemplating removing to London. I was shocked, and I wanted so much to protect you from a painful, destructive experience."

He lifted her hand to his lips, kissed it, then said ruefully, "My intentions were the best that day, but my execution was a disaster. I would have told you about Peg when I returned from meeting Magistrate Rawson, but you insisted upon staging that very public farewell."

The memory of it made Damon frown. "I still do not understand why you did that. It was the kind of trick Olivia would have employed."

"You thought it was a trick?" Lily cried. "Pray tell, to what end?"

"To manipulate me into marrying you," he said bluntly. "You know how I feel about manipulative women!"

"Yes, and after Olivia, I suppose I cannot blame you, but I was not trying to do so. I was afraid that if you got me alone, you would persuade me to stay at Hawkhill, even though it would cost me everything I had worked so hard for."

Lily looked down at the tumbled bedclothes, a faint blush coloring her cheeks. "You are very persuasive when we are alone." She lifted her gaze to his again. "I swear marriage never entered my mind. I know that it is out of the question for us."

He pulled her into his arms, hugging her to him, kissing her deeply, and thinking of all the wasted days and miserable weeks.

"What a mull I made of it that day," he said contritely. "I am so sorry, my love."

To his astonishment, she pulled away from him, looking terribly hurt. "Don't call me that!" she exclaimed vehemently. "I cannot endure it when you do not mean it!"

Damon was horrified. He had called her that because he meant it with all his heart.

Taking her face gently between his hands, he looked into her emerald eyes. "You *are* my love. My one and only love."

"But you do not believe in love!"

He smoothed her luxurious hair back from her face. "*Did* not," he corrected, "until you. You converted me, Lily."

And he would find a way to keep her with him always.

Just as he would always remember the joy on Lily's face at this moment.

Having said it in words, he set about proving to her with his body how much he loved her.

Much later, when Lily had gone to bring him breakfast, Damon lay in bed, his face turned to the pillow fragrant with her scent. Lily might think marriage was out of the question for them, but he no longer did. He would marry her no matter how much of a scandal it caused. He no longer cared about that. He cared about nothing but making her his wife.

A light knock sounded at the door. It was Lily's brother with Sewell. The groom had brought Damon fresh clothing, his toiletries, and a pair of crutches.

Raleigh, casual in fawn breeches and a shirt open at the neck, showed no inclination to leave with Sewell. After the groom went out, James asked Hawkhurst if they could talk.

Damon nodded. He knew what the major wished to discuss, and he opted to meet the issue head-on. "I am very much in love with your sister."

"Yes, I know. I saw the way you looked at her that first morning you came here."

"You seem remarkably sanguine about my being here."

"Only because she is wildly in love with you." Raleigh's face tightened, and he turned his head away from Damon to stare at the starburst quilt on the wall. "Frankly, I would much prefer a—er, regular relationship for her, but I understand the difficulty when an earl loves an actress."

"I intend to marry her."

The major's head swiveled, his expression shocked. "Now *that* will be difficult."

"It is not unknown for an actress to marry an

earl," Hawkhurst said defensively. "Craven shackled himself to a provincial actress and the Earl of Derby wed Elizabeth Farren. The latter even became a popular member of society, thanks to her husband's efforts. I shall contrive to do the same for Lily."

"But marriage to you would require that Lily quit acting," James pointed out. "We both know that it would be beyond the pale for a countess to appear on the stage."

That was very true. The Ladies Craven and Derby had both had to retire from the stage.

"I have come to respect how important acting is to Lily," Damon said slowly. It would be hard enough for her to surrender her cherished freedom, but quitting the theatre would be even more difficult for her. "I love her too much to *ask* her to give up something that means so much to her. My hope is she will do so voluntarily."

The major said, "But if she won't, you cannot marry her."

"No," Hawkhurst agreed. What a wonderful check for his consequence. Before he had met Lily he had thought that should he ever throw the handkerchief, his choice would consider herself a fortunate woman. Now if only Lily would accept him and relinquish acting, he would consider himself the most fortunate of men.

The door opened and Trude appeared with a breakfast tray for Damon, followed by Lily carrying one for herself. James took his leave with a conspiratorial wink at Damon.

Hawkhurst postponed putting his fate to the test for two days until he was up and about on crutches. In the interim, he sought to tilt the outcome in his favor by making love to Lily over and over with all the skill at his command. She astonished him with the depths of her answering passion, unfeigned and vital, as exciting as she was.

She had to accept his offer, he thought as he hobbled on his crutches into the tiny, crowded drawing room where Lily was writing at a little desk in the corner. He could not live without her. She looked up at his entrance, her face breaking into a smile that razed his heart.

He maneuvered his way awkwardly toward Lily between chairs covered with the same rose-patterned chintz that she had used in Bath. Damon supposed he ought to go down on bent knee to her, but he did not think he could manage that very well with the crutches. He settled instead for sinking into a chintz-covered chair by the desk.

Lily looked at him expectantly, waiting for him to speak.

Now that the moment to make his offer had come, Damon discovered to his consternation that he could not remember a single word of the eloquent speech he had rehearsed.

As he frantically searched his memory, Lily gestured at the room. "It is too small for you here when you are on crutches. You would be more comfortable at Hawkhurst House."

"Yes, but only if you come there with me." Seeing her shocked face, he blundered on, "Join me there, my love."

The pen dropped from Lily's hand, splattering the letter she had been writing to Sarah with black splotches of ink. So Damon wanted to proclaim to the world she was his mistress by moving her into Hawkhurst House!

"I know you pride yourself on your independence, my love," he was saying. "I understand your great fear of ceding control of your life to a man, but I swear to you I shall protect and cherish you forever."

"Forever is a long time to cherish a convenient!" she retorted acidly.

"Convenient?" He looked confounded. "I am asking you to be my wife."

Lily could only stare at him incredulously. "You cannot be serious!"

Damon learned forward and took her face between his hands. He caressed it gently with his fingertips. "I have never been more serious in my life."

For one incandescent moment, Lily was ecstatic, then her happiness snagged on the hard cruel shoals of reality. He bent his head to kiss her, but she pulled back from him in agitation.

"You cannot marry me, Damon! It would be disastrous for you. You would be ostracized by society."

He smiled at her with such love in his eyes, as soft as rich brown velvet, that it nearly brought tears to her own.

"No," he said with quiet determination, "I would see that we are both accepted as Lord and Lady Derby were."

But Elizabeth Farren had had to give up the stage to marry Derby. Lily had worked hard at the craft she loved, and she had finally reached its pinnacle. The thought of abandoning it now dismayed her. And frightened her, too. It had been her support for so long.

"I told you, Damon, acting is my life."

"You may give private theatricals here in London or at Hawkhill whenever you wish."

"But it is not the same." Amateur acting and professional theatre were worlds apart. He was forcing her to choose between the two things she loved most—acting and him.

"Oh, Damon," she pleaded, her voice cracking with emotion, "don't ask me to give up my career, I beg of you."

He captured her hands in his. "I am not asking you to do so. The decision is entirely yours, my love."

"But unless I quit the stage, it is impossible for us to be married, is it not?"

"Yes," he admitted.

Her heart was breaking at the awful choice she must make.

And making it even harder was the knowledge of what marriage to her would cost Damon. Lily was far less optimistic than he that he could force society to accept her or their marriage. If it did not, their union would be more disastrous for him and their children than for her. They would all be social pariahs because of her.

Hawkhurst might think now that being an outcast would not bother him, but he was wrong. Just as her father had been wrong. Luckily, it had not lessened his love for Mama, but it had hurt him terribly. Lily could not bear to see Damon as unhappy as her father had been.

What if Damon's love for her turned to hatred because of what she had cost him and their children?

Her soul withered at the thought. She had to refuse his offer for his sake and for that of the children who would never be born.

Her wavering resolve hardened. She must stand firm against him. So long as she refused to give up her career, they would not be able to wed. That was her most effective weapon against his cajolery.

Swallowing hard, she asked, "Pray what would I do with myself if I gave up my career? Become one of those idle women who spend their lives changing clothes and flitting from one squeeze to another with no purpose?"

"You will have a very important purpose," Damon protested, "as my wife and the mother of my children. One reason I want us to marry is that I long for us to have a family.''

''I would like that very much too,'' she admitted, wistful yearning in her voice. ''But it cannot be. I am sorry, Damon, but I cannot abandon the theatre.''

The wounded look in his eyes sliced at her heart. His hands released hers abruptly.

''Lily, if you loved me half as much as I love you, you would.''

''And if you loved me half as much as you say you do, you would not tell me that!''

''Listen to me, Lily,'' he pleaded. ''I did not even believe in love, but you taught me how wrong I was. Now, I want to care for you, protect you, give you my name, and make you the mother of my children. Doesn't that mean anything to you?''

Oh, yes, it did. More than she could possibly tell him.

''And what if you should become pregnant?'' he demanded harshly. ''Despite precautions, accidents do happen.''

''But not necessarily to us,'' she countered.

She wanted desperately to drive the bleakness from his expression, and she threw her arms around him, hugging him fiercely to her with all her strength. ''Oh, Damon, I love you more than words can express. We have been so happy the past two days. Why can we not go on as we are now?''

He held her hard against him. ''I love you, Lily, and I want you whatever way I can have you.'' His voice was so sad that she wanted to cry. ''I will accept your terms, but I hope very much that they will soon include marriage.''

Chapter 30

Damon had acquiesced to Lily's wish to continue their affair rather than marry only because he was certain he would quickly be able to change her mind. But she proved to be maddeningly obdurate about giving up her career.

Thinking to quiet her fears about her economic dependence on him if they wed, Damon offered her a marriage settlement that would ensure her a most generous amount of pin money as well as a large jointure should anything happen to him.

Every other woman he had ever known would have jumped at his offer, but Lily rejected it.

Adding to his frustration was her determination not to be kept by him. She would accept nothing from him but his love. At first, that had pleased him. He was so accustomed to having females beseech him for money and expensive gifts that he found it refreshing.

But it soon left him feeling thwarted and dismayed. He wanted to shower her with tangible tokens of his love for her, and she would not permit it. Lily would not even allow him to buy or rent a suitable house for them.

"What is the use of having a fortune if I cannot spend some of it on the woman I love?" he grumbled to her.

Their days had fallen into a pattern. On those that Lily had rehearsals and a performance, he would return to Hawkhurst House to take care of his affairs. Then he would dress for the theatre. He never missed one of her appearances, but he had not been in the greenroom since the night of his injury. He did not want to spur speculation about himself and Lily by appearing there. Instead he relied upon her brother to bring her home while he would visit his club until it was time for her to leave the theatre with the major.

They spent the days that Lily had no performance together, talking, playing chess, and making love. Once his ankle healed enough for him to abandon the crutches, they began exploring London together.

One day in early December, as a light wet snow was falling, Lily found Damon staring through a window of her lodgings at it. His expression was so melancholy that she asked him what was wrong.

"I want to go to Hawkhill for Christmas. It is my favorite time of year there."

"Then you must go."

He spun around. "Not without you!"

"I do not have performances that week. I can go with you."

His expression hardened in determination. "Only if you are my wife. I shall not take you to Hawkhill except as *its* mistress, not mine."

She touched his cheek lovingly. "Please, Damon, do not harangue me about marriage. We have been happy these past weeks, have we not?"

His jaw was rigid beneath her finger. "Not nearly as happy as I would be if you were my wife."

Hastily, she tried to turn the conversation by asking brightly, "Speaking of Christmas, what would you like from me?"

"An heir, or at least the start of one. Nothing else."

That would require Lily to marry him. Otherwise, any child she bore him would be a bastard with no right to his father's title, and they both knew it.

"That is impossible," she said quietly.

"It is very possible—except for your stubbornness."

After that Hawkhurst stopped trying to persuade her to marry him, but with each passing day, his determination to make her his wife grew stronger. Although he no longer brought up the subject to her, it was always on his mind. So was her plea: *"Don't force me to choose between you and my career, I beg of you."*

The more he thought about it, the more convinced he became that she should not have to make that choice. Damon had accused her of being stubborn, but it occurred to him he was guilty of that, too. What if she had asked him to choose between her and something that was as important to him as Hawkhill? Would he not have been unhappy—and obstinate as well?

She had a remarkable talent, and if he truly loved her, he should want her to make the most of it no matter what difficulty it presented. So let her continue to act after they married. It would set the *ton* on its collective ear, but he did not care. At least not for himself, but he wanted to guarantee Lily the place in society that was rightfully hers as his countess.

To do that was a challenge worthy of him! He began laying his plan as carefully as the Duke of Wellington ever organized a campaign.

Hawkhurst launched it with a visit to his own aunt, Lady Edith Purcell. After she greeted him, he told her, "I had a letter from Cassandra yesterday. She is overjoyed that you have agreed to chaperone her next season." He took his aunt's plump hands in his own and squeezed them affectionately. "I am most grateful to you. Now I must ask a second, even more difficult, favor of you."

"What is it?" Lady Purcell asked in alarm. "I have never seen you look so grave."

He freed her hands. "I have fallen very much in love, and I am about to marry. I want you to help me make certain that my wife is properly accepted by society."

His aunt could not have looked more incredulous had he told her the sun rose at noon instead of dawn. "I had no notion that you had the slightest interest in any female. Do I know her?"

"Not personally, but you know who she is: Lily Culhane."

"The actress? Surely you are quizzing me. I heard Major Raleigh is her lover."

"No, he is her brother."

"But that means . . ."

"Yes, Lily comes from two highly respectable families. She is the granddaughter of Sir John Drew and General Sir Francis Raleigh. She is also Lady Charing's niece and she will be my wife. I want to assure her the place in society that she deserves."

"She is the most popular actress in London. What an uproar there will be when it's learned she's quitting the theatre to marry you."

"She is not quitting it."

His aunt looked aghast. "But you cannot permit your wife to appear onstage.

"I can and I will."

In the end, as he had known she would, his aunt agreed to help champion Lily among the *ton*.

As he left her, she cautioned, "You will never get that old stiff-rumped General Raleigh to acknowledge her."

Hawkhurst smiled enigmatically. "Yes, I will."

His next call was on Lily's aunt, Lady Charing, a

fading beauty whose green eyes and generous mouth reminded him of her niece. She proved to be eager to help Lily in whatever way she could.

She confided tearfully, "After my sister died, I begged to take those poor children in, but Lord Charing would not permit it, would not even let me go to them or to attend my sister's funeral."

From the way she said her late husband's name, Damon suspected that Lady Charing, like Phoebe, had welcomed widowhood.

Hawkhurst's final call of the day was upon General Sir Francis Raleigh.

The unexpected visitor was ushered into the general's library by a flustered old retainer, clearly unused to having lords of the realm call.

Hawkhurst waited no more than two minutes before Lily's grandfather hurried into the room with a delighted smile on his wrinkled old face and effusive greetings on his lips. "Lord Hawkhurst, what a pleasant surprise."

Damon would wager that the general had been a tyrant to the men beneath him and a toad-eater to those above him. Age had taken its toll on him. His face and hands were sprinkled with liver spots, his body was gaunt, but he still maintained his military carriage. Hawkhurst guessed the old man's rigid posture had much in common with his character.

"To what do I owe the honor of this visit, my lord?"

"Your granddaughter."

The smile died on the old man's lips.

"I have no granddaughter, only a grandson. Perhaps you have heard of him, Major James Raleigh."

Hawkhurst made no attempt to hide his anger. "If Major Raleigh is your grandson, then you have two granddaughters, Sarah and Lily Culhane. Not that you deserve them."

Sir Francis said huffily, "I beg your pardon, my lord?"

"No, it is Lily's pardon that you should beg," Damon said icily. "You should be very proud of her. She is the finest woman I have ever known and a brilliant actress. Have you seen her perform?"

The general looked horrified. "I would not lower myself. Why are you defending her? But, of course, I should have guessed. The king of the greenroom. Is she your mistress?"

No, not his mistress, Hawkhurst thought, his lover. There was a difference. Lily had taught him that, as she had taught him so many other things—including love.

"She is about to become my wife," Damon said coldly. "Will you feel more inclined to recognize your granddaughter, General, when she is the Countess of Hawkhurst?"

The old man actually gasped at that. "You cannot mean to marry her. You will be cast out by society."

Clearly that was what mattered most to Lily's grandfather.

"If I am, Lily is well worth it. However, *she* would care if I were, and that is why I want to make certain *both* of us are accepted. I want her to take the place in society that is her right as my wife and *your* granddaughter."

"So you have persuaded her to give up the stage to marry you?"

"No, I do not require that of her. She wishes to continue to act, and she shall."

The general turned white. "You are mad to permit it!"

"No, with your granddaughter, I would be mad to oppose it."

The general's watery old eyes narrowed into slits. "I shall never acknowledge a vulgar performer as my granddaughter."

Damon could see where Lily had gotten her stubbornness. "There is nothing vulgar about Lily. You refuse to recognize your granddaughter because you fear what society might say because she is an actress? Are you that much of a coward?"

A flush replaced the old man's pallor. "I will not have my family and its proud name sullied by a cheap stage actress."

"It is not Lily's conduct that is a blot on your family's proud name, but that of another member of your family."

The general demanded in alarm, "Who are you talking about?"

"You! Furthermore, I shall see that all England knows of your reprehensible behavior."

"My conduct has always been above reproach."

"Has it? What about your shocking cruelty in turning away from your door your three orphaned grandchildren, forcing those poor penniless children to fend for themselves?" Contempt permeated Hawkhurst's voice. "I assure you that when I am done everyone will be quite as disgusted as I am by how your actions forced the eldest of them, a mere girl of seventeen, to go on the stage to support them. Against all odds, she succeeded in keeping the family together and even managed to scrape up the funds to buy her brother a commission, thereby giving the country a hero it would otherwise have been denied."

Damon paused to let the impact of his words sink in. Then he said icily, "I promise you it will be her courage that is applauded and your ignoble conduct that is condemned."

"This is blackmail," Raleigh sputtered.

"No, this is *justice.*"

"So you force me to recognize her."

"More than that. You must embrace her as you have done her brother—now that he is a hero."

The old man said nothing for a moment, then his stiff military posture cracked and his shoulders slumped in defeat. He looked tired and very old.

"You leave me no choice," he said bitterly. "But your efforts on her behalf are hopeless. Unless she gives up the stage, she will never win social acceptance."

"I will see that she does," Hawkhurst said with quiet determination.

The general stared at him. "By God, I believe you might."

Lily had no performance that night or the next, for which she was thankful. Usually she was bursting with energy and good humor, but today for some reason she had been very tired and oddly blue-deviled. She always looked forward to performing, but tonight it was a relief to know that she did not have to do so. It would be infinitely more pleasant to curl up in front of the fire in the drawing room with Damon and talk quietly.

When she told him after dinner that she would prefer that to a game of chess, he asked in concern whether she was feeling well. "You have not seemed quite yourself today, my love," he observed, taking her in his arms.

She told him about the odd malaise that gripped her. "I am certain I shall be fine tomorrow."

"You *look* magnificent." Damon's dark eyes perused her teal-blue gown, halting at the swell of her breasts beneath its deeply cut neck. He teased the tip of one breast gently with his thumb, and she winced. "Did I hurt you, my love?" he asked in surprise.

"I seem to be unusually tender tonight."

He studied her thoughtfully as he led her to the sofa before the fire. When they were seated, he put his arms around her and kissed her deeply.

Then he said huskily, "I have in my pocket a gift without monetary value that I hope you will accept as a suitable token of my overwhelming love for you."

With one arm still around her, he reached into his pocket and pulled out a folded paper.

"What is it?" she asked, much puzzled.

He handed it to her. "My name."

She opened the sheet and saw that it was a special license for them to wed.

He smiled at her. "I have a rector who will marry us tomorrow."

She tried to protest, but he laid a silencing finger across her lips. "I do not ask that you give up the stage after our wedding. You are free to continue with your career. Why do you look so stricken?"

Because Lily had thought he would never capitulate on that point. That he had done so touched her to the depths of her soul. But he had also robbed her of her most effective excuse for not marrying him. "But, Damon," she protested weakly, "it is unthinkable for a countess to appear on the stage."

"It is even more unthinkable that we cannot marry. I will settle for nothing less."

"I cannot shame you and your family by wedding you."

"You will honor me, my love, not shame me."

Lily swallowed hard. He would not feel that way when society turned its back on him and their children because of her. She could not bear to see his love for her turn to hatred as he realized the full price of what marriage to her had cost. "No, my dearest Damon, I cannot marry you."

He stiffened in anger. Lily looked into his dark eyes and flinched. He was furious with her.

She could not blame him. He was willing to sacrifice so much to marry her.

Far more than she wanted him to.

Far more than she would let him.

Lily put her arms around him, desperate to end this quarrel.

"Please, Damon, why cannot we continue as we have been? I love you so." She kissed him. "Please, make love to me."

He pushed her roughly away. "So I am good enough to sleep with, but not good enough to marry," he ground out. "Well, I promise you, Lily, that I shall not make love to you again until we are married.

She watched in disbelief as he stormed from the room. A moment later she heard the door of her lodgings slam shut.

Chapter 31

A t first, Lily thought Hawkhurst would not carry out his threat to ignore her until she agreed to marry him. Once his anger had cooled, he would return to her.

But he did not come back that night or the next.

Her brother, noting her red-rimmed eyes and Hawkhurst's absence, asked what they had quarreled about.

When she told him, he said, "No wonder he is furious at you. He has agreed to what you wanted and still you refuse to marry him."

Lily went to the theatre that night with a breaking heart. She played Zara in *The Mourning Bride* but could not concentrate on the role. She kept wondering whether Damon was in the audience. When the play was over, she knew it had been her worst performance since she had been at Covent Garden.

Embarrassed, dispirited, and blue-deviled, she went to the greenroom. Hawkhurst, of course, was not there. He had not been there since the night Iona had kissed him.

Several of Lily's admirers remarked on how quiet and subdued she was. When James finally came to take her home, she hurried up to him, relieved that she could escape at last.

As her brother took her arm, Hawkhurst strode

briskly into the room and up to them. His lips were smiling but his eyes were as hard and black as a moonless sky. Lily held her breath, suddenly apprehensive about what he meant to do.

In a loud, affable voice that carried clearly to the four corners of the room, he said to her brother, "I will take Lily home tonight, James."

The room fell instantly quiet. Everyone in it goggled at them.

Her brother, smiling broadly, immediately relinquished her arm to Damon. "Of course, my lord. She much prefers your company to mine."

Lily wanted to box her brother's ears. Her cheeks burned. She would only make matters worse by opening her mouth, so she silently allowed Damon to lead her toward the green baize door.

Lord Rudolph Oldfield, reputed to be the worst gossip in London, stepped into their path. "So the Hawk has offered the Lily a carte blanche?"

"No," Hawkhurst said brusquely, "I have offered her marriage."

The silence in the greenroom was so profound now that one could have heard a skirt rustle. Not a soul there would think twice about the Earl of Hawkhurst offering her a carte blanche, but marriage was truly shocking.

"Unfortunately," Damon told Oldfield, "she has refused my offer."

All over the room, jaws dropped in disbelief.

Oldfield nodded toward James. "So she prefers the major."

"Major Raleigh is Lily's brother, and I have his blessing to marry his sister. Not even her high stickler of a grandfather, General Sir Francis Raleigh, objects." Damon sighed mournfully. "But still Lily won't have me. Isn't that so, my love?"

Lily could not have spoken if her life depended upon it. She was so stunned that she let Damon guide her past Oldfield and out into the night where his carriage awaited.

When they were settled in it, she demanded in dismay, "Why did you do that? We will be the talk of London."

"Yes," he agreed, a cynical twist to his lips. "I have just guaranteed that your performances will be sellouts. You will no longer have to bother with the greenroom."

As the carriage lurched forward, she wailed, "How could you announce such a private matter to the world?"

"I want both the world and you to know that I would be proud to have you as my wife, Lily. I am desperate to convince you of that now that time is of the essence."

She stared at him blankly. "What do you mean, 'time is of the essence'?"

He frowned. "You do not know, do you?"

"No, I don't, and I cannot marry you. Oh, Damon, listen to me—"

The muscle in his jaw twitched convulsively. "I want to hear one word out of you, Lily! One word only, and that word is 'yes.' " He withdrew to the corner of the carriage as far away from her as he could manage. "Until then, we have nothing more to say to each other."

"This—"

He cut her off curtly. "Not one word, Lily, except yes."

"Very well, if he was going to be like that, she would say nothing. She retreated to her own corner, and they rode in tense silence to her lodgings.

Hawkhurst silently escorted her up the steps. She swept inside ahead of him. When she heard the door close, she whirled angrily to vent her anger on him and discovered that she was alone in the hall. He had left her.

Lily promptly burst into tears.

* * *

They were the choicest gossip in London.

Everyone from Lily's brother to Blandon Jerome made it clear to her that they thought she was a certified lunatic to reject Hawkhurst's offer.

Damon had been right when he had told Lily that he'd ensured her appearances would be sellouts. Everyone was clamoring for tickets to her performances, eager to see the actress who had refused to marry the king of the greenroom.

He, however, was pointedly absent from his realm.

James told her that Hawkhurst was much in evidence, gambling at White's or dancing at *haute ton* balls in the early hours of each new day.

She wanted to ask her brother who the fortunate women were that Hawkhurst danced with at those fashionable squeezes. Instead, she said testily, "Showing the world that he is not pining for me."

"No, he is showing the world he is not sleeping with the ninnyhammer he hopes to make his wife."

Lily sent Damon a note, asking him to call on her.

He did not come. Instead he sent her a note: *When you say yes, I will come. Then we will have something to discuss.*

Lily crumpled the paper angrily. Couldn't he see that she refused to marry him more for his sake than her own?

She missed him so. The days that had flown by when they were together dragged interminably now. She ached for him, ached for his company in bed and out. But, she thought forlornly, he was obviously unbothered by a similar longing.

Lily raised her head from the basin, feeling only marginally better. This was the third morning in a row that she had awakened sick to her stomach. Worse, what should have happened a month ago had not, confirming the unwelcome suspicion that she was increasing.

Much as Lily missed Damon beside her during the night, she was glad now that he was not here. He would have guessed immediately, as Trude had guessed yesterday and promptly told James.

"Now perhaps you will have the good sense to marry Hawkhurst," her brother had said. "Have you told him you are breeding?"

"No," she admitted. She would have to do so, but she was not certain that he was still in London. Christmas was only four days away, and he might have gone to Hawkhill. Nor was she anxious to tell him. The news was certain to worsen Damon's already foul humor and intensify his pressure on her to marry him.

She wondered bitterly whether he would refuse even to discuss her pregnancy with her until she said yes to marrying him.

Lily began to cry. Since she'd become pregnant, she seemed to want to burst into tears every other minute. She was becoming as bad as Phoebe.

Another wave of nausea racked her, and she bent over the basin again, feeling utterly miserable.

The door behind her opened quietly, but she paid it no heed, thinking Trude had come in.

As Lily retched again, a gentle hand held her forehead lovingly while its mate rubbed her back with soothing strokes. Her nausea receded. The scent of sandalwood drifted over her.

Much shocked, she looked up.

Damon was watching her, his face grave and his eyes full of love and concern.

She straightened, swiping at the tears on her cheeks. What could she tell him? she wondered in near-panic.

He smoothed her hair away from her face, then gently wiped her tears with his thumbs. "I think, my love, it is time that we talk about *our* baby."

The tenderness in his voice and the way he said "our" made her happier than she had been in days.

"How did you know?" she stammered. But, of course, her brother must have told him.

Damon smiled at her. "I suspected it before you did. There was your sudden malaise and the swelling and soreness of your beautiful breasts."

"Are you angry?" He did not look it, but she had to know.

"About the baby? No, I am delighted. I will be angry only if you continue to refuse to marry me. Then I will be enraged. I do not want my son born a bastard."

"You don't know that it is a son," she reminded him.

"Son or daughter, I don't care. I do not want the stigma of illegitimacy attached to any child of mine. That is why I told you time is of the essence. Marry me, and we will go to Hawkhill for Christmas."

She wanted that so much, but the price for him would be too high.

His eyes, the color of rich, dark chocolate, gleamed. "Marry me now, my love, and I will have the Christmas present I wanted."

"Damon, I cannot—"

"Listen to me Lily," he said firmly. "It is not only I who would curse you for refusing to marry me, but that babe you carry in your womb. Look at what your stubbornness will cost him. Instead of coming into the world well shod and hosed, the heir to a great title and estate, he will be born without name or claim to what is rightfully his."

Lily had not thought of that, and her head drooped sadly.

Damon tilted her chin so that he could see her face. "Can you do that to an innocent child, especially when he is your own flesh and blood?"

No, God help her, she could not!

"You have no right to deny our child its inheritance, Lily. If he is a boy, he may well grow up to hate you for what you have cost him.''

Damon was right, and her heart shriveled at the prospect. Lily was torn between what was best for her unborn child and for its father.

She tried to blink back her tears as she met Damon's unwavering gaze. ''But if I marry you, my dearest love, it will be you who will come to hate me for what I have cost you. I could not bear that.''

He hands stroked her face tenderly. ''I could never hate you, Lily. And what do you think you would be costing me?''

''The respect of your peers, your position in society—things you take for granted now but will soon miss.''

''I would miss you far more than anything else, my love.'' His mouth turned upward in his wry, teasing smile. ''Furthermore, having you for my wife is more likely to gain me the envy of my peers than lose me their respect.''

He pulled her into his arms. ''Nor will you be ostracized. Your grandfather, your aunt, and mine all stand with me ready to champion you in society. It will not be easy, but together we will pull it off.''

Her eyes widened in shock. ''Grandfather has agreed? I cannot believe that!''

''It is true. He is stubborn, but not as stubborn as you, my love. We will be accepted, I promise you.''

And Damon would never break a promise to her. Lily felt her maddening tears well up again. They spilled down her cheeks, and she could not stop them.

Damon pulled out his handkerchief. She tried to take it from him, but he insisted on wiping her tears away himself.

Then he wrapped her in his strong, comforting arms, his cheek resting against her temple. ''What do you have to say now, my love?''

''Yes, Damon—only yes.''

Epilogue

In the wings of Covent Garden Theatre, Lord James Damon Francis Giles St. Clair, Viscount Camberley, clapped his tiny hands gleefully, joining in the thunderous applause for his mother. Then he grinned at his papa, who was holding him.

"Your mama was brilliant again tonight, Jamie," Hawkhurst told his eight-month-old son.

The baby cooed happily.

Damon watched Lily with enormous pride as she took her bows.

Their marriage sixteen months ago had caused a sensation, especially when Lily continued to appear at Covent Garden. The *ton* had been scandalized, but Damon had kept his promise to Lily that it would eventually accept her. A few of his enemies had used his marriage to try to settle old scores with him, but he had prevailed. Most men envied him the magnificent creature who was his wife, and Lily had proved as skilled at charming the ladies of the *ton* as she had been at dazzling greenroom gallants.

Although Lord and Lady Hawkhurst attended only a select few soirees in London, it was not for lack of invitations. They were much sought after by hostesses, but they both preferred the company of each other to that of society.

When Lily's appreciative audience finally allowed

her to leave the stage, she hurried to her husband and son. Jamie held out his arms to her and she took him from his father. Undeterred by her stage makeup, which he was used to by now, the baby's chubby little arms encircled her neck tightly and he gave her a loud, smacking kiss.

Hawkhurst grinned. "I think I am jealous."

"You shouldn't be," Lily told her husband. "He could use instruction from his father on kissing technique."

Damon's gaze rested hungrily on Lily's mouth. "I could give him a demonstration now," he teased as they walked toward her dressing room.

She smiled up at him. "I hope you will as soon as I have removed this dreadful makeup."

He followed her into her cramped dressing room. In addition to a mirrored dressing table, it contained a cradle for Jamie and a sofa long enough for Lily to lie down on to rest between scenes.

"What were you saying to Jamie as I was leaving the stage?"

Damon sat down on the sofa. "We were discussing his mama's splendid performance tonight."

"The most splendid thing about it is that it is my finale for the season. Now we can go home to Hawkhill."

Whenever Lily appeared, the vast theatre was filled. People thronged to her performances, drawn by the novelty of a countess appearing onstage, but they left entranced by her acting talent. Her popularity meant that the management was quite happy to accept her on whatever terms they could get her. She was cutting back to a minimum her appearances and insisting that they be bunched together so that now she could escape London two months early.

Her husband was frowning at her. "Was tonight your finale?" he asked quietly.

"You know it was!"

"I thought so. That's why I was shocked to overhear the manager boasting tonight that you had agreed to his request to play your favorite role every night for the next two weeks."

Lily's eyes sparkled with mischief. "I did. The foolish man was under the mistaken impression that Lady Macbeth was my favorite role."

"It isn't?"

"No. He was most disappointed and chagrined to discover my favorite role is being your wife and Jamie's mother. And I do intend to play it every night for the next *six months* at Hawkhill."

Damon looked so relieved that she asked, "Surely, you did not think I would extend my commitment without consulting you?"

"No, I didn't. That's why I was shocked."

Lily started to put her son in his cradle so that she could change out of her costume and remove her makeup, but his father held out his arms for him.

As Lily handed Jamie back to him, she reflected that her acting career, which she had once thought she wanted more than anything, was no longer as important to her as her role as wife and mother.

She begrudged the time that she was separated from her son, and she longed to be back at Hawkhill where she and Damon had spent several idyllic months last summer before and after Jamie's birth.

Yes, marriage and motherhood had changed her in ways she had not expected. Yet, with Damon's help, she was able to juggle her two careers. She felt both fulfilled and so blessed.

With each passing day Lily had come to love and appreciate her husband more. When she saw the way other husbands treated their wives, she felt herself incredibly lucky. Damon was so solicitous and supportive of her—and, most of all, so loving and munificent.

No longer did she refuse to accept gifts from him.

He derived as much pleasure from giving them to her as she did from receiving them. A generous man was my lord Hawkhurst.

Lily exchanged her costume for her wrapper, then sat down at her dressing table and removed her makeup. "Are you certain you do not want to go to Lady Sefton's ball tonight?" she asked Damon, looking at his reflection in the mirror.

"Very certain. The only thing I want to do tonight is take my wife to bed." He gave her a seductive smile, full of promise, in the mirror.

She finished removing her makeup and turned to watch him playing with Jamie on the sofa. He was not at all an aloof, disinterested parent as his own father had been. Instead he was like her papa, delighting in spending as much time as he could with his son.

Jamie began fussing hungrily, and Lily took him so that he could nurse.

Damon grinned lovingly at his son and heir suckling at his mother's breast and said, "Now I know I am jealous."

Lily looked down proudly at Jamie. "He is perfect, isn't he?"

"Yes, just like his mama. And speaking of her, is there something she would especially like for her birthday?"

"Yes, I do want one thing very much."

"Then you shall have it," he said promptly. "Only tell me what it is."

Lily looked down at her son. His eyes were slowly closing in sleep. "Another baby," she said. It was time Jamie had a brother or sister. She knew that Damon wanted more children, too, but he had been reluctant to have her become pregnant too soon after Jamie's birth.

Damon frowned. "I do not want you to be exhausted by child-bearing."

She was touched by his concern for her. "I won't be. Indeed, I am disgustingly healthy. Please, Damon."

He looked from her face to that of his son. Jamie was sound asleep now, and his head had rolled away from Lily's nipple.

Damon smiled. "Well, perhaps you could talk me into it, my love, if you promise to give me a green-eyed, fiery-haired daughter just like her mama."

Lily's wrapper had parted over her legs, and her husband slid a warm, questing hand between her thighs. His fingertip unerringly found and caressed the hidden nub of her desire. Her eyes closed, and a little moan of pleasure escaped her.

When his hand retreated, she teased, "Do that again, and I will promise you anything."

As she put the sleeping Jamie in the cradle beside her dressing table, Damon went to the door and turned the key in the lock.

"Why did you do that?" Lily asked.

The look in his dark eyes sent a shaft of desire through her.

"I find, my love, I cannot wait until we get home to begin making your birthday gift."